The Asking Price

The Asking Price continues the compelling story of Kirsty and Craig Nicholson (begun in *The Good Provider*). Having escaped a harsh life of labour in the Ayrshire farmlands, they hope finally to build a future for their relationship. But the relentless demands of life in the mean backstreets of Victorian Glasgow take their inevitable toll, and soon, united only by their son Bobby, they are subjected to a world where grim poverty and dour respectability collide head on.

Jessica Stirling was born in Glasgow, and has enjoyed a highly successful career as a writer. Her previous novels include those in the best-selling Stalker trilogy – *The Spoiled Earth*, *The Hiring Fair* and *The Dark Pasture*, and in the Beckman trilogy – *The Deep Well at Noon*, *The Blue Evening Gone* and *The Gates of Midnight*. In her recent novels, *Treasures on Earth*, *Creature Comforts* and *Hearts of Gold*, she returned to the starkly dramatic Scottish setting which made her earlier novels such a popular success.

D0256315

Also by Jessica Stirling
in Pan Books

The Spoiled Earth
The Hiring Fair
The Dark Pasture

The Deep Well at Noon
The Blue Evening Gone
The Gates of Midnight

Treasures on Earth
Creature Comforts
Hearts of Gold

The Good Provider

JESSICA STIRLING

The Asking Price

Pan Books
London, Sydney and Auckland

The only men who truly lose are the many
who go on living continually as if sin
were a curiosity which did
not concern them.

Sören Kierkegaard.

First published 1989 by Hodder & Stoughton Ltd
This edition published 1990 by Pan Books Ltd,
Cavaye Place, London SW10 9PG

5 7 9 8 6

© Jessica Stirling 1989

ISBN 0 330 31405 X

Contents

PART ONE

Kirsty Nicholson opened her eyes and stared into the darkness. No sound came from the cot in which her son slept and she wondered what had wakened her at such an ungodly hour on a black and bitter February morning.

It could hardly be birdsong. Only sparrows and pigeons roosted on the ledges of the Glasgow tenement and it was far too early and far too cold for those crafty feathered urchins to be awake and squabbling. She lay on her side, cheek pressed to the pillow, nose and one ear like ice, and watched her breath form in a faint white cloud in the bed recess.

Through a gap in the curtain she studied the dim familiar shapes of kitchen furniture. The fire had gone out. No amount of tending, it seemed, would keep it alight through these dead cold, windless nights. She sighed. Now she would need to take out the ashes, set and rekindle the fire and wait, shivering, for a good half-hour for the kettle to boil so that she could brew herself a pot of tea and make a proper start to breakfast. She wished that there was money enough to hire one of the model gas stoves that stood shiny-bright in the window of Dawsholm Appliances, one of their Ready water-heaters too, but since her in-laws had turned up out of the blue in September of last year, 1897, there had been nothing to spare for household luxuries.

Gordon, Craig's young brother, had found work in a carpet factory but he was only 'a sweeper' and his wage contributed little to the domestic purse. With five mouths to feed, not counting the baby, Kirsty occasionally felt that she was tottering on the edge of poverty. This situation had come about simply because her mother-in-law, Madge, had decided that living under the wing of her firstborn in Glasgow was infinitely preferable to preserving her independence and struggling along on her own on the Carrick steading of Dalnavert.

There had been no direct contact between Craig and his mother in the period after he had defied her wishes and run off with Kirsty to Glasgow. When she arrived on the doorstep there had been no trace of that acrimony or of recrimination. Madge had breezed into the tenement apartment in a flurry of affability, dragging Gordon and Lorna with her. She had declared that she had relinquished the lease on the tenant farm and that wild horses would not drag her back to the country. Kirsty liked Gordon and Lorna well enough. But she resented the influence that Madge soon had over Craig and was annoyed that what had seemed at first a temporary arrangement had become permanent. She had not been consulted at any stage in the process. High-handedly Craig had assumed that she would be pleased to inherit a ready-made family. It did not occur to him that after all the tribulations of their first years of 'marriage', Kirsty might wish to have him, and the house, to herself. She still regarded herself as the house's custodian, its guardian, at least when Craig was on duty and, hearing the noise again, she sat up at once.

It could not be much after five o'clock. She had no need to rise before six. Craig never came off night duty with the Greenfield Burgh police before seven. Gordon would not roll, yawning, from his bed in the tiny front parlour until twenty past, Lorna ten minutes after that. Madge Nicholson would be last of all to get up. Even the baby, now that he was weaned, would sleep soundly until Craig came home and his daddy's deep, masculine voice wakened him. Who could it be? She was still troubled by fears that had plagued her in the months following Bobby's birth. He had been premature, so puny as an infant that all Kirsty's time and attention had had to be devoted to him, every minute of every waking hour. She had dwelt in a permanent state of anxiety, not only about him but about everything.

She swung her feet to the floor and grabbed her stockings, drawers, vest, skirt and blouse from the chairback. She dressed rapidly, stepped into her shoes and tiptoed to the cot. A beaded shawl was draped over it, making a sort of tent. Bobby's cheek, a sprig of dark hair and his button nose were just visible. When she placed her face close to his she felt, with relief, the tickle of breath against her skin. He would need changed as soon as he wakened. Meanwhile he was snug under layers of soft wool and the quilt that Nessie Frew had bought for him.

Kirsty straightened. Was the outside door open? She sensed the cold-stone emptiness of landing and stairs. Lorna, afraid of the dark, would not venture out to the closet on the half-landing but used the pot under the bed. Madge was also too lazy to make the trip and Gordon just never seemed to need to go at all. Kirsty's nervousness increased. Every change in routine made her apprehensive. Once, not so long ago, one of the villains that Craig had put away had escaped from prison and had come in search of revenge. In spite of Craig's assurances to the contrary she was terrified that it might happen again. Cautiously she opened the door that led from the kitchen to the tiny hallway. Doors to the parlour and front bedroom were closed. The heavy outside door, however, stood ajar. She groped for the hook above the coal-bunker and found to her relief that the lavatory key had gone. At that moment the outside door swung open.

"Gordon!" Kirsty exclaimed.

She would not have been too surprised to find him in his nightshirt, with an old stable jacket draped over his shoulders for warmth. But Gordon was fully dressed. A knitted muffler was wrapped about his neck and a snappy tweed cap pulled over his ears.

"Jeeze!" Gordon muttered. "That's torn it."

"Where have you been?"

He hesitated. "To the lavvie, of course."

"Don't lie to me, Gordon."

"*Wheesh*. You'll waken Mother. Go inside. I'm frozen to the bone."

"All right," Kirsty whispered. "But give me the key first."

When she returned to the kitchen minutes later she found that Gordon, on his knees, was raking out the ash-pan. He still wore his muffler and cap and his hands shook with cold as he tipped the ashes into an iron pail which would later be emptied into the midden in the backcourt.

"All right, Gordon, out with it." Kirsty kept her voice low so that the baby would not be disturbed. "Where have you been until this hour? Are you courtin' some lassie?"

The question amused him. "God, no! I'm only a wee boy, Kirsty. What would I be doin' with a girl in the dead o' night?"

"Don't play the innocent with me, Gordon."

"Promise you'll not tell Mother – or Craig?"

"No promises," Kirsty said.

She reached over Gordon's head and lifted the kettle. She carried it to the sink and filled it from the tap and placed it back on the range. Gordon busied himself with sticks and twists of newspaper. The lighting of fires, like all household chores, was considered to be woman's work. Gordon, though, seemed to know what he was doing. Kirsty said no more until he had struck a match and lighted the protruding fuse of newspaper. He sat back on his heels and looked up at her.

"Playin' cards," he said.

"Cards?"

"Three-card Brag."

"For money?" said Kirsty sternly.

"Well, it wasn't just for fun."

He was apprehensive but not frightened of her. He grinned. In spite of herself Kirsty felt her annoyance melt. At eighteen Gordon had a boyish charm that most women found disarming.

"Where do you do it?" she asked.

"At a pal's house. His name's Jimmy Moffatt. He plays the cornet in the band in the Gem theatre."

"Just the two of you?"

"Three or four of us. There's Harry Warden too. He's a bar-man in a pub in Byres Road."

Buskers and barmen sounded like the elements of bad company. Kirsty remembered how easily Craig had fallen in with a parcel of rogues soon after they had arrived in Glasgow, and what it had led to.

"Gordon, I saw you go to bed."

"I sneaked out again."

"How often do you do this?"

"Once or twice a week – when Craig's on night shift."

"Don't you know that betting's against the law?"

"Only makin' book or gamblin' in a public place," said Gordon glibly. "The coppers aren't goin' to crash into Jimmy Moffatt's kitchen and break our heads for havin' a friendly game o' cards."

"What does Mr Moffatt's wife have to say about it?"

"Hasn't got a wife. He lives with his old mother, and she's deaf as a post."

Kirsty knew nothing about gambling. She had seen the big pitch-and-toss schools in the distance once, in a field across the river from Scotstoun, and, more often, little groups gathered furtively behind the wash-house in the backcourt. She had watched young boys flicking cards into a cap or rattling dice in a jam jar. Personally she could not see much fun in it but she knew that football and horse-racing attracted men by the million. She had heard that even sober, sensible folk like Sergeant Hector Drummond and Superintendent Affleck had a wee flutter when Partick Thistle were playing Queen's Park or Belfast Handicap tickets were on sale.

"It's small wonder you look so washed out, Gordon, if you're goin' without sleep night after night."

"I can sleep on my feet all day," he said, "for all the mental effort the job requires."

"It's a start in life, Gordon."

"Some start! Sweepin' floors."

"Some boys of your age would be glad of the work."

"Most boys of my age are fit for nothin' better." He fished three or four small lumps of coal from the scuttle and pushed them through the spars of the fire-grate. "Is it the money you're worried about?"

She was only a few months older than Gordon and despised herself for sounding like a shrewish old scold, for trotting out those clichés by which the mothers in the close taught their sons morality and the rudiments of responsible behaviour.

She said, "I don't want to see you get into debt."

He grunted, fished in his trouser pocket and produced a grubby banknote. He held it out between his finger and thumb.

"Ten bob," he said. "Take it, Kirsty."

"Where did you get that? Did you steal it?"

"Jeeze, Kirsty! What do you take me for? I earned it fair and square. Here, take it."

She studied the note, pink and brown and wrinkled. It was more than she used to earn for forty miserable hours in Oswalds' bakehouse. Something in her recoiled from Gordon's lightness, the casual manner in which he flashed such a sum of money.

"Keep your – your gains, Gordon," she said. "I won't take your money."

"You take my wages."

"That's different."

"Sometimes, Kirsty, I think you're even more of a prig than my brother."

"Think what you like. I won't take cash that has a taint on it."

"Suit yourself." Expertly he folded the banknote and slipped it into his pocket again. He turned from her and contemplated the smoking coals. "I wish that bloody kettle would boil."

Ten shillings would put down a generous deposit on a new gas

7

stove, then they wouldn't have to wait for hours on these cold winter mornings for a kettle to boil. Ten shillings would buy Lorna a new pair of boots with fleece linings to wear to school. Her old pair were almost beyond repair. It would be money scrimped and saved from Craig's weekly wage that would have to pay for replacements. The gas stove and water-heater would have to remain dreams beyond her reach. She was tempted, hesitated: Really she could see nothing wrong in sharing her brother-in-law's good fortune. She thought, though, of the questions that Craig would ask. He would be bound to notice if she spent money that he had not given her, even on something like shoes for Lorna.

"Aren't you going to bed?" she asked.

"It's hardly worth it. I'll sit up an' keep you company."

"If Craig finds you up an' about he'll want to know the reason."

"Tell him you couldn't get the fire to light so you wakened me to do it for you."

"He'll never swallow that."

"Say nothin', then." Gordon got up, unwound the scarf from about his neck and draped it on a chair. "I'll concoct some story that he will swallow."

"I've come to the conclusion you're very good at tellin' lies," Kirsty said.

He put his arm about her before she could retreat, gave her a quick, affectionate squeeze and a peck on the cheek. "Ah, but I never lie to you, Kirsty, and never will."

"Set the table," Kirsty told him. "Do it quietly."

"Quiet as a wee mouse," said Gordon.

*　　*　　*

There was no escape from the paralysing cold. As night lengthened it manifested itself in a bristling frost that coated pavements and cobbles and turned the knurls of old snow in the gutters as hard as marble. It was not a pretty, sparkling frost but a grey, sifting thing that hoared the constables' coats and helmets and lined their eyebrows and moustaches like French chalk. It froze their lips too and made their words sound wooden, though that inconvenience did not stop young Ronald Norbert from prattling on and on, as he did every shift. By five o'clock Craig had had enough of Probationer Norbert and was tempted to strangle the idiot just to shut him up.

Ill-luck had saddled Craig with the postulant. He vowed that when the time came to make a report on Norbert's fitness to become a fully-fledged policeman he would be honest to the point of cruelty. It would serve no purpose, of course. Recruiting problems and a rash of resignations, common in winter, had thinned the ranks of the burgh force and the Chief Constable would sign on anyone who was keen to don a uniform.

"Think they'll cancel Thursday's parade because of the weather?" said Norbert.

Craig answered through clenched teeth. He had been asked the same question not two hours ago. "I told you, Ronnie, the Chief enjoys full musters. He won't cancel under any circumstances."

"He won't keep us there for hours, will he?"

"Twenty minutes at most." Craig was surprised at his own patience. "Twice around the parade ground, a general salute, a prayer and off we go home."

"Are you sure we don't get paid for it?"

"For the tenth time – no, we don't get paid for it."

"It's so inconvenient," said Norbert, "killin' time from seven to nine just to tramp round a stupid parade ground."

"If you don't like parades, Ronnie, withdraw your application and resign right now."

"I didn't say I didn't like them. I just said – "

"Put a bloody sock in it, eh?"

Ronnie Norbert was twenty-two years old, only months younger than Constable Nicholson. Craig seemed much more mature. He had been seasoned by experiences that had changed and darkened his character. He was tall and muscular and the moustache on his upper lip did not look jejune or foolish. He preferred to keep himself to himself, though this trait did not seem to have communicated itself to the young probationer who, after walking half a block in silence, started to chat once more.

"By God, I could do with a smoke."

Craig did not respond.

He was staring up at the edge of the roof of the Ollenshaw Oil & Colour Company's warehouse, which had a low pitch, so low that any enterprising thief could scamper along the ridge and prise open a skylight without much trouble. Ollenshaw was mean and employed only one night-watchman, old John Simpson. The warehouse had been raided three times in the past twelve months but Craig doubted if any self-respecting thief would poke his nose out of doors on a night like this one. Even so he scanned the roof carefully, and listened.

"Don't you smoke, Craig?"

"Not on duty."

"It's hard for me," Norbert bragged. "I've been puffin' the weed since I was ten. Consequently – "

"Shut up, Ronnie."

Ahead of the officers an arc lamp illuminated the entrance to the warehouse yard. The gate would be locked but he, Craig, would be able to see old John crouched in his cubby, eking out the meagre ration of stove coal that Ollenshaw allowed him.

Ronald Norbert said, "Aye, I was tossin' back whisky before I was twelve, an' all. Loved the stuff. Still do."

Ronnie was from the small Border town of Annan. His father was a seedsman and, if Ronnie was to be believed, quite well-to-do. With six brothers in the family there was not enough profit to support them all and Ronnie had struck out for Glasgow to make his way in the world. Craig's guess was that Ronnie had been run out of the family business because he could not hold his tongue.

"As for women – " Norbert began.

"I said, *shut it*."

"What is it? Do you hear somethin'?"

Ronnie Norbert was silent and still too. The officers stood motionless, both listening. But there was no sound at all in the grey air. Even the little groans and grumbles of the sleeping city seemed at that moment muffled.

"I don't hear a bloody thing," whispered Norbert.

"Keep it quiet, Ronnie."

"Right."

As soon as they stopped walking, cold gripped them. Even through layers of lambswool underwear, flannel and serge, it shrivelled their flesh. Fleetingly Craig thought of the kitchen at home, of a blazing fire in the grate, of hot porridge and hot tea, sizzling bacon and fried egg. He hoped that his mother would be up and about, wearing the fancy robe he had bought her. She was always bright and cheerful in the morning, which Kirsty was not.

He had put out of his mind the memory of his mam as a termagant who ruled Dalnavert with a rod of iron, how she bullied his dad and terrified them when they were younger. Growing up, becoming a police constable, had changed his perspective on many things. His attitude to his mother, as well as his wife, was one of them.

Ronnie Norbert said, "Do you want me to nip round the back? I could shin up the wall an' take a look along the roof."

"Nobody's up there, Ronnie," Craig answered. "The roof's like a glass sheet tonight. We'll give old John a shout, ask if he's seen anythin' suspicious."

The old man was watching for them. A constable came at approximately the same time every night. It comforted the old chap to know that the officers of the law kept an eye on him. He did not emerge from the box at the angle of yard and passageway, however, did not come forth to unlock the gate. He pushed open the window of the caretaker's box and called, "By gum, it's cold the night, lads, is it not now?"

"It's all that, John," Craig said. "Is all quiet?"

"Quiet as the grave."

"Have you been on your rounds?"

"Back ten minutes ago. All is safe an' sound."

"Are you sure?" put in Ronnie Norbert.

"Aye, I'm certain."

"Constable Nicholson thought he heard – "

"Ronnie, that's enough," Craig murmured.

Taking the probationer by the elbow, he gave the night-watchman a salute and moved on.

"Sometimes I don't understand you," Ronnie Norbert said.

"We don't want to scare the old joker, do we?"

"I suppose not," Ronnie Norbert admitted. "But if there was a noise – "

"Damn it, there wasn't."

The officers trudged north out of the warehouse district into a maze of old tenements that marked the bottom of Greenfield's thoroughfares. In one of those streets, Canada Road, Craig lived. In another, Ottawa Street, was the police station. At the nether end, though, the sandstone buildings were dark and sullen, defined only by hazy gaslight or a flicker of sparks from a recalcitrant chimney.

The streets were deserted in that dormant hour before night-shift workers crawled home to bed, and early birds set off for a day's labour. It was so cold now that even Ronnie Norbert's lips were sealed. The constables walked in silence, street by street, until they came to the door of the Buttercup Dairy, a seedy little shop, hardly wider than an arm's span, that sold skimmed milk, salted butter, fat back bacon and the worst sausages in Glasgow. The Buttercup Dairy opened its door at half past six to catch early-morning trade but it was an hour and more short of that time and its gate, of twisted and rusty metal, was still padlocked. Litter had blown against it and the man was sprawled amid the debris. One fist was frozen to the spars of the gate as if he had tried, vainly, to lift himself upright. His cap had come off. His hair was coated with frost and his eyes were wide open.

"Oh, God!" Probationer Norbert whispered. "What's that?"

"That," said Constable Nicholson, "is a deader, unless I'm much mistaken."

Kneeling, Craig groped for the man's wrist. No pulse. He slid a hand under the flap of the tattered jacket and pressed for a heartbeat. None, of course.

The man had been sick. A crisp bib of vomit hung from his chin. A bottle was still clenched in his right hand, plain glass, without a cork. It held a few drops of colourless liquid. Showing no distaste, Craig bent closer to the body and sniffed at the neck of the bottle.

"Arsenic?" said Ronnie Norbert.

"Raw spirits," Craig said.

"Isn't there blood? Isn't it murder?"

The probationer did not recoil. In fact, he seemed intrigued by the sight of the corpse. Hands on hips, he bent to study the remains for himself, hopeful that he would become involved in some dreadful and notorious case.

"Stab wounds?" Ronnie enquired.

"No, there's no trace of violence."

Craig unclipped a carbide lamp from his belt, shook it to let the gas accumulate and lit it with a match. He directed a milky beam on to the dead man's features.

Brows, lashes and stubble had caught spidery threads of frost but his mouth was shut and his expression, even in death, seemed fierce and defiant. Craig eased the head forward and examined the back of the skull. Rigor was already well advanced. He found no injury to the head, no tears on the back of the jacket. The clothing adhered to the pavement and came away with a thin ripping noise as Craig heaved the corpse into a sitting position and propped it against the gate.

Craig said, "It's my guess he died of exposure, or poisoned himself with the muck he was drinkin'. Anyway, he's stiff as a board an' there's nothin' we can do about it. Take down the particulars, Ronnie. Check the exact time on your watch. Make sure you get it right. We'll both have to make report in writing to the duty officer, and perhaps to the Procurator Fiscal. It looks simple enough but you never can tell what the surgeon will find."

"Maybe he *was* done in," said Norbert. "Is that what you mean?"

"You're a ghoul, Ronnie," said Craig. "I'll go back to the station and have Sergeant Drummond telephone for the meat wagon. You stay here, in the vicinity of the victim. Take a look along the street, see if you find anything that might be pertinent."

"Like what?"

"How do I know?"

"Do you want me to find the shebeen that sold him the spirits?"

"God, no!" said Craig. "Forget about the shebeen. He could have bought rot-gut any one of a dozen places."

Probationer Norbert had his notebook and pencil out and had taken off one mitten. He held the glove in his teeth and tried to steady his hands, to make his writing legible. It was cold, not shock, that made him shake so.

Ronnie Norbert said, "You didn't check his pockets."

"They're empty."

"No identification?"

"Don't need identification," Craig said. "I know who he is."

"Who is he, then?"

Craig said, "His name's Reynolds."

Norbert looked up sharply. "Sammy's old man?"

"That's him," Craig said. "That *was* him."

"Poor Sammy. Poor wee bastard," Ronnie Norbert said. "Who'll take the word? Who'll tell the boy?"

"I will," said Craig.

* * *

It was still pitch-dark and frost on the window panes had not yet begun to melt with the warmth in the kitchen. But the fire was bright now and the stove hot and Kirsty had clashed the pan and served Gordon a good breakfast.

Gordon liked his sister-in-law. If things had worked out differently he might even have been her husband. He had always fancied her, even when he was just a laddie running about Bankhead school playground. She had seemed much older than him in those days, calm and assured and mysterious. She looked even better now, though. Her hair had darkened, become more auburn. The sprinkling of freckles across her nose and cheeks had faded. It was difficult to recall that she had once been despised as an orphan brat from the Baird Home, mother a whore and father unknown, had been a servant-slave to Duncan Clegg up at Hawkhead Farm, away in the secret hills. He could not blame her for running away from that sly, lascivious wee bastard.

It was Dad who had given Craig money and urged him to run off with Kirsty, to strike out on his own and not become bonded to the run-down acres of the tenant farm at Dalnavert. Mother had been furious when she discovered that Craig had flown the coop. She would have journeyed to Glasgow to find her errant son and drag him back home if, for once, Dad had not stood his ground. What a half-year that had been for Lorna and him, caught in the middle of the angry war between their parents; then Dad had dropped dead of a heart seizure and, almost overnight, Mam changed.

At first she had tried to persuade Craig to give up his new life in Glasgow and return to take over the farm. Craig would have none of it, and when it became clear that she would not have her own way Mam had wasted no time in selling up. She had packed their belongings into five bags and whisked them, Lorna and him, off to Glasgow without shedding a single tear. Gordon had protested, just for the sake of it. In reality he had been infected by her eagerness to make a fresh start. Moving to a city had always been his dream. He could not say that he was sorry to leave the country and the place where he had been born and raised. But sweeping floors in a carpet factory for eleven shillings a week had not been part of the dream. He hated the gnashing chatter of power looms and filthy dust and the way the carpet weavers treated him, as if he was a bumpkin without a brain in his head.

It was Craig who had found him the job. He would have preferred to be a policeman like Craig, but he was too short in stature to meet the minimum requirement. Bossing them all, as was his way, Craig had planned Lorna's future too. She would stay at school for an extra year's instruction, then he, Craig, would find her a position as a clerk. All cut and dried – by Craig. Craig had taken command of all their lives; except that it was Mam who pulled *his* strings.

Gordon mopped up slick yellow-red egg yolk with a piece of bread, popped it in his mouth and pushed his plate away.

"Well, that'll set me up fine," he said.

Kirsty was seated opposite him, a teacup cradled in both hands. The baby, Bobby, slept still in his tented cot, undisturbed by the murmur of familiar voices and the timpani of crockery and pans.

"You'll not be happy until you get out of that factory, will you?" Kirsty said.

"I loathe the bloody place."

"Why don't you apply for a trade apprenticeship?"

"Two years learnin' how to manage a hammer an' chisel at a wage that wouldn't feed a sparrow," Gordon said. "That's not for me." ·

"What sort of job *do* you want?"

"Somethin' with scope for enterprise."

"I can't think what you mean."

"I don't want to sponge off you an' Craig one minute more than's necessary."

"Aren't you comfortable here?"

"'Course I am," said Gordon. "But it's not right, not for you."

"I – I don't mind," Kirsty said.

Gordon grinned. "Now who's tellin' lies? I've seen how Mother treats you. She doesn't give you your proper place. She's got Craig twisted round her finger. He spoils her somethin' awful."

"He's just tryin' to make amends."

"For runnin' off with you? Jeeze, it's the best thing he ever did."

"The house could become too small," said Kirsty, thoughtfully, "if the family gets bigger."

"Hey, are you expectin' another bairn?"

She was taken aback. "No, I am not."

It would hardly be surprising if she was, Gordon thought; though, as far as he could deduce, his brother and his wife never lay down together these days. Craig slept in the front parlour too because it was quieter and his shifts were irregular.

15

It was a larger house than most in the Greenfield but when the family grew the house would shrink accordingly; in that Kirsty was right.

Kirsty said, "Craig will never let you move out, even if you could afford a place of your own."

Gordon said, "I suppose Mother might decide to marry again."

"Do you think it's possible?"

"Well, she's seein' this bloke, Mr Adair – "

Kirsty sat forward in her chair. "What do you know about him?"

"Precious little. She won't talk about him."

"Is she ashamed of him, do you think?"

"Why should she be ashamed of him?" said Gordon.

"Perhaps he's married."

Gordon slapped his brow with his palm. "I never thought of that."

Kirsty shook her head. "No, Gordon. I'm sure your mother would never stoop to goin' out with a married man."

"She might," said Gordon, "if it suited her."

The clock on the mantelshelf chimed the hour. Kirsty rose, cleared dishes and put them in the sink. Chin on hand Gordon watched her perform her chores. He saw her take a clean egg-cup and a strainer from the cupboard, a spoon with a looped handle from a drawer. When Bobby wakened he would find everything ready for him. Gordon liked to watch Bobby being fed, to see how patient Kirsty was with the baby, how she coaxed him to eat. He wondered if Mam had been as patient with him when he was tiny. He supposed she must have been.

Kirsty returned to the table. He waited for her to take up the threads of the conversation once more, but she did not. She was usually quiet in the mornings, preoccupied with getting the day off right.

Her hand brushed affectionately over his hair.

"You look terrible, Gordon."

"Thanks very much."

"Change your shirt. Have a wash. I'll boil a kettle for you."

"All right." He yawned, stretched. "About this morning – ?"

"No," she said. "I won't say a word to Craig."

"Take the money, Kirsty. I'm sure you could use it."

This time, Gordon noticed, she did not even pause.

"No, Gordon," she said.

He nodded, got up, hugged her once more and went into the front parlour to change.

* * *

Ottawa Street police station was lighted and heated by piped coal gas. Chest-high bronze radiators gave off a fine fierce heat and a smell like burned turnip. As soon as he arrived for day duty Sergeant Stevens, a lean dry man from Islay, would order the windows to be flung open to drain the turbid air that had built up during the night. Sergeant Drummond, on the other hand, preferred to keep the windows sealed as long as possible to thaw out his coppers when they returned numb and sullen from the beat. Sergeant Drummond had even set up a special tea urn and saw to it that his men were served with mugs of piping-hot tea before being called to file their reports. The sergeant had had the nod for this irregular procedure from Lieutenant Strang, the duty officer, for Drummond and Strang had been outside, making rounds, and knew only too well how cold it was.

It had been a very quiet night. The log was almost devoid of entries. The cells in the basement were being used not for criminals but to shelter a few down-and-outs who had been scooped up for their own protection and would be fed and released, without charge, when daylight came. Police Court would be peaceful today too, which was just as well as Chief Constable Organ's monthly muster would go ahead as usual in the drill yard behind Percy Street headquarters. Mr Organ liked every officer to be there, if possible. He fair enjoyed the sight of all his uniforms marching under his paternal gaze.

Constable Craig Nicholson did not enter the station in haste. He did not display any of the agitation which a less stable officer would have been incapable of disguising. He did not pause at the radiator to warm his hands, though, but came directly to the desk, notebook already in hand.

"Found a deader, Sergeant," he said.

Sergeant Drummond reached immediately below the desk and brought out a buff-coloured form. He spread the printed form upon the counter, dipped a pen into the inkwell and, with belly pressed against the edge of the desk, nodded to Constable Nicholson to read off the details.

Craig provided all salient facts in order of their occurrence in the official jargon that fiscal authorities preferred. He concluded, "There was no visible evidence of wounding or injury. Evidence suggests that the victim was intoxicated at time of death."

"What evidence?"

"The bottle of spirits in his hand."

"Empty?"

"Almost," said Craig.

"Did you leave Norbert to guard the body?"

"I did, Sergeant."

"Did you find any identification on the corpse?"

"No, Sergeant. But I recognised him."

"Did you, indeed?"

"It's Sammy Reynolds' father."

Sergeant Drummond glanced up, pen poised. "Do you say now? Are you positive?"

"Yes, Sergeant."

"Have you seen the boy recently?"

"Saw him yesterday, Sergeant."

"Is he as daft as ever?"

"Aye, he is. In fact, I think he's gettin' worse as he gets older."

"He didn't appear – distressed?"

"No, Sergeant. He was blowin' his whistle and jumpin' about after us. As usual."

"I wonder where he is."

"He'll be at the Madagascar, I expect, in Rae's tenement."

"I think you'd better check on Sammy, Constable Nicholson."

"Aye, Sergeant. Will I break the bad news to him?"

"You'd better."

Sammy Reynolds was well known to Ottawa Street coppers. In particular he had attached himself to Craig who had once been responsible for arresting him on a charge of petty theft. In Craig, in the impressive uniform, Sammy had discovered a ready-made substitute for the authority that his drunken father could not provide.

"Sammy?" said the sergeant. "What age is he?"

"I think he's about fifteen," said Craig. "I doubt if he knows himself for sure."

"If no relatives are traced, relatives willing to take him in, I fear it will be the workhouse for the poor lad," said Sergeant Drummond, adding ominously, "or since he's not quite all right in the head, a ward in the asylum."

Craig said nothing but his mouth set hard as if the notion of Sammy Reynolds afloat on the boundless sea of parish charity angered him.

"I'll knock up the surgeon," said Hector Drummond. "I'll accompany the wagon to pick up the remains. Norbert can hold the fort until the end of the duty since it's only a half-hour or so. Meanwhile, you cut along to the Madagascar and see if you can locate Sammy."

"What will I do with him?" said Craig.

"Bring him back here," the sergeant said.

* * *

Lorna Nicholson was at an awkward age, neither child nor young woman. By turns she was sullen and rebellious, secretive, confiding, bashful and vain. She had a long oval-shaped face and a pretty mouth and, like the rest of the Nicholsons, a mind of her own.

Currently Lorna was obsessed with a little rash of pimples that had appeared on her brow. She would creep about with hands over her face and head hung down or spend hours trying to comb her dark springy hair over the blemish. To the girl's chagrin Kirsty had bought a jar of purifying cream from the chemist's. She had handed it to Lorna without a word and received, for her kindness, a murderous glare. Now, four or five days later, the blemishes had begun to smooth away and would soon vanish completely. Not that Lorna showed gratitude. That February morning she was making ready for school with the despondent air of a felon about to step on the gallows.

At least Lorna, unlike so many of her schoolmates, would be dressed for harsh weather. She had long drawers, long black woollen stockings, a lined vest, an overcoat, a tammy for her head, gloves and stout, if not fashionable, shoes. Thus protected, with a nourishing breakfast inside her, she would be shielded from the umpteen maladies that swept the classrooms and, before winter was out, would cull three or four weakly constituted children from the school rolls.

It was Kirsty, not Madge, who showed concern for Lorna's health and welfare, who fed her Scott's Emulsion, and Ipecacuanha Wine when the girl had sniffles or a sore throat. Madge would simply lay a hand on her daughter's brow, inspect her tongue, declare, "Oh, you'll live to fight another day," and pack her off to school regardless. Kirsty wondered if she would ever develop the knack of being unconcerned. She was far too devoted to Bobby to be so off-hand. She knew that her days would be shaped by his needs, by Craig's needs too. But on dark bitter mornings the prospect depressed her a little. The love she bore her son and her pride in her home did not seem quite enough to compensate for the feeling that she was trapped on a march down a road to nowhere.

Craig was late. White-faced with fatigue, Gordon had eaten a second breakfast and had gone off to the carpet factory. Lorna had risen, complaining of 'pains', and Bobby had wakened and demanded to be fed. At twenty-five past eight Lorna left for school. Still Craig had not returned. Racking her memory, Kirsty thought she recalled him saying something about a general muster that morning. Usually, though, he would return before a parade to snatch some breakfast, polish his boots and buttons and go off in the gathering light as if he relished the prospect of marching round the square at Percy Street. For all she knew, perhaps he did.

Changed, fed and comfortable, Bobby clung to her as she went about the kitchen doing her chores. He gurgled in her ear, reached out for everything with curious fingers. Soon she would put him in his cot again with his jingle-rabbit to keep him amused.

The clock ticked. Still no sign of Craig.

She had learned from the other police wives in the tenement that it was not riots and street fights that a constable had to fear but the trivial violence that erupted without warning; a stray dog turned vicious, a domestic squabble that ended with a copper catching a bottle in the face. Every little street farce and comic turn contained a mustard-seed of tragedy. She was always glad to see him come through the door, though she hid her relief and made her kiss of welcome seem casual. After all, she did not wish to embarrass him.

At a quarter to nine Madge Nicholson finally stirred. She had probably been lying awake for some time, luxuriating in the warmth of the double bed that she shared with her daughter, though she would have been up at once if she had heard Craig return. She would have appeared in the robe that he had bought for her, all soft and motherly and caring. She would have served his breakfast, folded his nightshirt over a chair to warm, would even have plucked Bobby from his cot and petted him, suggesting that he had been, somehow, neglected by his mother. Craig would seem to be taken in by the performance. He would grin and banter with his mother as he seldom did with Kirsty.

As usual Madge had not pinned up her hair. She was wrapped in the fleecy pink flannel robe with its Plauen lace trimming, fleecy sleeping-socks and dainty pink kidskin slippers. She had thick fair hair and a clear complexion. Even Kirsty had to admit that she was a remarkably handsome woman now that she had shed the trappings of farmer's drudge. A kailyard stridency could still be detected in her voice from time to time but when she applied herself she could shed her Ayrshire accent and adopt a timbre that made her sound like a large amiable tabby-cat. It was Kirsty, not Craig, who often saw the claws, heard the spitting hiss of ill-temper. Madge liked to keep Kirsty off balance. It was not her intention to destroy the marriage but merely to maintain the love of the breadwinner, her son, and dominance over his wife.

Madge had a life outside the tenement, however. She did not discuss what she did at concerts and soirées and whist drives, talked not at all of the man who courted her, attracted by her vigour and generous figure. Kirsty had to make do with church society, her friends at St Anne's, Nessie Frew and David Lockhart. For some reason Madge deeply resented those outside influences, the pleasures that Kirsty found in 'religion'.

Shaking out her thick, leonine hair, Madge came into the kitchen and made straight for the teapot on the hob.

"Where's Craig?"

"He's not home yet."

"I can see that," said Madge. "Where is he?"

"I think there's a parade today."

"Has Bobby been changed?"

"Yes."

"Has he eaten his breakfast?"

"Yes."

Madge poured tea, added sugar and carried the cup to the table. She seated herself, back to the fire, and fished a packet of cigarettes from the pocket of her robe. She lit one with a match, sipped the strong, black tea, inhaled a mouthful of cigarette smoke, coughed and sighed with satisfaction. Craig disapproved of women who indulged in nicotine but, alone with

Kirsty, Madge flourished the cigarette in a manner that she believed to be both ladylike and bohemian.

She glanced at the window. "Still freezin'?"

"Aye, there's no sign of a thaw," said Kirsty. "I can't wait any longer for the tap in the wash-house to unblock. I'll take the clothes to the steamie later."

The 'steamie' was a public wash-house used by all the women in the close when they had heavy things to be laundered.

"When I was your age — " Madge began.

Kirsty interrupted. "I know — you had to trample your dirty clothes in the burn."

"In all weathers too," said Madge. "Who told you about that?"

"You did," said Kirsty. "A dozen times."

The story was untrue. Bankhead Mains, where Madge had worked as a servant before her marriage, had had a well-appointed laundry room.

Madge said, "Dryin' will be difficult today."

"If I hang the stuff out it'll freeze in minutes."

"You'll just have to load the pulley."

Madge glanced up at the long wooden rack that was hoisted close to the kitchen's high ceiling. The spars were already festooned with stockings, drawers and napkins.

Madge said, "Best make sure it's all done before Craig has his dinner. He'll not be wantin' dripped on while he's eatin'."

"Will you look after Bobby while I'm out?" Kirsty asked. "I hate takin' him to the steamie with me. The dampness isn't good for him."

False politeness was the price she had to pay for enlisting her mother-in-law's help in matters that should not have required negotiation.

Madge blew smoke, cocked her head. "Can your 'posh' friend not look after him?"

The pettiness and repetitiousness of Madge's song-and-dance about Nessie Frew irked Kirsty but she did not rise to the bait, did not show her annoyance.

"If you mean Mrs Frew, she has quite enough to do without being burdened with a baby to look after."

"What does *she* have to do, tell me?" Madge said.

"She has a house to run."

"With servants to help her."

22

"One girl, that's all."

"Can the servant not – "

"I happen to know," said Kirsty, "that Mrs Frew has a previous engagement this afternoon."

"I wish I was a lady of leisure who could have 'previous engagements' when it suited me," said Madge haughtily.

She put her hands behind her head and gave her mane of hair another shake, a strange, girlish gesture, vain and sensual.

Soon she would cook herself a huge breakfast for, like her children, she had a farm-buddy's appetite. She would then repair to the front bedroom and spend an hour grooming herself. She would not appear in public until she was as smart as a painted pole, even if she was just taking Bobby out or doing some shopping. Madge's style impressed the other wives in the tenement. They took her for half a lady at least, and envied Kirsty for having such a well-bred woman in her household to offer wisdom and counsel.

"You've plenty of engagements," said Kirsty. "Why, you've hardly been in a night this week."

"You don't grudge me my pleasure, I hope. God knows, I've earned it."

"I don't grudge you anything," said Kirsty.

"I'm glad to hear it."

Bobby had so far ignored his grandmother. He had been twisting the limbs of his jingle-rabbit with ferocious concentration. Suddenly, however, he found voice, thumped the toy against the side of the cot and chanted crossly, "*Ayyy-ayyy-eyyy*."

"He needs changed, poor lamb," said Madge.

"He's been changed," said Kirsty. "Look, I'm not goin' to beg."

"Beg? Beg for what?"

"To have you look after him this afternoon."

"Oh, so that's it," said Madge. "I didn't say I wouldn't."

"Will you?"

"Of course I will." She tossed the cigarette-end into the fireplace and advanced on the cot, arms akimbo, face wreathed in loving smiles. "Won't 'e come wi' his gran den, wee darlin'? Down t' Mr Kydd's shoppie t' buy a barley-sugar, eh?"

Bobby rocked back, eyes round, as the woman leaned demonstratively over him. Madge was clever, though. She waited for the baby to ponder and decide. Only when he thrust out his arms to her and uttered a little grunting gabble did she pick him up. She pressed him against her breasts and gave him a smacking kiss on the cheek. Bobby chuckled.

Kirsty reached for her apron.

Madge went on, "I'll tak' care o' you, my wee sweetheart, while your mama's gallivantin'."

Kirsty flung a wet washcloth into the sink and spun round.

"Washing at the steamie is hardly gallivantin'."

Madge was all innocence. "I was just chattin' to my wee lamb, that's all."

"Well, I'll thank you to mind what you say."

It had been a long cold morning. She had achieved very little in the hours since she had got up and, for once, Madge's teasing sarcasm had got under her skin. Madge did not yield easily, though she preferred cut-and-run tactics.

"I'll say what I damned-well like. It's not your house," Madge retorted.

"It *is* my — "

Sounds from the stairs outside stifled the quarrel and made Bobby too fall quiet.

"Craig!" said Madge, and carrying the baby, stepped away quickly from Kirsty.

Craig it was, but he did not enter the kitchen alone.

He called out, "Is everybody decent in there?"

"Company!" Madge exploded. "Oh, my God! He's brought company, an' me lookin' like a hay-rick."

Craig peeped round the kitchen door. He had removed his helmet but still wore his muffler and greatcoat. He grinned and ushered before him a young ragamuffin in a jacket that was too short and trousers so large they had to be held up by twine. Tousled and filthy, he wore no shirt and no hat. Only a jersey with a sagging V-collar protected his thin body against the cold. Looped on an old leather bootlace about his neck was a rusty police whistle.

"You've heard me talk about Sammy Reynolds," said Craig. "Well, this is him."

Arm on the boy's shoulder, Craig steered the boy towards the fire. Madge drew the baby away from the stranger as if she suspected that he had escaped from a fever ward.

"What — what's he *doin*' here?"

"He'll be staying for a while," said Craig.

"*What!*"

"How long, Craig?" Kirsty asked.

"*He*'s not stayin' in my house," Madge cried. "Look at the state o' him. Dirt off the streets. How *dare* you bring such a — "

"His daddy just d-i-e-d."

Sammy remained upright by the chair that Craig had drawn out for him, motionless and awkward. He glanced from Craig to Kirsty, from Kirsty to Madge.

Kirsty said, "Does he know? Does he understand?"

"I think so," said Craig.

Kirsty had heard talk of Sammy Reynolds. He was soft in the head and neglected. He had made a hero out of Craig and believed that one day the rusty whistle about his neck would be replaced by a shiny new one, that he would become a member of Greenfield's burgh police force. It was laughable, pathetic, yet Craig would brook no serious teasing of Sammy's ambition though his dog-like devotion was frequently a nuisance and sometimes an embarrassment.

"Why isn't he cryin', then?" said Madge.

"He cried enough when I told him."

"Sammy," said Kirsty, "wouldn't you like to sit down?"

"Look at his hands," said Madge. "Filthy. Look at his hair. It's crawlin'."

"How did it happen, Craig?" said Kirsty.

Craig shrugged. "Drunk in the street, the bottle still in his fist. Froze to the pavement."

"Awful, just awful." Kirsty shuddered.

"Be that as it may," said Madge, "he can't stay here."

"Got no place else to go," said Craig matter-of-factly.

"He *must* have a family. He *can't* be alone," Madge protested.

"If he has relatives," said Craig, taking off his coat, "only God knows who and where they are. Sammy's lived in the Madagascar with the old man for seven or eight years."

"Letters? Papers?" said Madge.

"Not a scrap."

"The school — ?"

"The truant officers gave up on him ages ago," Craig answered. "They hounded the old man for a while to no effect, then got round the regulations by declaring that Sammy was over school age. I've no idea what age he is, really. Even Sammy doesn't know that. Do you, Sam?"

"Nuh, Mr Nicholson."

"Would you like a cup of tea, Sammy?" said Kirsty.

"Uh-huh."

He was shy but no longer distressed. When Kirsty pointed to the chair, he fitted himself into it at once.

Angrily Madge swung the baby away and plopped him into his cot where he lolled against the pillows, girning. She turned on Craig. "*You* may regard yourself as a servant o' society, Craig Nicholson, but it's not part o' your duty to drag home every dirty tink you come across."

"It's only for a day or two, Mother."

"*A day or two!*" Madge shouted. "If you think I'm stayin' in the house alone with that creature after dark — "

"For God's sake," said Craig wearily. "He has to go somewhere."

"Not here." Madge was adamant. "Let the welfare officers find a home for him. If you ask my opinion he should be locked away in the madhouse. Look at him. My God, he's *smilin'*."

Sammy's lips were pulled back to reveal broken brown teeth. It was not a smile of pleasure, Kirsty saw, but of uncertainty. Had he, she wondered, truly grasped the meaning of the news that Craig had given him? Did he know that his life had been dramatically altered? If he had been an ounce less stable perhaps he would not have sensed at all that things had changed, and that would have been a blessing.

"Did he have to be shown the — I mean, did you have to take him to that place?" she asked.

"No need for it. I found and identified the b-o-d-y. Bloody Ronnie Norbert an' me. That idiot Norbert was hopin' it was murder."

Madge had become aware that Craig was taking no notice of her protestations. "I thought you were on parade this mornin'?"

"Drummond will post me excused. I'm not bothered about missin' a damned parade," Craig said.

"More bothered about him, I suppose."

Craig ignored the remark. He tapped Sammy on the shoulder and demonstrated in dumb-show what he wanted him to do.

"You'll have to wash your mitts if you're goin' to eat at my table, Sammy," Craig told him. "See how I do it."

Sammy's head jerked, the smile fixed on his lips.

He had fluffy stubble on his chin and was well muscled. His

colour was similar to Kirsty's and he had freckles too upon his cheeks. Perhaps Madge was right to be concerned. After all, daft lads could be unpredictable in their behaviour. Kirsty put her doubts aside, lost in pity for the boy, with his vacant expression and faded uncomprehending gaze.

"I got a whistle, missus," he told her.

"So I see, Sammy," said Kirsty. "Listen, are you hungry?"

"Aye."

"Wash your hands then an' I'll give you something to eat."

Kneeling in his cot Bobby watched intently as the stranger stood elbow to elbow with his daddy at the sink, washed his hands under the tap and dried them, copycat fashion, on a length of clean towel, watched him come to the table and eat from the bowl of thick porridge that his mammy put down, watched him put away ham and sliced sausage and, still emulating Daddy, push his plate away with a lordly gesture of satisfaction.

"Grand," said Craig.

"Grand," said Sammy.

Fuming, Madge swept out of the kitchen and slammed the door behind her. She would sulk in the front room until she could catch Craig alone and bring all her powers of persuasion to bear on him. It was the first time that Craig had stood up to her, defied her. It seemed odd that it should be over a boy, a daftie. There was nothing sweet or appealing in Sammy Reynolds' appearance now, yet Kirsty felt for his plight. She knew what it was like to be at the mercy of strangers, an indiscriminate victim of charity.

"He can't go on living in the Madagascar, can he?" she enquired.

"Impossible," said Craig.

"Can he work?"

"I suppose he could, given the right sort of job."

"Can't you find him the right sort of job?"

"I never thought of that," said Craig.

Sammy wiped his mouth on his sleeve. He watched Craig light a cigarette. Craig rested both elbows on the table. Sammy copied the gesture.

"We can't take him in, Craig," said Kirsty.

"Oh, I know that," Craig said.

"I wish we could, but we haven't room."

He glanced up at her and she detected in his eyes a trace of an emotion that she could not identify.

Craig said, "I couldn't just drag him down to the station, Kirsty, not cold out of his bed an' his old man – you know."

"I understand."

Craig shrugged. "Mother's got a point, though. It's all laid down in law how cases like this should be dealt with. Some board or committee will decide what's to become of him."

"They'll put him away, won't they?"

"Aye, they might," Craig conceded.

"Can't you stop them?"

"How? I'm only a copper."

"Find him work."

"How?"

"David could help," said Kirsty cautiously.

It was months since Craig and she had talked like this, since she had had so much of his attention. Now she had managed to raise David Lockhart's name without it seeming calculated.

"Lockhart?" Craig paused. "What the hell could he do?"

"He might know somebody who would take Sammy in."

"Be a bloody miracle if he did."

"Or find him suitable employment."

Craig paused again. "If Sammy had a job, a paid, regular occupation, I could get him a place in a lodging-house. I'm sure I could."

"Would that keep him out of – you know?"

"It's a solution the welfare officers would accept with alacrity, I reckon. And it would save Mother from bein' upset."

Not a word about her wishes, her feelings. She had succeeded in bringing David to Craig's attention, however, and was grateful for that.

She said, "I'll take Sammy down there, if you like."

Sammy nodded. He didn't know where or to whom he was being led but he had taken to Kirsty, PC Nicholson's missus.

"Where?" said Craig. "To the kirk?"

"First to Walbrook Street."

"Walbrook Street?"

"If David isn't at home then Nessie will know where to find him."

"Why are you doin' this? To be shot of him?"

"I feel sorry for him," Kirsty said.

"Is that the only reason?"

"It's reason enough, Craig."

Craig got up from the table.

Sammy rose too.

"I'll set the clock for one," Craig said. "I'll go round to the station then and let Drummond know what's goin' on."

He stooped and lifted his son from the cot. As if to punish his father for ignoring him for so long Bobby dunted a soft fist against his father's nose. Craig slung the baby on to his left arm. Sammy, watching, stuck the rusty whistle into his mouth and blew, blew. No sound but a hiss came forth. Sammy blew harder. His cheeks turned scarlet and his ears stuck out. Bobby let out a yell of delight at the performance. Inspired, Sammy huffed and puffed at the whistle until his cheeks were moon-shaped and his eyes near popped from his head.

"Stop that," Madge shouted.

She strode into the kitchen, dressed, her hair pinned. "Leave my grandson alone."

The whistle tumbled from Sammy's lips, saliva dripping on to his chin. Madge grabbed him by the shoulder and dragged him back from Bobby who, frightened by his grandmother's temper, suddenly began to wail.

"Now see what you've done, you dirty devil," Madge shouted.

"Mother, for God's sake – "

Provoked by poor Sammy, Madge Nicholson's wilfulness showed as plainly as it had ever done in the old days at Dalnavert. Craig drew Bobby back from her, soothing the child with stroking motions of his hand. When he stepped away it seemed as if he had aligned himself with Kirsty so that for a moment she felt close to him, encircled by his love and his loyalty. It did not last long, however.

Madge planted her fists on her hips. "It's not right to bring riff-raff in off the streets. His kind – "

"His kind? What's that supposed to mean?" said Craig.

"Fine you know what I mean."

For no apparent reason Craig abruptly reverted to the flat, Ayrshire accent of his youth. "He canna help himself. God, Mam, but ye can be hard, times."

"I've had to be hard, son. Otherwise you'd never have got where you are."

"Aye," said Craig. "I've you to thank for that." He handed Bobby to Kirsty. "Now, I'm away to my bed."

"Leavin' him wi' us?" said Madge.

"No, Mother. I'm leavin' him wi' Kirsty."

"So what's to happen to him?"

"He'll be taken care of, never fear."

"By?"

"By me," said Kirsty.

Surprised at the ease of what seemed like a victory, Madge was suspicious. "What's goin' on here?"

Unbuttoning his tunic, Craig said, "You're gettin' your own way again, Mother. As usual."

"But – "

Craig put his hand on Sammy's shoulder once more. "You'll go with Kirsty, with Mrs Nicholson. She'll take you to see a nice man, Sammy. He'll find a place for you to stay."

"Stay here."

"Nah, nah, Sammy, that's not possible."

"Aye, stay here, stay here."

Kirsty took Sammy by the arm. Madge had been right about one thing; Sammy was not clean. From him she could smell a whiff of that same unwashed odour as her farm boss, Duncan Clegg, had exuded. She did not flinch, however, but gave Sammy a hug, Bobby balanced against her body.

"You and me, we'll go for a walk to see Mr Lockhart," she told him.

"So that's it, is it?" said Madge. "Any excuse will do, won't it?"

"What the hell do you mean, Mother?" said Craig.

"She's just usin' this poor boy as an excuse to go to see her – "

"What? See what?" said Craig, very softly.

Madge, though, would not speak the word. She did not dare challenge Kirsty outright by throwing down the accusation in Craig's hearing. Craig shrugged. He had his tunic top over his arm and his trousers partly unbuttoned, his collar off. Sammy was still leaning against Kirsty, elbow gently trapping her arm.

Craig said, "Now, you'll go along with Mrs Nicholson an' do what she tells you, won't you, Sammy?"

"Aye."

"Good lad," said Craig.

He kissed his son on the brow, turned and went out of the kitchen and across the hall to the small front parlour where he would roll into the cold bed and sleep until one o'clock.

The women stood motionless, facing each other across the

table, Kirsty with Bobby in her arms and Sammy pressed against her side.

She looked straight at her mother-in-law.

"My what?" she asked.

"Your lover," Madge Nicholson said.

*   *   *

Walbrook Street lay east of Canada Road towards the city's centre. It was a long, curved street of flat cobbles, tree-lined. Its elegant terraced houses were separated from the Clyde's wharves and quays by a bowling-green and by the high ramps of the Lanarkshire & Dunbartonshire railway. It was in Mrs Frew's boarding-house in Walbrook Street that Craig Nicholson and Kirsty Barnes, strangers to the city and to each other, had spent their first chaste night together, in separate bedrooms, of course.

Mrs Frew was prim and prudish but, as Kirsty was to discover soon enough, had a kind heart. It was through the intervention of Mrs Frew's brother, Hugh Affleck, a superintendent of detectives on the City of Glasgow force, that Craig had been saved from slipping into a life of crime and had eventually become a policeman too. It was also at Walbrook Street that Kirsty had encountered David Lockhart, a 'nephew of sorts' to Nessie Frew. David was now sole guest in the house, which had closed its doors to wayfaring clergymen and had become once more a private dwelling.

David was the elder son of missionaries. He had been born and brought up in China. David and his young brother, Jack, had been sent home to Scotland to complete their education, to receive advanced training in medicine and to take further degrees in divinity before they returned to the North China Mission. But David had renounced the paternal scheme, had chosen to defy his father and seek a parish post in Scotland. His decision had led to a great wound in relations with his parents and brother, one which David feared would never be healed. He was happy where he was, acting as ordained assistant to the minister of St Anne's parish church. In due course he would apply for a parish of his own, would move far out of Glasgow to pursue his calling as preacher and pastor. Both Nessie Frew and Kirsty dreaded that day.

There was a bond of unusual intimacy between Kirsty and David Lockhart, though they were not lovers in the accepted sense of the word. David had performed an emergency delivery of Kirsty's child, in a situation that had allowed no time for thought of consequences or niceties of behaviour. There was no doubt that it was David's prompt action that had saved Bobby's life, and Kirsty's too perhaps. He had received precious little gratitude from Craig Nicholson and, indeed, had even been estranged from Kirsty for a while because of it.

It was only when summer came again that Kirsty realised that she was in love with David Lockhart. How could she explain to somebody as plain and earthy, as selfish, as her mother-in-law that her love for David was not sinful? It was impossible. To Madge she would always be the daughter of a whore, to have in her, by nature's inexorable law, that streak of immorality which could never be contained by a husband, a home and a family. To Madge, David was a man first and a minister of the Gospel second, little different from the farmhands of Carrick, predatory and lusting above all else. Kirsty could not accept that all men were the same at heart, that appetite must always outrun sensibility, that affection must always be scheming in its courses. David was not like that, nor was Craig, really. She was poised between them, belonging in law to neither.

She was not embarrassed when Sammy clutched her hand. No doubt he thought he was protecting her. He seemed to have forgotten his father and the dreadful news that Craig had brought him earlier that morning. He was excited at the novelty, at walking abroad with Mrs Nicholson. He nodded to strangers, blew his silver whistle at carters, now and then gave a skip and hop, and grinned so happily that Kirsty did not have the heart to explain to him that he must soon leave her for the company of strangers. They walked quickly through the morning's cold haze and reached Mrs Frew's front door in about twenty minutes. Kirsty rang the bell.

Peggie, the maid, opened the door. She was a cheerful Irish-born girl, sturdy and robust enough to withstand Mrs Frew's moods and eccentricities.

"So it's yourself, is it, Mrs Nicholson?" she said, then winked at Sammy. "Brought a friend too, I see."

"Is David – is Mr Lockhart at home?"

"He is, he is."

Callers were common at No. 19. David had already acquired a reputation in the parish as a sympathetic young man who kept an open door for any members of the congregation who felt in need of help or guidance but were a little shy of broaching the minister in person.

"Kirsty, what a fine surprise."

David appeared from his study at the end of the gloomy hallway. He wore no jacket or cardigan, only a vest of fine grey cloth that, without the dog-collar atop it, would have given him more than passing affinity with a waiter in a sea-food bar or one of Glasgow's Italian restaurants. He was freshly shaven. A tiny blob of soap still adhered to his earlobe and it was all Kirsty could do to resist the temptation to take out her handkerchief and gently wipe it away.

David at home always seemed so different from the David who occupied the pulpit on Sunday evenings and preached strong logical sermons, from the man who assisted the Reverend Graham at Communion services or joined in hearty rough-and-tumble with the lads of the Boys' Brigade on Friday evenings. To several of the women of the congregation he was a dream son-in-law for their plain or untamed daughters and little Sunday School teachers and girls in Bible Study group went all fluttery when David was present and flushed to the roots of their hair when he gave them particular notice. There was one quirk in his character that some of the elders found puzzling. He refused to sermonise about his experiences in the mission field or raise his father's name to give weight to his words. Indeed, he would not talk at all about China or his training as a medical student. Curiously, because of this omission, there were those who doubted the seriousness of young Mr Lockhart's calling.

"And who is this you've brought to visit, Kirsty?"

"This is Sammy Reynolds."

Smiling warmly, David offered his hand, then, seeing that the lad did not comprehend the gesture, patted his shoulder instead.

"Come along in. It's far too cold to hang about on the doorstep." Kirsty gave Sammy a little nudge to coax him over the threshold and into the dark hallway. David went on, "Aunt Nessie's out. She's gone shopping, I believe. The fire in the study's pretty poor so perhaps you wouldn't mind if we talked in the kitchen."

"Nuh," said Sammy as if he had understood the point of courtesy.

Kirsty said, "Look up there, Sammy, and you'll see a pretty painting."

A stained-glass screen stood at the angle of the staircase. It was backlit by a gas-globe that, in memory of the late lamented Andrew Frew, was never extinguished. The subject of the painting was Scotland's patron saint, bearded, bald, scowling, imposing but hardly pretty. Nonetheless Sammy's attention was gripped by the grim image and he stood at the foot of the staircase staring up at it as if he expected St Andrew to boom out a greeting too.

"His father was found dead this morning," Kirsty whispered. "Sam's not quite right in the head, and Craig sent me round to see if you could find a place for him for a while, or some sort of job he could do."

David nodded. "No relatives, I take it."

"None are known. He lives in the Madagascar. The father was a habitual drunkard."

David said, "Craig's worried in case the court condemns him to an institution?"

"Yes, a mental asylum."

"Well, we wouldn't want that to happen," said David.

"Do you think you can help?"

"Come, we'll have a cup of tea and chat about it."

Sammy turned. The faint, parti-coloured light from the radiant screen softened and refined his features. He had closed his mouth. For an instant he appeared dignified, a quality that had eluded him all his life, and showed a kind of native intelligence. Taken in, Kirsty experienced a strange thrill of optimism, a belief that David really could work miracles.

"Sammy?" she said, querulously.

The daft grin spread at once over his face and the illusion of intelligence was dispelled.

He pointed at the screen. "Cross."

"That's right, Sammy," said David. "St Andrew had a cross too, like Jesus."

"Ma Daddy's gone t'heaven."

Kirsty caught her breath but David touched her arm to still her.

He said, "Will he be happy there, Sammy?"

"Aye."

"Sammy, where is heaven?"

"Up there. Up'n the sky."

"Will you go to heaven too, some day?"

"If I'm good, aye."

"Simple, isn't it?" David murmured. "I wish those old equations would still work for me."

Sammy said, "Mr Nicholson took him up there. Mr Nicholson'll take me too if I'm bad."

"Mr Nicholson's not – " David began.

Sammy said, "Daddy was a bad man but Mr Nicholson took him up anyway."

David uttered a small sound, not of laughter but of speculation. "But – "

"Is that no' right, missus?" said Sammy.

"Perhaps it is," Kirsty answered.

"It is, it is," said Sammy with absolute assurance.

David said, "Sammy, are you hungry?"

"Aye."

"Come on then. We'll see if we can find you a scone."

He took Sammy by the hand and guided him out of the hallway towards the warmth of the kitchen.

*   *   *

David's desire to find a place for Sammy Reynolds had much to do with innate decency and love for his fellow man. But it was also connected with a need to please Kirsty and to prove himself to her dour and difficult husband, motives that no kirk session would condone and to which David would never admit.

He spent the afternoon calling on congregational acquaintances, men well placed in business and commerce as well as church circles. He was candid with them, did not disguise Sammy's imperfections as an employee and received sympathy and promises but no definite, on-the-spot offer of a job that would suit the lad's limited capabilities.

It was around ten at night before David reached the exalted heights of Dowanhill Gardens where, in a divided mansion, the Reverend James Augustus, Clerk to the Presbytery, lived. Clerks were retained for long periods 'at the will of the Presbytery', whereas Moderators were spun around every six months. Therefore much of the power of governing the fourteen parishes, of which St Anne's was one, rested securely with old Gussie.

Reverend Augustus had been dining with a Liberal Member of Parliament and a fiery Celtic preacher in the Western Club that evening. He would have been much later arriving home if the MP had not had to dash off to catch an overnight train to London. As it was, Gussie had been home for only ten minutes and was treating himself to an extra glass of port in his study when he was interrupted by his dear wife, Annie, who informed him that a young assistant minister was at the door and very anxious to speak with him on a matter of some urgency.

In the Reverend Augustus' experience nothing that any unfledged assistant ever did was urgent. He suspected that the young fellow would be suffering some exaggerated crisis of conscience. He wished, heretically, that his Church had some convenient equivalent to the Catholics' Rite of Absolution so that he could pronounce it and be rid of the problem mighty quick. His attitude became less perfunctory, however, when he found that the caller was David Lockhart. He had known the young man's father in the good old days. He had also been impressed by the son's coolness and practicality, though he could not understand why young Lockhart had settled for drab old Glasgow in preference to the glories of the mission field.

Fortified against the cold with a glass of port and settled in a winged armchair by the fire in the snug book-lined study, young Lockhart wasted no time in coming to the point. The point was not, after all, of a personal nature but involved some weak-minded urchin who was in need of protection against the wheels of the legal system. In his years in the ministry Gussie had encountered zealots in all shapes and sizes. He remembered that David's father had been fired by a passion that was almost too hot for comfort. It seemed that the son had inherited the trait, though in more rational guise. Gussie was by no means out of sympathy with the new breed of parish minister to whom the ills of an unequal society seemed more heinous and more important than doctrinal schisms and secessions which in years to come, perhaps, would be regarded as but chaff on the wind of change. He lent an attentive ear to Lockhart's tale of woe. He was much taken with the assistant's sincerity and began to perceive that the missionary spirit was not lacking in David at all, that it moved in the son as it had done in the father and that the wonder of things was to be found in their composite character. He was already disposed to do what he could for the orphan, and David Lockhart was there to tell him how best he might intercede.

"The Peoples' Mission?" said Gussie.

"Yes, I've been there."

"Of course you have. You've preached there, haven't you?"

"Yes, sir – but I mean today."

"Ah! With whom did you speak?" said Gussie.

"First with Mr Arthur, the convener, and then with Mr Dugdale, the caretaker."

"What did they have to say to it?"

"They referred me to you, sir."

Yes, young Lockhart's determination to find a place for the lost lamb reflected the very essence of 'mission'. He had verily 'gone forth upon an errand'. Its commonplace nature did not devalue it in Gussie's eyes.

"What precisely did Mr Dugdale say?"

"He said that he could certainly make use of a boy to stoke the boiler and sweep the halls."

"He would, of course."

The Peoples' Mission was no tin hut. In spite of its name, of which Gussie did not approve, it had no evangelical function and was not concerned with cornering the market in drunkards and down-and-outs. The suite of halls provided a meeting-ground for the folk of the parishes and was quite as grand as the recently expanded accommodations of the Baptists and Roman Catholics.

Endowments and donations had built the halls. Competition was, it seemed, a healthy virtue when it came to raising cash. There were side rooms, parlours, ante-chambers, gas fires, steam radiators, and three large halls, in two of which the youth of the district could let off steam. The third hall was appointed as a bible class, a place where adults as well as children could listen to the Word of God in community and comfort. Attracted by its newness and luxury, local folk flocked to join the guilds, associations, brigades and study groups. Even little Roman Catholics smuggled themselves past Mr Arthur's watchful eye just for a heat and the odd free bun and to play with the hot-water taps in the big tiled lavatories.

"I was under the impression, sir, that the Mission was not yet fully staffed," said David Lockhart.

"It's true that we could do with extra labour," Gussie said. "But we can afford only a very small wage."

"How small?"

"Six or seven shillings a week."

"If Reynolds draws any sort of regular wage," said David, "I can secure him a bed in the Claremont Model lodging-house."

"That will consume most of his earnings."

"Yes, payment can be remitted directly to the superintendent, if that's possible."

"What does the boy do for clothing?"

"Clothing can be found, to fit his needs."

"Can he cope with the work?" said Gussie.

"He will do what he is shown."

"Parrot-fashion?"

"Yes, sir, in a manner of speaking."

"As there are organisations to deal specifically with the plight of orphans I do not wish to be thought to be setting a precedent."

"I will not ask again, sir."

"Oh, I expect you will, young man," said the Reverend Augustus. "Now, on a more personal note, I have a question I want to ask you."

Lockhart's cheeks flamed, the result of the port and the heat of the fire, Gussie assumed, not noticing the widening of the eyes and the way in which his young guest stiffened on the edge of the leather cushion. "What – what would that be, sir?"

"About your brother John."

"Ah! Ah, yes."

"Did I hear that he had returned to China?"

"Yes, sir, in October."

"Why, may I ask, was that?" said Reverend Augustus.

"My father requested him to return at once."

"Did he not complete his medical training?"

"Oh, yes. He obtained his degree in the summer term."

"But he did not go on to extend himself with a further degree in divinity, as you did?"

"No. No, he did not."

"I heard of this from his Presbytery who had him as a candidate under their care. What, if I may ask, was the reason for his rather abrupt change of plans?"

"He was, it seems, needed urgently in the northern missions."

"An epidemic, perhaps?"

"I cannot say, Mr Augustus."

"Did your father not tell you?"

"No, he did not."

"Or your brother?"

"I did not – did not have much communication with Jack during his last months of study."

"Was it because of *your* decision to remain in Scotland that your father asked John to return?"

"It may have been," said David. "Yes, I believe it may have been."

"Was your father afraid that John – Jack – would succumb to the temptation to stay here too?"

"Jack isn't like me. He was, to be candid, very upset at my decision. Even more so that my father would not permit him to complete his course in divinity."

"Will he not be a minister now?"

"There was talk of releasing him to study in the Bible College in Shanghai, but," said David, "I fear that may not happen immediately. There's been trouble again with the so-called people's soldiers, the Boxers."

"God works most mysteriously," said Reverend Augustus. "Perhaps the ministry's loss is medicine's gain. Have you looked at it in that light, David?"

"I've tried to, sir."

"Do you feel that you've let your family down?"

"I feel – no, I can't honestly say that I do."

"Scotland is the place for you?"

"Yes, sir. There's so much to be done here."

"There's good work to be done in every corner of the kingdom, God's kingdom, I mean. Will you not be missed in China?"

"My father – he – "

To save the young man further confusion and the pain of revelation, Gussie interrupted. "You are not supported from home, in that case?"

"No, sir."

"St Anne's is very fortunate indeed to have an ordained assistant who can survive on its meagre stipend."

"I'm helped, sir, by my uncle in Inverness. He makes me a small allowance."

"Very generous of him. He, I take it, approves of your decision to minister in Scotland."

"I think he does, sir. I think that Uncle George understands me in a way that my father does not," said David. "Of course, my aunt, Mrs Frew, allows me free room and board at her house in Walbrook Street."

"I remember Mrs Frew; a fine woman, very devout."

"Oh, very," said David.

"Well," said Gussie, getting to his feet, "I think that we've had a most satisfactory chat."

"About Reynolds, sir – "

"Of course, of course. I'll write in the morning to Mr Arthur."

"Also, if you would, Mr Augustus, to the court."

"Indeed, the court. That letter had better be delivered first thing, don't you think?"

"It would benefit Reynolds if it was."

"He may start work at once. Tomorrow, if you wish it."

"Thank you, sir."

David Lockhart was on his feet too. He had put down the wine glass, hardly touched, on a side-table. He was restless and tense but, Gussie thought, a very prepossessing young man.

The minister accompanied the assistant to the door of the study and there rang an old-fashioned hanging bell which would summon his wife to come and show the young man out. Gussie had no time for snobs who left such chores to a servant.

"By the way, David," he said, "why did this policeman bring Reynolds to your door? Is he one of your parishioners – the policeman, I mean?"

"His wife is. She's also a friend of my aunt," Lockhart explained. "I know her too – slightly."

The colour was still high on his cheeks, visible even in the wan light of the oil-lamps. Gussie could hear his wife puffing up the staircase. He put an avuncular hand on young Lockhart's arm.

"David, a word to the wise. Do not become too closely associated with policemen. Many of them are very worthy Christian fellows but the nature of their work tends to make them overly sceptical, even cynical. They are not saints, by any means."

"Craig Nicholson is a decent enough – "

"No doubt, no doubt," said Gussie. "Ah, here's my dear wife. She will find your overcoat and see you out. If you will excuse me, I will apply myself to writing those letters immediately."

"Do you not require to meet the boy, sir?"

"Reynolds? No, I'll look in on him when I make my weekly call at the Mission. I assume that he can survive until Wednesday without my blessing."

David Lockhart smiled. "I'm sure he can, sir."

"Goodnight to you, David."

"Goodnight, Mr Augustus."

Lockhart was shown downstairs into the hall and was soon out in the cold night air that shrouded the Gardens. Old Gussie went back to the port. He stood with his glass before the fire musing not on the nature of charity but on David Lockhart's character. He had been impressed. There, he thought, was just the sort of chap who, given a touch of ambition, might rise to high office in the Kirk.

"Good luck to you, son," he murmured, and raised his glass in a wistful toast.

*   * · *

For once Madge was at home. She had been restless all day and had sniped at Kirsty for no very good reason and, though the whole family had assembled for supper, there had been no warmth at table. Gordon had fallen asleep, slumped in his chair, and Craig had yelled at him to get away to bed at once. Bobby had cried and Kirsty had not been able to prevent him going the rounds from Craig to Madge to Lorna. Eventually he had reached her arms and had there fallen into a fretful sleep. It had been ten o'clock before some sort of peace was restored, with Lorna as well as Gordon gone off to bed and Bobby settled at last in his cot.

Craig, who had been round at the station twice during off-duty hours, had gone early to his night shift, but not before he had assured his mother that there was no chance of Sammy Reynolds being returned to their care. It was his opinion that 'the crowd at Walbrook Street' would take charge of the boy for the night.

In spite of the cold, Kirsty filled the basin at the sink with warm water and washed her hair. Dressed in an old robe of faded blue, with a Turkey red towel about her head, she felt like some Arabian woman on her way to the well. She could not, however, take herself to bed until her hair was completely dry.

It was almost eleven when knocking sounded on the outside door. Kirsty had a vague notion that, for some reason, it might be Sammy Reynolds come back of his own accord. She went into the hallway with trepidation for Madge was still up and about, and scowling.

"Who is it?" Kirsty asked.

"David."

She gasped. Her hands flew to the towel about her head.

"What – what do you want?"

"I'm sorry it's so late. If it's inconvenient – "

"No. Wait." She pulled open the door and admitted him. "It's unexpected, that's all."

He stood just over the step, staring at her turban. Kirsty could not make up her mind whether it was amusement or dismay that tightened his lips.

"Were you in bed?"

"No," she answered.

"I'll not come in," he said. "I would appreciate a word with your husband."

"He's gone on duty. You missed him by half an hour."

"Dash it all!" David exclaimed.

"Is it concernin' Sammy?"

"Yes. Yes, it is."

"Come in. Tell me the news."

"You're not – not alone, are you?"

As if in answer to the whispered question Madge's voice sounded in the kitchen. "Who the devil is it, at this hour?"

"It's Mr Lockhart."

"*Who?*"

"David Lockhart."

A muttered blasphemy, scuffling; Madge had begun to undress herself in front of the kitchen fire and now scrambled to make herself decent again.

"I'll not – " David said.

"Oh, yes, you will," said Kirsty. "Apart from anythin' else, it's time you met my mother-in-law."

"I saw her at Bobby's christening."

"Met her properly."

"All right."

· For a second they were close, cramped by the walls of the tiny hallway. At that instant Kirsty sensed that he wanted to kiss her. His desire was palpable. They were both enveloped in the scent of the soap with which she had washed. He had never seen her quite like this before, in her natural habitat, as it were.

"Kirsty?"

She flung open the kitchen door with alacrity.

David entered. Madge was tucking pins into her hair with one hand and fumbling with the buttons of her blouse with the other. One stocking was wrinkled, Kirsty noted, and the woman had a wild, dissolute appearance that contrasted with her own comfortable informality.

David wore a chequered overcoat and a faculty scarf was wound round and round his throat. He had no cap, no gloves and his hands and face were tinged blue with cold. Kirsty wished that she had been alone after all, wished that Madge would vanish in a puff of smoke.

"Do you remember Craig's mother – Mrs Nicholson?"

"Of course," said David. "I'm sorry to call so late."

"Not at all, not at all."

In spite of the fact that only that morning she had insulted and impugned his honour, Madge minced forward, gushing.

"Why, Mr Lockhart, what a surprise! Did you come all this way just to see Kirsty?"

"No. Craig," David got out as Madge drew him insistently to an armchair by the fire.

"You'll have a bite of supper, won't you, Mr Lockhart?"

"I – no, thank you all the same. I have to be – "

"You men! Always so damned – oh, excuse me – so polite. I know you'd love a nibble at somethin'. Ham?"

David glanced helplessly at Kirsty.

"Madge, why don't you make us all some tea?" Kirsty said.

"Yes," David said. "Tea would be very welcome."

Dragging herself away from the guest Madge crossed to the sink and noisily filled the kettle from the tap.

"Sammy?" said Kirsty. "What's happened?"

She listened as David explained what he had done for the boy and confirmed the fact that Sammy, that night, had been left in the care of Nessie Frew and Peggie. He told her that he had found employment for Sammy and would secure him a billet in the Claremont Model which had a trustworthy supervisor who would see to it that Sammy kept clean and was fed, and not bullied.

Although David made it all sound simple Kirsty knew that he had put a great deal of effort into securing a place for the orphan. She promised herself that when an opportunity arose she would thank him more effusively than was possible with Madge hovering, ears pricked, about them.

To have David here in her kitchen at such a late hour was

both exciting and embarrassing. David confused her as Craig never did, but the muddle of emotions was invigorating and pleasurable. She wondered what sort of a home David would make for a wife, what he would expect from a wife. It would not be a place like this, with underwear draped from the pulley and the smell of cooking-fat constantly present in the atmosphere. She associated him with Walbrook Street, saw that as his home. She thought of herself as privileged to have shared it with him, even meagrely and for such a short time.

"How's Bobby?" David asked.

He was kneading his fingers into his palms; they would be tingling and sore with the heat.

"See for yourself," said Kirsty.

It had been several weeks since last David had 'inspected' the child he had helped to bring into the world for he, David, had been given leave from his duties at St Anne's to visit his uncle over the New Year period. At Walbrook Street David would often take Bobby on to his knee and gleefully allow himself to be buffeted by the energetic child. But his fondness for her son took on a peculiar dimension here in the kitchen, close to the bed where Craig would take her in hard and urgent love-making in the dead of night.

Bobby stirred. David drew the quilt about his shoulders and, with a delicate touch, brushed a strand of hair from the child's brow. He would do the same, Kirsty felt, for any child, even one as grown-up and ugly as poor Sammy Reynolds.

Madge rattled the best flowered china on a tin tray. Swiftly and efficiently she had set out tea-things on an embroidered cloth. She poured the pale brew from the teapot too quickly and too soon.

"Mr Lockhart — sugar?"

"Please."

"All you men have a sweet tooth. Milk?"

"Thank you."

Madge craved David's attention. She could not bear to have him lean towards Kirsty, even towards Bobby. She offered him the cup and saucer, simpered, her mane of hair straggling and her blouse unevenly buttoned. David accepted the offering in the manner of any visiting clergyman but declined to be seated again and remained standing while he drank the hot weak liquid. He was not as he had been at the cot-side. Now he was poised, affable, professional, a little distant.

"You do not come to the kirk with Kirsty, then, Mrs Nicholson?" he asked. "Are you a member of another church?"

Madge was caught off guard by the question.

She blustered, "I – uh – I leave that sort o' thing to – to our Kirsty."

"You'd be made very welcome at St Anne's."

"Aye, I'm sure I would," she said, adding shrewdly, "but I wouldn't want to intrude."

"How could you possibly intrude? In God's house everyone is welcome, even sinners."

Kirsty could not be sure whether David was teasing. Change in direction had taken the wind out of Madge's sails. She retreated to the sink to wash a teacup that had not been used at all.

"Can Sammy cope with this job?" Kirsty asked.

"Cleaning out fires, sweeping floors. He'll cope admirably, I'm sure."

"What if it doesn't suit?"

"We'll have to find him another job in that case."

"Sammy isn't really your responsibility, you know."

"Well, Kirsty, I could argue that point," David said. "If he wasn't before, he certainly is now. Once you begin caring for somebody it becomes exceedingly difficult to stop."

He had been looking at nothing in particular until that moment. She was taken aback to find him looking at her, meeting her gaze.

She stammered, "Was – was it – difficult to find him a place in the Mission?"

"My father taught me patience, if nothing else," David told her. "He'd spend weeks, months on the conversion of one 'heathen' child. Half a day given to the welfare of a recently orphaned boy seems rather short-weight by comparison."

"Oh, yes, you've been in China, so you have." Madge flounced towards the assistant once more. "Oh, you must tell me what it's like there."

"Some other time, Mrs Nicholson. It's very late and I must be on my way."

David put the cup on the table and tightened the academic scarf about his neck. Kirsty resisted the temptation to straighten it. She kept her arms folded.

Madge said, "I'll tell Craig you called. You'd not know he was on night shift, of course?"

"No, Mrs Nicholson. I didn't know he was on night shift."

"Just as well I was here. I'm out quite a lot, evenings."

"I would have left a message with Kirsty."

"Aye," said Madge.

The woman was into the hallway before Kirsty could move. David gave Kirsty a little wink and she raised her hand and smiled.

From the hallway she heard David's voice. "Now, Mrs Nicholson, I trust we'll be seeing you at the kirk very soon. Kirsty, or Lorna for that matter, will show you the way."

When Madge returned to the kitchen all trace of friendliness had gone. Her eyes were hard and glittering.

"Why did he come here?" she demanded.

David had made the strange day seem right somehow. Kirsty refused to be intimidated.

"To put my mind at rest," she said.

"He was hopin' you'd be alone."

"In this house? I'm never alone."

"Oh, aye, you'd like fine to have us all gone so you could do what – "

"That's enough," Kirsty snapped, barely holding her temper. "I've heard enough out of you, Madge Nicholson. You may think what you like of *me* but do you honestly imagine for one damned minute that David Lockhart's that kind of man?"

"They're all – "

"Are they? Well, I expect you know more about men than I do," said Kirsty. "Anyway I'm not talkin' about other men. Let me ask you again, Madge – do you think David Lockhart would steal another man's wife?"

"I – I'm away to my bed. I've had enough o' your nonsense."

"No more of that talk," said Kirsty assertively.

"I'll – "

"Not one dirty word more."

"All – all right."

"Goodnight, then."

Madge grunted and swept haughtily out of the kitchen, leaving Kirsty alone with her child.

Kirsty glanced down at her fingers. She was trembling very slightly and yet she had not been aware that she had been so furious with Madge and her sordid innuendo. What was in her heart was her secret. If she loved David, she respected him far too much ever to try to entice him into loving her, in that way, in return.

The real secret, her secret and Craig's, would have shocked Madge into silence for sure; the fact that she and Craig were not married at all. They had never been wed before God or under law.

What would Madge have to say to that revelation? Would it have a salutary effect on Mrs Nicholson to learn that her son was living in sin with an orphan brat?

Kirsty would never tell a soul, of course, least of all Madge. She was not ashamed of it. Craig was, however, and in his shame lay her one small piece of power.

*   *   *

The weather in the streets that night was so bitter that Mr Organ posted notice for the issue of balaclavas to be worn under helmets. While it was possible to encase the limbs in combinations and hide jerseys and pullovers under your uniform the head and face remained vulnerable. Craig and Ronnie Norbert were certainly glad of the extra protection for the night shift went out into an arctic waste, all desolate and silent. The only sound of consequence was the dry steady clump of policemen's boots as the lads fanned out from the station to relieve their frozen colleagues at corner rendezvous.

Hot soup and mutton pies, courtesy of the sergeants' welfare fund, waited to fortify the off-duty officers and give them strength enough to make it home to bed.

Ronnie was prattling about his hot supper before they cleared the bottom of Ottawa Street. He went on and on about his gargantuan appetite and how much he could stow away until Craig and he reached Halifax Street. Here Peter Stewart waited impatiently. He was stamping up and down and beating his body with his arms to keep his blood circulating.

"Grand night, Peter, eh?" said Ronnie. "Found any deaders for us, then?"

Peter Stewart might be of Highland stock but he was not actually made of granite. He had accepted a free tot of rum from a kindly publican about ten past ten o'clock and had been sucking peppermint sweets since then to disguise the odour of spirits on his breath.

Ronnie sniffed and, as Craig and Peter exchanged notes, said, "Oh-hoh! You've been at the bottle, you naughty officer."

"For Christ's sake, Craig, tell him to shut it."

"Shut it, Ronnie."

Relieved at last, Peter Stewart turned and loped off towards Ottawa Street, his nose tucked down into his scarf.

Craig raised his hand, forefinger stiff, and addressed Probationer Norbert sternly. "Not a bloody word about drink, Ronnie. Got it?"

Ronnie Norbert laughed. "All right. Keep your hair on. I wouldn't shop old Pete just for tipplin' on the sly."

Ronnie had a handwarmer stuffed into each trouser pocket. The worms of charcoal smouldered nicely and a patch of warmth on each thigh gave him a feeling of superiority.

"Which way first?" he asked.

"Down Frederick Street."

The constables had gone no more than a hundred yards when they encountered David Lockhart. He rounded the corner from Banff Street, walking rapidly, hands stuck in his pockets and his shoulders hunched. Craig did not at first recognise him and became instantly alert at the sight and sound of such pedestrian activity in the slow and vacant night. The man came on directly towards them, passing into and out of the shadows between street lamps.

"Who the hell – " Ronnie began, tensing.

"It's all right, Ronnie," Craig murmured.

David stopped before them. His breath hung in a frozen cloud and he shivered visibly.

"What are you doin' out on a night like this, Minister?"

"I came to tell you that I've found employment for the Reynolds boy."

Craig nodded.

David went on, "I called at your house but you were gone."

"You could've left a message with my wife."

"I did. But then I thought that you might be anxious about Reynolds."

"Anxious?" said Craig. "Nah, it's all in a day's work."

Ronnie Norbert interrupted. "Christ, don't tell me somebody gave Sammy a job!"

"Assistant to the caretaker in the Peoples' Mission."

"Fast work, Minister," said Craig.

"I just happened to get wind that the post of – "

Craig said, "Hey, you didn't take him back to my house, did you?"

"No, he's safe in bed at Walbrook Street."

"Aye, that's where you should be an' all," said Ronnie Norbert, "by the look of you."

"Will I bring Sammy to the station tomorrow," said David to Craig, "or will you send for him when he's required?"

"I'll send for him."

"I thought I'd try to settle a permanent billet for him at the Claremont lodging-house."

"Aye, why not?" Craig said. "If he has a regular wage they'll take him in, I expect."

"What news on the father?"

"He died of drink," said Ronnie, "as we suspected."

"So far there's no trace of relatives," said Craig. "We think the old man came from Belfast, years ago. He's been living in that stinkin' cellar in Rae's tenement as long as anybody can remember. He paid the rent from odd shillings he earned by casual labour. Blewed the rest on booze, I reckon."

"So Sammy was brought up in the Madagascar?"

"Aye."

"Poor lad," said David.

"There's thousands worse off than him," said Craig.

"Well, at least we appear to have saved him from being committed to an asylum," said David. "I thought that would please you."

Craig was relieved to learn that Sammy would not be incarcerated and did not doubt that Sammy would fit into the routines of the Peoples' Mission. But he did not reveal any sign of his pleasure to Lockhart. He remained implacable, a little scornful of a man who had tramped miles through icy streets just to bring him news that could have waited until tomorrow. He sensed that Lockhart was waiting for him to speak, to give some praise, drop some word of gratitude, an expression of rapport between them. He considered it, paused, gave nothing in the end.

"We have to get along, Minister," Craig said.

"Yes, of course."

"Don't you linger," said Ronnie Norbert, "or we could find you dead in a doorway an' all."

They parted. Craig and Ronnie moved down Frederick Street and David Lockhart headed east along the river road towards Walbrook Street.

Craig increased his pace, forced Norbert to keep up with him.

A place had been found for Sammy in Greenfield. He was glad about that. He liked having the daft boy around, liked being worshipped. What was more, he had managed to do it without offending his mother. There was more to it, of course, something more subtle in his arrogance. For all his fancy, educated accent, smart clothes and dog-collar, Lockhart was uncomfortable in these mean back streets. He had shown himself to be too eager to please, too anxious to be admired. Men like David Lockhart had no place in the real world of Ottawa Street or Canada Road.

"By God, Craig, you know some funny folk," said Ronnie. "Toffs an' clergymen. Is that your wife's – "

Craig's mood did not alter. Arrogance, a feeling of strength and confidence, made him turn abruptly on the probationer. He caught him by the collar and ran him hard against a tenement wall.

"Listen, Norbert," Craig said softly, "I'm bloody sick of your chatter."

"But – "

It was as if he had Lockhart there, not Ronnie Norbert. There was no stuffing in Lockhart, no challenge. However much she might be attracted by his good manners, Kirsty would soon realise that there was nothing solid or manly there, that bloody Lockhart was a shadow compared with him.

"No bloody *buts*, Ronnie," said Craig, tightening his grip and, for a moment, stopping the breath in the young man's throat. "I'm the real copper here. You do what I say."

"Craig, listen, I – "

"Got it?"

"Aye."

"Aye what?"

"Aye, Constable Nicholson."

"That's better," Craig said, and with a thrusting gesture let the probationer go.

April

An evening out was no rare treat for Kirsty Nicholson. Church socials got her frequently from the confines of Canada Road. With Madge and Lorna to look after Bobby and see to Craig's supper she was not bound hand and foot to the house like most women in tenement society. Of course, Craig did not deign to accompany her. He cleaved to the traditional belief that men should follow their own courses and was as reluctant as the next chap to be seen in public with the mother of his children. He did not, however, forbid her a degree of freedom, within reason. But when she had another child, or three or four, and when Madge found a place of her own, things would be very different. Kirsty did not doubt that Craig would treat her then as all proud men treated their women and insist that she toe the conventional line.

Craig waxed sarcastic about her fondness for tea-parties and choral evenings. He would occasionally let slip a question as to whether Lockhart had been 'swanning it among the hens', whatever that meant, but for the most part he seemed indifferent to what went on at St Anne's and to the health of Kirsty's friend, Agnes Frew.

On that April Saturday Kirsty was being taken into town to Berkeley Street, to the municipal halls whose magnificent façades, complete with Doric columns and classical statues, towered like the Temple of Jerusalem over Glasgow's commercial terraces. Accompanied by David, chaperoned by Nessie Frew, she would be among the audience at St Andrew's Halls to hear the final address of Mr Tom Monroe's Scottish tour, an event not to be missed on any account.

Monroe's preaching had taken Glasgow by storm. His dogmatic down-to-earth style had caused an enormous stir of controversy among churchmen and in the public at large. Some saw in Tom Monroe's popularity a sign that the days of decay of the pulpit had come to pass. Others branded him as no more than a pulpit buffoon. But thousands had been touched by his plain speech and, if the newspapers were to be believed, had surrendered to his tenets of faith without reservation.

Tom Monroe was a phenomenon, no doubt of that. His mission to Scotland had been extended from three weeks to five. Only last weekend he had filled the vast arena of Henglers' Cirque two nights on the trot and might have put clowns and elephants and performing dogs permanently out of business if he had not had to tear himself from his native sod and embark on a summer tour of America. His lunch-hour lectures in St George's kirk had drawn thousands of lapsed Christians and religious outcasts in silk hats and frock coats and had left a milling mob on the pavements of Buchanan Street, baying for admission. The Press, however, made mincemeat of his theological statements, slated, berated and belittled him. They opened their columns to letters of vituperation from elders, deacons and infuriated ministers. Only the *Mail* took an opposite view, extolled the preacher as a working-man's Messiah, a poor miner's son from Ayrshire who had been exalted by divine hand and blessed with a gift that more educated brethren of the cloth had lost – the popular touch. Monroe's last public appearance in Glasgow was, therefore, a significant event.

Kirsty was stimulated by anticipation. She would not be fighting for a seat on the benches on the floor of the Grand Hall or queuing in the surrounding streets from mid-afternoon. David had acquired three precious tickets from the Reverend Graham who had heard Monroe once and never wanted to hear him again. She, Kirsty Nicholson, would be positioned in the front row of the Grand Circle with an unimpeded view of the great man when he stepped before the multitude.

Kirsty was troubled by what she should wear. She was aware that it was a serious, sober occasion but also that it would attract a flock of fashionable ladies. She did not wish to appear drab, to embarrass David and Nessie with a poor look. Plucking up courage she sought her mother-in-law's advice and, for once, Madge Nicholson was co-operative. Madge generously unlocked the door of the deep, camphor-smelling cupboard in the front room and allowed Kirsty to see the extent of her wardrobe. The array of clothes would not have shamed a baillie's wife, together with shoes, hats, gloves, all the bibs-and-bobs that Madge had acquired to wear when she whisked out of the house for a night on the town with Mr Adair.

The gust of fashion that had carried away the leg-of-mutton sleeve and heavily gored skirt had wafted several of Madge's costumes to the rear of the cupboard. The new outfit that had pride of place was front-flattened and belled about the hem but Madge made it clear that she did not intend to go overboard with matronly generosity and that that garment was not for borrowing. In any case, said Madge, Kirsty had no need for wadding and whalebone. She selected instead an outdoor costume in black and dusky pink which, said Madge, would be perfect for the occasion. She added a pair of shoes which, with little balls of newspaper tamped into the toes, would fit Kirsty nicely. Finally a hat with a brim of stiffened chiffon that was not too outrageously ornamental. Madge's skill with the needle far exceeded Kirsty's. The woman took in a tuck here and inserted a pleat there and, come Saturday, helped dress Kirsty in the full regalia.

Off duty, Craig had taken himself to the local football match with Gordon and was not about to admire his wife or his mother's handiwork. Lorna declared that the rig-out suited Kirsty far better than it suited Mam, a remark that did not go down well with Madge and that made last-minute trimming a brusque and hasty affair. At length, with a kiss and a cuddle for Bobby, and the issuing of last instructions to Lorna, Kirsty went out of the house and, excited as a child, sped down the stairs and into the road, started off for Walbrook Street where Nessie Frew and David would be waiting for her.

When David opened the door of No. 19, however, Kirsty could tell by his expression that all was not well.

"Aunt Nessie's ill again." He ushered Kirsty into the hall. "Her chest. It came on her last night. The doctor informs me that it's not severe but he advised her to stay in bed for a day or two. He's a sound fellow, knows what he's talking about. He gave her a draught to help her sleep and she's been drowsing all day."

All winter long the widow had suffered a bronchial affliction that, by its stubborn persistence, had given cause for concern.

"I'll sit with her," said Kirsty, hiding her disappointment.

David said, "She insists that we go without her."

"She can't be left with just Peggie. It isn't fair."

"Mrs Jagger has come round. She's kindly volunteered to sit with Nessie for part of the evening."

Mrs Jagger was the wife of St Anne's organist, a plump, amiable woman in her seventies who had known Nessie Frew, as wife and widow, for the best part of thirty years.

David was already slipping on his black overcoat. He wore his very best grey suit and looked, Kirsty thought, both sober and smart.

David said, "It would be a shame for you to stay at home in that outfit. It's very pretty."

"You don't think it's too – vulgar?"

"Of course not."

"David, we'll be – be without a chaperone."

"Five thousand Christian souls will be there," said David, showing no sign of apprehension, "and that will have to do in lieu of Aunt Nessie's watchful eye."

"David, are you sure?"

"Don't you want to go?"

"Yes, of course. More than anythin'. But – "

"No 'buts', Kirsty. Come. We'll hand in the spare ticket at the door. Somebody will be glad of it."

"I'll just say goodbye to Nessie."

"She's fast asleep," David said.

For an instant Kirsty wondered if he was telling her the whole truth. On the other hand Nessie Frew had always been a puzzling mixture of contradictions, prim to a fault but with a daring streak of romanticism in her heart. Kirsty could not quite believe, though, that Nessie had given David permission to go out alone with a young, married woman without an argument. She said nothing, however, let him guide her out of the house and on to the pavement.

He glanced at her, smiled broadly. "Ready, Mrs Nicholson?"

"Do you have the tickets?"

"Safe and sound." He patted his breast pocket. "Shall we whistle a hack – or shall we walk?"

"Walk, if there's time."

Suddenly she felt quite devil-may-care. The turn of events had added spice to the evening, just a whisper of naughtiness. She had been alone with David before, of course. He met her in the park sometimes when she was 'airing' Bobby in his perambulator. She had been alone with him in the parlour or kitchen of No. 19 when Nessie was elsewhere in the house. But this was different. This was a fine April Saturday and she was dolled up in the nicest clothes she had ever worn and was walking 'up town' with David.

"Take my arm, Kirsty."

"Do you think it's – "

"I'm only being a gentleman."

As soon as they had passed the gate of St Anne's and turned out of sight of Walbrook Street Kirsty linked her arm into David's and left, for a time, her guilt behind in the silky April twilight.

      ✱   ✱   ✱

The football league season was on its last legs. To judge by the state of some of the players it was just as well that Partick Thistle had already clinched the championship and that nothing crucial hung on the outcome of the home tie at Whiteinch, that the match with Port Glasgow Athletic was a dead issue even before it began.

As usual Paddy Smith had played the fool for most of the second half, to the delight of a small group of fans and the disgust of the majority to whom football was a religion and was not to be mocked under any circumstances. Paddy even managed to give away a goal, an act of charity to the Port, who were not in the Jags' class even on an off day. The final result of four goals to one for the Thistle excited the supporters not at all since a bigger win had been expected. There was speculation among the crowd that straggled away from the match that Paddy bloody Smith had taken out a 'winning score' line with some local bookmaker and that he was taking a hell of a risk of being banned for life if the League Association caught him at it.

Craig could not have cared less and Gordon was shrewd enough to keep his mouth shut, to say not a word about the fact that he was one of a handful of punters who had checked a slip for a 4/1 result and would collect from old Jimmy-One-Lamp, the carpet factory's runner, about six quid on Monday morning. Gordon did not take any special delight in the art and craft of the game of football. Unlike hundreds of thousands of Scots he was not addicted to its tactics and mechanics or devoted to its heroes. He did, however, assiduously study form and found that he could turn a pound or two by judicious and objective betting without having to get drenched or frozen half to death on Saturday afternoons.

Gordon had not expected Craig to accompany him to the match. Having patrolled football grounds in uniform and rubbed against too many rowdy fans in the course of his duties, Craig was even less enamoured of football than was his brother. Craig's hobby was swimming. In fact he had been on his way to the baths at Cranstonhill when Gordon had met him. Towel and bathing-costume were still stuffed in the pocket of Craig's coat. Gordon was conscious of the fact that his plan might yet founder if Craig decided to cadge a ride on one of the special brakes that carried supporters home to the hinterlands of Partick to round off his afternoon by an evening swim.

It had probably been the fine weather that had persuaded Craig to agree to accompany Gordon to Whiteinch, or one of his infrequent moods of fraternal good humour. It was not Craig's company at the match that Gordon wanted but his company afterwards, for he had set up the casual meeting in the street for a specific purpose.

"Are you for a pint, then, Craig?"

They were walking along the western end of Dumbarton Road, at the copper's pace, neither strolling nor marching.

"I'm thinkin' about goin' for a swim."

"A quick pint, that's all."

"Kirsty's out tonight," Craig said.

"So I heard."

"Up at some holy ceremony in Glasgow with her fancy friends," Craig said.

"She was fair excited about it," said Gordon.

Craig said, "She'll not be away yet. It'll be all fuss an' feathers until she's gone."

"Mam'll have our supper ready," said Gordon.

"She'll be goin' out an' all."

"Aye," said Gordon. "She usually does on a Saturday. Never mind. There'll be somethin' hot left in the oven. Are you for a pint or are ye not?"

"You're not old enough to drink legally."

"Nobody ever says a dickie-bird about that."

"Gordon, I'm a police officer."

"All right, all right. I'll settle for skoosh. How's that?"

"I could do with a pie right enough."

Craig hesitated. He studied the gilded façade of the recently opened public house at the corner of Cameron Street; the Northern Lights. It did not strike him as odd that Gordon had stopped walking, was loitering with the pub just in front of them.

"How – how about this place?" said Gordon.

"Hell, why not? But no hard liquor for you, right?"

"Right."

Gordon let his brother enter first, pushing through the swing doors of the public bar. The odour of beer slops, spilled whisky and tobacco spit had not yet taken full possession of the Northern Lights. It was clean and bright, stained glass, brass, varnished oak. The publican, an Aberdonian, looked smart and cheerful, if a wee bit Anglified, in a high-bibbed apron and cherry-red cravat. Slipping swiftly down over the shipyards' motionless jibs and the silent cranes of the dockland wharves, the westering sun tinted the tenement roofs russet and rose, and cast soft little wafers of coloured light into the bar's thickening smoke.

It was only ten minutes after the witching hour of five o'clock when public houses all over the land flung open their doors. But already the Northern Lights was packed. Even the bar parlour, something of an innovation in the district, had a crowd inside, including several so-called ladies. A whorled glass half-screen very properly segregated males from females, husbands from wives, though some very old men seemed to prefer the warmth of the parlour to the camaraderie of the public bar and sat nursing their drams among straw bonnets, mangy fur collars and glasses of port wine and sherry.

Gordon found a seat at a long table by the window while Craig ordered a half-pint of heavy beer and a glass of fizzy lemonade and brought them back from the bar. His attitude was not relaxed, Gordon noted. It was as if Craig could not shake off professional reserve, could not shed suspicion with his uniform. He went back to the bar and bought two cold mutton pies and carried them, one on each palm, back to the table.

"Not a bad howff?" said Gordon. "What do you think of it?"

"It isn't on my beat."

"Nice, though."

"I've seen worse," Craig conceded. "By Christmas, though, it'll be just like all the others. Spit, sawdust, bloodshed every Friday night."

"Maybe not," said Gordon. "Depends on who owns the place, I suppose."

"Owns it? He owns it." Craig gestured towards the Aberdonian in the bibbed apron and cravat. "He's the publican."

"Aye, but he may not be the owner."

"What are you haverin' about?" said Craig. "If you're not going to scoff that pie, I'll have it."

Gordon cracked the pie-crust with finger and thumb and sniffed the filling critically.

"Eat it, for God's sake," said Craig.

"I could have sworn I heard it mew," said Gordon, but took a mouthful nonetheless.

For ten minutes or so the brothers talked in desultory fashion. The rambunctious companionship that they had shared at Dalnavert had not survived. All Gordon's awe of his brother had gone, he knew not where. He could not reconcile the affectionate lad that Craig had once been with the stiff and somewhat selfish man he had become, and wondered whether it was the job or marriage that had altered him so.

It was important to hold Craig in the Northern Lights as long as possible, however, so he kept the conversation going and ate the pie and drank the lemonade slowly. He kept his eye on the swing doors and on the door from the parlour to the bar. The clock above the bar ticked away the minutes. The bar had become very crowded now as chill spring air drove men in off the streets in search of warmth, whisky and companionship. The soft roar of conversations was punctuated by bellows of laughter, raucous guffaws and the cackle of some old biddy in the bar parlour who could not hold her liquor or was showing off for the benefit of the old men.

All Gordon could see were backs and rumps, broad rumps and thin rumps, a sea of drab cloth grown deep about the bar.

Craig was becoming restless.

"Have another?" Gordon said.

Craig shook his head. "Come on, let's get out of here, for God's sake."

"No rush," said Gordon.

Craig buttoned his coat and tapped his bulging pocket to make sure that some light-finger hadn't hoisted his towel and costume. "I think I'll head for Cranstonhill. The pond's usually quiet about this time." He got to his feet.

Gordon looked about desperately. There were three men behind the bar now, all bobbing and weaving like demons while a pot-boy in a greasy canvas apron swept glasses from the tables on to a huge wooden tray. And then Gordon caught sight of his quarry. He had never clapped eyes on the chap before but he had gathered enough information about him to recognise him at once.

Mr Albert 'Breezy' Adair wore a double-breasted ulster in cloth the colour of tobacco leaf, broadly chequered, with a half-belt and horn buttons but no hood to spoil the drape of the shoulder line. A round-crown felt hat was perched jauntily on his head. He sported suede gloves and a whippy little cane, like a jockey's whip. He had a lean, waxed moustache and eyes as pale as gin, an excellent set of teeth that he showed off in a peal of laughter. Perhaps, Gordon thought, he was delighted at finding the new establishment, of which he was part-owner, thriving and the big scrolled money-drawers tinkling even at this early hour.

The fat barman raised his hand to signal, perhaps, where the counter was located. Breezy did not hurry. He stayed behind the crowd, rocking on his heels and toes, one hand in his trouser pocket and the ulster draped back off his elbow like a hussar's cloak.

"Recognise him, Craig?"

"Nope."

Craig was lying. Craig knew perfectly well who the well-dressed toff was.

"He's one of the owners of this place."

"Is he now?" said Craig.

"That's Breezy Adair, in case you didn't know."

"What's that to me?" said Craig. "I'm off to the pond. Good night."

Gordon scrambled to his feet and grabbed his brother by the arm. "Jeeze! He's courtin' our mother an' you pretend you don't care?"

"He can do what he likes."

Gordon pulled Craig close, both of them standing hard against the table's edge. In a low, seething voice, he said, "Don't give me any rubbish, Craig. You know damned well who Adair is. I can sus you out a mile off. You've found out all about him."

"I'm not bloody interested."

"He's not a crook, you know."

"Near as damn it."

"Ah," Gordon exclaimed. "I *thought* so. I thought you'd done some pryin'."

"He's well enough known."

If Breezy Adair recognised either of the young men he gave

no hint of it. He had been cornered by a tiny man, a gnome in flat cap and patched jacket who had separated himself from the throng and attached himself to Breezy and was pumping away at his hand and gazing up into his face with fierce red eyes. Breezy gave no sign of wanting to part from the company of the unappetising little man. He laughed and winked and bent confidentially to engage in gruff repartee.

"You're not goin' to run away, Craig."

"From what? From him?"

"Let's go an' introduce ourselves."

Colour drained from Craig's face. Dourness became a thunderous severity. "Get bloody stuffed, Gordon."

"Don't tell me you're scared."

"What he does — what *she* does — it's none of my business."

"I think it is," Gordon said.

Craig wrenched his arm from his brother's grasp.

"Listen," Gordon went on, "this bloke owns a slice of this place, plus a slice of the Spinning Wheel, plus a stake in Carruth's brewery, plus umpteen warehouses, plus God knows what all."

"I don't care if he owns the bloody world," said Craig. "I can't be seen shakin' hands with the likes of him. He's a bookie, for one thing."

"No, he's not," Gordon said. "Not personally."

"So you're the one who's been pryin', are you?"

"We'll just go an' say hullo, right?"

"You can do what *you* like," said Craig and turned away.

Craig was afraid, Gordon realised, not just embarrassed. He felt a certain disdain for his brother who would not confront opportunity or square up bravely to a man who had influence and power and was already, however tenuously, connected to their family. Craig beat a hasty retreat, was gone out of the pub in two seconds flat, the swing doors batting behind him. Gordon sighed. He had expected more of Craig, had expected him to take the bull by the horns, to discover at the very least what Mr Adair's intentions were.

Breezy Adair had made his way to the counter now. The customers had given him space and he was leaning on the bar with a glass of something expensive in his hand. Gordon went forward and waited politely. Breezy Adair glanced at him, let his gaze linger.

"Mr Adair?"

"That's me, son."

"I'm Gordon Nicholson."

"Are you now? Are you really?"

"I believe you know my mother – quite well."

"Of course I do," said Breezy frankly.

But he did not smile. The creases about his eyes had planed away and he looked older than Gordon had first judged him to be.

"I wonder," Gordon said, "if we might have a quiet word."

"Now?"

"If it's convenient."

The whippy little cane was hooked into the belt of the ulster to leave his hands free to hold the brandy glass.

"I can spare you ten minutes," Breezy Adair said.

"In private, if possible," said Gordon.

Breezy nodded. He lifted a section of the counter and kneed open a half-gate concealed beneath the cornices. The bar-hands were working like Trojans, pulling beer and measuring whisky. They ignored the owner as he opened the taproom door and ushered Gordon before him towards the top of a flight of steep wooden steps.

"What's down there?" Gordon asked.

"The vaults."

"Vaults?"

"Cellars," Breezy said. "Perfectly private, perfectly quiet."

"All right," said Gordon and went on ahead down into the pungent gloom.

* * *

If Kirsty had ever doubted that a wave of revivalism had swept through Glasgow this past year the size of the crowds that flocked about St Andrew's Halls would have dispelled her scepticism. Hacks, carriages, horse-buses, even a couple of hired brakes nosed and rumbled through the streams of pedestrians in Berkeley Street, West Granville Street and Kent Road.

Bands of bronze-coloured light illuminated the upper portions of the halls. The Free Church opposite, though dwarfed, had lit its lamps as if to remind acolytes of Mr Monroe that tomorrow the famous preacher would be gone but that sin would still be there, standing like a black rock unmoved by the torrent of words that had poured from the mouth of a mere mortal man.

The crowds were oblivious to the Free Kirk's gesture, were not solemn and sober, though it was not drink that buoyed them up but expectation. There was a bubbling excitement in the long queue that snaked away from the doors where entry to the unticketed ground floor was to be obtained for a fortunate five or six hundred eager souls.

"It'll be a miracle if half of them get in," said David. "A tenth of them."

"Perhaps there will be a miracle," said Kirsty.

David laughed. "Like the loaves and fishes, do you mean?"

"Well — "

"Our Lord never had to contend with municipal fire regulations. No, no miracles tonight, I fear."

She still clung to his arm, necessary now so that they would not be separated in the throng. She clung to him as he threaded his way towards the brass-and-glass door that would lead them out of the crowd and up plush stairs to the Grand Circle. Folks glanced at them, perhaps admiring the handsome young minister, wondering what kirk was lucky enough to have him in its pulpit. They would suppose her to be his wife. She wondered if they would think her pretty enough for him. She found that she was not embarrassed, not in the slightest, and gripped his arm more tightly as they came to the thickest knot in the queue.

"What about the spare ticket, David?"

"I'll hand it to the doorman."

"Give it to someone."

"What?"

"Please, David, give it to someone in the queue."

She had noticed their shabbiness. Ordinary folk done up in Sunday best. The good people of Glasgow drawn out by the promise of a show, church-goers like her. She wanted someone to share her pleasure. They paused while David fished in his pocket for the tickets and the woman fixed her gaze upon Kirsty. She was of indeterminate age, thirty-five or older, in a swollen green serge coat and with a plain brown hat pinned to mouse-brown hair. She had a moon face and tiny rosebud lips and spectacles magnified her pleading eyes.

"Lady, take me in wi' you," the woman said aloud.

She was not in the queue at all, Kirsty realised. But she exuded a desperate need to gain entry to the halls, to see Tom Monroe in the flesh, to be included in the great gathering.

"I – "

"Please, lady, please see I get in."

"David?"

Something in the manner in which David sized up the woman took Kirsty by surprise; a coldness that she did not associate with David but with Craig, as if he had put charity to one side and observed not somebody in a state of need but only a type that had become tedious in its familiarity.

"I can pay, sir. I'm willin' to pay."

The woman's nether lip quivered and her eyes filled with tears. David sighed.

"See, sir. See, I've a shillin' here. Take it, I beg you, an' let me have the ticket."

Others in the queue had become interested. At any moment a crowd would form around them, bartering with David for the extra ticket.

Flustered, David thrust the ticket into the fat woman's hand. "Here, take it. I want nothing for it."

"I canna let you – "

"Please," said Kirsty. "Do take it."

David drew Kirsty towards the door. The woman dogged them, crying out, "My name's Gladys McClure. Is he your man?"

With surprising lack of manners David shouldered his way through the queue, pulling Kirsty after him.

"What's his name?" Gladys McClure called. "What kirk's he from?"

Panting, the woman followed hard on their heels. Kirsty began to realise why David had been so curt with her. She wanted more than admission to the halls. She wanted to command their attention.

In the crowded foyer David handed over the tickets, received a salute in respect to his dog-collar from the doorman and was directed up the staircase.

Kirsty had no opportunity to enjoy the experience. She felt as if she was being pursued by Gladys McClure. David hurried on, dragging her behind him as if he was hauling her up an alp. A door at the top of the staircase opened. Suddenly she was within the hall, vast and breathtaking in its scale.

She recoiled from the sound that rose from the auditorium below, a gigantic whisper like the sea on a windy night. She could not look out but kept her eyes down, staring at her shoes

— Madge's shoes — as she picked down four steep steps from the aisle. She glanced up nervously. They were above and slightly to the front of the long polished length of the platform. She felt as if everybody in the hall was staring at her. David tipped down one of the plush seats and Kirsty lowered herself into it thankfully.

She gave herself a minute to settle and then peeped over the balcony rail. Floor and aisles were seething like an anthill. High overhead gas chandeliers swung on their chains in the void. She did not look up again but concentrated on the platform which rose in an amphitheatre of seats to columns of bronze organ pipes, hazy in the gloom.

Church dignitaries of several denominations, and their wives, had privileged seats on the platform, some civic officials too, marked by chains of office. They were there to be seen and pompously held their chins aloft, looking haughtily out over the multitude. Eight chairs in padded scarlet leather stood empty before a long table with a velvet cloth upon it, a lectern, carafes and water glasses. The empty chairs created an expectancy in the audience that communicated itself to Kirsty. She touched David's arm and smiled.

At that instant Gladys McClure plumped herself down beside them. "Are you a *real* minister, then?"

"Only an assistant, I'm afraid."

"Where?"

"St Anne's in Walbrook Street."

"I'm from Mr Flint's Mission in St Rollox. He's famous for his conversions," Gladys said.

"Ah, yes. I've heard of Mr Flint."

"Are you revivalists?"

"No," David answered. "No, we're not."

Without pausing for breath, Gladys said, "She's bonnie, your wife."

David said, "Did Mr Flint convert you, Mrs – "

"Miss. I'm just a plain miss. Marrit to the Mission, you might say. Wedded to the Word o' God."

"I see," said David.

Kirsty sensed that David was losing patience. He wanted to ignore the ardent, eager Christian, to shut her out, but the habit of politeness was ingrained. Behind her spectacle lenses Gladys McClure's eyes seemed huge. They had become her prisoners, trapped by kindness.

Kirsty said, "Have you heard Tom Monroe preach before?"

"If I'd heard Mr Monroe," Gladys retorted, "I wouldn't be here the night, would I?"

David said, "Did Mr Flint not receive an allocation of tickets for his congregation?"

"He'd none to spare," said Gladys McClure. "None to spare for me."

Bitterness speckled her piety like decay on the skin of a fruit. "I'll hear him tonight, though, won't I? Aye, we'll hear what Monroe has to say for himself tonight."

Gladys McClure had not come to the halls to be moved or uplifted. She had come, Kirsty realised, to judge.

It was a relief when the lights dimmed and the last few bodies were pushed through the doors and the audience became hushed. The platform took on a compelling luminosity. Into the concentration of light the platform party emerged from a low door on the side of the staging.

As each man appeared Gladys identified him.

"Mr Carter from the Institute. He's great.

"That's the Reverend Williams. I've heard him preach more times than tongue can tell.

"Yonder's the singer, Mr Jessamyn. Voice like an angel but they say he's too fond o' the bottle.

"See, that's Monroe himself."

Tom Monroe was small and almost ugly, with large, meaty hands and a shock of pure white hair. He wore no robes but only a black, vested suit with a high starched collar with a black tie in the vee. He was an ordained minister, of course, but eschewed the symbols of that office. He clumped to the centre and seated himself on a padded chair, folded his arms and glowered out at the assembly as if, even in poor light, he could weigh their collective worth and had already found it wanting.

Gladys nudged David with her elbow. "Who's that goin' up to play the organ?"

"I really have no idea."

"Huh!" Gladys snorted. "I see old Buchanan's leadin' the praise. No show wi'out Punch, eh!"

Kirsty was sorry that she had given in to charitable impulse. Gladys McClure's spirituality was twisted and egotistical. Whatever she received from religion it was not the bread of love or the wine of forgiveness.

The notes of the organ filled the hall, exalted and triumphant. The Reverend David Buchanan, one of Glasgow's most respected divines, rose from his chair and stepped to the platform's edge. He lifted his hands and bowed his head and intoned a short prayer before announcing that the evening would begin with a hymn of praise to the Lord. Kirsty closed her mind to Gladys McClure's failings and got to her feet.

Psalm 121: a comforting avowal of community belief in God. Like all church folk Kirsty knew the words off by heart. *I to the hills will lift mine eyes.*

After the psalm Mr Carter addressed the audience. He was a portly little man with a rude oratorical style. "What will be the lastin' effect of the great revival of religious interest in Scotland?" he began; and answered his own question by declaring that the new revivalism would be continuous and would bring people face to face with a most momentous crisis in social life, that God was speaking out at last through his missionaries, that God was saying, "According to your faith, so be it unto you." Mr Carter's address was punctuated by applause and Kirsty realised that this was not just another service but something that lay closer to the heart of the people. She did not feel particularly moved but she was greatly intrigued.

After Mr Carter had had his say the gaunt and aged Reverend Williams delivered a dry and practical address on the Church's rôle in society. He spoke of deprivation and starvation and indifference. The audience grew a little bit restless and Gladys sat back with her arms folded smugly as if she had heard all this nonsense before and was not impressed by it. David, however, listened with considerable attention, nodding discreetly from time to time.

After that address Mr Jessamyn sang 'Rock of Ages' in a ringing and sober baritone and got a tremendous ovation for his performance. And then it was time, at last, for Tom Monroe to speak.

One glance was enough to tell you that Tom Monroe was a man of the people, had sprung from the bosom of the masses, with the political overtones attached. Kirsty had seen his double in the streets of the Greenfield, except that Monroe was possessed by an inward fire, a zeal that other men lacked. It came alight when he stepped to the front of the platform to begin his address, his hair shaggy and bristling in the aura of the gas lamps. His voice was magical, deep and musical and resonant. Four thousand folk were rendered silent. In the hall you could hear a pin drop as the power of the voice transfixed them all and caused them to neglect, at first, the sense of the message that the voice proclaimed.

It was several minutes before Kirsty took in much that Tom Monroe was saying or where he was leading her. She, like all the others, was caught by the vivid word-pictures that he created, her judgment stilled by her imagination. Not even his grand pantomimic gestures could weaken his power. In three or four minutes he was well into his stride. He told the story of Gideon and his three hundred warriors, made of it an allegory of man's struggle and God's rôle in that struggle.

"Why," he cried, "if Gideon had been allowed to go with the thirty-two thousand he brought to the field in mere carnal energy, enthusiasm and human patriotism, the Midianites would have gone through them in the first shock of battle like wolves through sheep." As he spoke he crabbed along the edge of the platform, the light dancing about him. It was not accidental that he reached the first climax of exposition just as he reached centre stage. He raised his meaty, working-man's hands. "Aye, and every day there is the battle among us, the battle between Hell and Heaven and we, like Gideon, must go with God's word, trustingly, armoured with the Faith of our fathers."

The effect of his rhetoric was almost electrical and, for a moment, Kirsty felt that the battle was indeed her battle, the salvation that Tom Monroe promised was hers to claim. She was not alone in the experience. Cool-headed men and their vain, dressy wives were also swayed, roused, and also did not know how to respond. Only converts like Gladys knew what to do.

"*Hallelujah,*" Gladys cried, at the pitch of her voice, and got at once an echo from the body of the hall. "*Hallelujah. Hallelujah.*"

If Tom Monroe had stopped at that point he would have left every single soul in the halls elevated and amazed. But Tom Monroe did not know when to stop. He was driven by the force of his own conviction. He talked on and on, dropped catch-phrases like manna and was soon discoursing on sinfulness and greed and the necessity of seeking conversion. He spoke at length of his own coming to God. He told how marvellous an event it had been and how he had been changed by it in the roots of his being. He urged it willy-nilly on everyone as if it was something that could be earned by the sweat of the brow, like Sunday money, or willed down out of the clouds, or lapped up like the water that Gideon's men supped from their hands.

Eventually Kirsty began to separate matter from manner. What she took in now from the preacher's sermon made her feel guilty. He depicted a struggle from which she felt absolved, a war between evil and good. In the hour in which he occupied the platform not once did Thomas Monroe mention love.

*　　*　　*

According to religious zealots vice flourished in Glasgow like a great rank weed. If you knew just where to look you could find Satan in all his glory waiting to tempt you from the primrose path and lead you, blushing, to instant perdition. Up every staircase, along every shadowy lane, it seemed, were to be found 'maelstroms of depravity and abysses of pollution'. In case you were too shy to discover them for yourself the more popular religious publications would pinpoint exact locations and document the nature of the wickedness you could find within. Billiard parlours, dance saloons, drinking-clubs, gambling hells and bawdy music-halls were all described in tracts distributed not by the proprietors of these establishments but by their po-faced opponents. Many an impressionable young Christian must have learned the facts of life from such lurid articles and have been turned, like a perverse little weathercock, not from but towards these gaudy sins.

Bad conscience was not Madge Nicholson's problem, nor did she need the printed word to steer her to spots where fun could be found. She had Breezy Adair as guide and mentor and what there was to know about the seamy side of Glasgow life was known to Breezy as to no other. Breezy was by no means evil or even wicked. He was polite, considerate and good-humoured and no more ruthless in pursuit of an honest dollar than the next man. He had earned himself a modest fortune by the sweat of his brow and he had an appetite for good living that could not be contained by the strait laces of middle-class society. Breezy also believed that every citizen had a right to a share in material pleasure. In short, he gave folk what they wanted. French knickers, Turkish cigarettes, hip flasks, gold-plated watches, trinkets of all sorts, cheap Indian carpets, Scotch whisky, Continental port, rat traps and annular lamps, a wee flutter on the gee-gees or a night on the tiles with a passionate young vampire; Breezy could supply all of these things and more. Over the years, penny by penny, Breezy had salted his money into many enterprises. He owned nothing outright. He was never the bookmaker or the publican or the manufacturer. He bought, sold and traded other people's goods and services and skinned a good living without having to lift a finger for more than an hour or two each morning.

It had not always been so. Breezy had been raised by the rod according to Christian precepts. He had been born to a tenant farmer and his wife out beyond Garscadden and, like his five brothers and two sisters, had gone hungry, had wept on icy mornings when the tramp to the byre for the milking would have had the toes off you if you hadn't danced to the sting of Dad's stick on your thighs or had your lugs warmed by Mam's hard hand when you asked for something to eat before all the work was done. At twelve Breezy slung his hook and headed along the road to Glasgow. He never returned to the stink of sanctity, cow manure and poverty. He had lived rough in a cellar in Gower Street. He had taken 'commission' jobs, selling religious prints door-to-door and had learned the trick of filling his eyes with tears while offering a threepenny depiction of Mary and Joseph at the Infant's crib or some mournful collie dog draped over its master's grave.

Breezy had had a gift for selling. In a couple of years he had earned enough to buy prints directly from the engravers and to set up on his own. In due course he brought out all his brothers and sisters from Garscadden, all except wee Peter who was too daft to see the need to leave home and who died of pneumonia when he was sixteen.

The first decade in Glasgow was grindingly hard. Breezy suffered with and for his family, but they were always behind him; no regrets, no recriminations. They were unanimously agreed that anything was preferable to being whipped with one hand and served up the righteous pap of salvation with the other, especially when there was no hope of it this side of heaven. Breezy's parents still lived on the ramshackle farm. Dad still took the cart to the dairy every morning and hurled churns about as if they contained all the misery and hatred that he had milked out of life and in which, really, he revelled since suffering brought him closer to God. Twice a year Breezy's younger sister, Polly, went out there and gave Dad an envelope with ten one-pound banknotes in it;

Breezy's mite, for which he received no thanks, and wanted none. Breezy had never married. On several occasions he had been sorely tempted and he certainly did not lack for female companionship. In his time he had consorted with girls pretty enough to knock your eye out. But with so many sisters, brothers and in-laws, nephews and nieces and even the odd cousin, there were umpteen houses in which he could be assured of a warm and genuine welcome. It was only now, in his fifty-third year, that he began to experience the loneliness of bachelorhood and feel the need to take a wife. Why it should be a woman like Madge Nicholson that awakened such longing in his heart Breezy Adair had not a clue.

Madge was very proud to have attracted the attention of a well-heeled chap like Albert Adair. She was curious, though, as to why he should be smitten by a farmer's widow in preference to some sleek and slender girl, but she did not question him about it. She recognised in Breezy a sexual passion that was well under control. He made no bones about the fact that he wanted to have her in his bed but he did not take umbrage when she restricted familiarities to kissing and cuddling, and firmly refused to surrender.

Madge had met Breezy in the rooms of the Parisian School of Dance where she had enrolled to learn the latest steps and where Breezy had turned up to vet the place for his sister Heather whose daughter was all agog to take instruction. Breezy was only too well aware how easily a young girl could fall into bad company and he did not trust establishments in which he had no stake. Once Mr Adair clapped eyes on Mrs Nicholson, however, the cause of the niece was forgotten and it was Breezy himself who signed on for a course of lessons right there on the spot. Romance blossomed like a columbine. Breezy showered gifts on his lady love, took her to the best places to wine and dine and entertained her in the best boxes in the theatres. Naturally Madge loved every minute of it. Perhaps it was to preserve the courtship that she declined to submit to Breezy's advances. It was hardly moral scruple since Madge too was stirred by desire. She fancied being with a man who was not her husband, to revel once more, late in life, in the tingling pleasure of flirtation and capitulation. Indeed, she had never felt so amorously disposed towards any man, not even Bob far back in the old days when he had been ardent and arrogant and she had been his blushing bride. The truth, or part of it, was that she wanted to secure Breezy not just as a lover but as a husband and was holding on to what she had until he popped the question. But Breezy, it seemed, was leery of that final, irrevocable commitment, though he occasionally discussed the state in broad general terms just to see how she would respond.

This cat and mouse feeling added spice to their evenings and was in the air that Saturday when Breezy picked Madge up in a hired cab at the corner of Banff Street. He fell at once to kissing her on the brow and cheek. He drew her close so that her breasts were crushed against his manly chest. She could smell brandy on his breath but he was not drunk; Breezy never got drunk in her company. The cab carried them through twilit streets into the heart of Glasgow and discharged them at a narrow stairwell that wound up two flights to the Glenlyon Oyster Rooms. It was not the sort of place where gentlemen came to meet ladies but rather where they brought them after the meeting had been accomplished. It was a little too early for trade to be brisk but Breezy had reserved a table nonetheless.

Madge loved the shaded rooms, all corners and secluded bays, with waiters sliding silent as stoats between the marble cold tables and the bar. Candles in fluted rose-tinted bowls spread a flattering glow over each table, made it discreet and private. She loved too the briny tang of sea-foods, the rich odour of cigar smoke and the subtle sharpness of foaming champagne. Divested of hat and coat she seated herself behind a table in a padded corner and let Breezy pen her in with his gilded chair. Menu cards were brought. The business of ordering a hearty supper was gone through at some length.

Breezy seemed particularly chirpy tonight, she thought. He had a disconcerting way of studying her, eyes crinkled, and, as they waited for the cold smoked mackerel to start them off, he gave her cheek a tender little tweak, kissed her on the lips and murmured, "Ah-hah, Madge Nicholson. Ah-hah," as if he knew something that she did not.

When at length the mackerel had been put away and they were both tucking into mussel soup, Madge could contain herself no longer.

"What's got into you tonight, Mr Adair?"

"Not a thing, chookie, not a blessed thing."

Madge broke bread as Breezy had taught her to do, crumbled crust into the thick soup and spooned it into her mouth.

Twelve months ago she would not have known how to cope with all of this, would not have believed that she, a farmer's widow, the mother of three grown children, would be sipping and supping with a gentleman in an oyster room in Glasgow. The transformation had happened rapidly, however, and she had rapidly grown used to it. She dabbed her lips with a linen napkin.

"Did one o' your horses come in at a canter? Is that it?"

"Well, Partick Thistle won four to one."

"Did they?" said Madge. "And you had a bet on it?"

Breezy said, "It was a real nice day for a football match."

"Were you there?"

"I looked in for the second half." Breezy pushed the soup bowl to one side and a silent waiter whisked it silently away. "Your lads were there too."

"What lads?"

"Your lads, Madge. Your boys, your sons."

Choking slightly, Madge dropped her silver spoon and covered her mouth with her napkin.

"Gordon an' Craig," said Breezy. "You remember."

"You – you saw them?"

"I met them after the game."

"You – you spoke to them?"

"I spoke to Gordon. Craig had gone off by that time."

"How did you know who they were?"

Madge had avoided introducing her children to Mr Adair. It was not that she was ashamed of them, but she knew what a prig Craig could be and wished only to steer clear of embarrassment. She was also nervous in case too much came out about her past. She had not lied to Breezy, quite, but preferred her version of the truth to go unchallenged.

"I didn't. Gordon recognised me," said Breezy. "He's a charmin' lad, a lad after my own heart."

"My Gordon?"

"You should be proud o' him, Madge."

"What? Oh! Yes. I am, I am."

Breezy poured fizz into two glasses, handed one glass to Madge and returned the bottle to the ice-bucket.

"It was very, very interestin', Madge. Very."

She coughed again, resorted to the napkin again.

"What – what did he say about me?"

"Said hardly a word about you, chookie."

Madge did not know whether she was insulted or relieved. "What did you find to talk about, then?"

"Gordon wants me to find him a job."

Madge could not help herself. She flung the napkin angrily down into the soup bowl. "He did *what*? I'll kill that wee devil when I get home."

"Why, Madge? He's done nothin' wrong."

"He had no right to badger you. In any case, he *has* a job."

"Some job," said Breezy. "Sweepin' floors."

"I'll kill him, so I will."

A waiter, not much older than Gordon, glided to the table and, on Breezy's instruction, cleared away bowls, plates and crumpled napkins. He was back in a trice with fresh linen and a little brush with which he dusted crumbs from the cloth.

"Give us five minutes, Mario," said Breezy.

The waiter nodded and glided out of existence. Breezy reached over the table and clasped Madge's hand.

"For God's sake, Madge, there's no need to get so het up," Breezy told her. "Why shouldn't Gordon try to better himself? He's a smart lad as far as I can tell, and I'm no mean judge o' character, though I say so myself."

"He – he exploited a – a situation."

"Is that what you call it?" said Breezy. "I thought there might be a nicer word for it. Anyway, you can't blame him for being curious about me, can you?"

"Curiosity killed the damned cat, and it'll damned-well kill him when I get home."

"Madge, Madge! Gordon's a grown man, near enough. God, I'd been workin' on my own account for five years before I was his age. He might be a bit on the short side but he's got more than his share o' brains."

Madge slackened. She sniffed. "Do you think so?"

"He didn't just march up to me an' demand a job," said Breezy. "He was very polite about it."

"Oh, he would be polite. I brought them all up to be polite."

"Of course you did, chookie."

"It's a pity you hadn't met Craig. He's the real smart one in the family."

"Is he?" said Breezy, without conviction.

"It's Craig who looks after me."

"Uh-huh," said Breezy.

"Gordon would never make a policeman."

"Too short," said Breezy. "But you don't have to be five-feet-eight to work for me, you know."

"Don't tell me you'll offer him work?"

"Like a shot I will."

"What sort of job?" said Madge.

"Selling things; carpets to start with."

"Well, it sounds honest enough."

"My God, chookie, do you think I'd take your lad into anythin' shifty?"

"No, no," said Madge. "What does it pay?"

"Ten shillings a week, plus what he earns on commission."

"I don't like the sound of that."

"Believe me, he'll do well out of it."

"Where's the carpet shop?" said Madge.

"It's a warehouse. I'm not the owner, as such. It's on Dumbarton Road, at Partick East. He'll be working with me sometimes but mostly with my nephew Johnnie Whiteside. Johnnie'll show him the ropes all right."

Madge sniffed. "I'm sorry I flew off the handle."

"Make it up to me later," Breezy said.

On surer ground now, Madge simpered. "You've had your ration, Mr Adair."

"Come home with me tonight."

"Oh, so you think you can buy me by giving my son a job, is that it?"

"Of course that isn't it," said Breezy. "What do I have to do to convince you that you won't regret it?"

It had been on the tip of her tongue to answer 'Marry me' but Gordon's appearance in the equation had disconcerted her more than she would admit.

"I'm not that kind of woman, Albert."

Breezy sat back, lifted his champagne glass and sipped from it. "I'll just have to be patient, I suppose."

"Very patient," said Madge and, with a confidence that she had learned from her companion, snapped her fingers for a waiter to bring on the trout.

*   *   *

74

With a babble of conversations, some indignant voices raised in criticism and a murmurous undertow of general relief that the long sit was over, the crowd that spilled from St Andrew's Halls was noisy if not rowdy and showed no great inclination to dash off and disperse. Kirsty could not decide what her feelings were towards Tom Monroe. Her brain still reeled with his forceful imagery. But nobody had risen and declared that the Lord had come upon them, as had happened at the Cirque, and Kirsty had been less than impressed with Monroe's long account of his own conversion. What opinion David had of the performance was still a mystery. He had said little throughout though his eyes had never left Monroe while the evangelist occupied the stage. Kirsty was anxious to put questions to David, the more so as she would soon be offering herself for full Church membership. But that Saturday night the 'real' Church seemed quite remote as men and women from many denominations and many walks of life mingled upon the pavements.

Gladys McClure had dampened the pleasure of the experience for Kirsty as well as David. Gladys had been so voluble during the course of the sermon that several angry glances had been directed at the Circle and she had been advised to *wheesh* several times. David had almost managed to dissociate himself from her, though she addressed many of her strident asides to him and dug him with her plump elbow to rouse his attention.

Gladys clattered down the staircase in Kirsty's wake. Her cheeks were flushed, her coat unbuttoned and her spectacles bobbed against the bridge of her nose. She would not let them leave decently. She would seek to extract every last drop from the encounter. Kirsty was afraid that David's patience would snap at the last. Chased by Gladys, David dragged Kirsty past friends and acquaintances from his student days, though he would probably have liked to pause and talk with them. He might have made it into the street and have been clear of the building before Gladys caught them if the door had not been blocked by a convention of ministers and their wives.

Gladys' hand closed on David's shoulder.

She said loudly, "I could use my influence, get Mr Flint t'invite you t'speak at the Mission."

"Well," said David, "perhaps."

"Or I could come t'your church, hear you preach there. I'd tell you what I thought o' it."

"Public worship," said David, "takes place every Sunday at eleven o'clock and six thirty in the evening."

"I'll bet you don't speak wi' *his* conviction."

"No," said David. "I regret to say that I don't. Now, Miss McClure, we must be heading home, if you don't mind."

She was hard behind them, her body pressed against David's, her right hand on Kirsty's shoulder as if she might attach herself to them physically, like some dreadful creature out of legend.

"I'll walk wi' you a bit," she said.

"We're catching a tram," said Kirsty.

"I'll catch a tram too."

"But we travel in the other direction," said Kirsty.

Gladys prodded David. "When's your class?"

"My class? What — what class?"

David pushed himself through the doorway and stepped down on to the pavement below the shallow steps. He was gentleman enough to pause, to assist Kirsty, but he left Gladys to her own devices.

"Bible class, daftie," said Gladys.

Craig would have given the awful, persistent woman short shrift but obligation kept David from thrusting her away from him, from telling her to go to hell.

Gladys went on, "I'm comin' t'your class. I'm keen t'hear what you've got t'say for yourself."

She was still holding them, by elbow and by shoulder.

"*David? David Lockhart? Here.*"

The call came from a young fair-haired man who stood near the pavement's edge in the company of an elderly minister and two women, one of them young.

"Why, it's John Singleton," said David. "John's an old friend of mine, Miss McClure, so if you will excuse us now — " He tugged himself from Gladys' grasp and approached the group, leaving Kirsty too a step or so behind.

He shook hands with the fair-haired man. "How are you, John? I haven't seen you for an age."

"I'm well, David. Blooming, in fact. Have you a parish yet?"

"I'm still at St Anne's. Assisting Harry Graham."

Kirsty hung back behind David who had by now attached himself to the little group and had, it seemed, finally shaken off Gladys McClure.

"I'll see him again," Gladys muttered.

"I think – " said Kirsty.

"I know that one an' all," said Gladys. "He's the Reverend Tyler."

Before Kirsty could prevent it the woman had insinuated herself into the company. Kirsty followed her forward, uncertainly. David continued to ignore them both. It was as if they were equal, and neither of them important to him. At last Gladys felt the sting of insult.

"Lost your woman, Mr Lockhart?" she asked in a loud voice.

They all turned and stared at Gladys, at Kirsty.

The girl was very pretty in a sweet, unpainted way. She managed to force an uncertain smile. But her parents, the saintly stiff-backed minister and his upright wife, surveyed Gladys with glittering disdain. They had instantly identified the type and knew exactly how to deal with it.

"Is this person with you, David?" asked John Singleton.

"No," David answered. "I gave her a ticket of admission, that's all. She's not with me."

Gladys bared her teeth. She prodded her spectacles tight against her nose and clasped her hands tightly against the breast of her coat.

She shouted, "Ask him about *her*. Ask him what he's doin' wi' *her*. She's not *his* wife, you know."

Humiliated and stunned, Kirsty turned on her heel and walked rapidly away.

*   *   *

She had almost reached the corner of Granville Street before David caught up with her. She kept walking. Her toes dug into the little paper balls in the points of her borrowed shoes. Gladys had at last abandoned them. She had stung once, like a wasp, and flown away. But the others would be staring after David, speculating on what she, Kirsty Nicholson, meant to him. Perhaps there would be that same lofty disdain in their eyes as when they had studied poor Gladys McClure.

"She's a fool," said David. "You should not have taken offence."

Kirsty was relieved that he had followed her, had not abandoned her in favour of his posh friends. He did not touch her, however, did not take her arm. He strode by her side, at her pace, across Granville Street.

Kirsty said, "It was wrong of me to accompany you, without Nessie."

"Why was it wrong?"

"Because of what they'll think."

"Let them think what they like."

"They'll imagine – "

"Imagined sins mean nothing," David said. "It wouldn't be true, would it? Would it be true, Kirsty?"

"I don't know what you mean."

"Yes, you do. Tell me, would it be true?"

"We should never have given her a ticket."

"That's beside the point," said David. "She saw immediately how it was. Didn't she, Kirsty?"

He wanted her to put it into words. She longed to take his hand but Gladys McClure stood between them now. The woman had highlighted the shadowy nature of their relationship. Until now Kirsty had deceived herself into believing that a companionable friendship was possible and quite proper. It was a nonsense, a lie; Gladys McClure had shown her that much. She could not deny it. She said nothing. She walked on into the tail of Sauchiehall Street, heading west. David, mute and grim, strode at her side.

Above the Kelvin Grove stately mansions glowed in the April darkness and the trees along the pavements shivered in first bud. Parkway promenades were filled with young people in groups of five and six, with girls and boys linked arm-in-arm, couples, lost in love, clinging together in the shadows between the lamps, caught in the adventure of courtship, free as starlings. Kirsty envied them their freedom. She had never known that freedom. She had moved from servitude of one kind into servitude of another, into a 'marriage' with a man she hardly knew. All she had had out of it was her son, Bobby. The rest was nothing, the chaff of reality.

"Kirsty, aren't you going to answer me?"

She was suspicious of David suddenly, of his persistence, of his motives. Why did he want her to admit that she loved him? It was all wrong. She equated him with the well-to-do people on the pavement outside the halls. They were his sort of folk, upright, conventional, well-heeled and respectable.

"It's late," she heard herself say. "Put me on a tram, please."

"Aren't you coming back to Walbrook Street?"

"What for?"

"To tell Nessie about our evening."

"Mrs Jagger will see us."

"Oh, Kirsty, for heaven's sake – "

"I'll see Nessie on Sunday."

"Tomorrow."

"Yes, tomorrow."

"So you will come tomorrow?" David said.

"Why shouldn't I?"

"I thought you were angry with me."

"I'm not, not with you."

"Come back, then, just for a little while."

If he had put his arm about her she would have been lost. What *did* he want with her, from her? Did he want to be her lover, with all that word implied? What else *could* he want from a woman of her class? Craig Nicholson was her kind. She belonged in a kitchen in Canada Road. She could never have a place in David Lockhart's life, not a true place, a proper place. What he demanded of her was not possible. The compromise, the asking price, was too high. She stepped to the edge of the pavement.

Corporation tramcars clattered through the junctions, splitting on the down line to Argyle Street and up towards St Vincent Street's long hill. There were hacks and late-night carts, and rivers of pedestrians flowed from the doors of public houses. She peered at the trams, at the indicator boards above the horses and, when she saw one bound for Whiteinch, ran for it.

Partick folk, Greenfield folk, folk like her; they hopped on and off the running-boards as suited them, not bothering to wait for stages. There were small dwarf-like men in mufflers and walrus moustaches, all redolent of whisky, women in drab capes and tar-black bonnets, and a herd of apprentices who charged noisily upstairs to ride in state on the open deck.

"Kirsty," she heard him call out. "Kirsty, don't leave me."

If he wanted her he must pursue her once more. She must not make it easy for him, take all of the running upon herself.

"*Kirsty?*"

She paid her fare and found a seat inside the car. She kept her eyes demurely down. She was sure that David would slip on to the bench at her side, take her hands in his, forgive her everything; or perhaps she would look up and find him tucked into the conductor's corner, smiling at her fondly. David would understand what torment she was going through. He would tell her that he loved her for herself, that it was pure, decent, innocent. He would lie to her and she would believe him; and it would be as it had been before the evangelist's meeting. She stared out of the window at the street. Reflections in the glass; a young mother on the opposite bench had three tired bairns slumped against her body, their limbs thin and grubby, noses running; a middle-aged man in a commercial suit – worn cuffs, stained collar – ogled her and practised an introductory smile that was as inviting as that of a crocodile.

Kirsty kept herself shut off from the other passengers. The tramcar ground on, halted, ground on again. Coarse singing came from the upper deck, a variety-hall chorus. The horses' hoofs clacked on the cobbles and the car body creaked. Newspaper boys and hot-potato vendors cried their wares, echoes of the world outside.

At length Kirsty glanced to her right along the aisle between the seats. She glanced left. And then, blinking, faced the window once more.

She stared, blinking, at nothing, and struggled to hold back her tears.

David was not on the tramcar.

David had let her go.

*   *   *

Lorna had been the only one at home when Craig returned from the swimming-baths. She had made his supper, had brushed his uniform and had seen to it that none of his buttons was loose. Bobby was fretful. He cried and refused to lie at peace in his cot. He was red-cheeked and slavered a lot. Lorna said that he was cutting another tooth and had a touch of teething fever. She did not seem unduly concerned. She lifted the child and walked with him against her breast. She looked small and quite frail and Bobby seemed too large for her, as if she was mothering a changeling. Craig had felt a flash of pity for his sister. There was still some of the old affection between them, though they had both lost the light, dependent spirit that had existed between them when they were younger and lived on Dalnavert. He could not bear to hear his son cry, however, and left early for the night shift.

It was a fine clear night. Saturday was usually busy on the beat until one o'clock or so, after which the Sabbath took a hold and drunks fell to snoring and squabbling wives bathed their bruises and uproarious apprentices had sense enough to slink along the pavements and not attract the attention of the coppers since most of them were too young to tipple and did not want to waste a night in a cell. Craig liked a Saturday night, its diversions, its eventual peacefulness. He liked the varied rhythm of days and nights and felt most at home when he was out on the streets, patrolling his beat.

Since he was early he would go first to the Peoples' Mission in Scutter Street and walk Sammy Reynolds back to the model lodging-house. All the Ottawa Street coppers were wise to Sammy. They knew that he would wait in the Mission doorway, after Mr Dugdale had checked the shutters and locked the door. He would wait there until a uniform appeared, would not budge without an escort. Even Constable Norbert, recently fledged, took a turn at fathering Sammy, though Ronnie drew the line at letting the lad hold his hand. Sammy disliked Constable Norbert, if he disliked anyone at all, which put young Sammy very much in the majority in the Greenfield.

There was no need for Sammy to be accompanied home. He made the journey of a quarter of a mile every morning on his own. He would stop off to buy a roll and gammon for his dinner, though Mr Dugdale saw to it that Sammy got a fair share of leftovers when the Guild had a tea-party or the Boys' Brigade a bun-fight. But at night Sammy needed a friendly ear into which he would pour a garbled account of the day's happenings and any gossip he had picked up, all scrambled, about Miss Frobisher of the Bible School or Wee Corky, who delivered the coke, or Captain Glover of the Brigade who was very strict and never, ever smiled.

Craig felt a certain protectiveness towards Sammy. He would go out of his way to be the one who collected him from the Mission doorway. There were times when Craig envied the boy his simple routine of sweeping, scrubbing and raking out fires, the fact that he slept in a narrow cubicle and was untroubled by the complicated emotions that bedevilled a man possessed of all his mental faculties. To Sammy, only to Sammy, Craig occasionally blurted out his fears, doubts and frustrations. Sammy would peer up into Craig's face and nod gravely as if he understood the vicissitudes of adult life and burdens of responsibility, though he hadn't a clue what Mr Nicholson was talking about. Craig was careful not to mention names, just in case Sammy carried them unwittingly to Mr Dugdale or Miss Frobisher, but he railed against fickle women and rich educated men, mothers who had become silly and feckless, and brothers who betrayed you. Sammy would nod sympathetically and squeeze Mr Nicholson's hand to calm him down. Sammy was almost as big as he was now. Out of uniform it would have been ridiculous for a grown lad to take a man's hand, but the helmet and serge made it all right, except for Ronnie Norbert who had too much pride for his own damned good.

As he approached the carved stone doorway of the Mission Craig saw that the door had been closed and locked. There was nothing unusual in that. But Sammy was not standing in his customary place and Craig felt a little crimp of anxiety in his gut, though it was probable that some other constable had chanced by and had stepped in for service voluntarily. He quickened his pace – and saw the boy.

Sammy was seated on the steps, back to the carved stone corner. Sammy had a little girl on his knee. She was no more than three years old. Sammy had a hand about her waist and was stroking her hair.

Craig's mouth went dry.

Sergeant Drummond had warned him about the propensity of dafties to become 'nasty' when nature turned them into men. Drummond had also hinted to Craig what happened to feeble-minded males if they were caught pestering girls. They would be committed to an institution and kept there for the benefit and protection of society. Craig was forced to admit the sense of the law. God knows, even men with all their wits about them could be impelled into criminal behaviour by the violence of their sexual urges; and Sammy Reynolds had no wits at all. Sammy wouldn't know what he was doing, or why. He might have just enough social instinct to appreciate that what he was doing was not quite right and try to hide it. But he certainly was not hiding tonight. He was sitting in his usual spot waiting for a copper to come and take him home; except that he was fondling a girl child as if she was a doll he had found.

Craig spoke quietly. "Good evenin', Sam."

"Hulloa."

The girl was dark-haired, dirty. She was not in the least intimidated by the constable's uniform or, it seemed, by daft Sammy Reynolds. She was sucking her thumb. Her cheeks were hollow, streaked by recent tears. She stared up at Craig with big round moist eyes, and said not a word.

"Who's this then, Sammy?" Craig hunkered down by the step. "Is this a new friend you've made?"

"Jen."

"Oh, is that her name?"

"Jen. Jen."

Sammy did not appear to be excited. His hands on her hair were tender, soft in movement. She wore a heavy skirt and a knitted cardigan that was far too large for her. Her feet and legs were bare.

"An' where are you from, Jennie?" Craig asked.

"Jen. Jen. Jen."

"All right, Sammy. Tell me, Jen, where are you from? Where do you live?"

"Lives here."

"Sammy, let her answer, please."

"Lives here wi' me."

"What does Mr Dugdale have to say about that?"

"Mr Dugdale's gone."

The child was not going to respond without coaxing. She was probably too young to know her address.

Craig was undecided. He should take her straight to the station, with Sammy, and report the finding. He glanced along Scutter Street. How many people had seen Sammy with the child? How long had Sammy been alone with her? It was inevitable that if he returned to the station there would be an immediate 'enquiry' and suspicion would fall on Sammy Reynolds of a mischief of which he appeared to be entirely innocent.

The little girl laid her head against Sammy's chest and tugged on her thumb noisily. She was a trusting little minx, too trusting for her own good. It was not unusual to find bairns of tender years wandering alone in the streets. Lost children accounted for half the entries in the station log. In large families straying was commonplace, and a tiny child could easily be missed if Daddy and Mammy were drunk or distracted. Craig rocked, pondering, on his heels. No, Sammy could not have been alone with the girl for more than a few minutes. Mr Dugdale would certainly not have abandoned the child or left her to Sammy's tender mercy. To quiz Sammy about time was a waste of breath.

Craig said, "Where did Jen come from, Sam?"

"Down there." Sammy nodded at the lane that bounded the Mission building.

"Did you go down the lane to find her?"

"Came out. I saved her. Blowed my whistle."

"And had Mr Dugdale gone?"

"Locked the big door. He wented away."

Sammy's hand was passive about the girl's waist and he stroked her dark hair rhythmically, not lingeringly.

"I think her mam will be lookin' for her, Sam," Craig told him.

Sammy pouted. Clearly he did not want to part with her. If the routine of the coppers' collection had not been so ingrained Sammy might have toddled off with her to the lodging-house and have created a real sensation.

"Will you not help me find her mam, Sammy?"

After a prolonged pause Sammy nodded stoically and Craig reached out and detached the girl from Sammy's grasp. The boy did not resist but, oddly, the child closed her fists and clung to his jacket for a moment before she released her hold. Craig got to his feet. Jen was no light weight. He needed both hands to support her until she wriggled into a comfortable, compact position, tummy to his shoulder, and he was able then to offer a hand to Sammy.

"I think I'll see you home first, Sammy," Craig said.

"Nah. Find Mam."

"It's too late for you, old man. It would never do if Mr Black locked you out, would it?"

All memory of the dank cellar of Rae's tenement in the Madagascar had faded from Sammy's mind. He could not imagine a night spent on the streets now. Security had cost him his resilience.

"You find Mam," he said.

"Aye, I'll do that. Come on, take my hand."

Playfully the little girl leaned across Craig's shoulder and pawed like a kitten at Sammy's hair as they walked down Scutter Street. She said nothing, uttered no sound, but she giggled when Sammy tickled her fingers and hid her face coyly against Constable Nicholson's neck.

On reaching the Claremont they found Mr Black, the superintendent, standing on the step puffing on a nightcap cigar. He was a barrel-chested man in his fifties who had served time with an English regiment, the King's Royal Rifles, and had been wounded by the Boers at Laing's Nek back in '81. His hair was close-cropped and his grey moustache was trimmed as thin as a paper cut-out.

"Found me another lodger, then, Constable Nicholson?" He gestured at the child with the butt of his cigar.

"Lost or strayed, I think," said Craig.

"My, but she's a pretty one."

The Claremont was a symbol of enlightenment. It was kept warm and had excellent sanitary facilities and was subject to Mr Black's regime of discipline, strict but not cruel. The men who stayed there were not vagrants or down-and-outs but honest working-men who had no homes of their own. Mr Black, without fuss or sentiment, kept a fatherly eye on the three or four chaps who, like Sammy, were a bit short of the whole shilling. By now Sammy was rubbing his hair against Jen's arm. She giggled silently and fluttered her lashes and darted glances from Sam to Mr Black like a little coquette.

"Did a certain party find her, by any chance?"

"No," Craig lied. "I found her."

If Mr Black had his doubts about Craig's statement he gave no sign. He placed a hand on Sammy's shoulder.

"Come along, m'lad," he said. "You'll need a good wash before you turn in. I haven't dowsed the gas in the ablutions but you'd better look nippy."

"Aye," said Sammy eagerly, easily wooed from concentration on the girl by the superintendent's banter. He went up the steps and through the open door with hardly a backward glance. But the girl child, annoyed at being parted from her new-found friend, grizzled and drummed her knees against Craig's chest.

"Trouble for some poor male in fifteen or twenty years," said Mr Black. "Best get her off home."

"I think you're right, William," said Craig.

Still carrying the girl he started out for Ottawa Street.

He expected to find the girl's mother at the desk there, distraught and tearful. He would tell nobody that it was Sam Reynolds who had found her but would extend the white lie he had told to Mr Black. He was late for check-in now but he had a valid excuse. No mark would be put against his name, though Archie, who had the beat for the back-shift, would be fuming and champing at the bit to get off to his bed. He stepped it out, the child swaying in his arms. Still she had uttered no word and hardly more than a mew. It would be up to the sergeant and duty officer to coax a name from her or to inaugurate enquiries in the neighbourhood of Scutter Street. He felt good. He strode out. Trustingly the child clung to him. When he passed casual pedestrians they stood aside as if he was on a mission of mercy. They grunted approvingly for once, showed none of the hostility that coppers usually attracted.

Jen loved it when he walked fast. She clung to him with arms and knees as he whizzed along the pavements. He swung into the bottom of Ottawa Street – and almost collided with the woman. She uttered a stifled shriek and staggered. She too had been running.

The child was first to recover her poise. She wriggled in Craig's grasp and held out her arms to the woman. "Mammy, Mammy."

"Oh, God, thank God! You've found her."

"Mammy, Mammy. See, here's me."

All along the child had been perfectly capable of speech. She prattled excitedly, craned away from Craig and reached out to the woman.

"Is she your child?" Craig demanded.

"Of course she is."

"What was she doin' wanderin' alone in the vicinity of Scutter Street?"

"She strayed."

"What were you about, to let her stray?"

"Nothin'."

"Boozin', were you?"

"I was stone-cold sober, I'll have you know."

She was smaller even than Lorna, but not as slight. Her voice was low and melodious with a hint of an accent, Polish or Irish, perhaps.

"What's your name?" said Craig.

"Taylor."

"What Taylor?"

"Greta Taylor."

"Where's your husband?"

"I don't have no husband."

"Her father – "

"She belongs t' me, not to nobody else."

"Where do you reside?" Craig had not yet relinquished the

child who, now that she had been found, had become garrulous and restless and struggled to be free of him. "What's your full address?"

"None of your business."

"Aye, but it is," said Craig.

"Give me my bairn."

"How do I know it is your bairn?"

"Good God! Do you think I'd lie?"

She looked fierce. She had dark hair, not blonde as he might have expected from such a forename. She had great dark, dark-circled eyes with heavy lids. Her features were thin, though, but not gaunt. Behind the fierceness Craig sensed a terrible lack of assurance.

"If you won't answer me then you'll have to answer to my sergeant at the station," Craig said.

"Oh, God, you're not takin' me in."

"Letting a child get lost is — "

"She ran off. She's always runnin' off. She's a bad girl sometimes."

"Do you beat her? Is that why she runs off?"

"I don't beat her enough."

"Nope, I'll have to take you to the station."

Her hand was thin but not bony. It fluttered against his bare hand, palm brushing his knuckles. "Don't take me in, please."

"Have you somethin' to hide?"

"Give me my bairn, please, and let me get on home."

Craig studied her features in the street light, searching for guilt. He found none.

She said, "I was only at the supper shop."

"She was with you?"

"I couldn't leave her, could I?"

"It's too late for a young child to be out in the streets."

"We were both hungry."

"Which supper shop were you at?"

It was growing later by the minute. If he did not turn up for duty soon then Sergeant Drummond would have to send out a replacement to relieve Archie and there would be hell to pay when he showed up. He had put himself in a position where he had to take the woman in just to substantiate his story. He was also curious about her.

"At Banff Street corner," she said.

"That's miles away."

"No, it's not. Anyway, I told you she was a wanderer."

Craig did not doubt that the woman was telling him the truth, though it might not be quite the whole truth.

"What's your daughter's name?"

"Janetta."

"I thought she was called Jen."

"That's *her* name for herself."

"Jen. Jen. Jen," the child chanted.

"What happened to the hot supper?" said Craig.

"I never got the length o' the counter."

The hot supper stall at the corner of Banff Street was famous and exceedingly popular, and legal too. Craig recalled the taste of batter puddings and fillets of haddock all golden brown and dripping fat.

"How many have you?" he asked.

"How many what?"

"Children."

"Is one not enough?" she said. "Listen, you don't have to take me in, do you? I haven't done anythin'."

"I didn't say you had," Craig told her. "Nevertheless, I do have to report the incident."

"Incident? What incident? I lost my bairn. You found her. Once you hand her back to me I'll – "

"Waltz right back to the supper shop an' neglect her again?"

"God, but you're a right – "

"Careful," Craig warned. "Abusin' a police officer is a serious offence."

"Stop it. For God's sake, stop it."

Her concern over the lost child had been genuine. His bullying, however teasing, took all the fight out of her. Her shoulders sagged. He had enjoyed his minute or two of power over the woman. Now he felt gay and generous. He did not much care if she was a 'lady of the night' and had been up to her tricks in bed when the kid had escaped and gone for a toddle. He swung Jen and dumped her into Greta Taylor's arms.

"Get out of my sight," he said jovially, "before I change my mind."

Greta Taylor lowered the child to the ground and set her on her bare feet. She held tightly to the child's wrist, however. Perhaps a few wee smacks might be delivered to the saucy wee bottom as soon as he was out of sight. Hands on hips Craig waited for Greta Taylor to express her gratitude. It came grudgingly, an odd low throaty sound, like a tabby-cat might make, then she tugged the child by the hand and was past him and almost round the corner, hurrying.

"Stop," Craig shouted.

She halted at once. She did not turn around. She draped one arm protectively over Jen's shoulders and pressed the child against her skirts.

"You haven't told me where you live," Craig said.

"Benedict Street, at the Kingdom Road."

"Number?"

"Thirteen, ground floor. Why? Is this for the book?"

"Nope," Craig said. "Now, *shoo*. Go on."

Greta Taylor and her daughter took off. He watched them go, the rapid retreat familiar in those who had had a brush with the law and had escaped its consequences. He did not record her name and address or any mention of the incident in his beat book, though he told Sergeant Drummond about it as soon as he entered the station. It was nothing, Craig said, need not be filed. Drummond agreed with him and packed him off without more ado to relieve the anxious Archie outside the off-licence in the Windsor Road.

When he was alone, however, Craig did something that he had never done before; he left his beat.

It was impulse, pure and simple. He hurried round the corner to Banff Street, hoping that he would not encounter Constable Cropper on his way or run into the sergeant and the lieutenant out making rounds. When he reached the supper shop he jumped the queue and bought a batter pudding and a packet of thin, soft, greasy chips. He carried them out before him, like valuable evidence, to keep the smell from adhering to his uniform and walked rapidly to the Kingdom Road and down it to Benedict Street. He found the close at No. 13 and entered. The close was filthy and odorous. Drunken singing echoed in the stairwell and somewhere upstairs a baby shrieked as if it was being skinned alive.

There was, to Craig's surprise, a name-plate screwed to the wood of the doorpost. He examined it by the light of his carbide lamp for it was pitch-dark in the close and the gas lamps had been beheaded by some villain and closed off by the gas department with blobs of lead. The name on the plate was Taylor. He knelt

and placed the savoury, steaming parcel on the floor in front of
the door, rose and rapped loudly with his knuckles. That done he
retreated at once to the street outside. By the close mouth, out of
sight, he loitered until he heard the door open, heard her enquiry,
her exclamation, the chatter of the child. He heard nothing else,
no masculine voice. Grinning, Craig turned and trotted out of
Benedict Street and on to the riverside.

Ten minutes later he was back on his beat. Nobody had missed
him. Nobody knew that he had forsaken his appointed course
– nobody except Greta Taylor and she, Craig was sure, would
forgive him.

June

It had been a peculiar spring all round, Kirsty thought, as she
wheeled Bobby down Walbrook Street under a high, hot-blue
sky. The perambulator, a Cornwall, was becoming too small
for him now for Bobby was growing like a stalk of wild barley.
The pram was far too good to use for lugging laundry to the
steamie or to bring up coal from the merchant's, but she would
not sell it. It had been a gift from Mrs Frew and she would keep
it, even if it did take up much room, in case she had another
baby. Admiring the pram, which she often did, she felt guilty at
her neglect of Nessie Frew these past weeks. She had cut down
drastically on her outings to St Anne's and visits to Walbrook
Street. In consequence she had spent more time with Bobby. He
had thrived under her care, had become quite petted in fact and
would kick up a dreadful fuss when he was left with Madge or
Lorna. Craig could not stand it when the baby was rowdy and
he became surly and snappish. He never took Bobby out, never
went out with Kirsty. He was, Kirsty had heard, 'flying high' at
Ottawa Street – though she could not imagine why – and was
tipped as a runner in the promotion stakes.

It could not be her behaviour that had darkened Craig's mood.
She had been attentive and obedient to him since that April
night when she had gone to hear Tom Monroe, since she had
conformed to type, had realised that it was wrong to love David
Lockhart in any manner at all. It was Gordon who had annoyed
his brother. Gordon had gone to work for Mr Adair and had
taken to the job – requirements mysterious – like a duck to water.
Madge Nicholson's relationship with Breezy had been brought
into the open. Mr Adair even called for her at the house now.
He had been introduced to the other members of the family.
Kirsty liked the chap, found him down-to-earth and not at all
given to airs and graces, though his apparel showed him to be
well off. Craig had steadfastly refused to meet Mr Adair. Craig
made no bones about the fact that he considered Breezy to be
the next best thing to a crook. The more dour and sullen Craig

became, the more Madge fawned over him. At times she was sickeningly maternal. She danced to Craig's every command, obeyed his every whim, treated him, as Gordon put it, 'as if he was a bloody plaster saint'.

The edge of poverty had been thoroughly blunted now that Gordon was bringing home a wage. Gordon was generous to a fault and shelled out to Kirsty exactly the same sum for housekeeping as Craig did.

"But what do you do, Gordon?" Kirsty would ask.

"I told you. I sell things."

"What things?"

"I told you. Carpets, mostly."

The question was soon rendered unnecessary for evidence of the staple of Gordon's trade was all around them. Gordon had floored all the rooms, the narrow hall too, with a warm selection of Brussels loop-pile and cuts of soft Wilton velvets. He had refused to listen to Craig's offer to pay for the ends and for the laying.

Good carpets made the house seem much grander, though everybody sneezed for a fortnight as the pile of the Wilton gave off a rich dust, and Craig made derisory comments about the quality. The neighbours were less critical. Mrs Walker and Mrs Swanston soon found an excuse to climb the stairs and inspect the Nicholsons' floor coverings. Gordon was quickly nabbed to fit their rooms out too with hemmed pieces at cost price. Even the Pipers invested in three lengths, but only when Gordon found them a pattern that resembled tartan. Mrs Walker went the whole hog, of course, and plumped for Chenille Axminster so that she could lord it over the others. Gordon was not averse to selling along Canada Road. He had a whole warehouse of stuff to flog and had already promised Kirsty linoleum for the kitchen and a copper-and-brass suspension lamp for the hall, no doubt hoping that he could start a run on these items too.

"In six bloody months we'll be livin' in a palace," Craig declared, "an' there won't be room for us to turn round."

"In that case," Gordon retorted, "we'll just have to move to a larger house, won't we?"

Craig could not contemplate a removal. He was tied to the burgh, to the low-rent tenement property, as long as he remained on the Force — and Gordon knew it. What was more — another thorn in Craig's flesh — Gordon had paid for Lorna to go to

Prossers' Commercial College as soon as she left school in June
and once she had her diplomas Gordon promised that he would
find her a job in one of Mr Adair's offices.

Inch by inch, it seemed, Craig was losing control of his family
to Mr Albert Adair. It would only be a matter of time, surely,
until Madge succumbed to the man's blandishments, married
him and moved out of No. 154 for good, taking Lorna with her.
Kirsty was no longer certain that she wanted the Nicholsons to
go, for they buffered her against Craig and against the loneliness
of a 'marriage' that she now regarded as a mistake.

Kirsty would not have been in Walbrook Street at all that fine
June afternoon if she had not received a letter from Nessie Frew.
She had hardly had a moment alone with Nessie since April. She
had taken Lorna to kirk services with her and had gently turned
down all invitations to return to No. 19 for a cup of tea. She was
afraid of meeting David face to face. When she saw him in the
pulpit or at the lectern, when she heard his voice, her heart still
gave a sad little thump and she had to force herself to think of
Bobby and of the loyalty she owed to Craig on her son's behalf.

Mrs Frew's stiff, formal note could not be ignored, however.
She could not, in all conscience, refuse a direct invitation to call
on her old friend at three o'clock. Kirsty was nervous of the
meeting. In the letter Nessie indicated that she had something
on her mind and 'wanted to have it out in the open, for good and
all', to be assured, perhaps, that she was not the cause of Kirsty's
coolness and to find out the real reason behind it.

Kirsty braked the pram outside No. 19, unstrapped Bobby,
lifted him into her arms, climbed the step and rang the doorbell.

Nessie, in person, opened to her. Winter ailments and spring's
lingering illnesses had taken their toll of the widow. She seemed
frail and stooped now. On Sundays her stiff formal garments
tended to hide signs of aging but in a summer frock, with the
sunlight upon her, the changes were distressingly obvious. It was
as if she was withering, not blooming, in the balmy summer days.

"Oh, you came, did you?" At least her voice had not lost its
sharpness. "I didn't really expect you."

"Your letter – "

"On such short notice," Nessie Frew added.

"I brought Bobby."

"So I see."

"Hasn't he grown?"

From his perch in Kirsty's arms Bobby stared at the old woman as if trying to recall her. It had been several months since last he had sat on her knee and been fed custard from a spoon.

"See," said Nessie Frew, "he's forgotten who I am."

"No, he hasn't. He's just shy."

"Come along in. We're not going to talk on the doorstep, I presume."

Kirsty handed Bobby to the widow and dragged the perambulator up the steps and into the hallway then followed Nessie into the kitchen. Peggie was already taking off Bobby's little summer coat, chattering away to him in her Irish brogue, an accent that Bobby seemed to find both fascinating and comprehensible.

"We'll take tea in the parlour," said Mrs Frew. "And perhaps you'd be good enough to give Bobby some of that nice junket from the cold cupboard."

"I'll do that, mum."

Bobby, who had been so petted at home of late, let Kirsty go off without a murmur of protest. He bounced on the servant-girl's lap and jabbered to her happily.

In the back parlour nothing at all had changed except that a brass ashtray on a wooden stalk had been placed by the side of the best armchair and that four or five weighty books lay on top of the cabinet. *Sermons to Young Men* and *Faith and Life*; two titles caught her eye. Clearly they belonged to David.

Now that she had Kirsty to herself Mrs Frew seemed unusually tongue-tied. She enquired after Craig and Lorna with a prim formality, delaying the important issues until Peggie had brought in the tea-things, and the reassurance that Bobby was fine with her and was 'eatin' up his junket like a warrior'.

Bread-and-butter in thin slices and a yellow seed-cake; Kirsty did not presume to reach for the teapot and serve as she would have done eight or nine weeks ago. She accepted a piece of buttered bread, for politeness, and watched Nessie dispense tea.

When that was done Nessie put her awkwardness aside and came right out with it.

"What happened between you two?"

"Nothing happened."

"Did David forget himself? Did he overstep the mark? I'm your friend. You can tell me the truth, Kirsty."

"No," Kirsty said. "Oh, no."

"He hasn't been himself either."

"He's not ill, is he?" Kirsty said.

"Not ill, no." Nessie hesitated. "He's love-sick."

"What?"

"I think you heard me the first time."

"But who would — "

"Kirsty, do not pretend you don't know."

Kirsty said, "We should never have gone to hear Tom Monroe together, not without you."

"Is that when it happened?"

"Nothing did happen, I tell you."

"All right. No call to get snippy."

Buttered bread lay on a flowered plate, one small dainty bite taken from the slice. Kirsty could eat no more. Her mouth had gone dry. She had heard what she wanted to hear, and the truth frightened her.

Kirsty said, "I'm — I'm sorry. I didn't mean to snip at you, Nessie."

"Just because I'm old does not mean to say that I can't remember what it was like to be in love. Has David told you how he feels?"

"Of course not. It would be — improper."

"Did you not know of his feelings for you?"

"I — I — it's not a surprise."

"And in return?"

"I — I — I don't know."

Nessie Frew might profess to live by strict Christian principles, to adhere to the sober, bourgeois morality of her class but she was also a woman who had once loved a man who had not been free to marry her. She would carry with her to her dying day the remembrance of that sweet sinful spell in her life. But Kirsty was made cautious by the woman's choice of words. They were too archaic and too romantic to be taken without a pinch of salt.

Kirsty did not believe that David was 'love-sick'. He might be troubled by conscience, yes, and might want her, but surely his feelings would be temperate and controlled. Men did not suffer from loving as women did. She tried to keep calm, to give nothing away. How could she admit that she longed for an overwhelming passion to take both David and her and lift them up like a wave and carry them out of their senses. That longing to be swept away, rendered unheeding, uncaring of consequences, was dangerous and silly and she did not think that it was love at all but something set apart from the real world.

"Do you not like him?" said Nessie.

"Yes, I like him. I – I admire and respect him."

"Oh, come now, Kirsty. Do you not trust me with the truth?"

"I would trust you before anyone," said Kirsty cautiously. "But I've told you the truth."

"David won't talk to me about it."

"Perhaps it's not as serious as you think."

"I'm sure he's in love with you, dear."

"I wish you wouldn't keep sayin' that."

"It shouldn't embarrass you. If I was your age and a gentleman like David thought I was – "

"I have a *husband*, Nessie, in case you've forgotten."

Nessie Frew sniffed. She had never really approved of Craig Nicholson; yet it seemed ridiculous that she of all people would not only condone but would encourage a relationship between her beloved nephew and a woman who was already married to another man.

"Husbands are as husbands do." Mrs Frew nodded sagaciously though Kirsty had no idea what she meant by the statement.

"Besides," Kirsty said, "David's an ordained minister."

"St Anne's isn't the only parish."

Kirsty blinked. "Is there scandal?"

"Not that I've heard," said Nessie Frew. "David's very popular with the congregation and with the elders."

"But we have been seen together."

"These days, nobody thinks much of that."

"Well," said Kirsty, "even if I wasn't married to Craig I wouldn't be for the likes of David."

"Snob!"

"Oh, that's unfair."

"It's perfectly fair," said Nessie Frew. "It is not up to you to say whether or not he thinks you good enough. I was good enough for my Andrew and he was better placed than David at the time."

"He wasn't a clergyman, though."

"No, but he was a Christian."

"And was he married?"

Nessie considered a reply but did not give it. She just shook her head, frowning over the neglected tea.

Kirsty said, "Why did you really ask me here?"

"I don't wish to lose your friendship, Kirsty."

"I'll always be your friend, Nessie."

"Good, good."

"But you mustn't make it awkward for me, or for David. It *is* difficult, I admit."

How could she explain her feeling of inadequacy without making it sound like rank conceit? She wondered how David's feelings towards her would change if he caught her on her knees on the tenement's stairs, hands red and skirts soaked with suds, her hair straggled in rats'-tails. He probably would not even recognise her. There would be nobody like her in David's life. His mother would be neat and well groomed, even in China. The servants in his Uncle George's house in the Highlands would be better turned-out than she was. David's upbringing, his education, his experience of life all seemed to rise like a cloud before her. She could not fantasise about David as Mrs Frew seemed to be doing, helplessly and without calculation.

"I thought as much," said Nessie Frew, pursing her lips with a certain smugness. "Difficulties are there to be overcome, dear."

"By prayer?" said Kirsty, and immediately regretted her sarcasm.

"None of us know quite how God works out our fates."

Nessie Frew had shed the aloofness that had been apparent earlier. She was displaying again that devious, childlike self that hid behind sober respectability.

Kirsty touched the old woman's wrist. It felt as thin and brittle as a twig.

"I'm sorry," said Kirsty.

"How can I make you see, when you're so young, that the years fly away from you? So fast. So fast. One day you're old and you wish — "

"I know," said Kirsty, though she did not.

"He'll bind you."

"Who will?"

"Your husband. Craig."

"I'm bound to him by marriage, yes."

"Did you know what that meant when you did it?"

"I — I don't regret it," said Kirsty.

"I feel sorry for you," said Nessie.

"But why?"

"He doesn't love you, Kirsty."

"If you mean Craig – "

"He wants the convenience of a wife, that's all," said Nessie Frew. "Having you there to cook his meals, wash his shirts and raise his children. He'll give you no thanks for it. He doesn't consider it important."

While she spoke Nessie's hand tightened on Kirsty's as if to save herself from slipping further into a pool of indefinable regret. She could not have learned such cynical lessons from her marriage to Andrew, surely? What else was it that brought tears to the old woman's eyes now? Kirsty could not understand that so many of the things she had envied were nothing but a substitute for a more enduring form of security, a love without loss.

"But Craig will always look after me."

"Yes, I expect he will," said Nessie.

"What is it? What's wrong? Tell me."

"I'm frightened."

"Of what?"

"Dying."

"Ah!" said Kirsty.

*   *   *

He must not lose heart. This was what ministering was about, a far cry from the tepid fellowship of St Anne's Church, platitudinous sermons and tea with the Ladies' Guild. He knelt by the bed and tried to summon up phrases that would make his prayer meaningful and bring comfort, to remember 'suitable' quotations to cover the death of a child who had never lived, a tiny stillborn creature in a tiny unvarnished coffin on a table in the middle of the kitchen.

The family's name was Finnegan, Belfast Irish. Old man Finnegan had not even thought it worthwhile to lose a half-day's pay from the cattle dock. He had strolled out early with his pipe in his mouth and his cap tipped at its usual jaunty angle without a sign that he was leaving anything valuable behind. There were already eleven mouths to feed. The woman was worn out. Her sisters informed him that she was only thirty-three years old and had had three stillbirths before now, in among the live ones. The sisters were very like her, reddish, haggard and lean. They were Protestants. There was no injunction upon them to make so many children. They just did not seem to know how to stop.

There was one man present, Angus McColl, a brother-in-law. He was a member of the congregation of St Anne's, a decent, hard-working chap who had won a struggle to wean himself off drink. It was McColl who had invited him to come and do the necessary for the Finnegans. McColl would pay for the little funeral too, unless he was mistaken. McColl was the only one who would accompany him to the Children's Corner of the new cemetery behind building-ground at the end of Wolfe Road. Wolfe Road: it was small wonder that the place had already become a legend, that children screamed the name to scare themselves and that bizarre stories of hauntings abounded. Wolfe Road cemetery was raw, new and remote, but already brothers were buried there, sisters, cousins, schoolmates. The unfulfilled lives generated a theatrical terror among the young, and no belief at all that their relatives' souls had gone to rest. David detested Wolfe Road. How could he possibly explain it to this poor, exhausted, ungrieving and unbelieving woman when he could not explain it to himself?

Isaiah 40. Verse 11: "He shall feed his flock like a shepherd: he shall gather the lambs with his arm, and carry them in his bosom, and shall gently lead those that are with young."

Smelling the sour odour of the bed, tasting dust, David bowed his head.

Harry Graham had told him, "You'll get used to it. In the fullness of time, you'll get used to it." He did not think it was right to want to get used to it, to become ungrieving like the wretched woman on the bed, or uncaring like her husband.

Inches from his brow Mrs Finnegan stirred. Behind him one of the sisters murmured, "God be praised." Nobody wept yet. Perhaps when they reached Wolfe Road and the coffin was lowered into the ground Angus McColl would weep.

". . . having our whole trust and confidence in the mercy of our heavenly Father and in the victory . . ." He intoned the words without inflexion, could not explain them.

The stench in the room was overpowering. The morning had been warm, the curtains drawn. The sisters had been there for hours. He must go on to Wolfe Road. He must walk dutifully behind the one-horse, two-wheeled carriage with the tiny coffin buckled like an accordion case inside. No flowers. No wreath. Money wasted. None to spare on futile gestures.

The woman stirred again. He glanced up. He hoped for tears.

She was dry-eyed, impatient. Her head rolled a little on the bolster, her lips pursed. She disapproved of him. A cut-price minister. Doing no good. He cut off the prayer and got to his feet. One by one the sisters rose too. An elderly neighbour crossed herself furtively. One of 'the other kind'. He was surprised that Finnegan had let a Roman Catholic cross his doorstep.

McColl had attended to the Certificate, had hired the undertaker. The infant had been carried to full term, had never drawn breath. She had emerged into the world with soul departed. The midwife had given a statement to that effect.

"Do we – ?" McColl muttered.

"Yes," David said.

He stooped over the bed. He squeezed Mrs Finnegan's hand. She was impatient to be rid of him. She wanted the whole thing over with. How could he blame her for that? He threaded a route through the furniture, opened the door to the landing.

Hazy sunlight filled the close from the stair window. The undertaker's men were waiting by the landing rail. Six or seven little children were on the stairs, chewing and slavering. One of the undertaker's men had given them toffees. There was an air of contentment among the gathering. They frowned at the minister's appearance, shrank from him and crept reluctantly down the stairs.

"All ready?" said the undertaker's man.

"Yes."

He walked downstairs. He passed among the children. He had nothing for them, no sweets, no cakes. He hurried down to the ground-floor level and out to the mouth of the close. He could hear sounds above him like echoes in a cave. It was warm in the street, pleasant. He wanted tobacco, a smoke, but had no time. McColl joined him.

Pressed side by side against the wall they watched the tiny coffin pass. No awkwardness, no dunting or bumping. The little thing was light and easy to carry. The undertaker's men slid it quickly into the back of the carriage. The horse was not black, wore no plumes, no decoration. None of the women emerged from the house. The children came down, though. They congregated, whispering, at the angle of the first landing and watched from there.

"Do we – "

"Yes."

"How far is it?"

"About a mile."

"They won't drive fast, will they?" said McColl. "I haven't much puff these days."

"Walking pace."

An undertaker's man fumbled with straps, closed the door on the coffin.

"It was good o' you to come, Mr Lockhart."

"Not at all, Angus."

Only two, a minister's assistant and a compassionate brother-in-law; they lined themselves square with the back of the carriage, heads bowed. They matched the rumbling pace of the vehicle and followed it round the corner, turned east towards Wolfe Road.

David was relieved to be out of the tenement, walking in sunlight. He glanced surreptitiously at his watch. It was ten minutes to three.

With luck he would be home for tea.

* * *

"I'm an old fool," said Nessie Frew. "I don't know what upset me. I suppose it's because I've no children of my own. I have to worry about somebody."

"Do you worry about David?" said Kirsty.

"I worry about both of you," she said. "I think sometimes that when I'm dead and gone nobody at all will remember me."

"Hughie – Mr Affleck – he'll – "

"Perhaps, perhaps," said Mrs Frew curtly. She did not want to be drawn into a discussion of her brother's merits. "But when I'm unwell it comes home to me just how I've wasted my life."

"Oh, nonsense!" said Kirsty.

"It's true. You can't understand what it means to be old, to have nothing left but a few memories."

"Do you still miss your husband?"

Nessie shrugged her thin shoulders. She had dried her eyes and was a little embarrassed at her show of emotion.

"Andrew isn't really gone from me," she said.

"What you hope for, Nessie, isn't possible."

"Oh, I know it," Nessie admitted. "When I waken in the night, though, and the house is cold and empty I think how nice it would be if we were all here together – you, David and I."

"That can never be."

"I know, I know. He'll go off soon to a parish of his own and you'll be tied up with your children and your man."

"Whatever happens," said Kirsty, "I'll still visit you."

"When David goes, you'll go too."

"No, I won't," said Kirsty. "Look, why don't you take in guests again?"

"I'm not fit for it now."

"Peggie's a good girl. She'll help."

"No. That's over," said Mrs Frew. "In fact, soon it'll all be over."

Kirsty said, "And then you'll be with Andrew again."

To Kirsty's astonishment Mrs Frew only gave a soft little *huh*. It seemed that age had diminished the beliefs that had sustained her, that the old verities were not imperishable after all.

"Why don't you talk to David about it?"

"He's young too."

"He can't help that, Nessie. Talk to him. I'm sure he'll be able to explain – "

"Listen," Nessie interrupted.

From the kitchen came laughter. Bobby chuckled. It sounded oddly deep and grown-up. The clatter of a spoon on tin drowned out the sound.

"Peggie's got him playing the drum," said Nessie. "She's a terrible lass, is that one."

"At least he's happy," said Kirsty, "if not exactly quiet."

"Why should he be quiet? Let him make himself heard. I'd like a bit of commotion about the place." Nessie Frew's gaze roved about the walls and up to the handsome plaster ceiling. "I'd like this house to shake, just for once."

"I'll see if he's all right," said Kirsty.

"Leave him be," said Nessie. "He's enjoying himself."

"Shan't be a minute."

Nessie shook her head at such excessive motherly concern and poured herself a cup of lukewarm tea as Kirsty went out of the parlour into the hall.

David had just let himself in through the front door. He was poised, key in hand, looking at her. At first glance Kirsty thought that he seemed older. His square handsome features were drawn, his shoulders stooped. He held a bible in his right hand, the book pressed against the cloth of his jacket, black and hot in the warm sunlight. Perspiration glistened on his brow and he moved stiffly, without his usual grace. The tin drum clanged and clattered loudly behind her. She heard her son's laughter become less adult, rise to a shriek of delight as he laid into the pan or biscuit tin with all inhibitions cast aside. David slid the bible on to the hallstand. He came towards her swiftly.

Kirsty gasped when he put his arms about her but she did not retreat or resist. She let him hold her close, pressing her close, his cheek against her hair.

"Oh, God, Kirsty," he whispered, "I'm glad you're here today." He kissed her mouth, released her. "I've missed you."

"Who is it?" came Mrs Frew's voice from the parlour.

She laid a hand lightly against his chest. She could taste the slight salt sweat of his kiss upon her lips.

"Only David," Kirsty said, as he took her once more in his arms.

*　　*　　*

Blood-feud had a long dishonourable footnote in the annals of Scotland. Highland and Lowland families had indulged themselves in the sport generation upon generation and many barbarous acts stemmed from oaths and allegiances whose origins were lost in the mists of time. What remained of the war-cry and the clash of claymores was a thin unspecified hatred in the hearts of young and old in the cold stone streets of the city and its suburbs. The participants were, on the whole, too stupid to realise that inherited prejudice was a disease that destroyed its agents and advocates as well as its victims.

The 'clans' were well known to the forces of law and order: the Sheddons, the Fitzgeralds, the family Ross, the Bully Boys from Jackson Street, 'the Greens' from Windsor Road. Religion was at the back of it, a red-handed bigotry, much of it imported, that stood in lieu of conviction and belief in God. Protestant hunted Catholic; Catholic defended against Protestant. Mysterious lines were drawn along lanes and vennels, little enclaves formed in certain tenements, with a feudal devotion to territory as substitute for religious principle. Most notorious of all the gangsters was William King – King Billy – a petty criminal who had never worked an honest day in his life.

Billy earned his bread by trading on the fear he inspired. He extorted from local shopkeepers and small businessmen a weekly tithe which ensured that their windows did not get smashed or their stock catch fire. Billy was no Daniel Malone. He made a bare living out of his activities and had served several prison sentences for his pains. He was unpredictable when sober, dangerous when in drink. His gang was made up of young working-lads who were impressed with his power and envious of his idle life-style. King Billy and the grandsons of Patrick McMahon had been engaged for years in a sporadic war, one that had its origins in far-off Ireland, the green isle upon which none of the boys had ever set foot.

Hogmanay and the Trades' Fair Holidays put extra money into the pocket and fired the blood with booze, and the police were always on their guard then. But clashes could occur at any time, without rhyme or reason, and street violence knew no special season. June was just as good a month as December or July to let off steam, and on that placid peaceful evening King Billy's lads were on the warpath before anybody knew quite what was happening.

Billy was forty-two years old. He had no wife and resided with his father and mother in a single-end in the Kingdom Road. Father, at least, approved of all that his son did and thought the whole system rotten and the police tyrannical to pursue his boy with such fervour. Billy was small but strong. Street fights had left scars, a crushed nose and wrinkled tissue about the eyes. His thin black hair had begun to recede and he brushed it self-consciously downward now. He was not attractive, unless you had a penchant for brutality, drank heavily and smoked like a foundry chimney. Even if he managed to avoid the gallows, the consensus of opinion was that he would be lucky to reach fifty. Billy had one sterling quality: a strange sullen patience. Many a copper had abused Billy in the hope of persuading him to lash out and collect another year or two behind bars, but Billy let all the taunts and jibes and insults wash over him as if he was blind and deaf. Nobody, not even his father, quite knew what made Billy tick.

Billy 'pulled his boys out' about a quarter to nine on that fine young summer night. There had been a fist-fight between William Dunbar, twenty-three, and Joseph McMahon, sixteen. Joe McMahon had been discovered on Billy's territory, a narrow stretch of wasteground behind a stand of old tenements. Willie

Dunbar had gone to teach him a lesson in geography. McMahon had broken for cover in Vancouver Lane but had been spotted by other stray members of King Billy's gang and had been driven into a backcourt and trapped there.

Greenfield's streets were by no means deserted at that hour. Children were still out playing and women hung from their windows to enjoy the evening air. It was not until a gaggle of young girls ran screaming out of a close that the trouble became public and the alarm was raised. Fathers and brothers rushed out to scoop up their youngsters and whisk them safe indoors. Joe McMahon was defending himself gallantly with a dustbin lid and a stave wrenched from a backcourt fence. He was being bombarded with stones and slates by the three lads from Benedict Street and knew it would take a bloody miracle to get him back to his home ground unscathed.

Who it was that sprinted to the McMahons' tenement in Windsor Road to summon reinforcements was never established. Within three or four minutes, however, the McMahons and their allies were galloping to Joe's rescue.

The rival gangs met in an uneven front along and behind Riverside Street. Stones flew through the calm shadows. Boots, fists and staves were used as weapons. The noise was cacophonous, echoing out of closes and up stairwells. Some thirty young men were involved, in clusters of three and four, in knocking hell out of each other. Tenement windows, above ground-floor level, were flung wide open. The good folk of the district crammed into them to watch the sport. It had been four or five months since there had been a real ding-dong. Cheers rang out for King Billy's heroes, jeers for the villains from Windsor Road, and one lone voice in the wilderness cried for order to be restored.

Constable Flynn, whose beat it was, was occupied with a small, elderly, almost boneless drunkard who had collapsed on the public thoroughfare and was too bottled to stand up and give Archie his name. Archie was engaged in dragging the drunkard towards Banff Street where he hoped to flag down a patrol van to haul the obstruction off for a night in the cells. If the battle had drifted east Archie would have missed it altogether and it would have passed into Constable Nicholson's jurisdiction. As it happened, there was a chase, a stand, a brawl. Children and startled citizens fled in all directions. Even at a distance of a quarter-mile Archie twigged that something nasty was afoot. He dropped the drunkard like a sack of potatoes and took immediately to his heels, running towards the commotion and blowing his whistle loudly.

Gordon Nicholson was closer to the tide of battle than Archie. But Gordon had lots of things on his mind and did not pay much attention to the racket in the backcourts. He put it down to obstreperous children's games of Kick-the-Can or Leave-the-Gaol. Gordon was working, and when Gordon worked it would have taken an earthquake to shake his concentration. He was also late, anxious to get back to the carpet warehouse before Johnnie Whiteside, Breezy's nephew, grew tired of waiting, locked the safe and left the premises. In a money-belt about his waist Gordon had twenty-four shillings in small change and he preferred to have his collection recorded and secured at the end of each day.

Ever ready to expand his markets Gordon had persuaded Johnnie Whiteside, his boss, to let him organise a deferred payment system whereby carpets and rugs were supplied at a modest down-payment and Gordon, like any ordinary tallyman, tramped round the houses once a week and shook a shilling or a couple of bob out of the householder. If a family found it could not pay, Gordon did not threaten them with violence. He simply doubled the tally for that week. So far there had been few problems. Gordon had selected his clients with care and made sure that his manner and appearance were such that the clients on his books deferred to him as if he was a gentleman and doing them a great favour.

He had been to call on the Harrisons, his last collection west of the Kingdom Road, but had tarried there a little longer than he had intended. The Harrisons had a daughter of sixteen who had taken a real shine to him and would flirt coyly while her mam brewed him a cup of tea. Gordon was not averse to being adored but the exercise had made him later than ever and he came downstairs at the double, buttoning his fancy jacket and settling his broad brown cap on his head. He was debating whether or not to blow a shilling or so on a hack or simply wait until morning before checking in the night's takings. With this on his mind he did not really hear the yells in the backcourt or the shrill blasts of Archie Flynn's whistle. He was moving too fast, as usual.

He came skipping down the stairs to the ground-floor level and headed straight for the close mouth into Riverside Street. He was almost out on to the pavement when three men came around the corner and tumbled into the shelter of the close. At first Gordon thought they were after his money-belt. He hunched his shoulders and wrapped his arms about his belly and stopped dead in his tracks. But the men were oblivious to his presence. They were pummelling each other furiously. One of them had a slat of wood which he wielded like a cricket bat, flailing about him. Without a word Gordon backed towards the close's rear exit. If he had not glanced behind him he would have backed straight into the unholy trio who blocked that route of escape. All three were armed with iron bars and looked grim and bloody, not the sort of chaps who would listen to reason or be taken in by boyish charm. Gordon did not hesitate. He rushed forward, jumped around the brawlers and out of the close on to the pavement.

Billy King, of course, had not been on the retreat, not him. He had merely been leading the McMahons deeper into his territory and getting himself into a position from which he could slip into hiding as soon as the polis made an appearance. When the boy came leaping out of the close at him King Billy did not pause to ask questions. He caught his assailant with one hand and swung him round and drove a fist into his face and, as the boy fell, kicked him hard with his knee. Gordon did not know what hit him.

Billy was mildly surprised when he peered down at the body. It was not one of his crowd and it certainly did not look like any of the McMahons. The boy was natty and neat and small. And the boy wore a money-belt. Tally-men, it seemed, were getting younger every year. Billy dropped to one knee. He drew a blade from his vest pocket and sawed through the leather strap of the money-belt, removed it and stuffed it into his jacket pocket. He got to his feet, tucked the blade away out of sight, and peered down at the body once more. He kicked the boy's head, thoughtfully, and looked up.

The copper, a big bugger, was horsing up Riverside Street. He was peeling away on his whistle and wagging his truncheon. He was still some distance away, fortunately, for Billy did not like having to grapple with coppers. He took eight or ten paces towards the constable then stepped unhurriedly into a close. He walked unhurriedly through the passage and into the backs, clambered over a wall behind the middens and headed for the close that would take him safely out into Benedict Street.

It was some fifteen minutes later that Constable Norbert turned Gordon over. Archie had gone flying past the body on the pavement, assuming that it was just another of the Bully Boys who had bitten the dust and who wasn't going nowhere.

Constable Norbert didn't recognise the younger Nicholson, who was still insensible and could not identify himself or protest his innocence. In consequence, Gordon was flung into the back of a patrol van and was driven post haste to Ottawa Street with the other villains to be booked and charged with riotous affray.

* * *

Bobby lay asleep on her lap. He had been over-tired and over-excited by his visit to Walbrook Street and had grizzled and whined for a couple of hours until, just as patience was running out, he had dropped off in Kirsty's arms. She sat with him now in the chair before the fire in the warm kitchen, waiting for Craig to come in off the back-shift. His supper was in the oven and she had not quite given up hope, though it was nearing midnight. Six months or a year ago she would have been worried to death but she had grown accustomed to the uncertain hours and suspected that Craig had been called upon to do an extra shift and had not managed to let her know. Gordon too had not returned but that was a much more common occurrence and Kirsty hardly gave her brother-in-law a second thought. He would be out with his chums again, playing cards or billiards somewhere.

Bobby gave a little groan. Kirsty tucked the shawl about his bottom and made him snug.

"Put him to bed, for God's sake," said Madge.

Madge wore a dressing-robe and slippers with fluffy baubles. She sat opposite Kirsty puffing on a cigarette and nursing a cup of tea.

"When I'm ready," said Kirsty.

"It's not good for him. I raised three – "

"I know, I know."

"If you hold him too long in that position you'll bend his spine."

"His spine's all right," said Kirsty.

Madge had been nagging at her all evening. She had patronised her, insulted her, and Kirsty wished fervently that the woman would take herself off to bed. She tried to relax. She hummed a wee melody to Bobby, more to soothe herself than her son.

"Where *is* he?" said Madge.

"I told you, Madge, it's just an extra shift."

"You don't care, do you?"

"Of course I care."

"As long as you have your fancy friends, you don't care about your husband."

"I'm not going to squabble with you, Mother. Not tonight."

"You saw *him* today, didn't you?"

"I told you that too."

"I thought you'd learned sense."

Kirsty did not answer. She was alert now, however. It would be unwise to underestimate Madge Nicholson. She gave no outward sign that she was on her guard and crooned to her son in a whisper.

Madge put down her teacup and sat back. She folded her arms under her bosom. She had not yet set her hair in curling-papers and it hung heavily about her face like a helmet. The cigarette, still in her lips, wagged when she spoke. "I'm surprised that the officers o' the church haven't had him on the carpet."

"For what?"

"Cavortin' with a married woman."

"Cavortin'?" Kirsty shook her head. "Do you think we dance reels up an' down the aisle?"

"If only Craig had eyes to see."

"There's nothing *to* see."

"I'd still like to know what he did that night you spent alone wi' him."

"What night?"

"At 'the Halls'."

"Alone wi' five thousand other folk."

"That's as maybe."

"For your information," said Kirsty, "David Lockhart's a perfect gentleman."

"When you come down to it there's none o' them gentlemen."

"Perhaps," said Kirsty, "you're associatin' with the wrong kind of man."

"I hope you don't mean – "

"Mr Adair," said Kirsty. "Unless there are others."

"How dare you – "

"Mr Adair, who's done so much for you and for Gordon that he must be gettin' something in return."

"Are you tryin' to imply that – "

"You'll waken Bobby, shoutin' like that."

"I'm not that sort o' woman," Madge hissed.

"I don't know what sort o' woman you are," said Kirsty, "but when's it going to dawn on you that I'm not wicked?"

"I worked my fingers to the bone to keep body an' soul together," said Madge, "an' this is all the thanks I get."

"What *are* you blethering about, Mother?"

"I deserve – I deserve a second bite at the cherry."

So that was it; Madge felt that she had earned herself a second chance at happiness – and did not quite know how to cope with it.

Madge went on, "I'll have you know I'm not that old. My life's not over yet, Kirsty Barnes."

"And mine's hardly started," said Kirsty.

"I beg to remind you, lady, that you picked my Craig for yourself. Nobody forced you to marry him. I was never for it. I make no bones about the fact that I never thought you good enough for him – and I haven't changed my opinion."

Checking her anger, Kirsty got up and lowered Bobby gently into his cot. He stretched the length of it now, the crown of his head almost against the spars. He gave a little disgruntled wriggle and then settled, thumb against his lips.

"There," Kirsty said. "His spine should recover in due course." She turned. "Now, what was that you were sayin' about Craig being too good for me?"

Perhaps it was Kirsty's control that intimidated her mother-in-law or perhaps the woman felt that she had gone a shade too far. For whatever reason the fishwife's shrillness was gone from her voice.

"I – I didn't really mean – " she said.

"It's what you said," Kirsty told her.

"I just meant that you wouldn't have been *my* choice."

"Well," said Kirsty evenly, "if I'd had any opportunity to meet other young men, any freedom, I doubt if *I*'d have chosen *him*."

"What?"

"You heard," said Kirsty.

"If my Craig ever thought – "

Kirsty shrugged. "But I didn't, so I'm stuck with him, with all of you."

"Oh, that can be easily remedied," said Madge. "If you don't want us here you just have to say the word."

"And then what?"

"We'll – I'll – "

Kirsty raised her hand, finger pointing. "Careful, Madge."

"Mr Adair has asked me to marry him. Several times."

Madge had been trapped into the admission and realised it too late. She sat motionless, staring into space and then, damage done, tossed her mane of hair haughtily and tried to retrieve the situation. "But I'll not abandon my children."

Kirsty laughed. "Gordon's making enough money to support himself in grand style. And Craig has me to look after him."

"Lorna still needs me."

"Aye, but for how long?"

Unwittingly Kirsty had gained the upper hand in the argument, had turned the tables on her mother-in-law. She could not resist exploiting her advantage.

"In a year or two, when she has an office job, some young man will fall for Lorna, and – " Kirsty went on.

"Stop it. You're wishin' her wee life away."

"In any case," said Kirsty, "Lorna's more than welcome to stay here with Craig an' me – if, that is, Mr Adair can't be bothered with bairns running under his feet."

Madge's protests had been extinguished. She looked at the cigarette in her fingers and tossed it into the grate. "I *would* marry him, you know, if things were right."

"Things are right," said Kirsty.

"What if you decide to leave him?"

"I'm not goin' to leave him."

"What if you decide to run off with your fancy-man?"

"David? David's no – "

"He might have an education an' sport a dog-collar but, underneath, he's just like all the rest of them." Madge paused, squinted slyly at Kirsty. "He's had what he wants from you, hasn't he?"

"Madge, you really have a wicked – "

"In that house in Walbrook Street," Madge continued. "Come on, you may as well tell me. He's had what he wants already, hasn't he?"

111

Kirsty hesitated. Outraged denial formed in her throat. All question of having got the upper hand, of having put Madge in a corner about her intentions, fled. She stared at her mother-in-law, at the smug expression on her face, and gave in to impulse.

"Not yet," she said.

*　　*　　*

Gordon recovered consciousness without the aid of the reeking bottle of sal volatile by means of which Assistant Police Surgeon Penman was coaxing patients in the holding-cells back from the land of Nod. It was Mr Penman's duty to see to it that none of the ruffians actually snuffed it before they could be booked and charged and shuttled off to Percy Street. After two or three seconds Gordon realised where he was and what had happened, and set up such a howl of protest that big Archie Flynn was sent downstairs to help shut him up. Archie recognised Gordon at once. Within minutes the constable had him separated from the villains and brought up to the sergeants' room where Hector Drummond, stealing time from pressing duties at the desk, brought him a mug of tea and offered apologies.

Sweating, out of breath but not flustered, Craig entered the station some fifteen minutes later. He had collared one of the McMahons, a vicious little fifteen-year-old named Bernard who, still spluttering with bloodlust, had swung at Craig with a length of chain. Craig had immobilised and disarmed him without much difficulty. He had secured the boy's wrists with manacles and had frog-marched him the length of Ottawa Street while spectators hurled abuse, not at little Bernard but at the big bad copper.

Bedlam in Ottawa Street station: fathers, mothers, brothers, a wife or two, several priests and a pair of cheapjack solicitors were all milling about in the waiting-area to the tune of weeping, wailing, gnashing of teeth, false promises, horrible threats, defiance, repentance and hysteria. Sergeants and duty officers were doing their best to cope, though none of the little lambs seemed willing to admit guilt in any degree; had been a victim of chance, bad company, mistaken identity, extreme provocation, did not belong here, had never done such a thing before, was related to the Provost, the Lord Chancellor, the Pope himself, and would pull down the very halls of justice unless he was released without a stain on his character.

None of this was new to Craig. He had survived three previous riots and one violent strike.

He grinned as he hoisted Bernard to his feet at the desk.

Sergeant Drummond's soft Highland accent had hardened. In a voice like the Crack of Doom, glowering into Bernard's pink pupils, he shouted, "NAME, LAD?"

Bernard gave it without quibble.

Only when formalities had been completed and Bernard led away by Lieutenant Strang did Sergeant Drummond tell Craig that his brother was waiting for him in the sergeants' room.

"Can I go?" said Craig.

"Day shift tomorrow," said the sergeant. "You'll be required in court at nine thirty, so come here first."

"Right," said Craig.

"Go."

Sipping tea and puffing on a cigarette, Gordon did not appear to be much injured or in pain. A basin of cold water was by his feet and from time to time he would dab at his swollen face with a sopping wad of lint.

Helmet tipped back, hands on hips, Craig stood before him. "What happened to you, then, sonnie boy?"

"Wrong bloody place at the wrong bloody time, I reckon."

"How's your head?"

"It's not so bad. My side hurts, though. I think the bastard booted me."

"Just one of them?"

Gordon nodded.

"Think you could recognise him again?" Craig asked.

"Maybe," said Gordon. "I'd recognise my money-belt, that's for sure."

"He stole your takings?"

"Twenty-four shillin's."

"Funny," said Craig. "Robbery wasn't on their minds to-night."

"Well, some bastard robbed *me*."

"I'll put it in the report."

"I just want to get home, thanks."

"Does it hurt when you breathe?" said Craig.

"Aye, right here."

"Cracked rib, I suspect. I've had one of those. Can you stand up?"

"Sure." Gordon eased himself gingerly to his feet.

"I'll fetch Mr Penman to take a look – "

"Get me home, Craig, for God's sake."

"Might be a punctured lung," said Craig. "You could conk out in the night and I'd be responsible."

"Craig, I am not goin' to die. I'll see a quack first thing tomorrow, I promise. Breezy knows this doctor – "

"Where did the incident happen?"

"Riverside Street."

"Did you get a look at him?" said Craig, innocently. "Can you describe the thief at all?"

"Yeah," said Gordon. "He wasn't so young, not much taller than me, and he had a broken nose."

"Dark hair? Wearing a reefer coat?"

"I think so. Can't be sure," said Gordon. "Have you caught the bastard, Craig? Is he locked up down below? Can you get my money off – "

"Hold your horses, Gordon. I thought you just wanted to cut along home?"

"I do – but I want my money back an' all."

"One thing at a time." Craig held out an arm, crooked at the elbow. "Come on, sonnie boy, you can hang on to me."

"What about my twenty-four bob?"

"Leave that to me," said Craig.

*　　*　　*

Kirsty wakened at the sounds from the hall. She thought at first that it was Gordon and that her brother-in-law had been, for once, at the bottle. It did not sound at all like Craig who, when the hour was late, entered No. 154 very quietly and cautiously.

She had been drowsing, not in a deep sleep. She had been caught in a thick, whorled dream, not unpleasant, and had no notion of the time.

"Gordon, is that you?"

"It's both of us," Craig answered and, a moment later, touched a taper to the gas lamp.

Kirsty blinked, swung her legs out of the bed and reached for her cardigan to cover her breasts. Gordon was seated on the chair by the fire, holding one hand over his face.

"Sorry about disturbin' your beauty-sleep, Kirsty," said Gordon sheepishly.

"What happened?"

"Street fight," Craig told her. "The usual rumpus. Our Gordon got caught in the middle of it an' took a bit of a wallop."

"I'm really all right," said Gordon.

"You don't look all right to me," said Kirsty.

She opened a small cupboard beside the larder door and brought out a bottle of Gentian Violet, the household's all-purpose healing agent, and some linen swabs cut from an old sheet. She filled a bowl at the sink and carried the Violet, the cloths and the bowl to the table by Gordon's chair.

"For God's sake," Gordon murmured, "don't waken my mother. I don't want her fussin'."

Kneeling, Kirsty applied a cold swab to the bruises on Gordon's cheek and brow. She felt him wince. In his cot Bobby stirred and, as if in sympathy with his uncle, gave a deep groaning sigh before he dropped back into deep sleep once more.

"Jeeze," said Gordon, "you're not Florence bloody Nightingale, are you?"

"An' you're no wounded hero," Kirsty told him.

"That's for sure."

Gordon forced a brave grin while the Gentian ran down his cheek like a tear.

"He may have cracked a rib," Craig said. "Help him off with his shirt, Kirsty, and get him through to bed."

"What about you?" said Kirsty.

"I have to go out again."

"At this hour?"

"Duty calls," said Craig. "I'll be back for breakfast, then I've a court appearance at nine."

"When will you sleep?" said Kirsty.

"All day tomorrow."

Gordon wiped liquid from his eyebrows with his fingertips and squinted at his brother over Kirsty's shoulder. For a moment it seemed that he was about to put a question. Kirsty hesitated, holding the dripping swab over the bowl. She did not catch the look that passed between the brothers or Craig's discreet gesture, his shake of the head.

"Look after him," Craig said, and was gone.

She did not hear him pause in the narrow hallway, open the lid of the bunker and remove the iron-headed hammer which was used to break coal and, Craig felt, would do just as well to break bone.

* * *

She did not open to his knocking. At that hour and in that street Craig could hardly blame her. Brow to the woodwork he told her in a low voice, "It's Constable Nicholson. Let me in."

"What do you want with me?"

"I have to speak to you."

The letterbox, at waist height, clicked and hinged inward, drawn by a string. Craig stooped and found himself staring into her eyes.

"Now do you believe me?" he said.

She unbolted the door and admitted him. The tiny hall was made smaller by two huge wicker baskets heaped with clothing, and a rope, stretched taut between hooks, draped with shapeless woollens; so much fabric that it deadened the sound of their voices. The smell was like that of a sheep fank at shearing time but to Craig it was not unpleasant.

Greta held a candle in a tin holder, the flame scant and wan. She had flung a cardigan over her shoulders but it did not decently cover her and a thin cotton chemise showed him the shape of her body. The collar of the chemise was decorated with a baby-pink ribbon that drew Craig's eye to her breasts. Taller than he remembered her she seemed somehow stronger too, rounded by subtle shadows. Craig leaned against the door and pressed backwards with his elbows until the latch clacked.

"Brought me another puddin', have you?" Greta said.

"No, tonight it's your turn to do me a favour."

"I told you once, I don't do – "

"Business, Greta, just business."

"Your business or mine?"

"Where's the wee girl?"

"In bed. Asleep."

"Who else is here?"

"Not a soul."

"What's through that door?"

"The front parlour."

"Don't you rent it? Don't you have a lodger?"

"I prefer my own company."

"Let me see it," said Craig.

"See what?"

"The front parlour."

She leaned past him, turned the handle and pushed the door open. He peeped into an oblong room, sparsely furnished but neat. A double bed, covered with a shot-silk counterpane, had not been used that night.

"You sleep in the kitchen?" he asked.

"It's warmer there."

"The bairn with you?"

"Aye."

"Nobody else?"

"Look, come out an' say what you're here for, copper."

"I'm here to track down Billy King."

Surprised, she paused. "I haven't got him hid."

"I reckon you know who he sleeps with, though."

"Why should I – "

"He's got a bunty in Benedict Street," Craig said. "I want to know her name and address."

"I have nothin' to do with the likes o' King Billy."

"Come on, Greta," Craig said. "Maybe you earn your crust by takin' in laundry for rich folks – "

"Hah!" she said.

" – but you can't live in Benedict Street an' pretend you don't know what goes on here. So who's King Billy's special bunty?"

"I'm no damned washer-wife, I'll have you know."

"All I want from you, Greta, is the bunty's name."

"If I don't tell you, what'll you do?"

"Rub your arm up your back."

"You wouldn't do that to me, would you?"

"I might," said Craig.

"And then what?" said Greta.

"Don't be scared that Billy'll find out who put the finger on him," Craig said. "I won't breathe a word, *not* if you tell me what I want to know."

"That's an old trick," Greta said. "I get it if I do; I get it if I don't."

"Take your pick," Craig said, shrugging.

They were crushed together in the tiny hall. The candle lit her face from below and shadows hid what her body had to offer. He gave her no warning, reached urgently to his right and flung open the kitchen door. He had a sudden fear that perhaps King Billy was standing only feet away, a razor or a carving-knife in his fist.

By the flicker of the fire in the grate he could see an oilcloth cover on the table, a big cream jug and a brown earthenware bowl. The kitchen too exuded the smell of moist wool.

"Don't wake Jen, I beg you," Greta said. "There's nobody hidin' here, I promise."

"The bunty?" said Craig.

"Her name's Mary Shotten."

"Is he there?"

"Yes, he went in earlier tonight."

"How can you be sure?"

"I saw him. I'm not deaf and blind, you know. I heard the barney in the street. I bolted my door double-quick then I keeked out of the window. I saw Billy come out of the lane and walk down to Mary Shotten's. He went in."

"Which house?"

"Third down, opposite. She's on the top floor, left," said Greta. "Are you goin' to arrest him?"

"Nope."

"What, then?"

"Just goin' to have a friendly word, that's all."

"With Billy King? God, you must be – "

"Unofficially," said Craig. "If you don't object I'll leave my helmet an' tunic here for a while."

"I've no desire to get involved with coppers."

"Ten minutes, that's all."

"What are you goin' to do to him?"

"I told you – have a quiet friendly word."

"What's that in your pocket?" Greta said.

Craig removed the coal-hammer and held it between his finger and thumb. He could not contrive to make it look like a tool and not a weapon.

Greta said, "Good God! You *are* goin' to do him."

"There's no risk to you," Craig said. "I'll give you a half-crown for your trouble."

"You're a callous beggar."

"What about it, Greta?"

"Well, I'd rather you used that thing on him than on me."

Craig laughed and handed her his helmet. She placed it on top of the woollens on the larger basket, folded his tunic and put it there too, his leather belt and holster last of all.

He could not tell what she really thought of him. She had set the candle on the floor and the light showed off her limbs through the thin cotton garment. She had dark, dark, dark eyes, calculating and secretive. He stood before her in shirt and trousers and tucked the hammer into the waistband.

She studied him. "What's old Billy done to you?"

"Duffed my brother."

"Then arrest him. See him sent away."

"Short on evidence," Craig told her. "Anyway, I like it this way. All over and done with, clean and quick. No questions asked. Just him and me. Man to man."

She showed something of herself, a smile, a flash of small, vulpine teeth and a dimple that incongruously pocked her cheek.

"I'm glad it's not me you've got it in for."

"Do you want the half-crown?"

"Nope," she answered. "Not this time. This time the favour's for free."

*   *   *

"Mary," he crooned. "Mary, are ye no' there, my love?"

He drummed on the door with his knuckles.

"Come on, Mary, come on, come on."

She answered in a hoarse whisper, without opening the door. "Ga awa'. I'm busy the night. I've an old friend stayin' wi' me."

"Oh, Mary, come on."

"Who the hell *is* that out there?"

"Billy sent me."

"Billy sent ye? But Billy's here."

Craig smashed the coal-hammer into the lock box. He heard Mary Shotten scream. He used the hammer again, then stepped back, hurled himself at the door and rammed his boot into the lock box. The door flew open. The edge caught the woman and sent her reeling. She screamed once more, not piercingly but in warning. Craig hit her with his forearm and dived into the kitchen. Evidence: Gordon's money-belt lay coiled on the bare wooden table. He glimpsed it as he sprang at the man on the bed. Billy had been slow to waken, had not got his feet on the floor. Craig brought the hammer down on the crown of

King Billy's shoulder. The knife spun and skittered away across the linoleum.

Craig flung Billy back on to the bed and pressed the shaft of the hammer against his throat. Billy was no threat, no worthy adversary. He seemed fuddled with drink and sluggish. He wore his shirt and was bare-legged. A bandage with trailing ends was wound about his head. Craig pressed the butt of the shaft against Billy's Adam's apple. Billy's eyes were comically crossed. He did not struggle at all.

"Hullo, Billy," Craig said.

Instinct told Billy King that Craig was a policeman and, following his usual practice, he said not a word at first. If his damaged shoulder was paining him he gave no sign of that either.

"I've come for my brother's money," Craig said. "Will you hand it over nicely or will I do for your other fin as well?"

"Brother? What bloody brother?"

"The bloke you robbed on the street."

"Dunno what the – "

"Oh, Billy!"

Craig drove his fist into King Billy's stomach.

Billy King gasped but did not retaliate.

The woman had come quietly into the kitchen. Craig was aware of her. She was lean and tall and gawky, younger than he had supposed her to be. She seemed timid, not the sort to stick him with a carving-knife or brain him with a frying-pan. She stood quietly behind the table, dabbing at her nose with her wrist. She wore only a shift and bodice and had no breasts to speak of.

"Oh, Billy!" Craig said again, admonishingly. "I'm not out for blood, man. All I want is the cash you stole."

"You're a friggin' copper."

"'Course I am."

"You got no right t' be here," said the woman. "You got no warrant. You aren't even in bloody uniform."

"Ask Billy about rights," Craig said. "Tell her about rights, Billy."

Craig released the man and stepped back from the bed. Billy did not move. He was sprawled against the wall, damaged arm flung out and bandage trailing. He looked like a cheap engraving of a hero of the line.

"She's right, Billy," Craig said. "I'm not in uniform. I'm not really here at all. You could have a fair whack at me an' nobody would be any the wiser."

Billy's mouth hung open. He shifted his right hand to his jaw and stroked the bristles on his chin.

"Just you an' me, Billy," Craig cajoled.

"Bugger off."

"Scared, Billy?" Craig asked.

"Bugger off."

"If you want rid of me, you just have to tell her to shell out the money."

"Gi'e him the cash, Mary," Billy said, without hesitation.

Dismayed at King Billy's meekness the woman began to protest.

Billy cut her short. "In my troosers."

"I thought you were a fightin' man, Billy," Craig said. "I thought you'd give me a hard time. I was lookin' forward to knockin' the sufferin' hell out of you. I'm disappointed."

Billy laughed, wheezily. "I'm no' daft, copper."

"I doubt if the lads would recognise you, lyin' there on your back, refusin' a fair fight."

"Gi'e him the bloody money, Mary."

Craig said, "If it's in your mind to nobble me some dark night when you've got three or four accomplices with you, Billy, I wouldn't advise it. You're not man enough to take me, not you or your bloody gang."

"Mary, get him — "

She raked through the pockets of her lover's trousers and spilled cash on to the table, banknotes as well as silver and copper coins.

"How much?" said Craig.

"There was twenty-four shillin' in the belt," Billy said.

"I didn't ask you that, Billy. How much is on the table?"

The woman counted laboriously while Billy King lay motionless, scowling from under swarthy brows. Craig waited, the hammer in his hand. He felt poised, daring, amused.

"Well?"

"Sixty-six shillin'," Mary told him.

"Aye, that'll do," said Craig.

King Billy made no protest as Craig plucked up the notes and coins and slipped them into his trouser pocket. Mary watched him, her head cocked quizzically. She wasn't a bad-looking woman, Craig thought. He was tempted to pull her to him and make her kiss him, get a squeeze at her breasts just to discover if they were as small and hard as they seemed.

"Will there be anythin' else, copper?" Billy said.

"Nope, I've got what I came for."

"Some copper!" said Mary Shotten.

"Right," said Craig. "That's it. Bye-bye."

He felt light as a bubble in the strange dirty-grey kitchen. He moved to the door.

"Remember, Billy, keep your nose clean or I'll be back."

"I'll no' forget," said Billy King.

"Some bloody copper!" said the woman again and Craig, grinning, left them to lick their wounds.

* * *

The child, Jen, was still asleep in the bed recess, screened by a flowered curtain.

"Did you get what you wanted from him?" Greta asked.

She had put on a gingham dress, small cinnamon checks, and had pinned up her hair with a matching ribbon. She was still bare-legged and barefoot, though.

"I did," Craig told her.

She had laid out his tunic, helmet and belt on the table and he put on the jacket and buttoned it, taking his time. She was a queer wee creature, Craig thought, a creature of contrasts.

"Do you want somethin'?" she asked.

"What?"

"Somethin' to eat?"

"No, I'd better get along."

"Did you settle old Billy's hash?"

"Sure."

"An' did you enjoy it?"

"What?"

"Was it fun, takin' him to task?"

"Sure, it was fun."

"Did you take her to task too?"

"Who?"

"Mary Shotten."

"I saw her, of course," Craig said.

"Pretty, don't you think?"

Greta Taylor was fishing for compliments. Craig was suddenly uncomfortable.

He said curtly, "Too skinny for my taste."

Greta laughed softly.

Craig stuck the helmet on his head and felt better at once.

"What do you do for a livin', Greta?"

"Sell clothes," she told him. "I buy the best stuff I can from rag-wives, patch it, wash it an' sell it again."

"Keeps you alive, does it?"

"I manage," she said.

"So there's no man to take care o' you?"

"If you mean her daddy, no, he's dead."

"Dead?" said Craig. "I'm sorry to hear it."

"He was never mine, anyway," said Greta. "I only had a loan o' him, you might say. He was a salt-sea sailor. He drowned in the Baltic."

"He had a real wife somewhere, I suppose?"

"In Dundee."

"How did you find out he was drowned?"

"The mate o' the ship wrote an' told me how Tom was swept overboard in a storm. Lost at sea, they call it."

She did not seem particularly distressed.

Craig said, "Did the mate not come to visit you afterwards?"

"What's that intended to mean?"

"I thought – "

"Don't think," the woman said.

Craig said, "Where do you sell the clothes?"

"At the Irish Market," she said. "I've a legal licence an' all. Want to see it?"

"No need. The Irish Market isn't in my province."

"Oh, I thought maybe you'd come along, you an' your hammer, an' beat the – "

"You're a saucy bitch," Craig said.

"An' you shouldn't be here."

"I know it," Craig said. "Do you want the half-crown?"

"Stuff your half-crown."

"Business must be good."

"Business is fine."

"All right. I'll thank you for your assistance," Craig said, "an' be on my merry way."

Greta Taylor ushered him into the hallway and opened the door. "Don't call again," she said and, with that benediction, closed the door behind him and dropped the bolt.

*   *   *

For once Kirsty did not hear Craig enter the house. He had removed his boots on the second landing and had crept upstairs silently.

It was early but it was not dark. She assumed that the rest of the household were all fast asleep, though it would not have mattered to Craig in his mood if they had been awake and listening. He was roused as she had never seen him roused before. She heard his breath a split second before he touched her.

She opened her eyes and stared up. He was naked, had taken off all his clothes. He put his hand across her mouth and shook his head, telling her to be quiet. She had sense enough not to protest. He wanted her, wanted her immediately, and would take her in spite of her reluctance. He thrust his hips against her to let her realise his need. Kirsty nodded. He put an arm about her shoulders and pulled her from the pillows. He tangled his fingers in her unloosed hair and tugged her against him, rubbing himself against her.

"Take it off," he told her, thickly.

"What?"

"Take everythin' off."

He peeled the blankets from her. He planted a knee on the bed, kept the other foot anchored on the floor. In the half-light he seemed thin but not puny, all sinew and stretched muscle. He was too impatient to wait for her to obey him. He grasped the hem of her nightgown and furled it over her thighs and belly. He dragged it upward until the folds caught on her breasts. She winced and fumbled with the cotton tie. He put his hands upon her, upon her bare breasts and pushed her backward against the wall. Her bottom was raised and tilted by the pillows. Her shoulders were braced against the bed's panel headboard. It knocked upon the wall and she was tense with the fear that the sound would waken Bobby. Craig rubbed against her indiscriminately. He said nothing, made no tender gesture, did not even stoop to kiss her. Struggling, she got the nightgown over her hair and tried to slide down, to put herself beneath him. He was too impatient even for that. He cradled her bottom and jerked her against him so that her knees splayed wide and she was open to him. He wriggled frantically. He fitted his knees between her thighs, his narrow hips slipping down, stretching her. He fitted himself into her and arched his back. He swung forward and drove into her.

The headboard knocked and knocked against the wall. Kirsty was distracted by it. She rolled on her hips and tried to clasp him in her arms. She was racked by the position and gasped when he rocked against her. She had never felt such penetration. She did not know whether it gave her pleasure or pain. The headboard knocked and the springs under the flock mattress twanged. It was all so loud, so desperate, so uncaring. She was ashamed that she had joined with him, that her will was not strong enough to resist the strength of his desire. Heat, however, mounted in her parts and her breasts became heavy with each thrust, each surge, each rocking angry motion up and forward and back. Now that she had firm hold of him he drew his hands from under her and slapped them against the headboard, smothering its sound. Kirsty closed her eyes.

Craig's muscles clenched. She clenched her thighs about his hips. Involuntarily she lifted herself up. She braced herself, taut too. She reared against him as he thrust and panted, panted and, with a short grunting cry, came to his climax. She matched it a moment later with three short choked groans. He fell against her, his head buried in a corner of the pillow that was crushed beneath her. He was spent but still hard within her. Kirsty groaned again, softly, as he withdrew. He flopped sideways, satisfied, and sagged against the inner wall.

After several seconds he stirred, touched her shoulder.

"Did you want it?" he whispered.

"Yes," she answered, dutifully.

"Really?"

"Really," Kirsty said.

"I thought so. I damned-well thought so."

"Do you want more?" she asked.

"Hell, no," he said, and laughed.

— PART TWO —

August

Breezy could not be certain when he became impatient to marry Mrs Margaret Nicholson and carry her out of tenement town to a mansion on the hill, when he finally lost not just his heart but his head. He had always been a schemer and set about persuading Madge that he was the man for her in a most deliberate manner. The proposal, climax of the courtship, would be unconventional, to say the least of it, but entirely true to the spirit of their relationship and to Breezy's character and reputation.

It had been a fine warm fortnight and grew warmer still towards the end of the month. Trades holidays were over, Clydesiders had all gone back to work and only the upper crust remained at leisure, romping over grouse moors or cruising the Hebridean waters in hired yachts. Breezy did not favour holidays. He preferred the city and its conveniences. But he was not above taking a little breather and had no difficulty in setting up an excursion for the last Thursday in August.

On a lovely, languorous, hazy-blue day, Breezy and Madge rode down to Balloch by train. There, in the bustling wee town at the tail of Loch Lomond, they picked up a pony-and-trap from the yard of the Railway Inn. A picnic hamper and a cold-box containing wine were stowed under the seat and with Breezy at the reins the couple set off up the lochside. Breezy was not as expert as he professed himself to be and it was just as well that the pony was obedient and seemed to know what was required without much instruction from the driver. At length, Breezy and the pony between them got the trap out of the inn yard and across the bridge over the Leven and out on to quiet roads and lovely country lanes that meandered among emerald pastures and fields of grain heavy and ripe for the harvest. So far everything was going swimmingly and exactly according to plan.

It was very hot indeed. Soon Breezy was obliged to take off his linen jacket, collar and tie and roll up his shirt sleeves. Madge, though, revelled in the heat. She was clad in a frothy frock with a huge floppy hat to shade her from the sun, a parasol to hand

129

if she required it. She lounged contentedly in the curve of the trap as Breezy navigated away from civilisation in search of a quiet rural corner where he might have his way without a soul to disturb him.

Bulls snorted and whisked their tails. Cows' udders swung half-full. Ripening barley gave off a fecund odour and swayed sensuously as the trap climbed away from the loch shore and into the foothills below the moor. Tiny isles dotted the mirrored surface of the loch like tabs of fur and the sky above was as blue and smooth as bonded paper. Madge said little but seemed almost to be purring in the pleasure of the day. Breezy had no doubt that, with a chicken leg or two inside her and several glasses of wine, he would at last be able to undo her defences. She certainly made no objection when he steered the trap out of the lane, through a broken gate in a drystone wall and out on to rough, secluded pasture.

A trickle of water, seeping off the moor, spread, brown as tea, over flattened stones. Breezy braked the trap, untethered the pony, put it on a rope and let it drink and crop as it willed. Hands on hips, he looked around. There was no living soul in sight except in the far distance where field-hands, tiny as gnats, followed a reaping machine down a dip towards the loch. On the water small craft plied, strung on puffballs of smoke or with long oars glinting in the sun, for there was no breath of wind today to fill sails.

Breezy paused. He was filled with strange smouldering desire which, he hoped, would communicate itself to Madge as soon as he touched her. He was not even sure that he could contain himself until after lunch. He wondered if he was man enough still to do it twice in one afternoon, fortified between with cold meats and alcohol. He shaded his eyes and looked round at the woman.

"Is this not the place for us, Madge?" he said. "Country born and country bred as we are. Will you come an' join me?"

"I will if you help me down."

He placed his hands about her waist, braced himself and took her weight. She seemed to be as light as a girl to him at that moment and he felt as if he was a strong young ploughman just reached his manly prime, the pair of them stepped out of a painting or out of a famous old poem or song. True, his forearms were pale and his moustache too trim and spruce, but it was easy, on the edge of the great shaggy moor, to believe that he was a hardy Scots lad who could sweep all resistance before him and that Madge was not quite the lady he would make of her but a sonsy Highland maid who would come eagerly to his arms. He was more in love with her there and then than he had ever been with anyone before. He could not imagine that she would not be aware of his ardour, would not surrender to him in fine style.

He swung her to the ground, and, with hands still about her waist, dipped under the brim of the floppy hat and kissed her. Her lips were dry and warm and her skin seemed to burn against his.

"Shall I fetch a blanket, Madge?"

"Well, I'm not going to sit on the grass."

"Wait," said Breezy.

He clambered up into the trap, drew the hamper and cold-box from under the seat and tucked one under each arm. Madge watched him, rotating the parasol in one hand, her head tipped back slightly. Breezy knew that she felt as he did, intoxicated, rejuvenated by the setting and the weather, young again in heart and soul, her fancy tickled by it all. Cold-box and hamper tucked under his arms, Breezy leapt nimbly to the ground.

The hamper bounced away down the slope and the cold-box clattered after it. Heels skidding on the flat stones of the water-course, Breezy fell. He could not protect himself. He came down with an awful thump in the slick tea-brown water. He sat up at once and let out a yell of pain and a string of curses that would have turned a navvy's ears bright red.

Madge shook her head.

"Idiot!" she said.

"God Almighty!" Breezy moaned and, in a sitting position, clasped his left ankle with both hands. "Jeez-us!"

Madge discarded her parasol and, without hesitation, stepped into the trickling water.

"Can you stand on it?"

"I think it's broken."

"Havers!" Madge said. "Come on, stand up."

She took Breezy's hands and yanked him to his feet. She supported him while he danced one-legged, touching the injured foot to the ground and lifting it again, moaning and yelping.

"It is. It's broken."

She held him while he hopped to the grass. She helped him down and kneeling at his feet removed his elastic-sided boot and gently turned his foot this way and that. Breezy winced but did

131

not cry out. He bit his lip not just against the pain but against the realisation that the day was shot, that his plan too had come a cropper.

Madge said, "Aye, it might be broken right enough. What in God's name possessed you to go jumpin' about at your age?"

"I slipped, I just slipped," said Breezy. "What the hell do you mean — at my age?"

"An old man."

"I'm not bloody infirm, Madge."

"You are now," she said.

"Is the bone stickin' out?"

"Don't be daft, Albert. Even so, it's the doctor for you. There's bound to be one in Balloch. That leg'll need splinted, I think."

"What about — what about our picnic?"

"Put that — an' other things — right out of your head, Albert Adair," Madge told him. "An unset bone can be very dangerous in old people."

"*Old* people!"

"Gangrene could start up. You could lose the leg."

"Madge, for God's sake — "

She was sympathetic but beneath her concern he could sense amusement.

He said, "I don't think it's funny."

She let out a hoot. "Aye, but it is. Here's you tryin' to play the gallant lover an' you can't even keep your feet on the ground."

"Don't laugh at me, Madge."

"I can't help it."

"We can't stay here now," Breezy said dolefully.

"I know. Come on, I'll help you into the trap."

"But who's going to drive?"

"I am," said Madge.

A half-hour later Madge brought the trap into Balloch at a fair clip and an hour after that, with Breezy's left leg encased from sole to shin in stiffening plaster, the couple hobbled on to the train that would carry them back to the city.

Madge made her companion as comfortable as possible in the compartment, propped in a corner with the leg stretched out along the seat. She had had the foresight to remove from the hamper a couple of chicken legs and from the box one bottle of wine and a corkscrew before she returned them to the inn. She opened the bottle as a man would, holding it between her knees. The chicken legs lay on her scarf, greasy but appetising. She had taken some sun and her cheeks were dusky, her hair a little unkempt. Breezy, ankle throbbing, watched her, reassured.

She passed him the uncorked bottle.

"Sook on that," she told him.

He drank obediently to ease his thirst and wash away his disappointment.

"An' gnaw on this."

He nibbled on the chicken leg, watching her still as she swigged unselfconsciously from the bottle.

The whistle shrilled, steam hissed, the carriage vibrated. Holding the wine bottle at arm's length Madge lowered herself to her knees on the floor of the compartment and pressed her body against his, to hold him safe and sound as the carriage lurched into motion. Breezy put an arm about her and rested his cheek against her hair. He could smell the scents of the country from her. He held her until the train attained rolling speed and the Leven flickered past the window, shoals of river craft on its tidal banks, and green trees cowled the track and cast shadows into the compartment. She hoisted herself carefully on to the seat by him and accepted the drumstick that he offered her. Lovingly he watched her eat.

He said, "I worship you, Madge."

"Aye, I know you do."

"What do you want from me?"

"A big house," she said, shrugging. "Lots of fine furniture an' a place for my children."

"I wouldn't mind that," said Breezy.

"I'll need to stay with you tonight."

"What for?"

"To look after you."

"Nonsense. I've got servants — "

"Nursin' is what you need. You need somebody to tuck you into bed an' make damned sure you stay there."

"Madge, I had — I mean, I was going to — "

"I know fine well what you intended, Breezy."

"I'm sorry."

"Sorry for what?"

She took a casual bite from the drumstick and turned her head a little so that she no longer met his eye.

Breezy took a deep breath. "Will you marry me, Madge Nicholson?"

Sunlight cut through the corner window and illuminated her face, smoothed away the evidence of the years and made her appear astonishingly youthful.

Breezy held his breath.

She dabbed her mouth with the back of her wrist and turned, smiling.

"Of course I will," she said.

*   *   *

The windows above the sink, open top and bottom, admitted all the sounds from the streets and courts, the price you had to pay for a breath of air in the stifling kitchen. It was all Kirsty could do to bring herself to kindle a fire in the range to boil a kettle and melt lard in the frying-pan. She did not feel well, felt thick, stupid and a little sick even at that early hour. Bobby had wakened in a temper, had climbed from his cot and, bare but for a vest, had clung to Kirsty's skirts, girning, while she summoned energy to face the day's routines. Clad only in drawers and a towel, Gordon was trying to shave, jockeying for space at the sink, while Bobby stamped and whined and demanded attention from him too.

Craig was also in a foul mood when he returned from night shift. He had been involved in one of those demeaning farces that seemed to take up so much of a policeman's time. He had spent three hours in pursuit of a mongrel that was reported to have savaged a child in Kingdom Road. The child, he learned later, was fourteen years old and had no doubt been tormenting the poor dog. Nevertheless the report had to be taken seriously. The chase had been prolonged, across backcourts, over stinking middens, through the pipe of the Kingdom burn, before the little terrier tyke had been trapped in a wash-house, netted and roped and taken away to be destroyed by a man from the Humane Society.

Sweaty and leg-weary, Craig found no peace in his domain. Hardly had he seated himself to unlace his boots before Lorna appeared from the parlour.

"Where's Mam?"

Cut-throat poised, Gordon turned. "Is she not in bed?"

"Nope," said Lorna. "She's not in the closet either. I've just been."

"Didn't she come home last night?" Craig asked.

"Nope."

"Well, why the flamin' hell didn't you tell somebody?"

"I didn't know till now, did I?"

Gordon arched his throat and scraped bristles with the steel blade. "Been on the tiles with Breezy, I expect."

"All night!" Craig exclaimed.

"Keep your hair on," said Gordon.

"Aye, I don't know what you're goin' on about," said Lorna.

"She's been with him *all night*," Craig shouted.

"So what?" said Gordon.

Tired of being ignored, Bobby butted his father with the crown of his head, butting and butting at his thigh like a little ram until Craig plucked him up and dumped him back in his cot. Bobby scowled furiously, promptly clambered out of the cot again and lowered himself to the floor.

"*Get back in there, you*," Craig yelled.

Stunned by the anger in his father's voice, Bobby shrank into a ball against the base of the cot until Lorna took pity on him and lifted him into her arms.

"Don't shout at Bobby," said Kirsty. "It's not his fault."

"Where's my bloody breakfast?"

"Here's your bloody breakfast."

She slapped a half-cooked egg from the frying-pan on to a plate and clattered the plate down on to the table.

"It's still raw."

"Aye, well, how can I cook without a fire?"

A wave of nausea came upon her. If she had been alone she would have lain down upon the bed but she forced herself to remain upright, to give no sign of her condition.

She should have told him before now. Her pregnancy had been confirmed yesterday evening in Dr Godwin's consulting-room in Banff Street. She should have told Craig before he went out on shift. She could hardly tell him now; he would regard her news as another thorn in the crown of suffering that he was obliged to wear.

Craig snatched a chair and seated himself at the table. There was no steam yet at the kettle spout and porridge lay like clay in the pot.

Gordon said, "Hey, I've a bottle o' beer, if you're interested."

"Naw," said Craig. "Anyway, what are you doin' wi' bottles o' beer?"

"Forget I asked," said Gordon.

"What do you want to eat, Gordon?" said Kirsty.

"I'll catch a bite at the stall at the Cross."

Craig plastered the runny egg on to a heel of bread and bit into it. Yolk dribbled down his chin and freckled the oilcloth.

"Mucky pup," said Lorna.

"Shut your mouth."

Lorna was no longer in awe of her brother. She had been a student at Prossers' Commercial College in Glasgow for four weeks and, in that short time, had gained in confidence.

"Did Mam tell you where she was goin' by any chance?" Craig said.

"Out for a day in the country," Lorna answered.

"Which bloody country?"

Gordon put a hand on his brother's shoulder but Craig shook it off. He crammed the remainder of the sandwich into his mouth and washed it down with milk swigged from the jug. Kirsty felt that he was deliberately trying to provoke her by his display of bad manners.

Gordon said, "I'll find out where she is."

"How?"

"Somebody at the warehouse is bound to know," said Gordon. "Breezy's never out of touch for long."

"Jesus!" said Craig. "What a world we live in when you have to ask strangers where your own mother spent the night."

Lorna said, "I think she'll marry him."

Craig lowered the milk jug. His moustache was dappled white. "Who says she will?"

Lorna said, "She told me. She told me she thought Breezy was ready to pop the question."

Bobby had both arms around Lorna's neck and was pressing silly kisses against her cheek. She did not dissuade him and held him firmly against her, one hand under his bottom, the other about his waist.

Craig said, "Did she happen t'tell you what answer she'll give?"

"Doesn't have to," said Lorna.

"She'll not refuse?" said Kirsty.

"'Course she won't," said Lorna.

For an instant it seemed that Craig might explode, might hurl the milk jug against the wall. Instead he placed it carefully on the oilcloth and stroked the milk from his moustache with his forefinger.

"We'll see about that," he said.

*   *   *

The boxes that contained the Zephyrs had been gathering dust in the warehouse for years. Some impetuous Adair had bought the fans on the cheap from an Indian importer who had gone liquid. They were of German manufacture and, unlike their market rivals, were neat and handsome objects, operated by a handle and not a pincer-action device which tired wrist and fingers very rapidly. Gordon found the consignment behind some rolls of carpet and, on checking the Purchase Book, discovered that the cost of the fans had been written off that very January. Any sale now made would account as found profit. It did not take Gordon long to invent a patter and gun up a couple of tricks to impress potential customers. He would show how the air-flow could whisk a feather across a room or blow out a candle at five paces. He put one of the Zephyrs into his best mock-leather travelling-case and set out on that stifling morning to try his luck around the houses.

Fans were generally useful for clearing smoke from kitchens, removing unpleasant odours from sickroom and nursery and for drying ladies' hair. It was for their cooling effect on the brow that the fans would be bought today, however, and Gordon was keen to strike before the weather changed. Auto-Rotary fans were catalogued to sell at eight shillings so Gordon offered the Zephyrs at three and — lo and behold — sold nine of the things by dinner-time. He brought the order slips back to the warehouse about two o'clock and instructed the delivery lads to get the goods to the customers and collect the cash before the temperature dropped. If the hot spell continued for another three or four days he felt sure he could shift all four dozen Zephyrs in that time. Pleased with himself he went into the office for a fresh pad of order slips.

Breezy was arranged in the chair behind the roll-top desk. He appeared to be as natty and cheerful as ever in spite of the fact that his left leg was encased in plaster and stuck out awkwardly, foot resting on a feather cushion on a separate wooden chair.

"Clearin' out dead wood, I hear," Breezy said.

"Not much goes past you, does it?"

"What are you chargin'?"

"Three bob."

"That's fair. As I recall, the item cost was only tenpence," said Breezy. "Take it while you can, I say."

"What happened to you, then?"

"Fell off a mountain."

"I hope you didn't take my dear old mother with you?"

"Not her," said Breezy. "She was the hero of the hour. Drove me back to a doctor toot-sweet, she did."

"As a matter of interest," said Gordon, "where is she?"

"At my house."

Gordon paused, then said, "Must be awkward, that plaster."

"It is awkward," said Breezy. "Painful too."

"So Mam sort of – looked after you last night?"

"Played the Nightingale to perfection."

"My brother was none too pleased at her being out all night long."

"Will he be any more pleased, d'you think, when he discovers he's about to acquire a brand-new stepdaddy?"

"You?"

"Well, I don't mean Harry Lauder."

Gordon was taken aback by the news. In spite of Lorna's warning that a marriage proposal was imminent it still surprised him. He flashed his best salesman's smile, however, and stuck out his hand.

"Congratulations."

"You don't object?" said Breezy.

"God, no. I'm delighted."

"What about your brother, though?"

"I can't speak for Craig."

"He can't stand me, can he, Gordon?"

"Candidly, he thinks you're a crook."

"Is that all?" said Breezy. "He won't be the first to bark up that tree."

"An' he won't want Mam to go."

"Still a mammy's boy, is that it?"

"He's not soft," said Gordon.

"I know he's not soft," said Breezy. "Will he cause a fuss, son?"

"He might," said Gordon. "Listen, Breezy, is there a risk?"

"Risk?"

"Is Craig liable to find anythin' he shouldn't?"

Breezy said, "It's not *all* above board, let's put it like that. Can you not bring him round?"

"I can try, I suppose," said Gordon. "But he's a stubborn bugger."

"We plan to find a house real soon an' to tie the knot in December," said Breezy. "It's not as if Craig's being abandoned on a stranger's doorstep. He's got a nice wife, a son, a house."

"What about us? Lorna an' me?"

"Your mother wants you both to stay with us."

"How do you feel about it?"

"I feel fine about it," said Breezy. "In fact, I'll be disappointed if you don't take up board and residence."

"I gather," said Gordon, "that you don't have it in mind to rent a room-and-kitchen?"

"If a man marries late in life," said Breezy, "he isn't going to deprive his wife, or himself, of some of the nice things the world has to offer, is he?"

"You do love her, don't you?"

"Surprisingly – yes."

"Surprisingly?" said Gordon.

"I never thought I'd fall for a lady who had connections in the Burgh police."

"How much *do* you have to hide?"

"Not much," said Breezy. "Some old bones in old cupboards, that's all. Nothing that would send me to the jail."

"Is the book-keeping all right?"

"The book-keeping is immaculate."

"In that case, why are you worried about Craig?"

"I'd like it better if he liked me."

"He doesn't like anyone," Gordon said.

"Why not?" said Breezy, surprised.

"I wish I knew," said Gordon.

*   *   *

He could not put a name to it, could not quantify the sense of loss. From the moment that he learned that his mother had spent the night with Breezy Adair, however, Craig knew that he was doomed.

The guilt he had felt those years ago when he had left Dalnavert without a word to her, when he had given up everything for Kirsty Barnes, came flooding back. He had tried hard to make it up to his mother, and he had failed. In addition he deeply resented Adair's effortless success, just as he resented Gordon's off-the-cuff charm. Soon they would be gone and he would have no chance to prove himself, to force them to respect him. He would be left with the wife and the wean, the job, the tenement house, the shackles of a marriage that gave him no comfort, that made him seem dull and old and ordinary.

Clasping at straws Craig decided that he would try to find something that would reduce Mr Albert Adair's stature, some activity that could be classed as an offence against the law and, using that for a lever, would try to bring the old devil down.

It would not be easy. Gossip abounded in the Ottawa Street station but nobody had a bad word to say about Breezy or his boys. He was not regarded as a menace to society, as anything other than a businessman who had done very well for himself. If he was into illicit bookmaking and the transportation of un-licensed goods – what of it? There were worse things going on day-and-daily in the streets of the Greenfield. Besides, Breezy did not reside in the burgh; officially he was Partick's problem, in so far as he was a problem at all.

When Craig rose at half past one o'clock in the afternoon he found that Kirsty and Bobby had gone out and that he was alone in the house. He cooked himself a second breakfast, more substantial than the first, and ate it slowly. He brooded over a second cup of tea, wondering how he should approach this problem, trying to make of his confusion of emotions a simple puzzle, something that could be solved by pragmatism, appli-cation and cunning.

It was as hot as hell in the kitchen now. The curtains hung motionless over the open windows and in the backcourts there was a weird suffocating stillness as if everybody had been smothered while he slept. Sweat prickled his body, naked from the waist, and his mind was sluggish. He could think only of his mother, of all that she had once meant to him, of his daddy too, small, patient, meek; lost in a haze of whisky, impotent, unmanned and enduring. He wished that he was working the fields of Dalnavert still and might discharge his frustration and anger by swinging the big iron sledge-hammer or, since this was August, by riding bareback on one of the big horses that pulled in the corn harvest to Bankhead's threshing machine.

In time memory too became a kind of torment to him and he stirred himself, washed at the sink, put on a clean vest and a cotton shirt with a pointed collar, flannel trousers and shoes. He draped his striped jacket over his arm, lit a cigarette and went out of the house. Now that he was on the move, anger diminished and the irretrievable longings went out of him. He had a notion now of what he would do to pass the long afternoon.

One of the Piper boys was seated cross-legged in the cool of the close, squeezing a tune from a chanter. He looked very young and sun-browned. Craig could not imagine why he was not at school. The boy took the reed from his lips.

"Hot, intit, Mr Nicholson?"

"Aye, it is that."

Craig went out of the close into the street. The plaint of the pipe followed him as he walked along Canada Road, hugging the narrow band of shade by the tenement walls.

Fifteen minutes later he found himself in Benedict Street. He was neither excited nor afraid. He seemed to stand apart from himself, observing without passion what that other self was up to. He walked to the close and went in. He knocked on the door, not expecting her to be at home, prepared for disappointment. She opened the door.

"Greta," he said. "I was just passin' an' I thought I might – "

She hesitated for a fraction of a second only.

"Come in, Constable Nicholson," she said.

* * *

In spite of the heat Mrs Frew wore a shawl of fine white wool about her shoulders and a rug about her knees. David had carried the wicker chairs into the garden and had placed them in shade, facing the old red-brick wall which, at this season, hung thick with ivy. He had brought out a novel for his aunt to read but the book lay open in her lap, a faded ribbon marking her place. Nothing about Nessie Frew was as it had been a year ago. Even her voice had weakened, become less sharp and certain.

When Peggie showed Kirsty through the kitchen and into

the back garden she found a peaceful scene. David was seated opposite his aunt, a wooden tray on his knee and a pencil in his hand. He had been writing a sermon and had filled one of the sheets of lined foolscap with his small quick script. He wore his pale grey linen vest but no jacket and had removed his collar and rolled up his sleeves. He was surprised and delighted to see Kirsty and her son and rose at once to greet them.

Peggie had been on her way out to the new Italian Café to buy a jug of ice-cream and to see if she could find a punnet of Lanarkshire strawberries for which Aunt Nessie had expressed a desire. Peggie offered to take Bobby with her and Kirsty readily agreed. Her son had been restless all day and she hoped that the exercise would tire him enough to make him sleep that night. Bobby went off with the servant-girl without a qualm, toddling manfully by her side. David joined Kirsty at the front door of No. 19 and together they watched Peggie and Bobby until they rounded the corner by St Anne's and passed out of sight.

Sunlight baked the street and the houses of the terrace and across the bowling-green an arc of water glistened in the air and formed, for a second, a faint dissolving rainbow against the frieze of masts and derricks. Kirsty reached back her hand and David touched her fingers. She trusted his will to be stronger than her own, respected that strength in him more than anything. She would not challenge it just to satisfy her vanity or from a selfish need to have him prove that he loved her.

"I'm expectin' another child," she said.

His fingers tightened. "Has it been confirmed?"

"Yes, by Doctor Godwin."

"All's well?"

"Everythin' seems to be in order."

"What did Craig have to say to the news?"

"I haven't told him yet."

"How far are you gone?" said David.

"Nine weeks."

David said, "I don't suppose you'll want me to deliver this one on the doorstep?"

Kirsty did not respond to his attempt at humour.

She said, "I was afraid this would happen."

"Afraid? Surely you've nothing to fear? Just because Bobby came early doesn't mean to say – "

"I'm just afraid, David, that's all."

"Let's go inside."

She followed him into the hallway.

There was no coolness to be found even in No. 19's deep gloomy hallway. The house smelled dry and musty as if all the old dry ghosts that the place contained had gathered listlessly in daylight, too enervated to wait for dark. The gaslight behind the stained-glass screen on the stairs had been extinguished and even St Andrew had dwindled sullenly into the shadows.

David and Kirsty lingered at the angle of the hall and kitchen passage.

"Do you not want another child, Kirsty?"

"Yes. Yes, I do."

"What is it then that makes you apprehensive?"

She looked at him, straight at him. She did not need to explain. He understood her predicament only too well.

She said, "Would you hold me, David, just for a moment?"

"Of course."

It was not spontaneous as it had been the first time and, at first, his arms felt awkward about her. She put her head against his shoulder and heard him sigh, felt him relax. A consoling resignation came over her, as she had hoped it would.

"I wish," she whispered, "I wish it was your child, that's all."

He gave her a hug and gently released her.

"You won't leave him, Kirsty, will you?"

"I can't."

"Because you love him?"

"Not that, not even that."

"Simply because he's your husband?"

"Craig isn't my husband."

"But – "

"Between Craig an' me there are no statutory bonds," she said.

"But you've lived together as man and wife for – "

"Almost three years."

"I see," said David. "He refuses to marry you, and that's why you're so distressed about having another child."

"*I* won't marry *him*."

"Good God!" said David. "Why not?"

"I won't give in to him now."

"Give in to him? Kirsty, you're not making much sense."

"I'm sorry."

David seated himself on the stairs.

"Well, Kirsty, I'm astonished."

"Bobby is baptised. That's all that matters to me."

"I'm not clear on the fine print of the law," David said, "but it would seem to me to be much more sensible if you and Craig legitimised what is, by now, a marriage presumed."

"It's presumed all right," said Kirsty.

"Kirsty, why have you told me this?"

"I thought you should know the truth."

"Who else knows?"

"Nobody. Not a soul."

"This can't make any difference to us," David said. "Craig Nicholson will never let you go."

"Oh, I know that," said Kirsty. "He can't. We're tied by 'habit and repute' and that's a damned sight stronger than any vow."

She seated herself on the stair by David's side and smoothed her skirt over her knees.

David said, "I wonder how Craig managed to register Bobby without certificate and proof of marriage."

"I don't know how he did it, but he did," said Kirsty. "Was it wrong of me to have Bobby baptised?"

"No, I can't say that it was wrong," David told her. "I really don't know what to say, to tell you the truth. I shan't tell anyone, of course. Have no fear about the wrath of the Presbytery descending on you."

"I hadn't thought of that, to be honest."

"Kirsty, this doesn't change anything."

"I know. I can't think why I told you."

"Because," he said, "you know I love you."

"Yes."

"Bobby's Craig's child. The new baby will belong to Craig too. And you're Craig's wife by consent. I can't take you from him, Kirsty."

"Because it would ruin your career?" she said.

"Oh, it would do that all right."

"Sometimes I almost wish you'd gone back to China."

"Perhaps it may come to that yet," said David. "I can't say where I'm going or what I'll be called upon to do."

"God's will?" Kirsty said.

"The Kirk's will."

"Another parish in another town," said Kirsty. "I know it'll come to that sooner or later, David."

"No parish on God's green earth will take me with another man's wife in tow," he said. "Lord knows, there are plenty of scandals within the Kirk, things hushed up and brushed under the carpet. I suppose some ministers wrestle with conscience and others abandon all moral responsibility. But I don't feel in my heart that I owe myself totally to God, that everything I do is directed."

"David!"

He laughed. "I used to wonder, as a lad, how it was that God's will always seemed to coincide exactly with my father's."

"Do you think we're sinners?" Kirsty asked.

"No."

"When Craig's family leave, when we're alone again, perhaps it'll be different. Better."

"What if it isn't, Kirsty?"

"Craig hasn't done me any real harm."

"What if it isn't?"

"I'll just have to put up with it, won't I?"

She got to her feet and abruptly returned through the kitchen to the garden. David followed her, frowning.

In the wicker chair Mrs Frew appeared to be asleep, motionless, frail and wispy. They stood quietly behind the woman's chair, hand in hand in the shadow of the house. What, Kirsty wondered, would there be for her when she arrived at that late stage in her life? What memories and regrets would drift across her thoughts on some hot August afternoon at the end of a summer far hence?

"Where are my strawberries?" Nessie Frew said, without opening her eyes.

"They'll be here soon," David told her.

"I thought you'd gone to Lanarkshire to pick them yourselves."

"Patience, Auntie, patience."

"I've no time left to be patient," the old woman said. "I want my strawberries now."

*   *   *

The apartment was at ground level and the disposition of the buildings about the court protected the kitchen window from the full glare of the afternoon sun. She had laid on only a tiny fire, a handful of coals that seemed to have no flame at all at centre and to release no heat from the streamer of brown smoke that trembled up into the vent.

Soft garments soaked like puddings in a big zinc bath on the board by the sink. The fragrance of washed wool was clean and cool in Greta's house. Pulley ropes were draped with clothes, hung there not to dry but to await repair. On a frame of light wood were items of intimate wear also in need of mending.

Greta had put her chair before the open window to catch the light and any trace of breeze. Tins of hooks and buttons, threads and needles were arranged on the linoleum by her feet and a linen bed-sheet was swathed over the chairback. She drew out a second chair from its place at the table and planted it before her, facing into the window.

Craig seated himself, legs crossed.

"Where's the wean?" he asked.

"Gone to the park."

"Not on her own, I hope."

"Mrs Thomas took her."

"Who's Mrs Thomas?" he asked.

"Mrs Thomas is a neighbour. Next landing up. She's got five weans of her own, if you must know."

"How does she earn her bread?"

"Nosy devil, ain't you?" Greta said. "She has a husband. He works on the Merkland dock."

She had taken her place on the chair again. She lifted the sheet and resumed work on it, patching. He watched her nimble fingers ply the fine needle. She did not look up. She wore a pale blue delaine shirt tucked into the waist of a dark blue pleated skirt and her feet were bare. Craig gazed at them. They were clean and white, as if she had been trampling the clothes in the bath.

"How long has she been gone?" he asked.

"Not long."

"How long until she comes back?"

"Long enough."

Craig said, "Will you sell all this stuff?"

"Eventually, aye."

"What about this?" He gestured to a muslin camisole that was spread wide on the rack. "Will you sell this?"

She did not look up. "Somebody'll buy it."

"What for?"

"Because it's pretty an' has lots o' wear left in it."

"Some girl?"

"Some young girl, I expect," Greta said.

She had not asked him what he wanted here or why, of all places, he had chosen to pass time on that simmering afternoon in her kitchen.

"What about these?" Craig said.

She flicked her gaze over the garment, let it linger on Craig's face for a split second. He lifted the frill of lace at the hem of an Empire chemise and lightly let it fall again.

"That's not an easy seller," Greta said.

"Looks nice to me."

"The high waist is out o' fashion," said Greta. "Some old lady might be glad of it, though."

Craig hesitated, then brushed his palm against a pair of nainsook knickers. "These?"

"I'll be lucky to sell them at all."

"Why's that?"

"They're mine," said Greta soberly.

"Are they now?" Craig said. "What are they doin' there, then?"

"It's too hot for knickers."

"What do women wear underneath in hot weather?"

"Ask your wife."

"I'm askin' you."

Greta shrugged. "Nothin' at all."

Casually Craig said, "I don't believe you."

"Do you want me to prove it?"

"Aye."

She put the sheet carefully to one side. She stood up. Craig stretched out his legs and cocked his head, watching her. She looked directly at him, unabashed.

"Won't you take my word for it?" she said.

"Nope."

She stooped, caught the hem of her skirt and slowly straightened, lifting the skirt until it caught in folds about her hips.

"Now do you believe me?" she said.

Craig did not reply. He said nothing, staring.

"Is this what you want, Mr Policeman?" Greta asked.

"Come over here."

There was still no sense of urgency. He felt as if he was treading water just below the surface, alone in the deep end with the shimmering weight of the pool above him. She was quite without shame. She sidled closer, skirts held up. She did not draw back when he put his hand upon her.

"Why did you come to me?" she said.

"Because I wanted this," he answered.

"If I won't do it, copper, what'll you do to me?"

"Stand still," Craig told her.

"No, go on, tell me; what'll you do to me?"

"Run you in," Craig said.

She laughed huskily and twined her arms, at last, about his neck.

"Do it then," she said.

*   *   *

When Gordon got home to the tenement in Canada Road he found the family at supper. To his dismay, however, his mother had not returned and, God forbid, might not come back at all that night if she was still playing the Nightingale for Breezy.

Craig was at table, supping broth. He wore serge trousers and his heavy shirt and his brow was glossy with sweat. Lorna was at table too, Bobby on her knee. She was feeding her nephew who, sated with sunshine and strawberries, was too tired to make a fight of it and champed on the spoonfuls of potato and flaked meat with sleepy resignation.

"Where is she?" Craig asked as soon as Gordon entered.

"She's fine. She's fine."

Gordon had brought home a demonstration fan in the fond hope that it might divert attention from the news that he would be obliged to impart. He handed the Zephyr to Kirsty.

"Aye," said Craig, "but where *is* she?"

"Breezy broke his ankle," said Gordon.

He told the story, making a joke of Mr Adair's misfortune. Craig was not amused but, to Gordon's relief, he did not seem to be his usual volcanic self and ate dourly.

"You still haven't told me where she is," Craig said.

"Well, I – "

At that moment the door opened and Madge burst in.

Craig glared at her but continued to chew the slice of cold roast pork that he had stuffed into his mouth.

"I'm to be *married*," Madge declared. "I'm to be married to *Albert Adair*."

Kirsty hugged her mother-in-law, congratulated her and generally made a fuss. She could not deny Madge her spell of glory, the understanding and rapport that existed between women.

Madge swept off her hat and unwound the chiffon scarf from about her throat. "I'll have a ring tomorrow. A diamond cluster, I think. Breezy says that money's no object."

"Christ!" said Craig.

"Breezy will be buyin' a new house for me. He wants Gordon an' Lorna to come along too. You'll have a room all to yourself, pet, with a wardrobe and a dressin'-table an' your own mirror."

"That'll be nice," said Lorna drily.

Craig said, "For God's sake, have you no sense at all?"

Madge had been expecting an outburst from her eldest and swung on him immediately.

"It's none of your business, Craig," she snapped. "I don't require your permission to get wed."

Round-eyed, Bobby followed his father with his gaze as Craig got to his feet.

"I think it is my business," Craig said. "Jesus, Mam, I've provided you wi' food, shelter an' clothin' since you turned up on my doorstep. The least you could do is discuss this daft proposal before you leapt into Adair's bed."

Madge handed her hat, gloves and scarf to Kirsty as if she was about to do battle physically with her son.

"You knew that Albert was after me," Madge said.

"Seems like he got you an' all," Craig said.

"That's enough, Craig," said Kirsty.

"I don't care what you think," Madge said. "The truth is I've always been a perfectly respectable woman – an' still am."

"You spent the bloody night – "

"He had a broken ankle."

"Pull the other one," Craig said.

"I had to look after him."

"By climbin' into his – "

"Craig, *stop it*," Kirsty interrupted.

As if drawn by a weighted rope, Craig lowered himself ponderously to his chair. He glanced up at Lorna and his son. "For God's sake, Lorna, wipe his mouth an' get him to bed."

"I'll do it," said Kirsty.

"Lorna can do it. She's not bloody paralysed, is she?"

"What's that?" said Madge. "Is that pork?"

"Aye," said Kirsty. "Bought fresh today."

"I could do with a bite." Madge positioned herself in front of Craig. "If I have his lordship's permission to partake of food at his lordship's table, that is."

"For God's sake, Mother, sit down," Gordon said.

"Well, Constable?" Madge said.

"Do what the hell you like," said Craig.

Madge remained on her feet. The aggression had diminished, the bravado. "I thought you'd be pleased for me, son."

"I'm pleased for you, Mam," said Gordon.

"Craig?"

He held the cup in both hands and sipped from it, eyes fixed on the belly of the teapot. He gave no sign that he had heard her.

Madge shrugged and sighed and, after a moment, slid her hands behind her head and flounced out her hair.

"God! but it's stuffy in here," she said.

"I can cure that," Gordon said.

He went to the dresser and brought down the Zephyr. He positioned it close to his mother, cranked the handle and made the blades spin.

"See, is that not better?" he said.

"My, my! It's a fan, so it is," Madge said, as a stream of air wafted across her bosom and throat. "*Ooooooh*, that's lovely. Keep it up, son."

Without a word Craig got up and stalked out of the kitchen.

When, a quarter of an hour later, Kirsty went to look for him she found that he had left the house; helmet, holster and all.

* * *

Lockhart was the last person that Craig expected to meet in Scutter Street, and the last person he wanted to see on that particular evening. He could not ignore the minister, though, and hesitated as Lockhart approached.

The sun had gone down but there was still a faint hazy twilight in the streets and lots of folk about, taking a breath of air before bedtime. Lamplighters came and went, threading the closes, and a strange goblin-like music floated over the tenements from a street-harmonium some blocks away.

"Been at the Mission, have you?" Craig said.

"Yes. I've been tutoring some of the boys from the Brigade in bible study," David answered.

"Bright sparks, are they?"

"Bright enough. Where are you headed? Off duty or on?"

"On."

"Would you be going to collect the Reynolds boy, by any chance?"

"What d'you know about Sammy?"

"Sammy's famous; the policeman's mascot."

"Are you bein' snide?"

"Of course I'm not," David said. "I'll walk down with you, if you've no objection."

"Why?"

"Don't be so prickly, Craig. I've an interest in Sammy Reynolds too, remember."

"Come on then."

David turned and together the men headed for the door of the Mission about which some older boys in Boys' Brigade uniform loitered, laughing. As soon as they caught sight of the minister and the copper, however, they fell silent and slouched off towards the corner of Riverside.

"Hardly a smart body o' men," Craig said.

"They do their best," said David. "Discipline is all they require to make them shape up. By the way, I saw Kirsty today."

"Did you?"

"She called to visit Aunt Nessie," David said. "Didn't she tell you?"

"I believe she mentioned it, aye."

"She's looking well."

"Did she tell you anythin'?"

"About what?" David said.

"She told you about my mother, didn't she?"

"Your mother?"

"Well, she *is* goin' to marry Adair," Craig said.

"Ah, you must be pleased for her."

"Adair's a bloody crook."

"Is he? Is he, really? I thought your brother worked for him?" David said.

"My precious brother'd do anythin' for money."

151

"What will happen after the marriage?" David said. "I mean, will Gordon and Lorna go to live with the happy couple?"

"Sure they will. Good riddance, an' all."

"You'll have plenty of room in the house then," David said.

"Room for what?"

"In case you decide to have more children."

"You'd know about that, wouldn't you?"

"Pardon?"

"You bein' a doctor."

The lights in the window of the front hall of the Mission went off at that moment and, a second later, Mr Dugdale emerged from the door, Sammy Reynolds at his side. Sammy had started the day dressed in a knitted pullover and thick socks but somebody, one of the 'afternoon ladies' like as not, had made him take off the pullover and had replaced his knitted socks with a pair of white cotton. The boy had tucked his trousers into the top of the socks and looked almost sporty as he bounced down the steps. He did not seem in the least surprised to find both the policeman and the minister waiting for him.

"Heard you speakin', Mr Lockhart."

"Did you enjoy it, Sammy?"

"Mosses, it was."

"What?" Craig said.

"Mosses. Mosses. All about Mosses."

"Moses," David said.

"Aye, Mosses. Sailed in a wee boat."

Mr Dugdale laughed. "Get awa' wi' ye, Sammy. I'll see you at eight tomorrow. An' remember, if it's a hot day, leave that pullover at the lodgin'."

"Aye, Mr Dugdale."

Sammy looked expectantly at Craig and held out his hand. Craig, embarrassed, tried to ignore it.

David said, "Show me the way, Sammy."

To Craig's consternation, Sammy gave Lockhart his hand and they moved away from the steps of the Mission towards the Riverside corner.

The harmonium was still puffing out a tune. The sound came from the direction of Ronnie Norbert's beat and Craig was surprised that Ronnie hadn't stemmed the racket; it was falling late now and there were many in the tenements to whom music would bring no pleasure. As if he, Craig, had somehow willed it the harmonium cut off in the middle of 'The Bluebells of Scotland'.

"Awww!" said Sammy. "Gone."

He glanced at Craig and thrust out his free hand, a curious little challenge implicit in the gesture.

"Two hands tonight, Sammy?" David said.

"Aye."

Craig gave the boy his fist and, with the lad between them, the copper and the minister headed for the model lodging-house.

"Swing," said Sammy.

"Naw, naw, Sammy. You're too damned heavy for that caper."

"Swing, eh?"

"What does he want from us?" said David.

"He wants us to swing him between us, like a bairn," Craig said.

"I wonder how far back that memory goes."

"What?"

"Who last gave him a swing; how long ago it was."

"Swing," said Sammy.

"I never thought o' that," said Craig. "I suppose somebody must have, once."

Craig held the recollection of a leafy lane behind the Bankhead kirkyard, a huge sheet of blue sky, his hand in his dad's hand, his hand in his mam's hand, feet off the ground.

"I saw your wee friend Jen today," Craig said.

"Jen?"

"Aye, Sammy, don't you remember her? She was asking how you were, an' she sends you her love."

He had erased the old memory with a new one. He wanted something of the afternoon to come out. Talk of Greta's child was as much as he dared risk.

"I thought you'd remember Jen," he said.

Sammy skliffed his feet on the pavement and seemed to have nothing on his mind except how he might persuade the men to give him a ride in mid-air.

Suddenly, though, he said, "Jesus loves me too."

Craig snorted.

"Jesus loves me," Sammy insisted, "this I know."

"What's he talkin' about?"

"Canny see Jesus, but."

"No," said David. "But Jesus can see you, Sam."

Disturbed a little by the turn in the conversation, Craig said, "Hey, Sammy, do you really want a swing?"

"Aye."

"What about it, Lockhart? Can you support his weight?"

"I can try."

"Right then, Sammy," Craig said. "Pick 'em up."

The boy tucked his knees under him. Suspended between the minister and the copper he pendulumed to and fro, chuckling, as they hauled him across the end of Scutter Street.

"How long can you keep this up, Lockhart?"

"As long as you can, Nicholson."

Craig grinned at the challenge, braced his muscles to take the strain and put all thought of making it back to Greta Taylor's house out of his mind until morning.

─── *October* ───

The stinging grey rains that lashed Glasgow that first week in October did not dampen Madge Nicholson's spirits one bit, for life, thanks to Breezy, moved from one peak of fulfilment to another with hardly a space between. He had taken her, for instance, to a discreet third-floor office in a block in Argyle Street and had had a selection of engagement rings spread out for her approval. On Breezy's recommendation she had selected a fine diamond three-stone half hoop which Breezy had paid for there and then in hard cash, discreetly out of her sight.

"How much did it cost, dearest?" she had asked him later.

"Now, now, Madge, mustn't be rude."

"Oh, go on, tell me."

"Ninety-five, if you must know."

"Pounds?"

"Well, not pennies, shall we say."

"Breezy Adair, you're too good to me."

"Mutual, I'm sure," Breezy had said and had kissed her on the mouth, not caring who saw them.

He took her to lunch that day in the Buckingham Hotel and in the palm-fronded dining-room told her that he loved her to the end of time and kissed her across the table; and the string quartet hidden behind the plants, given the signal, played a few bars of 'The Love of My Life', and made Madge weep with happiness.

Afterwards Breezy hired an open carriage and had them driven along Great Western Road. It was a calm, dry, cloudy afternoon, just before the rains set in. Madge thought that he was taking her to the Botanical Gardens for a stroll and hugged him as the carriage rolled along.

Trees flanked the thoroughfare, leaves touched with autumnal tints, the dome of the Winter Garden snow-white beyond. Opposite to the gardens the façades of the terraces where the rich lived were screened by trees too.

"Classical Greek by inspiration, so I'm told," Breezy informed her, pointing with his Malacca cane. "Only twenty years old, however, and hardly even weathered yet. Handsome, eh?"

"Not as handsome as you, Albert."

"They're not as old as me, of course," said Breezy. "Don't you like the architecture?"

"It's very handsome, yes."

"Well, I like 'em. So I thought we'd just have one." He leaned across her and pointed again with the cane. "That one, in fact."

On cue the driver rolled the carriage to a halt at the kerbstone and Madge gazed in awe at the terrace's delicate iron railings, corbelled eaves and noble pillared doorways.

"You – you *bought* one of those?"

"Signed on the dotted, yesterday."

"How – how many rooms?"

"Oh, the whole house."

"The whole – "

"Eight rooms on two floors. Servants' quarters additional," Breezy said.

Madge collapsed beside him. "Eight rooms! My God!"

"Two each," said Breezy, "if Gordon an' your Lorna come to stay with us. You don't object to me just stormin' ahead, do you, Madge?"

She kissed him. "Albert, I don't know what to say. It's so – so grand. Can we go in?"

"In two or three weeks," said Breezy. "It hasn't been vacated yet."

"How on earth will we furnish it?"

"From the stores, of course," said Breezy. "But I'll leave all that to you."

It was left to Kirsty to bear the brunt of Madge's unbridled enthusiasm for her new house on Great Western Terrace. Lorna and Gordon were out much of the time and Craig was openly scathing about the scale and location of Adair's new property. Odd though it seemed, Madge needed the young woman's consolation, her support. Breezy had given her more than she had ever dreamed of. The happy ending to the fairy-tale had not depended at all on patience and perseverance, and Madge was so conscious of her luck that her assertiveness changed, temporarily, into a kind of panic.

"What if he doesn't like me? What if I disappoint him?"

"Madge, he *loves* you," Kirsty would assure her. "He wouldn't have done all this if he *didn't* love you."

"He says he loves me but – I don't know, I don't know."

"Do you want to call it off, Madge?"

"God, no! No. No. But what if his family hate me?"

By then Madge had met most of her new relations. Dinners and supper parties had been arranged and each of the occasions was, for Madge, an ordeal. As far as Kirsty could tell, though, Madge had carried all before her. Gordon told Kirsty that he'd heard that the Adairs were relieved that Uncle Breezy had at last found a wife and that she was a sound, down-to-earth person. Apparently there had been some close shaves in the past with young women who would not have fitted at all into the family circle, whose aspirations were not just materialistic but positively grasping.

As the day of entry drew closer Madge's doubts dwindled and her thoughts focused entirely on the house on Great Western Terrace. Stone and marble and carved wood symbolised achievement in monumental form, far better than anything raised in her wildest dreams. Rain or no rain, a half-hour after Breezy had had a set of keys delivered, Madge and Kirsty were in a tramcar heading north. Bobby was left in the care of Jess Walker, for Craig, off night duty, was still asleep.

Madge had visited the empty house with Breezy, just once. She had waxed so lyrical and so long about its splendours that even Gordon and Lorna had turned a mite sarcastic and had eventually retreated unbidden to bed. Nothing that Madge had told her, and Madge had told her everything, had prepared Kirsty for the reality of the splendid terrace. It was three times as large as No. 19 Walbrook Street and had an elegance, a balance in all its parts that quite took her breath away.

Entrance was by a marble-floored hall from which a grand staircase flowed upward past wood-panelled walls. The dining-room seemed to have been borrowed in scale from a proud municipal property and the upper-floor drawing-room could have contained all the rooms in Kirsty's house and still have had space to spare. Cornices, carvings, fireplaces all had a timeless simplicity of design that made Madge and Kirsty converse in hushed tones as if they were in a cathedral and not a private dwelling-house.

Some rooms were lighted by electrical fitments and it was one of the electrical devices that epitomised the house's luxury for Madge.

"See this, Kirsty," she said.

"What is it?"

"It's called an electrical servant," Madge said. "Watch."

They stood before a wooden hatch set into the wall of the drawing-room and Madge dabbed at an ivory button and, cocking her head, listened to the whirring, grating noise that sounded in the hidden shaft, a sound that both Madge and Kirsty could associate with power, as if a miniature traction-engine was installed in the depths below. Madge held a hand to her ear and smiled beatifically as a bell *pinged* behind the hatch. She slid open the door – and there were deep empty shelves, four of them, filling the space within.

"Amazin', isn't it?" said Madge.

"Absolutely amazin'."

"You try."

Obediently Kirsty slid the hatch into place, dabbed the ivory button and listened again to the whirr and the grating of invisible cables within.

"Where does it go?"

"Right down to the kitchen," Madge told her. "We'll come up here after supper, after dinner, touch this button an' *ping*, next thing you know we've got our coffee. We don't even have to see a servant."

"Oh, that's very convenient."

Madge played with the electrical servant, sending it down and bringing it back up again, while Kirsty walked the length of the room to the window and looked out at a view of trees and the gardens.

She understood why Madge was excited but personally she found the house daunting. Perhaps when it was decorated, carpeted and furnished it would be less intimidating, less grand. When she thought of moving up in the world she fixed as her ideal the house in Walbrook Street which, though it had plenty of rooms, was cosy and shabby and on a scale which she could encompass and accommodate. She doubted if David's uncle, up in Inverness, lived in a house as grand as this one. She could not imagine what sort of man would have the audacity to demand so much from a dwelling-place. Even Kirsty had her weakness, however. She found herself coveting the bathroom, the long, deep, tiled bath whose curving taps would deliver streams of piping-hot water on demand.

It was in the bathroom too that she finally realised the import of it all. Madge had once washed other folks' clothes for her daily bread and now she would have servants of her own, would never have to scour another pot or chap her hands on a scrubbing-board, not as long as she lived. It would be a life of ease for Madge Nicholson, of pampering and indulgence. Somehow, even to Kirsty, it did not seem quite right. For a while on that wet afternoon in the intimidating house that her mother-in-law would command, Kirsty felt a certain resentment at the randomness of fate, at the fact that she would have been happy with so much less, and would forever be denied it.

She was twelve weeks into her pregnancy and still had confided in nobody except David. She feared Craig's reaction to the news. It had been weeks since he had last made love to her and she resented the fact that he had become absorbed in his own childish hurt. She could not put it off much longer, though, and would, she promised herself, tell him before the weekend.

"What's wrong with your face?" Madge said.

Kirsty started, turned from the window.

"Nothin'. I'm fine."

"You don't like the house, is that it?"

"It's wonderful, Madge. Truly it is."

"We've had our differences in the past, I know, but you'll always be welcome to visit me, even if his lordship won't come with you."

"That's – that's very kind."

"It'll not be my way to forget my humble origins," Madge said, "or the poor folk who have to live in the Greenfield."

"I'm sure it won't," said Kirsty.

They went downstairs again into the marble-floored hall which seemed as cold and solemn as a tomb in the slanted grey light that leaked in through the transom.

With the bunch of keys in her hand Madge paused and drew Kirsty to her side. It was rare for Madge to touch her but now she held on to Kirsty's arm with tight, conspiratorial affection.

"You will tell him how nice it is, won't you?" she said.

"Aye, of course I will."

"I want you to tell him he's got to come here."

"Madge, he won't listen to me."

"Aye, but he will."

"I think he's jealous of Mr Adair."

"No, it canna be that," Madge said. "Our Craig's not daft. He knows full well he could never do what Breezy's done."

"What does Craig want, Madge?"

"More than you've managed to give him so far."

"How can I do – "

"He's a man. He wants it all." Madge, impatient with this examination of motives, released her. "Never mind that. Just you tell him what a fine place his mother's going to be occupyin' an' persuade him to behave properly."

"Towards you?"

"Aye, towards me," Madge said. "Who else?"

Suddenly Kirsty realised that Madge's gestures of friendship had nothing to do with kindness or affection, contained no generosity of spirit.

"You'll do it for me, won't you, dear?" Madge said.

"I'll – I'll try."

"I knew I could depend on you."

Madge heaved open the heavy front door and peeped out into the rain.

"Tell you what," she said, "we'll take a cab back to Canada Road. My treat. Why don't you pop over to the stand at Kirklee and fetch one for us, eh?"

Kirsty hesitated. She was tempted to tell the woman what to do with her charity, her patronage, but she did not want to spoil the afternoon now by flying off the handle.

"All right," Kirsty said and stepped quickly out into the drenching rain.

*   *   *

It had been months since David had heard a word from the North China Mission. He had ceased to write to his parents, to Jack, who did not, in any case, reply.

He had noticed a note of apology creeping into his last letters and he had resented it. He did not feel that he had done anything very wrong in electing to stay in Scotland and seek a parish there. Father, of course, would never forgive him for his betrayal and Jack, it seemed, had developed a grudge against him too. He had heard nothing at all since April.

Jack's letter arrived in the middle of October. It brought David no comfort. His brother's style was direct and cold, not bantering as it had once been. Politics, not religion, made up the substance of the four short pages.

'Old Buddha', Dowager Empress Tz'u Hsi, was at her wily tricks again, stirring up the notion that all foreigners were devils and that the ancient gods were all on the side of the Harmonious Fists, the rebels. David had gleaned something of the situation from short reports in *The Times*. Fanshi's remoteness, his family's vulnerability, had cost him sleep. He had prayed for them regularly, in that vague wish-dreaming way that had become a substitute for proper communion with God.

"They say," Jack wrote, "that we build hospitals so that we may mutilate their children, churches so that we might lure their women into bondage, that we shelter fugitives from justice in our missions. Some Americans, whom I met in Nanking, are very worried about the future here. Father, however, will have none of it. He remains blissfully confident in the absolute loyalty of his flock. He seems to believe that the God of Israel will protect Fanshi against attack. He actually seems to look forward to a battle royal between Christ and the eight million spirit soldiers that the Boxers claim will descend from the skies when the time comes to sweep the land clean of foreigners. Father believes that Protestantism, not mere Christianity, is bound to triumph."

David read the letter in the kitchen of No. 19 Walbrook Street. The fire was warm. There were eggs and sausages on his plate, hot buttered toast in a silver rack, coffee in the pot, and Peggie pottering about to set a tray for Aunt Nessie.

"Bad news, Mr Lockhart?"

"Not particularly, Peggie."

"They don't write you often, do they?"

"They haven't much time," said David.

There had been trouble with rebels and bandits before. He had heard shots and jabbering once or twice and had been hurried away, with Jack, to the shelter of the church with Mother and a dozen trusted servants. It had been exciting. He had had no sense of danger when he was a child. Besides, it had all been over in a couple of hours, the rebel band put to flight by gallant Christian converts armed with three rifles and a fowling-piece. His father had preened and prayed and boasted for a week after each incident, and Jack and he had played at Boxers and Christians, shooting each other with sticks and falling about on the ground behind the church.

He scanned Jack's letter again. How strange that he could not bring his father's features to mind. He could see his mother clearly enough, her pale, saintly little face, and long, pale throat, her feathery hair and dainty, busy hands. But his father's face had faded from his memory like a daub kept too long in a damp room.

If there was going to be serious trouble in China he should not be here in Scotland. He should be with them, in body if not in spirit. The Presbytery had been encouraging him to apply for one of their vacant charges. He had been sent to preach in several empty pulpits. Gussie had interrogated him about his intentions, had suggested that he might still have release to return to China. It did not seem to have crossed Gussie's mind that he might wish to seek demission for another reason.

Peggie interrupted his chain of thought.

"Will you be takin' in her tray this mornin'," she asked, "or will I be doin' it?"

"I'll do it."

He folded Jack's letter and slipped it into his vest pocket, took the tray from the servant and carried it to the back parlour.

Nessie was up and dressed. She huddled over the coal fire, though, as if the first wet taste of winter had thoroughly chilled her bones. She was not so old, really; about sixty-four or -five. In the parish David had encountered women a good twenty years older than his aunt who were still hale, hearty and active. He could not understand the nature of her illness, or why it had undermined her so suddenly. He wondered if she had lost her will to survive and, however much she feared the act of dying, encouraged it.

"Good morning, Auntie. How are you today?"

"Not so bad." She glanced up at him without a smile. "It's wet again, I see."

"Miserable."

"I shan't go out, in that case."

"Very wise," David said.

It had been months since she had ventured from the house. She had not even attended service for ten or a dozen weeks now. She left the running of the house to Peggie. David drew out a little table and put the tray upon it. Nessie peered at the boiled egg as if she expected it to hatch.

"Soft, I hope?"

"Try it," said David.

He watched her tap and crack and flake away the shell and pierce the membrane with the tip of her spoon. Yolk ran yellow and, without interest, Nessie began to eat.

"I had a letter from Jack today," David said.

"How are they all?"

"They seem to be well."

"Still sulking?"

"Father is, I expect."

"Perhaps I should write to them," said Nessie.

"If you feel up to it," said David.

She laid down her spoon and pushed the tray away from her a little. "I'm not going to be here much longer."

"Now, now – "

"What will you do then, David? It'll have to be sold, you know, this house. Hugh, Edith and my nieces must have their share. However much I dislike them, it can't be avoided."

"If you insist on being morbid, Aunt Nessie, perhaps you should send for a lawyer."

"Oh, that's all done," she said. "My will is drawn up, signed and witnessed."

"I see."

"I assume that the Vacancy Committee will expect you to take a charge by Whitsun?"

"The Presbytery have been pushing a little, yes."

"I'd better pop off before then, hm?"

"For heaven's sake, Auntie – "

"Hughie wouldn't know how to cope with an infirm female in decline."

"He would never abandon you. He'd take you to live with him, I'm sure."

"I'd throw myself in the Clyde first," Nessie said. "If, by some unfortunate chance, I drag on for another six or seven years I'll be a terrible burden to – "

"Will you *please* stop this nonsense."

She glanced up at him again. He detected some of the old shrewdness in her eyes. "You've seen what happens to old women, David, those who have no kitchen corner to huddle in."

"But you *have* a kitchen corner. You've — "

She gave a little shake of the hand to silence him. He could almost hear her bones rattle like a wizard's talisman.

"I want you to see that Kirsty receives what I've left her," Nessie said.

"Am I to be your executor?"

"No, Mr Marlowe will act in that capacity."

"If you're trying to make me promise to look after Kirsty — she has a husband to do that, Aunt Nessie."

"He's too much of a man to be the husband for her," the old woman said. "She's a good girl, David, a nice girl. I would have liked a daughter like her, if it had been given me."

David said nothing. He had not the heart to explain that he might be three hundred miles from Kirsty, or five thousand for that matter, that he might even be relieved to escape from the feelings that Kirsty engendered in him. He could not admit to Nessie that he was beginning to realise that he had not been called into the ministry by God but only by a habit of obedience to his father, by training in the faith and not by inspiration. To Nessie, still, kirk and creed were a part of life but not life itself, as they must be for a minister.

"Why are you frowning?" Aunt Nessie said. "You'll spoil your good looks if you frown like that."

"I'll do what I can for her, for Kirsty."

If he had not met Kirsty he might never have known the truth about himself. He would have buried his doubts, found comfort in the manse, in the respect of his parishioners, would have become a good quiet middle-ground man like Harry Graham or a charitable administrator like Gussie, and the clamour of doubt would have died quickly away. But he wanted Kirsty and he did not know yet if he had the strength to be without her.

The old woman hesitated. She toyed with the sticky egg-spoon for a moment or two. "In the end there will be nothing. I'm reconciled."

"Oh, Nessie, don't you have any belief left?"

"In God the Father?" she said ruefully. "In the communion of saints and the forgiveness of sins? No, I don't think I do."

"In the life everlasting?" David said.

"I held the faith, David, but it seems I was never held by it."

"I'm — I'm sorry."

"It's not your fault. If it's anybody's fault, it's my own. All of my life, near enough, I skated on the surface and depended on example and obedience to save me from falling through the ice. I've come to the conclusion that the Kirk did not tell me the whole truth."

"What truth is that, Auntie?"

"God's generous, David – and we should be generous too."

"I don't know if – "

"Dogma, doctrine and theology; not at breakfast, David, please."

Butter on the toast had cooled and thickened and the remains of the egg had congealed in the broken shell.

"Is there no sort of consolation, Aunt?"

"Of course there is," she said.

"What?" David said. "What is it?"

She smiled to herself, and shook her head slightly.

"Won't you tell me?" David said.

"You'll find out for yourself, in time," she said. "At least, I hope you will."

"Aunt Nessie, if – "

"Now, if you will, please take away this tray."

"You've hardly eaten a thing."

"I've had quite enough," she said.

Carefully he stooped and lifted the tray away from her.

She sat upright in the chair now, prim and fragile. She looked calm and patient, like some elderly shaman who would take her secrets to the grave.

"Why are you so concerned about what will become of Kirsty Nicholson?" David blurted out.

"It's you I'm concerned about, David."

"Is it the same thing?" he said.

"Of course it is," said Nessie and, with an imperious little gesture of the wrist, waved him away to the kitchen before he could fathom it out.

* * *

He would come to her, sometimes, in the morning before he went home. He liked the quiet hour when he was pumped up with fresh air and exercise and had been thinking of her for most of the shift. She would be tousled and lazy and would not rise to greet him but would wait for him where she lay, in the bed set into the wall.

How she knew when to leave the door unlatched was one of the mysteries. Once or twice Jen would waken before they were done, would come padding through innocently from the big bed in the front room where she slept now, separate from her mother. The child's attention, her friendliness, would embarrass Craig and tint his desire with irritation though he knew that he and not the child was to blame.

In the street at that hour he was conspicuous. He would drape an old coat over his uniform and hide his helmet under its folds but that just seemed to make him more obvious and he did not like the feeling that disguise imparted. If he lingered overlong in Greta's arms he had to brave the first flush of the morning's workers on Benedict Street and the Kingdom Road, not just midden-men and bakers but shipwrights, dockers and carriers too, and he felt guilty when they nodded and wished him the best of the day. At length, Greta and he agreed that it would be better if he confined his visits to the night hours.

Most of the folk in Benedict Street were aware that Greta Taylor had taken another lover. Some laughed at the idiot for risking his reputation and his job for the likes of her and others muttered vociferously against a woman who was low enough to give herself to a copper.

Mary Shotten told King Billy and Billy smirked and filed the information against that day when he would take revenge on the half-mad policeman and would not have to raise a fist to do it. Isa Thomas, Greta's friend, was kept informed of all the intimate details of the affair but she was as discreet a confessor as you could hope to find and told nobody, not even her husband, what Greta told her.

Benedict Street was well off Craig's beat. He feared that he would run into one of the senior constables who patrolled it and would be reported to Lieutenant Strang for being there, though horse-sense told him that he could talk himself out of it once or even twice since he had, so far, resisted the temptation to slip away from his post during duty hours. Craig thrust all unpalatable facts to the back of his mind, however, and let himself be driven by his need of her, twisting the old, stalwart forms of pride into new shapes and competing with all the other men who had had her in the past.

On that October evening, however, the weather washed away most of his doubts and apprehensions. With rain drumming on the window, the fire crackling in the grate and the child sound asleep in the room bed, Benedict Street was the place to be and Greta the person to be with. There was no need for disguise. The streets would be quiet, puddles webbed with rain, gas lamps swaying in the wind. He loved the wild wet weather and its contrast with the stuffy, cluttered interior of his home in Canada Road.

Kirsty had been complaining of a belly-ache and Mam thought she might have a chill in the stomach. Gordon had been engrossed in counting the day's take, hogging half the table, and Lorna, po-faced as usual, had been seated by Gordon's side to make note of the tally on white-paper cards. His mother had been babbling on about Adair and the wonders of the house the crook had bought for her, and Bobby, with a runny nose, had been whining because he did not like the taste of the soup that was offered him.

Supper almost untouched, Craig had left home early and headed for Banff Street and then on, directly, to Greta's house, a double black pudding supper in a paper wrapping warm in his hands. If Jen was not in bed yet he would feed her pieces of the pudding and one or two chips and then she would be put down and would fall asleep, and he would be alone with Greta. It was early in the evening to be calling but he did not think she would object. Whistling, he entered the close at No. 13 Benedict Street. It was only a quarter past seven and he was not due to report for duty for more than three hours. He was in a hurry and did not see the stranger, almost collided with him at the mouth of the close.

The man was startled too and backed away, growling an apology. Craig experienced a moment's panic at the unexpected encounter, imagining that it might be King Billy or one of his cronies, but the stranger was not of that ilk at all. With his ulster overcoat, Homburg hat and suede gloves he might have been a factor's agent or a bailiff on a call. Craig had only a glimpse of his features and no opportunity to stop the fellow and interrogate him before he was off out of the close and away down Benedict Street at a fast lick.

Greta opened the door in a flash in response to his knock. It had not been bolted. She was not, as he had half expected, dressed in a peignoir or floral dressing-gown but wore a white blouse and sober black skirt and had, for once, shoes on her feet.

"Who the hell was that?" Craig said.

"What?"

"The bloke who just went out?"

"Not out of here," Greta said. "He didn't come out of my house. You didn't see him come out of my house, did you?"

"I bumped into him in the close."

"Ah, well, you see."

Craig brought the steaming brown paper package from under his cape and handed it to her before he took off the crackling garment.

"Fishy sort of bloke," he said.

"How – fishy?"

"Posh. A toff."

"In Benedict Street?" Greta laughed. "Never."

"Ulster coat an' a Homburg."

"Be a tally-man, I expect."

"Some tally-man!"

Greta took his arm and led him into the kitchen.

"You're extra special early tonight," she said.

"Aren't you pleased to see me?"

"'Course I am. I'm always pleased t'see you."

The kitchen seemed altered somehow. It was just as clean and soapy as ever but all the garments had been removed from the pulley and the racks and folded into bundles on top of the dresser board. Craig made no comment. Jen was not in the kitchen. He took Greta in his arms. She held herself a little away from him, hugging the black pudding supper to her bosom.

"Can you stay long?" she asked.

"All evenin'."

"Good. Now take that lot off while I put this lot on a plate."

"Are we goin' to have it on the table?"

"We'll have it anywhere you like," Greta said, archly.

Oilcloth had been replaced by linen; teacups and a china pot he had not seen before. He took off his tunic jacket.

"Been entertainin', Greta?"

"Isa Thomas was down earlier."

"Best china for Isa, eh?"

"I had the set out t'wash it, so I thought I'd give us both a treat."

"Where's Jen?"

"In the room."

"Is she asleep already?"

"No. Playin', I think."

Without asking Greta's permission he stepped back into the hall and opened the door of the front room.

The little girl was dressed for bed in gown and robe, socks on her feet. She knelt over a slate on the floor. The slate was brand-new and there was by her side a box of brand-new chalks. She drew, flourishingly, on the slate with a stalk of blue chalk. Craig hunkered down by her.

"What's this you're drawin', Jen?"

"Man."

"Aye, so it is. Does he have a name?"

"Nuh."

"Does he not have a big coat on?"

"Nuh."

"Does he not have a funny hat?"

"Nuh."

She was too young to be deliberately deceiving, but perhaps the instinct was already in her.

"Where did you get these nice chalks?"

"Fr' Mammy."

"From Mammy, eh? When did she give them to you?"

"Ah'm drawin'."

Craig suddenly felt a twinge of guilt at interrogating a mere child. He had no real reason to assume that the toff had come from Greta's house, in spite of the linen table-cloth and best china. He stroked Jen's hair which was soft and fluffy as if it had been recently washed.

"Time to wash handies an' go for sleepies," Greta said from the doorway.

How long had she been there, watching and listening? She had removed her skirt and blouse, shed with them the respectability that had disconcerted him.

"Maaammmy?" Jen protested.

"Now," said Greta, firmly. "An' remember t'say your prayers."

A quarter of an hour later the child was tucked up and almost asleep in the bed in the room and Craig, with tunic and boots removed, was seated at the table munching his share of the black pudding supper. As he ate he watched Greta as she moved about the kitchen. The undergarments clung to her body and she was not ashamed of what he could see, of what she showed him.

His voice thickening, he said, "How is it you never ask me for money?"

"I don't take money from men."

"I don't mean like that. I mean for your – your needs."

"I make enough."

"I can't see how what you take at the Irish Market pays your bills."

"Well, it does," she said. "Anyway, I sometimes sell to the shops too, when I get good enough stuff."

"I didn't know that."

"There's a lot you don't know."

"I'll bet there is," Craig said.

He finished the last of the chips and wiped his hands on the towel she gave him and lit two cigarettes, passed one to Greta. He liked to see her smoke with no refinements and an appetite for tobacco that seemed to bring her closer to him. She stood with her back to the fire. It was almost as he had visualised it, rain on the windows, coals crackling, Jen asleep.

"There's a lot about you that I don't know," Greta said.

"I'm just as you see me," Craig said.

"I doubt it."

"Because I'm a copper?"

"Because you've a wife at home."

At the mention of Kirsty he felt a wave of anger within him. Kirsty had no place in this kitchen, in this street. He had assumed that Greta would understand how he felt about that and was annoyed at her tactlessness. He swung round in the chair, was astonished to see that she was no longer behind him, that she was in bed. The curtain draped the recess and the light from the gas mantle illuminated her legs and belly.

She had slipped out of her undergarment and retained only her bodice which was partly unlaced. She supported herself on one elbow, allowing him a view of her body and a glimpse of her face. Her hair cascaded darkly about her shoulders and one breast was exposed, dark-nippled and heavy. She was not at all like Kirsty but her arrogance and coarseness stirred him as he had never been stirred by Kirsty's gentle compliance. He was not obliged to pretend that he loved Greta or to disguise the fact that he wanted her only for pleasure.

"How long do you have left?" she asked.

"Full two hours."

"Don't waste a minute then," Greta said.

Craig moved towards the bed, thinking of nothing except what they would do to each other and together before duty called him away.

*   *   *

The onset of bleeding was sudden, sudden and shocking. She was alone with Bobby in the kitchen when it began. Bobby had been fractious all evening, would not settle. She had struggled with him for fifteen minutes, lifting him back over the bar of the cot three or four times. Finally she smacked his legs to teach him that he could not always have his own way, that he must do as he was told and lie down.

Lorna had lost patience with her nephew and had slipped off into the front parlour to complete the arithmetic with which Gordon had entrusted her. Gordon, in haste, had departed soon after Craig and Madge, in turn, had dolled herself up and gone out to meet Breezy for dinner and a discussion of wedding arrangements.

It did not seem to Kirsty that she had strained herself in her struggles with her son. All day long she had nursed a slight backache, a weight in the loins. She had come around to believing that Madge's diagnosis was right, that she had caught a chill. She promised herself that if she did not feel better by tomorrow she would call upon Dr Godwin, just to be on the safe side. And then it was too late.

Flooding, cramping pains beset her and there was nothing that Dr Godwin or anyone could do to save the infant that had been forming within her these past thirteen weeks and that was, in as many minutes, lost.

She soon realised what was occurring but even in her panic there was shame. She wanted to protect Bobby and Lorna from the display of pain and from the mess of it all. She staggered back from the cot, clutching her stomach, thumbs pressed into her groin. Sensing that something odd was happening, Bobby stopped sobbing. He stood upright in the cot and, with elbows on the bar, stared at his mother with an implacable hostility as if this was a new ruse to trick him into sleep.

Fierce contractions doubled Kirsty up. She gasped and braced herself against the table. The pains were not kneading now, pulsing, but had become violent and constant. Both fists buried in her lap she hobbled to the door and pushed into the hallway.

"Lorna," she cried, "look after Bobby."

She unlatched the outside door and picked her way down the stairs.

The odour of rain filled the stone close, all earthy, like the stench of the byre at Hawkhead. A damp aura hung about the gas lamp. She crouched down and crabbed along the wall and on to the half-landing.

"Kirsty, what's wrong?" Lorna called.

"*Go – back – inside.*"

She was anxious still to protect Lorna against the reality of womanhood, the awful casualness of nature. It was in her mind that she might be able to rouse Jess Walker who would know what to do for the best, but it was happening too fast now. She was losing it there on the public stair. She slumped against the locked door of the lavatory.

"*Lorna?*"

She closed her eyes. She prayed that one of the Piper boys would not come whistling up the stairs and find her in this state. She could not bear to be looked on by a man, a young man. Lorna touched her.

"Oh, God, Kirsty! What ails you? Will I run for Dr Godwin?"

"No, bring – bring the key."

She tried to suck in a series of deep breaths as if this was true labour. Hopeless.

She heard a door open in the close below, footsteps on the stone stairs, a voice: "Is that you, Mrs Nicholson? Is everythin' all right?"

Lorna returned.

"Who – who is it?" Kirsty gasped.

"It's Mrs Swanston. Will I tell her you're – "

"Just – just open the door."

Kirsty staggered into the dark, dank closet. She collapsed against the door and closed it with her shoulder.

Faint now, she wrestled with her skirts. She was oblivious to the squabble of voices on the half-landing as pain sprang abruptly away from her body and, shivering, she cowered against the pedestal until expulsion was complete.

*   *   *

Neighbours took care of her. Calum Piper was sent to fetch Dr Godwin from his house in Dowanhill. Bert Swanston went round to Ottawa Street and left word with the sergeant that Craig should be notified. Meanwhile Kirsty was tucked up in bed and given a snifter of whisky from a bottle that Jess Walker scrounged off her husband. Distressed by the tears and the hubbub, Bobby wailed and was taken into the front parlour by Lorna and soothed, and soon fell asleep in his auntie's arms. In due course Dr Godwin arrived. He gave no sign that he was annoyed at having been dragged away from his dinner but examined Kirsty thoroughly and intimately. He told her that she had been fortunate that the abortion had been 'natural', that as far as he could discern no portion of the placenta had been retained. He was concerned that sepsis might set in and treated her accordingly to avoid it. He left a sleeping-draught in a brown bottle and promised to return the following forenoon. Jess Walker stirred the sedative into a glass and gave it to Kirsty as soon as the doctor left. Kirsty did not resist. She craved sleep, longed for oblivion, felt too drained to suffer sorrow over her lost infant. That would come soon enough.

Lamp dimmed, curtain drawn, Jess Walker stationed in a chair near the bed, Kirsty let herself sink into sleep. She was aware that she would have to waken eventually, to face guilt and a sense of failure – and Craig.

*   *   *

The house was silent, save for water dribbling in a pipe and a gout of ash dropping into the grate. Kirsty wakened with a start and sat up. It did not hurt at all.

Surprisingly she felt quite well, though she was cold. She put her hand to the pad that Dr Godwin had applied and found that it was dry. Indeed, she felt very dry all over, arid and parched. The aftertaste of the sedative was bitter on the back of her tongue.

She touched the curtain, parted it a little. She could see nobody in the kitchen. She felt relieved. She needed a drink. She moved her hips, raised her knees and lifted back the blankets.

"So you're awake, are you?" Madge said.

Her mother-in-law had been hidden by the high back of the fireside chair. She was dressed in the fleecy robe that Craig had bought for her. Her hair was fluffed out and angry and her voice grating.

Kirsty stretched bare feet towards the floor.

Madge loomed. "What do you want? Do you need the pot?"

"No."

"Are you goin' to be sick?"

"No. I'm thirsty."

Madge remained planted by the side of the bed.

"He's disappointed in you," she said. "He's very hurt."

"Where is he?"

"He came when he was sent for," Madge said. "Don't think he didn't."

"Where is he?" said Kirsty again.

"He says he felt like a right bloody fool, since you hadn't seen fit to tell him."

"Has he gone back to work?"

"What could a man do here, except get under my feet?"

"I thought he might have – "

"We're all disappointed in you," Madge said.

Kirsty eased forward. She was stiff, tense in her muscles. She lifted herself to her feet gingerly, swaying and light in the head.

"Why didn't you tell him?" Madge said.

Only that afternoon she had been with Madge in the great empty mansion. It seemed like weeks ago, months ago. She had been carrying her baby then. Now she was not.

She wanted somebody to hold her.

She did not want to be blamed. She had been punished, had she not? She felt a strange melancholy, like resignation. But she did not want *them*, not even Craig, to know of it. She tried to stand up but her legs betrayed her. She fell back into a sitting position on the bed.

"Is it a drink you're after?" Madge said.

"Yes."

"Do you want tea?"

"Just water."

"Sit where you are."

"I can get it myself."

"You always were an independent bitch – when it suited you."

Independent – she had never been that. She needed something that Madge would not comprehend, something that did not exist among the Nicholsons. She would have loved her wee baby, the wee baby that God had denied her.

"There'll be time enough for tears, m'lady, when Craig gets

back." Madge held the cup of water out to her. "I hear old Godwin says you'll soon recover."

"Yes."

She took the cup and drank, drank it all, held the cup out for more.

"Have you any idea what time it is?" said Madge.

"No."

"It's a quarter short of four."

"In the afternoon?"

"In the mornin'."

"Is it still raining?"

"What?"

"I just wondered," Kirsty said.

"Why didn't you tell us? Why didn't you at least tell me?"

"I wanted to be sure."

"For God's sake, girl, you were three months gone. Was it not his?"

At first Kirsty did not understand.

"Was Craig not the father?" Madge said.

"It was mine, my baby."

"Aye, but who spawned it?"

"Craig."

"In that case why did you keep it a secret?"

"It was Craig's baby."

"How can we be sure of that now?"

The empty cup in her hand looked tiny, like a thimble. Her body had absorbed the water like sand. She was less confused now, her mind clearing. Sorrow was round and smooth inside her head, and rang with the woman's accusations like a glass rubbed with a moist finger.

"I've never lain wi' anybody else," Kirsty said.

"Why didn't you tell him?"

"I — I didn't want to bother him."

"Bother him? Bother your husband?"

"Could I have some more water, please?"

"How old, exactly, was it?"

"Since the end of June."

"An' definitely Craig's doin'?" said Madge.

"Yes," Kirsty said. "Yes."

"Do you want tea this time?"

"Just water."

Madge refilled the cup from the tap at the sink and brought it back to the bed. She swung Kirsty's legs under the blankets and made her lie down against the pillows.

Propped awkwardly, Kirsty supped water from the cup in Madge's hands. She could not meet the woman's eye, bowed her head meekly.

"I'm sorry," Kirsty said. "I'm so, so sorry."

"Aye, an' so you should be," Madge Nicholson said.

*   *   *

Through a narrow gap in the curtain Kirsty watched the Nicholsons come and go about the breakfast table. The only thing that made it different from other mornings was that she was not part of it.

She could see Craig's narrow back, braces dangling, shirt-sleeves rolled up, elbows twitching as he worked his knife and fork. Madge's fleecy pink robe blotted him out. Smoke wisped from the frying-pan in her hand as she tilted it to slide another rasher of bacon, another fried egg on to her son's plate.

Gordon had shaved already, slicked down his hair, fastened his collar and put a tiny nut-shaped knot in his bow tie. Gordon was ready for the day. Through slitted eyes Kirsty studied Gordon as he in turn watched Craig, warily.

Bobby must still be asleep. She felt no immediate longing to have her son near to her. His energy was too demanding for her to cope with just yet. She was still dry, still weak. She felt flat, compressed into herself by the disgrace of it, by failure and melancholy guilt.

The Nicholsons spoke in murmurous undertones.

She listened, listlessly.

"You mustn't blame yourself, son," Madge was saying. "There was nothin' you could do for her. I doubt if she even knew you weren't there. Anyway, you had your job to do."

"She should have told us," Craig said.

"Oh God, aye, she should have."

"Perhaps she wasn't sure," said Gordon.

"What do *you* know about such matters?" said Madge.

"Not much," Gordon admitted.

"The doctor says she was thirteen weeks – " Lorna began.

"We can all bloody count," Craig interrupted.

"I'm just thankful it didn't happen later," said Madge.

"The later it happens," said Gordon, "the more dangerous it is for the mother, I suppose."

"I meant nearer to the weddin'," said Madge.

"I'd forgotten about the weddin'," said Gordon.

"How could you, Gordon?" said Lorna with, Kirsty thought, more than a trace of sarcasm.

Craig said, "She'll get over it."

Madge said, "Aye, she's strong if she's nothin' else."

Craig said, "Godwin's comin' this mornin'. I'll speak to him."

"No, I'll speak to him," said Madge.

Gordon said, "What if the doctor finds – what's it called – complications?"

Craig said, "I'd better wait up."

"You'll do no such thing, son," said Madge. "I'm not havin' you sacrificin' your health."

"I could stay home today," Gordon said.

"Don't be bloody stupid," Craig told him. "It's none o' your business. It's a woman's thing. Leave it to Mam."

"What if she needs an operation?" said Lorna.

"She won't," said Madge.

"What if she does, but? It'll cost a – " said Lorna.

Gordon said, "I've got some spare cash put aside."

Craig said, "I thought I told you to keep out of it."

"What if she can't have any more?" said Lorna.

"More what?" Craig said.

"Children," Gordon said.

Kirsty hardly dared breathe. Until that moment she had thought only of the child that was gone from her, not of the children who might never be conceived.

"Don't be daft," said Craig.

"It can happen, though, can't it?" said Gordon.

"Aye, but it won't happen wi' her."

"How do you know, Craig?" said Lorna.

"Ask Mam, if you don't believe me."

Madge said, "Aye, it *can* happen – in some cases."

"See," said Lorna.

"But she's young an' strong," said Madge. "The doctor would've told us last night if she'd been damaged."

"How would you feel about it, Craig?" said Gordon.

"About what?"

"Only havin' one?"

"One what?"

"Baby," said Lorna.

"It'd be no skin off my nose," Craig said.

Gordon rose abruptly from his chair.

"Time I was out of here," he said.

"Can you not be quiet," said Madge. "You'll wake her."

"Perhaps she's awake already," said Lorna. "I'll have a look."

"Get away from that bed, girl," Madge snapped.

"What if she wants somethin'?"

"She can ask for it."

"Jesus!" said Gordon.

"I thought you were leavin'," Craig said.

"I am. I am."

Gordon vanished from her view. She heard the door close then saw Craig turn and glance at the bed, the smoke of his cigarette billowing about his face. She waited, tensely, for him to come to her.

"She seems all right," Craig said.

"Leave her," Madge said. "Get away to your bed, son. You need a good long sleep. It's been a sore trial for you more than anyone."

"Aye," Craig said. "Aye, it has."

Kirsty closed her eyes tightly. Doors opened, doors closed.

Madge parted the curtain and stared down at her.

"Oh, so you are awake, are you?"

"Yes."

"Do you want somethin'?"

She wanted Craig's forgiveness, or so she thought, but she would not beg for it. She touched her tongue to her lips, dry lips, dry mouth. She longed for a drink of cold, cold water. She would ask for nothing, though, deserved nothing.

"Well?"

"I'm fine," Kirsty said.

*　　　*　　　*

It was six days before she dared leave the house alone. In that time Craig spoke to her hardly at all. He did not once mention the lost child or discuss Dr Godwin's verdict. He offered no recrimination, no consolation. He seemed afraid to be left alone with her, however, to come near to her, as if she carried still some subtle contagion. Madge remained aloof and brusque. Only Gordon offered anything like sympathy. If her depression had not been so deep and arid she might have clung to Gordon and given him her tears. But Gordon too was a Nicholson.

Dr Godwin could not explain the reason for the miscarriage. He examined her on two more occasions, found no trace of infection, no tumour or pelvic defect. He told her, in a serious tone, that one out of every five pregnancies ended in abortion, that nature did not always play fair.

Kirsty cried a little. Dr Godwin patted her hand.

"Will I – can I have more children?"

"Ah, so that's it. Yes, of course you can."

"Will I lose them too?"

"Not if you're careful."

He left a tiny jar of blue pills and told her to call round to his consulting-room in Banff Street in a week or ten days' time.

She told Madge and Madge told Craig. Craig seemed to absorb the information without being in the least affected by it. At least there was no rage in him; for that she had to be thankful. But as the days passed she found herself resenting his apparent indifference and feeding on that resentment to make herself strong again.

Kirsty wakened Craig early, about half past one in the afternoon. She had prepared a hot meal, beef and potatoes, for he liked a second breakfast to be served as soon as he got up. Lorna was at college, Gordon out on his rounds and Madge had rushed off to tour a furniture warehouse with Breezy. Bobby played on the carpet before the hearth. He had been reserved and well behaved all week. He sensed that something was amiss in the routine that governed his welfare and he did not clamour for attention and was watchful and cautious.

Kirsty waited until Craig had finished eating and was stretched in the armchair by the fire, smoking. He did not speak, did not allow his glance to fall upon her. He watched Bobby as the child played with a box of wooden bricks that Gordon had brought in for him.

Kirsty said, "I'm goin' out."

"Did Godwin say you could?"

"I'm leavin' Bobby here."

"For how long?"

"An hour or two, that's all."

"Are you goin' to the doctor's?"

"To church."

"On Thursday?"

"I'm goin' to prayers."

He stirred, flicked the cigarette into the hearth and sat forward, forearms on his knees.

He said, "Bit bloody late for prayers."

"Will you look after him?"

Bobby stared up at his father, offered him a red wooden brick. Craig did not take it. He remained slumped forward in the chair like an old man.

"All right," he said.

Kirsty nodded curtly and went into the front room to dress.

*   *   *

Peggie answered the doorbell.

"Why, Mrs Nicholson, this is a surprise. She'll be very pleased to see you, I'm sure."

"Is David at home? Mr Lockhart, I mean?"

"He's down at the kirk."

"Oh, is he at a meetin'?"

"Not as I know of," Peggie said. "Will you be comin' in to wait for him?"

"I think," said Kirsty, "I'll walk down to the church."

Peggie said, "You'll not be wantin' me to tell Mrs Frew that you've been an' gone?"

"I think not," Kirsty said.

"Best," said Peggie. "She's not quite herself today. She's sleepin' in her chair."

"Is she sick again?"

"No, just a bit out o' sorts," said Peggie. "Best to say nothin'. Call again when you can."

Melancholy had sharpened her perceptions. She knew that Nessie might not live much longer, that the long cold winter might see her away. She felt a slight pang of disloyalty at not going into No. 19 to offer comfort to her old friend but she had need of comfort herself. She turned away from the house and headed at once for St Anne's.

Brown leaves were plastered to the pavement and, though the sky remained cloudy, rain had blown away on a stiff, almost wintry wind from the river. She pinched up the collar of her coat and walked nervously to the church.

David might not be alone. It was more than likely that he would be with Harry Graham or one of the elders or women from the Flowers & Fabric committee. She tried to pretend to herself that she was just an ordinary parishioner in need of a minister's counsel, but it was not so. She did not want answers from Mr Graham or Mr Augustus. She wanted to see and speak with David and with no one else.

The church's main gate was padlocked, the big wooden door closed. A light showed in a side room, however, and the dainty wrought-iron gate that led up the side of the building was unlatched. She was very nervous now and her fingers trembled as she opened the green-painted side door and stepped into the stone-floored corridor within. The vestry entrance to the church was propped open with a chair and the heavy velvet curtain that muffled sounds from the corridor was tied back with its thick soft velvet cord. She peeped inside and, to her chagrin, saw three men there in the church.

The kirk officer, Mr Yuille, looked unfamiliar in a stained brown dustcoat and cloth cap. The others were strangers; a tall middle-aged chap in rusty tweeds, and a youth in corduroys and dirty roll-necked jersey. All three were standing at the back of the organ pit. Mr Yuille held up a lighted lantern. Lengths of varnished timber and two heavy wooden panels were laid against the organist's bench together with three startlingly new bronze pipes. An array of carpenter's tools spilled from a canvas bag that was open on the floor.

"Kirsty?"

She turned and peered into the gloom of the corridor.

He wore his grey suit and dog-collar, a pencil stuck incongruously behind his ear. He came towards her.

"Kirsty, what on earth are you doing here? Is something the matter?"

"Yes."

"Is it Aunt Nessie?"

"I lost my baby."

She began, at once, to cry.

David folded her into his arms. She crumpled against him.

"Kirsty, Kirsty." He held her tightly while she wept. "Poor lamb, poor lamb."

A discreet cough from the direction of the church door: "Is there somethin' the matter, Mr Lockhart?"

"Mrs Nicholson's a little distressed, Mr Yuille, and in need of my help," David said, without letting Kirsty go. "If you can proceed no further without the plans I suggest you take the men into the kitchen and make tea for them."

"Aye, Mr Lockhart."

"Come on, Kirsty," David said. "Come into the vestry where it's warm."

He kept one arm about her and guided her along the corridor and into the end room, square, wood-floored, dominated by a massive table. A gas fire purred and there was a friendly aroma of pipe-smoke in the air. Sheaves of plans and elevations were spread out upon the table. David closed the door with his heel. Kirsty was still crying. She hugged him as if she was afraid that he too might leave her to founder in incommunicable misery.

"All right, Kirsty. It's all right now."

She choked, gasped for breath.

David pressed his palm against her midriff. "Breathe. Deep breath," he told her. "I'm here now. Breathe."

It was as if some taut membrane within her had torn of its own accord, some remnant of the birth that had never been. She gasped, sobbed, and let the tears flow and, gradually, felt the aridity go out of her, that terrible dryness.

"No – one. No – nobody – "

"Yes, Kirsty. Yes, I understand."

"Why? Why was it?"

"It wasn't punishment," David told her. "You mustn't assume that you were being punished."

"How can I help it? It *was* because of us, wasn't it?"

"No, Kirsty. No, no."

He helped her to a chair, the seat padded in cracked blue leather. He drew it closer to the gas fire and knelt by her side, one hand on her knee, the other brushing away the tears from her cheeks gently and tenderly.

"When did it happen?"

"Last Thursday, in the evenin'. It was so quick. I'd no time to do anythin'," she said. "No time. It was all over an' done with in minutes."

"Did you lose much blood?"

"Yes, but it stopped soon – soon after."

"No residual bleeding now?"

"No."

"You consulted Dr Godwin, I suppose?"

"He came at once. He's been twice since."

"You're all right now, aren't you? Physically, I mean?"

"I want to know why," she said.

David sat back, resting his weight on his heels. He still had the pencil behind his ear.

He said, "What did Godwin tell you?"

"He said there was no reason, no reason at all."

"That's not the sort of answer you want, is it, Kirsty?"

"No," she said. "Tell me the truth, David."

He removed his hand from her knee and rubbed the tip of his nose with his knuckle, heaved a huge sigh.

"Didn't Craig – "

"I didn't tell Craig," Kirsty said.

"You didn't tell him that you were pregnant?"

"I intended to but – "

"He should have been told, Kirsty."

"I wanted to pretend that it was ours."

"Ah!"

"An' I think that's why it was – "

"God didn't take the baby away," David said. "There was no transgression, nothing to punish."

"I did want it, you know."

"Is Craig angry with you?"

"He says nothin'."

"Is it forgiveness you want, Kirsty?"

"I don't know what I want. Can't you tell me?"

"There's nothing to forgive," David said.

"But it died inside me."

"Kirsty, I can't tell you why it happened."

"Because of us."

"Stop it, please."

"It won't be stopped. It won't go away."

He rose suddenly and stepped back from her. She looked up at him, imagined that he was trying to distance himself from her pain and her bewilderment, from dread. But she had already drawn him into her hurt and could not release him from it. He took a handkerchief from his pocket and blew his nose.

"I didn't mean to upset you," Kirsty said.

David tried to force a smile. "Bit undignified, isn't it?"

"You care, don't you?"

"You know I do."

He pulled himself together and, seated on the edge of the table, took her hand.

He said, "I should be able to offer an appropriate piece of Scripture, but I think you want more than that."

Kirsty said, "I can't imagine what He looks like. I can't hear His voice and when I see His face it's just like old St Andrew in Aunt Nessie's screen. It's not real to me, not even very interestin'."

"He's all around us," said David. "And within us."

"Was He in my baby?"

"I don't know, Kirsty. I'm sorry."

The deep bass note of the organ in the church made her start. Bass was followed by treble, shrill and out of pitch, phantom sounds though not mysterious. At that moment too Mr Yuille knocked upon the vestry door and enquired if the minister and Mrs Nicholson would like some tea.

David pulled open the door. He did it, Kirsty thought, to appease the elder's curiosity and to assure the officer that no impropriety was being committed.

"Kirsty, do you wish tea?"

"No, thank you." Ashamed of her tear-stained state, Kirsty got to her feet. "I should be gettin' back home."

Mr Yuille said, "I – er – I trust it wasn't bad news brought you here, Mrs Nicholson."

"It was a personal matter, Mr Yuille," David told the man and then, with the officer watching, led Kirsty along the corridor to the painted door and out into the side lane.

"You're not going to call on Aunt Nessie, are you?"

"No, not today," Kirsty answered.

"I don't think we should say anything of this to her, do you?" David said. "It would distress her terribly."

"I won't say a word."

"How do you feel now?"

"Better."

"Are you sure?"

"I'm sure."

He kissed her on the mouth then turned and hurried back into the church.

Kirsty stood for a moment on the path, looking after him, and then she walked to the gate and through it on to the pavement by the gable of St Anne's.

Sunlight tinged the cloud, indirect and insubstantial but sufficient to edge the stonework and solidify the pennant of brown smoke that fluttered at the china-factory's chimney. She took a hesitant step away from the gable's protection and felt the wind tug at her hat and the skirts of her coat. From within the church she heard the boom of the bass and its answering treble, in harmony at last. She turned towards Dumbarton Road to buy a loaf and some herring for her husband's evening meal.

David had provided no answer or explanation yet she felt relieved of the burden of her solitary suffering, as if the touch of his hands and his lips had been enough, and all the rest of it would be pared away in due course of time.

─── *December* ───

If any of the lesser members of the great trading clan of Adair
had reservations about Breezy's marriage they made certain that
Breezy did not hear of them nor did they discuss the wisdom
of the chieftain's choice with outsiders. Like all close Scottish
families the Adairs knew when to present a united front to the
world, when to confine scepticism and speculation to private
conversations among themselves.

Some in-laws and hoity-toity nieces, and a couple of the nephews,
considered Mrs Nicholson to be decidedly *déclassée* but none of
them was hypocritical enough to condemn her as an opportunist
since they had all been raised in the worship of Mammon and
trained to regard marriage as a perfectly valid means of attaining
the high moneyed state to which they all aspired.

Sister Polly and brother Donnie, a broker in the Glasgow
Exchange, were relieved that Breezy had taken a mature and sensible woman to wife. They had feared that he might have a fit of
middle-age and trip off with one of his young doxies and find himself at the altar before he knew it, might breed away lumps of the
inheritance that had been earmarked to provide security for their
children later in life by having a platoon of children of his own.

Sister Polly and brother Donnie were close to Breezy and
always had been. Donnie had done a fair reckoning of the cost
of the whole marriage shoot and knew for an absolute fact that
Breezy had sold off several blocks of income shares to meet it and
to purchase the ridiculous mansion and lavish on his lady-love
credit lines for all the best warehouses in the city, and not just
those in which the Adairs had stakes. The house, one supposed,
was always a cash asset; but the cost of the wedding celebrations
had come to seem mad, particularly to Donnie who lacked his
brother's fun-loving, extravagant streak. Even Polly, however,
was forced to agree that Breezy had gone a bit over the score and
decided to have a quiet word with him about it, while making
it crystal-clear that she did not blame Madge Nicholson in the
slightest for the spending spree.

Breezy was not put out by Polly's solicitude. He just laughed and treated her as if she was twelve years old again and helping him fasten his cardboard collar before he went on the streets to peddle steel engravings of the Sacred Heart and the Shepherd's Collie. He understood her concern over the welfare of the top end of the family fortune but did not relent or promise to draw in his horns.

"Once in a lifetime, Polly, once in a lifetime. Anyway, as you well know, I'm not short of a bob or two. Look what I'm gettin' for my money: not just a wonderful wife but a stepson who's smart enough to be my own flesh-and-blood and a pretty young stepdaughter who will blossom into a fine young lady when a few sovereigns are sprinkled on her head."

"Donnie tells me you've been selling shares."

"Pieces of paper, that's all."

"Banknotes are also pieces of paper."

"I'll buy more shares in a month or two," Breezy had said. "The money rolls in, the money rolls in."

"I hope you'll remember to stop."

"Stop? Why should I stop?"

"Albert, this isn't like you at all."

"Come now, Polly, I've never been mean."

"No, that's true, but – "

"It gives Madge pleasure and, to tell the truth, I haven't had so much fun in years."

"But to saddle yourself with that mammoth house? Donnie wonders why you didn't just refurbish your rooms in Curzon Street."

"Because my rooms in Curzon Street reek of years of loneliness."

"Oh, come, Albert, you've never lacked for company."

"Gregariousness, Polly, is not love."

"I see. All this spending is a symptom of love, is it?"

"Of course it is. What else would it be? Senility?"

"Donnie requires to be reassured."

"Reassure him, then. Tell Donnie to come along and drink at my wedding and let brother Breezy worry about payin' the bills, as usual."

"You're not worried about paying the bills, are you?"

"Hell, no, Pol. I'm not worried about anything."

Among the younger Adairs were a pair who had been trusted

with many of Uncle Breezy's darker secrets; they *were* concerned for the old boy's mental stability. Being young and hot-blooded they could not imagine what Uncle Breezy saw in the farmer's widow or why he would choose monogamy in preference to the free and easy existence of a man about town. If Breezy had plumped for some elegant young damsel from the upper bracket they would have nodded sagely and considered it, at his age, a wise move. But to give up his freedom and the goodwill of four or five hand-picked young beauties for a specimen of old rustic charm was, to John Whiteside and Eric Adair, an act of sheer folly.

Breezy had always been fond of the ladies. He was not ashamed to associate with girls who were not of his 'class', a word he abhorred. He was not daft enough to flaunt his street girls openly, though. He wined them and dined them and brought them to roost in small hotels that catered for such discreet associations. No money would change hands on such evenings of pleasure, a touch that relieved the girls of the feeling that they were being paid to be nice to Breezy and that erased from the man's mind the doubt that he could only get it if he paid for it.

Young though they were Johnnie and Eric had run Breezy's line of communication with the girls for three or four years. They saw to it that special favourites did not go short of bread and milk, received, in effect, a little pension in memory of days and nights gone by. It was typical of generous old Uncle Breezy to spend his money in that way, and it meant that now and again he could find a partner for a business associate if a little cream was needed to clinch a lucrative deal.

It did not occur to Breezy that he had betrayed his sister Heather, John's mother, or his brother Donnie by drawing his nephews down into vice. He was not fey, of course. He knew that the boys would make hay here and there since they were both Adairs and sensual as well as sensible. But slap-and-tickle had done him more good than harm, he reckoned, and he saw no reason why it should not be the same for his nephews.

It was accepted that, in due course, Johnnie and Eric would take over the running of the warehouse and some of the street businesses. What role Breezy would find for Gordon remained to be seen. In the meantime he would put Gordon out to the best training possible for a smart young man, let him start at the bottom, earn his commissions and his advancements. Naturally

Gordon was not to be told of past indiscretions even though Breezy's days of roving were well and truly over now.

John Whiteside was twenty-six years old, Eric Adair a few months younger. They had been bosom chums since childhood, allies at the Academy and, these last seven years, mutual partners in managing Uncle Breezy's shady ventures. They had chosen to ignore their parents' pleas that they educate themselves with degrees and diplomas and had marched united into the carpet hall to learn, eagerly, all that they could about making money.

They were not openly hostile to the interloper, to Gordon Nicholson. They quickly realised that Gordon was here to stay. Having shrewdly assessed his character and intelligence they conferred and agreed that he was much like themselves. They were not, however, prepared to take him at once into their charmed circle, to make an outright friend of him. Gordon, in turn, was not unaware that he had to prove himself to Johnnie and Eric as well as to Breezy Adair. He was relieved that they did not try to thwart his energetic schemes. They too were energetic, if less obviously so, and were concerned only with turning profit for the firm by any means that could be vaguely classed as legal.

It was to obtain an edge on Johnnie and Eric that Gordon agreed to move from Canada Road and live with his mother and stepfather in the grand mansion on Great Western Terrace. He would, if the truth had been known, have preferred to stay put, close to Kirsty, but he could not ignore the convenience of living on the Terrace or the trappings of privilege that would be his to share. It did not take Gordon long to persuade Lorna to join him.

"It'll be all right, Gordon, won't it?"

"Of course it will. Hell, Lorna, I don't know why we should be so shy about movin' into a palace complete with servants, carriages an' electrical lights."

"I'll miss Kirsty. Bobby too."

"You can call on them any time, any day."

"I thought yon house was spooky."

"It's not spooky. It's just large. Once Mam's got it furnished it'll seem like home in no time. We'll both wonder how we ever managed in poky wee places. Is it Breezy you don't like?"

"No. He's all right, I suppose."

"What is it, then?"

"I dunno. I just don't feel right about it."

"But you will give it a try?"

"I suppose so."

By mid-November it had been settled. Gordon and Lorna had been allocated rooms in the house on the Terrace, rooms that Madge promised to see furnished in the grandest manner possible.

As the month progressed Madge spent less and less time at Canada Road, to everybody's relief. Kirsty too was finding the woman's conceit wearing, for Madge had escalated her opinion of herself to that of Lady, with a capital letter. She had been seduced by the trappings, by the deference shown to her by shop hands and warehouse assistants, and persuaded herself that she had acquired style along with money.

"I hope she remembers who she really is when this damned wedding's over," Gordon had said to Kirsty.

"Breezy will bring her back to earth, I'm sure," Kirsty had said to Gordon. "He'll clip her wings."

"Or take to the bottle," Gordon had said grimly.

Since Kirsty remained much out of favour with Madge, who still seemed to blame her for the miscarriage, it was poor Lorna who had become her mother's confidante and companion. She had no say in the matter, being just a daughter. She was dragged round stores and fashion salons every evening after she finished her stint at college and was expected to throw herself into fits of rapture as, item by item, Madge arrayed herself 'like Solomon' for her day of glory.

The novelty of dressing-up had no appeal for Lorna. She considered herself far too plain to be redeemed by wearing frills, ribbons and floral ornaments. But she did her duty as best she could until sister Polly, sensing disaster, stepped into the scene. Polly whisked Madge off to dressmakers and milliners of her, Polly's, acquaintance and made sure that the bride would not make a fool of herself by appearing at the altar or the wedding reception done up like a dish of fish. Craig was the only fly in the ointment of Madge's happiness. He refused to commit himself to being at her side on the walk down the aisle of St Martin's Old Parish Church. He grumbled that he might not be able to obtain a release from his duties; a nonsense, of course. On the surface he did not appear to nurse anger now but evinced an indifference to the flow of Madge's affairs that was even more hurtful. Gordon tried to bring Craig round, and failed.

Lorna fared no better and all Madge's pleading and ranting was to no avail.

Driven by desperation Madge showed Kirsty a flag of truce and asked her once more to use her powers of persuasion on Craig.

"Don't worry, he'll be there," Kirsty had said.

"No, he won't. He'll shame me by not turnin' up."

"He won't miss your weddin'."

"He's capable of anythin', that one."

"He'll want to swank down the aisle in his uniform."

"His uniform?" Madge had said.

"He can apply for permission to wear it, you know."

"Who told you that?"

"Mrs Walker."

"He'd look real smart in his uniform," Madge had said. "But I'm not too sure that Albert would like it."

"I'll tell Craig that."

"What? Why – "

"You'll see," Kirsty had said. "He'll be there."

But it was not just the opportunity to flaunt his policeman's uniform that brought Craig round. Breezy Adair had a hand in it too.

Distressed by Madge's sorrow at her eldest's behaviour, Breezy placed a discreet telephone call to Sergeant Byrne at Percy Street, found out how the land lay and requested a wee tiny bit of unofficial pressure. Sergeant Byrne spoke with Sergeant Drummond and Sergeant Drummond in turn had a paternal word with Constable Nicholson who was made to understand that duty was not just something a police officer did at the station but that it was part of his life all round.

At supper, that evening, Madge tackled her son once more.

"Have you made up your mind yet?" Madge said. "If you won't give me away then I'll need to find somebody who – "

"I'll do it."

Everybody stopped eating and stared at Craig.

He flushed slightly. "I'll be there. I'll be bloody there."

"At the church?"

"Aye."

"To give me away?"

"Aye."

"In your uniform?"

"Aye. Are you happy now, Mother?"

"I'm so happy, Craig. So happy I could cry."

"Hallelujah," Lorna said, and went back to eating her fish.

* * *

Breezy threw his bachelor party two nights before the wedding day. Craig and Gordon were both invited but, to nobody's surprise, only Gordon turned up.

The China Clipper was an expensive but rowdy eating-house in Glasgow's West Nile Street. The supper-room was beamed like a fo'c'sle. Tarry ropes, marlin spikes, brass bells and swags of sailcloth abounded and after two or three tots of the house speciality, hot Banana rum, you could easily imagine that you were pitching about on the Yellow Sea and that the room and not your head was doing the swimming.

Fish soups, steaming plates of cod dressed with *sauce de la matelote*, dark and bloody venison and bowls of curried veal soon soaked up the first flush of alcohol. Before the wines could take effect Breezy seized the opportunity to wish all his friends a fond farewell and Johnnie Whiteside delivered a long bawdy speech, which would have been bawdier still if the bride's son hadn't been present; then there was a general scramble for bottles and decanters to see who could get conked the fastest.

Gordon was surprised at the diversity of the gathering. There were a hundred men and more in the long low room, all of them friends of the groom; such a cross-section of society that it might have been assembled for a panoramic portrait of Democracy. There were fine gentlemen from the Exchange, though not brother Donnie, fat publicans, brewers with queer accents, salesmen and accountants, wine merchants, and a number of small shifty men in patched jackets who fell on the food like wolves and seemed impervious to the effects of massive quantities of strong drink. Gordon was introduced to assorted cousins and nephews and spoke with other men who somehow contrived not to give their names away. He began to understand why Craig had ducked the party, for the presence of a copper would not have been welcome to the street people, though it was churlishness and not diplomacy that had kept Craig away.

Gordon enjoyed himself but he remained a little guarded and did not imbibe freely of the wines and spirits that flowed like water and, on the whole, kept the best of his wits about him which, as it happened, was just as well.

Some time after two o'clock he found himself in a hansom with Johnnie and Eric. Apparently they had been instructed by Breezy to see him safe home. Johnnie and Eric were also comparatively sober for they had learned that there were times and places to let yourself go and times and places where you did not. Besides, they had no intention of letting the evening be spoiled by falling down drunk. They had other plans and knew exactly where to find a certain kind of adventure even at that late hour of the night.

Gordon rocked in a corner of the cab, lulled by the clack of the horse's hoofs and the rumble of the vehicle's wheels on the uneven cobbles. He was thinking of his mam, how she would quit the Greenfield tenement tomorrow to spend the night before her wedding at Polly's house, how she would not return, how everything had changed so much in the last three years, how everything would change again tomorrow.

Cigar clenched between his knuckles, Johnnie Whiteside patted Gordon's knee. "How d'you feel, old spud?"

"Slightly kippered," Gordon answered.

"Not too kippered?" said Eric.

He was shorter than his cousin, broad-chested, but some peasant strain had come out in him for his legs were a little bowed and he walked with his toes turned in. Dark brown hair and insolent brown eyes came off his mother's side of the family, for Donnie had married a haughty Irish beauty, Nuala Magee.

"Too kippered for what?" Gordon said.

He was inexperienced but not naïve; he knew perfectly well what Eric Adair meant.

"Do you know, old spud," said Johnnie, "I do believe our little violet has never tasted the joys of the flesh."

"Balderdash!" said Eric. "He's a country lad. I'll bet he's rolled in the straw with girls galore."

"Fiver says he hasn't."

"I accept," said Eric. "How will we prove the bet?"

"Ask him."

Gordon did not respond, though he had both eyes open now.

"Tell my sceptical friend how many times you've done it, Gordon," Eric said.

"None-ce."

"None-ce?" said Johnnie. "What kind of a word's that? Is that a country expression? Does it mean a dozen, three dozen? Twice a night for a year?"

"I never have," said Gordon.

"Good God! D'you hear that, Eric?"

"I hear but I do not believe."

"I'm only a wee laddie, chaps," said Gordon.

"Old enough and ugly enough, I'd say."

"Absolutely, Johnnie, absolutely."

"Well, Gordon, tonight's the night."

"I think," said Gordon, "I'd prefer to choose my own time, an' my own girl."

"Girl? Who said anythin' about a girl? Did.you mention a girl, Johnnie?"

"Certainly not. It's a woman for you, old spud. A matooor woman."

"Adair's law," said Eric. "If you're old enough to pee, you're old enough to — "

"Pay for it?" Gordon said.

"Oh, it's the cost that worries you, is it?"

"You know me, Johnnie," Gordon said. "Tight as they come."

"But this one's on us, on Uncle Breezy."

Gordon did not allow his agitation to show. He did not wish to go with them, to become the client of a whore, yet he would not give them the satisfaction of seeming to be afraid.

Reaching out he plucked the cigar from Johnnie's fingers and sucked on it slowly, then he handed it back and glanced casually from the window.

"Who is she?" he asked.

"A charmer, just your size."

"What d'you say, Gordon, old spud?"

"You're sure I won't be charged?"

"She'll do it for love," said Eric.

"In that case," said Gordon, "lead me on."

In due course the cab rolled into Greenfield via the Kingdom Road, into that stretch of territory where, last summer, he had had his ribs cracked by Billy King. He had not expected the 'charmer' to live so close to home.

For some unaccountable reason he was filled with wistful sorrow. He realised how much he liked the Greenfield. He did not want to leave it, leave Canada Road. He wanted Craig to ship out, to take his brother's place in Kirsty Barnes' heart, and her bed.

"Here, cabbie, just here," Johnnie called.

"Best if you go in first, John," Eric whispered. "Sort of prepare the way, don't you think?"

The cab jolted as John Whiteside clambered out. Gordon shifted position and watched Johnnie enter one of the closes.

He said, "It isn't exactly a Persian garden, is it?"

"Ah, but beauty lies within," said Eric. "Besides, you can walk home from here afterwards."

"What about you pair? What's your pleasure?"

"The same sort of thing, but elsewhere."

"Out of the Greenfield?"

"Each to his own," said Eric.

Johnnie Whiteside returned. He put his head around the canvas, grinning. "She'd just love to have you visit, old spud. Can't wait to welcome you with open arms."

Gordon took a deep breath and hoisted himself out of the cab. He was aware of the hunched back of the driver, and how studiously the old chap ignored the younger men and their disgusting antics.

"I'll accompany you," said Johnnie.

"You're not goin' to — "

"To effect a proper introduction, that's all."

Meekly Gordon let Johnnie Whiteside lead him into the dismal close and along it to the first door on the left. The woman was waiting for them. She was small and dark, wore a flowered robe tied at waist and collar. Her hair was loose about her shoulders and she was scowling. He had expected her welcome to be effusive and professional but it was not. He could smell a strange clean odour, like soap, from inside the house. He found it, and the woman's attitude, quite reassuring, the whole thing functional and unromantic.

"Here's the man himself," said Johnnie. "He's all yours, my love, and he's a first-time sailor."

She tutted, stepped back and gestured to Gordon to enter the hall.

Johnnie, leaning on the doorpost, grinned. "Oh, how I envy you, Gordon. It's not every lad who makes it into Greta's front hall."

She closed the door purposefully on Whiteside and walked

past Gordon into the kitchen. Not knowing what else to do he followed her.

The gas had not been lit and the kitchen was red and mysterious in the glow from the fire. Great bat-like shadows clung to the walls. He glanced up, saw clothing draped from pulleys overhead and two zinc basins crouched on the board by the sink. He was uncomfortably aware of the bed in the recess, its blankets tumbled down. He did not want this woman. He had not one iota of sexual desire in him. It was far too cold-blooded. He was afraid that she would set upon him in some manner that he could not imagine. Under his breath he cursed bloody John Whiteside for luring him into this awkward situation.

She stood with her back to the fire, glowering.

"What's wrong wi' you, then?" she snapped.

"Nothing's wrong with me."

"Is it me you don't fancy?"

"I'm not in – in the mood, that's all," Gordon said.

"What's 'mood' got t'do with it?"

"I know Johnnie paid you for – "

"Johnnie paid me nothin'. What do you take me for, for God's sake?"

"I'm sorry."

"If you don't want it – "

"I don't," Gordon said.

"Why did Whiteside bring you here, then?"

"How well do you know Johnnie?" Gordon asked.

"Too damned well for my own good."

"In that case you'll know I'm tellin' the truth when I say he did it just to embarrass me."

"Are you embarrassed?"

"Aye, a bit."

"Don't you even want to kiss me?" she said.

"I wouldn't mind doin' that."

"Hah, you're just like all the rest. You want to be coaxed."

"I don't want to be coaxed," said Gordon. "Listen, have you got a front room in this house?"

"Aye," she said. "Why?"

"Is it carpeted?"

"As it so happens – "

"Let me have a look, at the carpet I mean."

"There's somebody in the room, so you can't."

Gordon said, "Somebody — not a man?"

"Dinna be frighted, wee laddie." She mocked the trace of the accent she had caught in his speech. "It's no' a mannie, only ma wee bairn."

"Never mind the carpet," said Gordon. "Tell you what, will you go an' look out into the street? See if the cab's gone. If it is, I'll be on my way."

"You're serious, aren't you?"

"No offence," said Gordon, "but I'm not for this."

She turned abruptly and dabbed a taper into the fire and lit the gaslight from it. She peered at him, advanced on him. He retreated a pace, bumped against a laden clothes-rack.

"I know you," she said.

"I — I don't think so."

"What's your name?"

"Gordon," he said.

"Would it be Gordon Nicholson, by any chance?"

"It might."

"Damnation!" she exclaimed. "God, I'll kill that bastard Whiteside next time I see him."

"What's my name got to do — "

She put a hand on his shoulder, not caressingly, and swung him round to face the door.

"Out," she said. "Out. Out."

"What did I — "

"What you don't know won't kill you. Now — out."

She steered him firmly through into the hallway, opened the door quickly and gave him a push that ejected him into the close. She said not a word of farewell but slapped the door shut on him as she had done to Johnnie.

Gordon was left in the close, staring at the woodwork. He may not have wanted her but he resented being rebuffed in such a manner.

And all because his name was Nicholson?

Hands in his overcoat pockets he strolled out of the close. The cab was gone, the street deserted. He did not know exactly where he was but turned towards the river and, at the street's end, paused and squinted up at the name-plate that was screwed to the front of the last tenement: Benedict Street.

Picking up his pace he walked along Riverside Street. He was thinking clearly now. It was not his association with John

Whiteside that had turned the woman against him. Craig: it had to be Craig. She had made him out as the brother of a policeman, and was leery of any involvement with the law; in her trade who could blame her?

Big brother, *in absentia*, had saved his bacon, had kept him pure. He would invent a lie or two to tell Johnnie and Eric but he would not mention Greta Taylor to Craig for he doubted if his brother would find the situation amusing and might, out of spite, just run the lady in.

Blind to the truth, Gordon lit a cigarette and hurried on home to bed.

*   *   *

The marriage went off without a hitch. The bride was attired in ivory silk set with tiny pearls and silver embroidery and was so well groomed that not one person in the kirk or upon the pavement outside thought her to be mutton disguised as lamb, for which sister Polly had to be thanked. Breezy looked raffish in black frock-coat and striped cashmere trousers and Lorna was as pretty as a picture in white silk.

Craig's policeman's uniform did not seem at all out of place in the gathering and he was so sober, straight-backed and handsome as he walked down the aisle with his mother on his arm that many a little heart fluttered in the bridegroom's pews and even Kirsty felt again a touch of the romantic foolishness which had drawn her to Craig at school.

In the gallery of the kirk neighbours had assembled to give Madge support and see her on her way. After much discussion it was decided that Bobby was just a wee bit too young and unruly to be incorporated into the swing of things and he had been left in charge of Jess Walker, who had him on her knee upstairs. Bobby did manage to make his presence known, however, for at that solemn moment after Mr Millar had asked Madge if she would take Albert to be her lawful husband his shrill treble rang out, "*Gamma, Gamma. See Bobby up high.*" Furs swayed and hats bobbed and a ripple of amusement lightened things for just a second before Madge, cheeks aflame, managed to mumble her promises and silence settled again.

Gordon glanced at Kirsty and grinned but Kirsty was looking over at Craig who had his arms folded as if he was in the witness-box in the Burgh court-house. He wore a flinty frown that indicated that he saw nothing funny in his son's behaviour. Jess Walker had prudently armed herself with a big bag of sticky toffee and promptly stuffed a piece into Bobby's gob and no more was heard from Master Nicholson for the rest of the ceremony.

Kirsty was not sorry that Craig had left her in his brother's care while he attended to his duties, such as they were, and chose to ride back to Great Western Terrace in a carriage with Donnie and Lorna instead of with her. Cheering and whistling accompanied the carriages as they trundled off. Good luck pennies were thrown for the children. Kirsty and Gordon in a hansom waved too and tossed coins out to keep the mêlée going. Kirsty spotted Jess Walker with Bobby in her arms and leaned out and waved specially to her son who, all sticky, did not seem to recognise her in her fancy feathered hat and remodelled coat and stared blankly at her as if she was a stranger.

Gordon lit a cigarette, blew smoke and sank back.

"Thank God that bit's over."

"I thought it was all very nice," said Kirsty.

"Aye, women always do."

"Your mother looked lovely."

"I suppose she did, really."

"Is it strange?" Kirsty asked.

"Very strange," said Gordon, who had no need to ask what she meant. "If, three years since, somebody had told me I'd be a guest at a posh weddin' and that my old mam would be the bride – well, I'd have laughed in their face."

"It'll be odd for me too, when you've all gone."

"I thought you always fancied havin' the house to yourself."

"Oh, I did."

"Changed your mind, have you?"

"Got used to the company, I think."

To Kirsty's surprise Gordon reached over and touched her hand, the gesture tender and sympathetic.

"If it's any consolation," he said, "I'll miss you too."

"Will you?"

"'Course I will. Aye, I know it's only a tuppenny tram ride down Byres Road and I can visit you any time, but it won't be the same, will it?"

Kirsty shook her head.

Impulsively she put an arm about him and gave him a hug.

She felt a queer desire to confess to Gordon that she was afraid of Craig and of the hollowness of their relationship, how that hollowness would become the core of their marriage and only habit, a pernicious bond, would keep them together. But this was not the time or the place for confessions, though Gordon did not seem to realise it. He leaned his head on her shoulder. He was not much taller than she was, and they were snug in the cab and protected by their overcoats.

"I'll not take you for granted, Kirsty," he said. "I want you to remember that if you ever need a pal, I'll be there for you. I'll not let you down, whatever might happen."

She thought of David, of how she loved him without quite trusting him. She still suspected that David would desert her if ever he found out what she was really like, how she had been formed by her childhood in the Baird Home and a girlhood shut off on the bleak acres of Hawkhead Farm. She had no secrets to keep from Gordon, though, for he was cut from the same stuff as she was.

He disengaged his arm and relit his cigarette which, neglected, had gone out. He struck a match, held it in his cupped hands, glanced at her again.

"I don't think you believe me," he said.

"Yes, I believe you, Gordon."

"I mean it, every word."

"I know you do," she said.

* * *

Kirsty had not been inside the house since it had been decorated and furnished. She was taken aback by its opulence and grandeur and saw at once from the setting that Craig and she would now become 'the poor relations', that the see-saw of fortune that had kept Craig aloft of his mother, brother and sister had tipped him low, that never again would he have a material hold over them. On the other hand, as she moved among them, she realised too that not all members of the family to which she had become tenuously attached were as well-to-do as Breezy or the sisters and brothers who had studied the art of material acquisition at the master's knee; not all, it seemed, had shaken off their earthy origins.

Feuds, jealousies and petty squabbles, closely observed, marred the image of a family united. Rank snobbery was apparent in the younger generation who obviously despised the likes of Uncle Willy Todd, a dealer in horses, and Aunt Evelyn Mungall who had come dropping off the end of a publican's family. What those swaggering, half-educated nephews and pretty, elegant nieces thought of her, Kirsty could not imagine and did not care to try.

For the most part, though, the kinsfolk made her welcome. She was taken around by sister Polly, treated to champagne and compliments and protected against questions that became too pointed.

An hour passed in social preliminaries before she found time to look for Gordon and Craig. She noticed Gordon tucked into a corner by the grand piano in the upper drawing-room, deep in conversation with a tall, haughty young man. It took her longer to spot Craig in the throng. He had changed out of his uniform into a black, vested suit, his Sunday best. In the long perspective of the drawing-room among all the unfamiliar faces he seemed more determinedly aloof than the worst of the Adair nephews. He carried a champagne glass in his fist, a cigarette dangled from his lips. He had gathered about him a little flock of admirers, those giggly, goosey girls who had first seen him in church and who were flirtatiously drawn to him, Kirsty supposed, by his dark good looks and the feeling that he would be proud and ruthless like the hero of some daft, female novel.

While Polly gave herself over to chat with two very old ladies, Kirsty studied Craig as if she had never seen him before. She wondered if he was flattered by the girls' attentions, if he felt twinges of desire to be with one or other of them. She could deduce nothing at all from his expression or manner. He remained stiff and arrogant, without charm. He hardly glanced at the girls who clamoured to catch his eye and seemed to be scanning the room. Thinking that he might be looking for her Kirsty raised her arm and gave him a discreet wave.

He saw her, she knew, but ignored her, turned his head away, as if the sight of her somehow disconcerted him.

"Shall we move on?" said Polly.

"I think we should," Kirsty said.

*   *   *

Now that his final duty to his mother had been discharged he would do no more, would refuse to make any sort of speech, offer any toast in the round of formalities that would begin as soon as bride and groom joined their guests. He was tense, awkward and felt conspicuous. He would not admit it to himself but the house awed him by its magnificence and he retreated into scheming. He nurtured malice towards the man who had thieved his mother from him, who had somehow punished him for a failure to achieve success and fulfil all that had been expected of him.

He was briefly diverted by the girls. He gave no hint that he might be susceptible to their winsome ways, though he sized each one up as if he was a potentate who might pick and choose one of them for his bed. That game too soon dissatisfied him. He knew what he was to them; a man in uniform, a married man, son of Breezy Adair's new wife. He felt trapped, suffocated in that huge, gilded room. He saw Kirsty waving to him, like the daft bitch she was. He did not want her hanging on to him, telling him what a wonderful place this was, what a wonderful time she was having. He drifted away from the girls, out of the drawing-room and on to the grand staircase.

Paintings in fancy frames; he was too close to them to see what scenes were depicted on the huge, sighing canvases. He could only speculate on what each one had cost and how such a load of money could have been earned honestly. He went down to the hallway and into the dining-room on the left where the buffet was laid out.

The long room with its long tables, candelabra, red-coated servants, crystal and silver and trays of rich food wallowing in rich sauces fuelled Craig's bitterness and frustration. He should not have been subjected to this. Part of him longed for the swank that only money could buy and part of him rebelled against it. What did any of this have to do with the likes of Sammy Reynolds or Greta Taylor, with starving children on the streets of the Greenfield? He hated, at that moment, the disparities and inequalities of the city. God, he would have been happier hammering stobs into hard ground on the hill of Dalnavert for the rest of his life, going home of a night to a farmhouse and a good, loving wife.

"Aye, so you're the polis, are ye?"

Craig held a plate, laden with cold cooked meats, and flinched when the stranger touched him.

It was out before he could help it. "Who the hell're you?"

"Sinclair."

202

The stranger did not seem in the least dismayed at Craig's abruptness. He was a man of about sixty, with a mop of white hair, a ruddy complexion and a bow-window paunch under a striped waistcoat.

"I'm one o' the cousins," he said amiably. "We farmed further out, by the Hogganfield. But the place was lost when Daddy died. I hear you were brung up on a farm tae."

Sinclair's plate was heaped with pieces of chicken laced with a creamy sauce in which were embedded several small dark wrinkled objects.

Craig said, "What do you do for Breezy?"

Sinclair grinned and winked. "Och, that'd be tellin'."

"I'll bet you're a turf accountant."

If he had been less confused Craig would have approached the subject more cautiously.

Still grinning, Sinclair said, "You've got them a' worrit. They think you'll be takin' out your wee black notebook t'mak' note o' their names an' addresses."

"For what reason?"

"I just do this an' that," Sinclair said.

Sinclair's speech might be rough but, Craig noticed, he managed to juggle the big oval plate and a glass of whisky with an ease that he, Craig, could not emulate. Sinclair was obviously used to such fancy affairs.

"So you're not a turf accountant?" Craig managed a grin too. "I'm not on duty tonight, Mr Sinclair."

They moved out of the dining-room into the hall, put their plates down upon a polished oak table and, with forks, began to eat.

Sinclair said, "I've met your wee brother. A sharp lad, him. He'll go far. It wouldnae surprise me if he wound up in a house like this in due course."

"He's here already," said Craig. "He's a family lodger, has a room upstairs."

"Braw," said Sinclair. "Real braw."

Sinclair supped from his whisky glass and then, twirling his fork expertly, scooped chicken into his mouth.

Craig said, "What are those black things?"

"In the sauce do ye mean? Capers," Sinclair told him. "Listen, son, if you've any sense at all you'll tak' advantage o' this burst o' good fortune."

"It isn't my good fortune," said Craig. "I'm not marryin' Adair."

"Aye, but you should learn what's duty an' what's not," said Sinclair. "Family loyalty means everythin' to the Adairs."

Craig juggled with his fork, got a fragment of chicken to his mouth but dripped sauce on to the marble floor. He looked down at the blob self-consciously and rubbed it with his heel, smearing it.

Sinclair said, "In five or six years you could be eatin' chicken with every meal an' suppin' good malt whisky every night."

"I'm a policeman."

"I know ye are."

"Retire from the police, is that what you mean?"

"Naw, naw," said Sinclair. "Anythin' but."

"Well, you can't buy much whisky on a copper's pay," Craig said, "so I'll just have to learn to be content with my lot."

"A loyal copper could be useful," said Sinclair.

"What does a house like this cost?" said Craig. "Ten thousand, fifteen thousand pounds?"

"Och, more."

"How did he get it?"

"He started young."

"I suppose it's too late for me, then?" Craig said.

"It depends what you have t'sell."

"Funny, I thought you'd say that."

"You helped nail Malone, did ye not?"

"What's that got to do with it?" said Craig.

"Aye, Malone was an evil bastard."

"Are you implyin' that – "

"I'm no' implyin' anythin'," said Sinclair. "But we'd never have truck wi' the likes o' Malone."

Craig ate more of the chicken, his elbows on the polished table. Good manners would mean starving to death. He knew that Sinclair had been sent to sound him out – but by whom? He did not need details as to what he might have to sell, what services he might be able to render for money. He had worked with Daniel Malone long enough to know how much a congenial policeman could be worth.

Craig said, "I suppose there's a chance we'll meet again."

"Every chance."

"So what's your first name?"

"First name's Sinclair. Second name's Smith."

"Sinclair Smith."

"That's it."

"Where do you live, Mr Smith?"

"We don't a' dwell in splendour like our Albert. Most o' us are just plain folk."

"In the Greenfield, is it?"

"Near enough."

"Is that where you carry the bettin' book?"

Sinclair Smith held up his glass in surprise. "Well, will ye look at that. Empty, b'God. Time for a refill. One thing about caper sauce, it fair gives a man a thirst."

"Listen, if I wanted to talk – "

"I don't think you want t'talk, son. I think ye just want t'ask questions."

"No, I – "

Still grinning, Sinclair Smith nodded and turned and waddled off into the side room where liquor was being served.

Craig gave a little grunt. He had bungled it. He should not have been aggressive and impatient. He lifted his plate and, using his fork like a spoon, polished off the chicken and returned the plate to the dining-room. He had no need to repeat the name. He would remember it. Sinclair Smith. He wondered just how high up Breezy's monkey-puzzle tree the cousin was situated and what he might know of Breezy's dealing with the street people. He lit a cigarette and, feeling more relaxed, sauntered out into the hall again in the hope that another of Adair's shifty relatives might come and make a pitch.

Next time he would be more careful.

* * *

Members of a five-piece orchestra, resplendent in tails and boiled shirts, had arrived in the upper drawing-room. They had unpacked their instruments and set up their music stands and the strains of 'The Tea Garden Waltz', the season's favourite, had begun to lure guests up from the dining-room. When the majority of the guests had reassembled in the long upper room Breezy would sweep Madge into his arms and, to cheers and applause, would lead off the evening's dancing.

Sinclair Smith had done what was asked of him. Now he had a full glass of malt whisky and had lit his pipe and was looking forward to a wee rest. He would seat himself away up by the window and puff and sup and admire the ladies as they danced. He climbed the stairs laboriously and did not see John Whiteside in the shadows of a tall rubber plant that guarded the top of the staircase.

"A word, Sinky, if you please."

"Aye, I thought you'd find me."

"What did you make of him, of Nicholson?"

"I think you're barkin' up the wrong tree, Johnnie. I think he's honest. I think he's too honest for his own good."

"Think again, Uncle."

"Oh, so you know otherwise?"

"Absolutely," John Whiteside said.

"What do ye want me t'do now?"

"Not a thing," said Johnnie. "You can leave Constable Nicholson to me."

*   *   *

Craig had seen the tall young man many times in the course of the afternoon and evening but had paid him no particular attention. He had marked him down as one of the gang of crooks who managed Breezy's warehouse. Gordon knew him and had talked to him as if he was a chum. Craig, however, was not daft enough to believe that he would ever trap one of the young brigade into revealing details of the Adairs' less savoury dealings. He suspected that they would treat him with the same sort of disdain with which they treated everyone who did not have the advantage of their breeding and background.

Craig returned to the dining-room, ate a dish of fruit pie and cream, then went across the hall and had one of the servants pour him a glass of beer.

Later, he reckoned, after Breezy and his mother had gone off on their short holiday, the house would throb with drunken antics and the celebration would eventually decline into a disreputable affray. He would be gone long before that happened. He would have to trust to Gordon to see to it that Lorna came to no harm.

He had hardly seen his mother since they had returned from church and had not felt obligated to offer his congratulations or even to seek her out for a few polite words. He could think of nothing he wanted to say to her now. He felt isolated, cut off from his family, even from Kirsty. He loitered in the hall, sipping beer.

Music floated down the grand staircase. Girls scurried out of the dining-room as if jerked by ribbons, tugged by the sound of the fiddles. If he went upstairs Kirsty would expect him to dance. He could not dance. He had never learned, had no inclination to begin. If he went upstairs it was possible that one of the Adair girls might drag him on to the floor and everybody would smirk and sneer at his clumsiness. He looked towards the front door. An etched glass panel broke up the light from the road outside and the lamps of horse-drawn traffic flickered like fireflies in it. He finished his beer and set the glass on the polished table. He was tempted to pick up his uniform and slip off without a word to anyone, let Kirsty find her own way home. Let one of the bloody Adairs pay for a cab for her.

He had change in his pocket. He could hire a cab at the corner and be in Greta's house in a quarter of an hour. What time was it? He took out his watch. Only a quarter to eight o'clock. God, he felt as if he'd been in this bloody place for hours. He lit another cigarette, tossed the match-end on to the marble and watched it burn itself out.

His mood had shifted once more.

What the hell was wrong with him?

"Are you not dancing?"

She had come off the tail of the line of girls that had whipped out of the dining-room. She was young, not much above sixteen, he reckoned, had her hair in ringlets still, a heart-shaped face, thin lips and enormous brown eyes like a spaniel's. She wore a dress that was a scandal for a girl of her age, the bodice straps just clinging to her shoulders, her breasts almost visible. She knew that she was well developed and held herself forward like a squab to let him admire what she had.

"I'm drinkin'," Craig said, "not dancin'."

"I know you. You're Craig Nicholson."

"Who told you my name?"

"Everyone knows who *you* are. Anyway, I spoke to you upstairs."

Her brown eyes were fastened on his face. She was trying to fascinate him, and she was good at it. She spoke in a voice as soft and deep as plum velvet.

"What's your name?" he said.

"Amanda."

"Mandy?"

207

"No, Amanda," she said. "Won't you kindly come upstairs and give me the pleasure of a waltz?"

"I told you, I prefer it here."

"Don't you like me?"

"I don't even know you."

"You could get to know me," she said.

Craig said, "I'm married."

"I know you are. She's upstairs. You don't have to answer to her, do you? You're a policeman. You can do what you like."

"I wish I could."

"I could take you down below stairs and show you the electrical servant."

"I've heard all about the electrical servant."

"Wouldn't you like to see it?" she said.

"Listen – "

"You could kiss me. Nobody would have to know."

She said it in a whisper and the sound of her voice alone made his flesh tingle. He had an urge to go with her, to lurk in the dark of the servants' stair and put his hand inside the bodice of her gown, see if that would teach her a lesson. His cheeks flushed at the thought. Christ, what sort of family would breed a tart like this?

"Bugger off, girl."

"Oh, that's not nice."

"I told you, I'm married."

"Suit yourself," she said.

She whirled and went skipping up the staircase to the half-landing where a knot of girls waited, giggling.

Craig's face grew hotter. Now he had to find Kirsty, just to protect himself against these shameless rich girls. He started towards the staircase.

Servants were clearing dishes in the dining-room. He could hear the hum of the famous electrical device as it rose and fell in the shaft. From upstairs came cheering and applause. His mother must be dancing with Breezy Adair.

The staircase was deserted, top to bottom. He climbed it slowly, anger welling inside him like blood in a contusion. The upper drawing-room was packed. Everybody was there now. Dark-suited gentlemen filled the doorway. Silks gleamed within. Whisky and perfume, pomade, cigar smoke, gas all mingled into the soft haze that lay over the top of the staircase.

He stepped on to the top landing.

"I say, haven't we met before?"

It was the supercilious tall nephew, Gordon's chum; he had been hiding behind a potted plant.

"Nope," said Craig, without hesitation.

"Are you sure?"

The specimen placed himself directly before him, his head held back, his chin tilted. They *had* met before. Craig's mouth felt dry suddenly. In a flash he recalled the occasion, that night in October in the close in Benedict Street.

"You are Constable Nicholson, are you not?"

It was spoken in the formal manner of a court official putting a question to the accused.

"What if I am?" Craig said.

"I never forget a face, old spud."

"Are you Whiteside?"

"*Hmmm*," the nephew murmured. "Now, let me see, where could it have been that we met before?"

"We've never met before."

Whiteside smiled, shrugged. "Perhaps you're right."

He stepped to one side and, without another word, let Craig pass on into the crowd in the upper room.

* * *

For the first time in months the house was empty, the fire gone out. Kirsty lighted it again immediately, stooping over the ash-bucket in her evening dress, still with the big feathery hat on her head.

She was annoyed with Craig for dragging her away from the party but she had not protested. One look at his face and she knew that he was close to losing his temper. She had not asked him to explain their sudden, early departure. She had said nothing at all to him as they rode down on the horse-tram from Great Western Road to the stop at the head of Canada Road.

The night was cold and damp, as the day had been. He had taken her arm as they had walked from the far end of Canada Road but the gesture was neither amorous nor even courteous. He held her as if she was one of his prisoners bound for a night in the cells. He carried his uniform in a big crackling brown paper parcel draped over one arm and his helmet and boots in a bandbox that sister Polly had found for them.

They reached home about half past eight o'clock. The life of the Greenfield was still going on in the tenements. Jess Walker was very surprised to see them at such an early hour. Bobby had just fallen asleep in a bed in the Walkers' front parlour. The child was soggy and fretful as Craig carried him upstairs. He took his son directly into the front room and put him down in the bed that Madge had shared with Lorna.

New sleeping arrangements had not been discussed. Nothing of consequence had been discussed. Craig had hardly said a civil word to her in weeks. She wondered, as she kindled the fire, if Craig expected her to move into the front room too, or if he had other plans. She would be reluctant to abandon the hole-in-the-wall in the kitchen. It was comfortable and convenient and she had grown used to sleeping alone.

Once the fire had caught she took off her hat and dress. She draped the dress in camphored tissue-paper and hung it up in the now empty cupboard in the parlour. It looked forlorn on the rail where, until recently, Madge's splendid wardrobe had hung. She picked up Craig's uniform and brushed it. It was cold in the front room, in her petticoats. She put a shawl about her, took the uniform and carried it into his room, draped it over the wooden chair.

Craig had already unpacked his helmet and boots. When she entered she found him seated in the half-dark on the end of the bed, buffing the boots' toecaps with a rag. He had taken off his trousers, vest and jacket and had tossed them over the bed-end. In his combinations and black stockings he looked like a sportsman ready to run or row. He smoked, the coal of the cigarette glowing in the gloom.

Kirsty said, "Why did we leave so early?"

"'Cause I was sick of it."

"Your mother won't be pleased."

"She'll get over it."

"It looked – rude."

"None o' that bloody lot would know what 'rude' means."

"What have you got against them, Craig?"

"They're snobs, snobs o' the worst kind."

Kirsty said, "Are you sleepin' here?"

He worked the rag over the boot toe.

"Where else would I be sleepin'?" he said.

"With – with me."

"I'm fine where I am," he said.

"Don't you want to share the bed with me?"

"If I do," he said, "you'll only do it again."

"Do what?"

She drew the ends of the shawl over her breasts, shivering. She watched him take the cigarette from his lips and drop a globule of spit upon the coal-black glossy leather. He rubbed it in.

"Have another one," he said.

"Another baby, do you mean?"

"Aye, only next time it would be worse, because *she* won't be here t'take care o' us."

"Dr Godwin said – "

Craig cursed the doctor quietly.

Kirsty stiffened. His wounding words did not strike deep into her, however. She did not feel in the least tearful, and that surprised her.

"Why did you marry me, Craig?" she said.

"I never did marry you, remember?"

"No, you just bought me a ring instead."

"Isn't that enough for you, all of a sudden?"

"It's enough for me," Kirsty said. "Is it too much for you, perhaps?"

He glanced up at her suspiciously.

"Don't pick a fight wi' me, Kirsty. Not tonight especially."

She drew in breath. "Do you want supper?"

"Nah."

"Will that be all, then?"

"Aye, that'll be all."

She nodded, turned, crossed the hall into the kitchen and closed the door behind her, firmly but without heat.

211

January

Midnight brought the old year to an end and, without hesitation, ushered in the new. In just twelve months, as optimists kept reminding you, the whole damned century would go to its grave and give the golden age another shot at being born. At this time of the year the pagan remnant was at its most obvious, eager to propitiate the gods that the holy men had never quite managed to throw down. Even before whisky began to flow there was a terrible cheerfulness in the air and the streets of cities, towns and villages the length and breadth of Scotland rang with bells and shook with rattles and the jovial greetings of 'first foots', those tall, dark men who, if you could find them, were welcomed as harbingers of good omen and carried with them over the threshold the symbols of plenty, a lump of coal, a fish tied with ribbon, a bun and, naturally, a bottle.

Calum Piper stood in for his father who, like Craig, had drawn the dreaded Ne'erday shift. Young Calum had lungs like a bull, though, and strutted tirelessly up and down the pavement in front of No. 154 and played in the New Year on his bagpipes, kilt swishing about his boyish knees. All the neighbours flung open their windows to listen and cheer him on and none dared admit at that sentimental season that they really could not abide the flayed-cat wail of the old war-pipes.

Kirsty stood at the bedhead and looked down at her son who, cocooned in blankets, slept through the din. For some reason she had an alarm clock clutched in one hand. She had not opened windows or doors. She would risk the ire of the household gods just to keep her son from being disturbed by the revelry of a rough world that cared not a jot for sleeping bairns or those lamentable souls who had nothing at all to celebrate and who only wanted peace.

Soon the neighbours would come for her, would spill into her hall and kitchen, dark-haired Jim Walker in the lead, perhaps, and she would uncork the bottle that Craig had left out and would cut the great slab of currant bun that she had baked and

would put on a show for them, would laugh and offer greetings
and let the lads kiss her, daringly, on the cheek. Mrs Swanston
would hug her and would whisper a reminder in her ear about
the tragedy of the year gone, as if she needed reminding, and they
would be brave together for a moment or two until Jess Walker
would call out, "That's enough o' that now. We'll toast the year
that's come in and not the year that's awa'," and there would
be murmurs of agreement and a clink of glasses. Soon after that
they would all ebb away into the Pipers' house to scoff the huge
steak-pie that had been perfuming the close all afternoon and the
menfolk would get down to some serious drinking. She would be
invited, would be welcome across the landing. One of the young
Piper girls would be told to stay and listen for Bobby, and it
would have been all right, except that Kirsty wanted none of it.
She was not in a companionable mood. She was faintly depressed,
though not melancholy; she doubted if the feeling would go away
no matter how broadly she smiled or how many times she was
kissed on the cheek.

David was far away in Inverness. Gordon and Lorna were at
a grand party in Breezy's house, to which she had been invited
but which Craig had refused her permission to attend since, if he
was on duty, a twelve-hour shift at that, she must be here to feed
him when he returned, and no argument against it.

She had seen little of the Nicholsons since Madge's wedding,
and had seen Madge not at all. Gordon had dropped in now and
then, usually during the day, when he was in the Greenfield. He
would scrounge a cup of tea or a bowl of broth and blether for
half an hour, then depart again at the double. Lorna had called
in twice, on Sundays. But something had gone out of Kirsty's
relationship with her in-laws, as if Craig's animosity had sucked
it away. Even Gordon did not seem so affable and candid, though
he assured her that he was happy up on the Terrace and tolled off
the benefits of high living with a sheepish grin; yet she sensed
that Gordon too was uncomfortable with her and put it down
to her shabbiness, to the contrast with the luxurious life-style
that Breezy Adair offered.

Breezy belonged to the old school which did not make much of
Christmas, though Lorna had turned up with a basket of presents
for Bobby and a long embossed card which conveyed good tidings
from Albert & Madge to Craig & Kirsty, a card that Craig would
not display but tore up and tossed on the fire.

In spite of herself Kirsty was yielding to Craig's grudge against the Adairs. The weeks between the wedding and New Year had been calm, not marked by restored affection or contentment but passive. Craig's shifts defined the shape of her days and his conversation, what there was of it, was directed at her now as if he hoped to impart to her by repetition an understanding of the monotonous nature of his job. There had been no love-making, however. Craig had shown no inclination to share her bed.

Kirsty suspected that Craig had some plan afoot to ruin Breezy Adair. As far as she could make out from talk with Gordon, Breezy's misdemeanours were confined to involvement with street betting in which she personally saw little harm. Mr Graham would occasionally preach a sermon about the evils of gambling and she supposed that a few men did get carried away by betting fever and lost pounds or pennies that should have gone to feed their children but she agreed with Gordon on that score, that the fault was in the man and not the game.

The clock in her hand gave an ominous click, signal that it was about to break into strident chatter. She pressed the spring that switched off the mechanism and put the clock down. She bowed her head as midnight struck and bedlam broke out in the street.

Even with windows and curtains closed there was no escape from the roar. She was not moved to go out on to the landing, to make public the emotions that stirred in her. However unsentimental she supposed herself to be there was still powerful significance in the calendar festival. Bobby gave a tiny nasal cry. Kirsty seated herself on the side of the bed and stroked his hair. He wriggled and settled again, oblivious to the racket of Calum's bagpipes and shouting in the close. She wondered, apprehensively, how long it would be before the neighbours stormed her kitchen.

"*A happy New Year tae wan'n' a'.*"

It was, she thought, a battle cry not a greeting. She listened to more of the same, bellowed by a big male voice, already oiled; Andy McAlpine, probably. Constable McAlpine was notoriously fond of the bottle. On the ground floor John and Morven Boyle, Free Kirk members, would have already made their gestures to goodwill and, being Temperance, would probably soon go to bed.

"*A guid New Yeeear.*"

When the knock sounded upon the outside door she went at once, bound by convention to be hospitable. It was not McAlpine,

Jess Walker or one of the Pipers who stood there, however, but David Lockhart.

Kirsty felt joy leap in her heart. She flung the door wide open. A Piper peeped from across the landing, a young one. Barefoot and nightgowned, she had stolen from her bed to share the fun, but the racket was still confined to the mouth of the close.

"Oh, David, I thought you were in Inverness."

"I got back a half-hour ago."

"Come in, please. Come in."

He wore a strange-looking hat, tweed with ribboned flaps, and a heavy tweed coat, not new, the colour of marmalade. He took off the hat and stepped into the hall. Kirsty closed the door and put her arms about him.

"David, what a good first foot you are – "

"It's Aunt Nessie, I'm afraid."

"Oh!"

"She's very close to death. She has asked for you, Kirsty."

The joy went out of her. She felt a moment's pique. It was not fondness that had brought David to her but Mrs Frew's dying wish. Depression settled on her once more, even in David's company.

"Can you come?" he said. "Immediately, I mean?"

"Bobby's asleep. I've nobody to – "

"A neighbour, perhaps," David said, "if Craig's not about?"

"He's on the Ne'erday shift."

"Well – a neighbour, then."

"Will Nessie not last until mornin'?"

"I doubt it," David said.

"Who sent for you?"

"Hughie," David said. "He telephoned the Inverness police station and they sent a man out to my uncle's house this morning. I left at once, of course."

"Why didn't Mr Affleck send for me too?"

"Perhaps he did," said David, "and you weren't at home. I don't know."

It was true that she had been out for a full three hours that afternoon.

Kirsty said, "Did Nessie really ask for me?"

David hesitated. "No. I came directly here from the railway station. I haven't been to Walbrook Street yet. I've a hack waiting outside, unless the cabbie's deserted me and gone off home."

"Why, then?"

"I want you to be with me," David said.

"*A haaapppy New Yeeeaar in 'ere. Open up in the name o' the law. Ha, ha.*" The revellers had reached the top landing.

Kirsty yanked open the door and confronted Andy McAlpine who, already staggering, had been tippling all through Hogmanay. He had a quart bottle of shebeened whisky in his hand and he was waving it about like a brass-band conductor. He was pursued by his wife, Joyce, angry and anxious at her husband's condition, embarrassed too.

"*Haw, ma lovely, ye canny turn awa' a guid first foot.*"

"Andy, for God's sake," Joyce hissed, plucking at his sleeve. He shook her off. If only Jock Piper had not been on duty he would have sorted out the loud-mouthed constable in short order. The wee Piper was giggling and, glancing downstairs, Kirsty saw Mrs Piper and Calum, Jess Walker and Mrs Swanston gathered on the half-landing by the closet door, unsure of what to do since they did not wish to be too closely associated with a drunkard so early in the night.

Kirsty said, "I've got somebody ill, Mr McAlpine."

"He's no' here. He's on the bloody shift, I ken."

"Andy, come away downstairs."

"Are you — you refusin' — "

"I have a first foot," Kirsty said.

The sight of the minister had a sobering effect on the constable. He squinted at David, at his voluminous tweed coat and, focusing, at the dog-collar around his neck.

"Hell're you?"

"He's a minister, Andy, can y'not see? Kirsty's got company. She'll take a drink out your bottle later."

"Well, I never thought," said Andy McAlpine reasonably. "I never thought she'd get at it, like her bloody man." He made an exaggerated bow, staggered, braced himself against the doorpost and then slipped. He landed soft. His wife stooped over him and hauled him up again, while the Piper girls fell over themselves with laughter in the door opposite.

"Aye, I'll — I'll — I'll no' say a word t' Craig, sweetheart." Andy McAlpine winked. "I'll let y'get on wi' your — your prayers, eh."

Kirsty turned to look at David. "Do you think the hack will still be there?"

"Yes."

"We'll take Bobby with us."

"Yes."

"He's in the front room."

She left the door open, let the neighbours see just what was going on. They were distracted by the antics of McAlpine who was trying to persuade the Pipers' seven-year-old to shake his hand and make him welcome into the house, until, that is, young Calum folded away his bagpipes and took charge.

Kirsty locked the guard over the fire and turned out the gas. She put on her coat, a Sunday hat and a scarf. It took her no more than a handful of seconds and when she returned to the hall she found that David had already lifted Bobby from bed and held the child in a great swaddle of sheet and blankets in his arms. It was as if they were fleeing before the advance of an enemy, Kirsty thought, and took a moment to pack clean clothes for her son into a shopping-basket.

Jess Walker and Mrs Swanston were loitering by the closet door, curious and bewildered. Kirsty explained to them what had happened and, having locked the house door, gave the long key to Jess and asked if she would see to it that Craig was given it in the event that she did not return before noon.

"Can Craig not be told?" Jess Walker asked. "Should he not be there too?"

"No," Kirsty said. "It's my presence that's required."

She followed David down into the street, leaving a peculiar vacuum behind her for several seconds, a silence less respectful than bemused.

The cabbie had waited. He was an old man, old as the year that had gone, Kirsty thought, with a stiff grey beard and a hood to his cape. He would be one of those who cared less for celebration than the money that was to be made at that season. She climbed into the cab. Bobby stared at her, unstirring and unprotesting, over the hem of the blanket, safe in David's arms.

Five or six minutes later the cab rolled to a halt in front of No. 19 Walbrook Street and David, Bobby and Kirsty got out.

*　　*　　*

New Year duty in the Greenfield was not the trial it was for the officers and men of the City of Glasgow police. They had to contend with the vast crowds that gathered about the Tron and in

George Square, congregations that contained a high proportion of 'keelies', young hooligans, intent only on stirring up violent mischief, and in the course of the short winter day with six or eight football matches that frequently ended in riots, major or minor, in spite of the fact that all the public-houses and wine-shops were closed by law. There were few such massings in Greenfield, though it had become a tradition for young folk to drift along to the Burgh Hall and wait there for the bell in the clock tower to set the New Year loose, to sing and chant and dance about for an hour or two before dispersing. Chief Constable Organ had instructed his men to lie low during the festivity, though horses were saddled and twenty brawny constables assembled in the Percy Street stable yard ready to break and go at the first hint of trouble.

From Ottawa Street the constables went out in pairs. The public holiday was covered by three long shifts of twelve hours each, a system that tried the duty officers and sergeants no end since it meant an irregular muster for a whole blessed week. Nonetheless the system seemed to work and the good people of Greenfield celebrated noisily but without much nuisance. The incidence of domestic affrays shot up, of course, and cells would be crammed with drunks awaiting the glare of daylight or the next opening of court, and if Partick Thistle was slated to play at home there would be a certain tension in the late afternoon, though that would not be Craig's concern since he would sign off at eleven o'clock and would be home in bed by noon.

Fortunately he had drawn Archie Flynn as a partner. Archie and Peter Stewart were his only chums on the Force. He was bloody thankful he hadn't drawn Norbert, who had become overweeningly conceited since he had trapped three robbers who were obtaining entry to the safe in a sacking warehouse office by the use of threats with weapons. Norbert had got them locked in a store, more by luck than design, and had been commended by Mr Organ for his courage and ingenuity. Besides, Archie was a hearty big devil and would relieve him of the necessity of being genial when wild young lassies fancied a bit of a twirl on a copper's arm, or half-piddled wee punters sought amnesty by shaking a constable's hand up to the elbow. Archie could do it. Archie would enjoy cavorting with the general public while he, Craig, kept his eye peeled and stood polite but aloof from those citizens who got carried away by the brotherhood of the season. By 5.00 or 6.00 a.m. it would all be dead, except for the occasional loner reeling home or some bibulous party that refused to be extinguished by exhaustion and, on that day, there would be no midden-men or bakers or milk-carts to disturb the last hours of the duty.

Before they went to relieve Boyle and McKenzie they made a detour to the model lodging-house and handed over to Sammy a parcel of small gifts from his pals at the station; nothing much, a gingerbread, a cheap canvas belt with a butterfly clasp, a whisky bottle filled with non-alcoholic raspberry cordial with which the boy could toast his friends. Sammy was excited by it all, hopping distractedly, crying out clichéd greetings, altogether too excited to linger long with the coppers. He would be looked after well enough, given a certain amount of rope by the superintendent, but would probably collapse about two o'clock, burned out, and would sleep through the worst of the model's bleak celebrations.

To see Sammy so lit up made Craig wish yet again that he was less burdened by responsibility and had more of that innocent fire in him. It made him wish too that he had not separated himself from Greta Taylor in the wake of the wedding, that he had not allowed his fertile imagination to shape a conspiracy out of what was probably only a coincidence. He had not called on Greta for over three weeks and wondered, hurting, if she missed him at all and why she had not come to look for him. He should have asked Whiteside point blank to explain what he was doing down in Benedict Street at seven o'clock at night, whether he knew Greta Taylor or did not. But he had not had all his wits about him on that awful evening, and regretted his omission now.

Craig was strung between the knowledge that he would surely make a fool of himself if he netted one of Breezy's bookies or even found one of the houses that the Adairs used as a betting shop. A small fine would be the law's only punishment. It would be paid not by the illustrious Albert but by some lackey, a nephew or cousin. He had browsed through a tome on the Scottish Liquor Laws too, but found nothing there to give him hope that he might ever do more than inconvenience his stepfather and cost the man a sum that would hardly be missed from his bottomless coffers.

So far as taking revenge on Adair, on striking legally at the clan, Craig did not know how to proceed. He was stuck. Not only was he thwarted in his aim, he had even begun to lose enthusiasm for plotting and to wish, a bit, that he had not been so proud and stubborn in the first place.

For all that he ached to be back in Greta Taylor's arms he had denied himself that capitulation. He would allow things in general to settle down before he tried to restore that relationship. The scare with Whiteside had awakened him to danger. It was not wise for a constable to harbour secrets, and his career, still, must come before all else.

"Well, this is a queer way for grown men t'bring in a New Year," said Archie.

"I suppose there's worse."

"Aye, but no' for me."

"I hope you're not carryin' a bottle," Craig said.

"Ach, I thought about bringin' along a taste o' whisky but I knew you'd disapprove."

"Drummond will be out on inspection tonight, for sure," Craig said. "He'll be smellin' breath all over the district."

"Drummond likes a dram himself," said Archie.

"Aye, but never on duty."

"I wouldn't want to wind up like Drummond, would you?"

"Not me," said Craig.

"I suppose no' bein' married makes a difference," said Archie. "I wonder if he's got a bunty hid away some place."

"Drummond? He's past it."

"So you think it's a young man's game, Craig, eh?"

Craig did not approve of the drift of the conversation. They had come round by the warehouses to the east of the Kingdom Road and cut now towards more populated streets where there would be distractions to take Archie Flynn's mind off women.

It was an hour past midnight. An hour into the New Year. Craig's thoughts turned towards Greta. He could not help himself. He speculated on what she might be doing, who she would be with, if she had found some other, better lover to warm her bed. And then, strangely, as if he had conjured her up by wishing and willing, he spotted her in the street. She was not alone. She travelled with two other women, minus children. They were moving quite rapidly down the end of Riverside Street, that short stretch of it which trailed on to Craig's beat. He was in no doubt at all that it was Greta. He recognised the dark hair, the busy, jaunty walk. He could hear one of the other women laughing. He hesitated. He could not just let her go past, not tonight.

"Archie, wait here a minute."

"What? What is it? Is it trouble?"

"Naw, naw, man. Just wait here."

Archie frowned, shrugged and stood his ground. Craig strode diagonally across the bottom end of the Kingdom Lane and switched direction at the corner where the burn ran under a section of cobbles. He came back, not hurrying now, towards her, screened by the butt of one of the old cottages which had been converted into a cooper's store. It would seem that he had encountered her quite by chance, without motive or volition. When he stepped around the corner he almost bumped into her. The other women were older than Greta. One of them, he guessed, might be Isa Thomas, the neighbour and friend, but he did not press for introductions. He put a hand gently on Greta's arm and checked her. She started when she recognised him under the helmet.

"So it's you again?" she said, in a quiet, sarcastic voice. "The bad penny."

"Watch it, Greta," Craig said. "You're on my beat now."

"Goin' to run me in again?"

"Not here," he said. "Not now."

The women had gone on. They went silently around the corner by the cottage store and, Craig guessed, stopped there to wait for their friend. If one of the chums was Isa Thomas then she would know who he was and would not be apprehensive. On the other hand if the women were strangers they would be angry and afraid at having Greta waylaid by a policeman. He didn't much care. He had, he realised, no idea what Greta had told her friends about him, if she had told them anything at all.

She wore a silk shawl with long fine plaited tassels, a flounced skirt and black button boots that looked, from what he could see of them, to be new.

He tipped back his helmet, leaned forward and kissed her on the brow. "Happy New Year, Greta."

She did not return the greeting. She seemed not so much embarrassed by the encounter as shy. It was not a quality he had seen in her before.

She sighed. "You haven't been round."

"I know. I meant to but – "

"I thought you'd found another girl."

"Greta, I'm not a flirt."

221

The dark eyes darted to his face. He adjusted the helmet, folded his arms, became the constable on the beat. He did not know who might be watching from one of the loud, lighted windows or from the shelter of a close up the street. He did not know what Sergeant Drummond would have to say about administering kisses while in uniform, let alone stopping for a chat with an attractive girl.

"Too busy for me, is that it?" she said.

"Aye, partly."

"Are you not comin' back?"

"Yes, I'll be round soon. Listen," Craig said, "have you ever met a bloke called Whiteside?"

"No."

"Johnnie Whiteside?"

"Never."

Craig said, "Where are you off to, Greta?"

"Now, you mean?"

"Aye, for New Year?"

"To see a friend."

"A man?"

"No, not a man. A friend."

"Where's Jen?" he asked.

"God, but you're a copper to the bloody bone, Craig Nicholson. I'm not goin' to stand here an' – "

"All right," Craig said. "I'm sorry. I'm just surprised to see you this far east, that's all."

"It's only half a mile – "

"I apologise," Craig said. "What more do you want?"

"I want you back," she said, without coyness.

"When? Tonight?"

"Tomorrow night," she said. "Can you?"

"I'll be there," Craig said.

Now she smiled, shoulders lifted, head tilted, and let her lids lower heavily over her eyes.

"I'll be waitin'," Greta said.

She had told him nothing about where she was going, who her friends might be or where she had stowed her daughter for the night. She had told him only that she did not know Johnnie Whiteside and Craig, in thrall to her again, was willing to swallow her denial whole. She slipped past him and went around the corner out of sight.

Craig remained rooted, looking over his shoulder. He heard

the women's laughter and it did not seem to him to be chiding or derisory, just gay and youthful. In fact he wanted to laugh too. He wanted to shout out at the top of his voice. He did not know what had got into him all of a sudden or why, just as suddenly, the year ahead seemed bright with promise.

Grinning, he strolled back to join Archie.

"Who the hell's that, man?" Archie said.

"Just a wifie from Benedict Street."

"Bonnie," said Archie. "Very bonnie."

"Aye, I suppose she is."

"She your bunty?"

"Don't be so bloody daft."

"If she was mine," Archie said, "I'd brag about it."

"Well, she isn't yours," Craig said. "An' she isn't mine either."

"More's the pity, eh?"

"Dig out your bottle, son."

"What?" said Archie, startled. "I told you I don't have a bottle."

"Liar!" Craig said. "Fish it out, Archie, an' give me a dram to keep me goin'."

The big constable reached sheepishly to his deep pocket and unbuckled his belt a little to loosen the bottle that he had hidden against his ribs. He held the gill in the flat of his palm, put it stealthily to his mouth and uncorked it with his teeth. He passed the bottle to Craig who took it and, after glancing this way and that, sipped a mouthful of the fiery liquor.

"Jeeze, Craig," said Archie, "I didn't know you drank."

"There's a lot about me you don't know," Craig Nicholson said and, blowing out his cheeks, sipped and swallowed again.

*   *   *

First-footing was an activity not confined to the Greenfield or working-class neighbourhoods. In Walbrook Street too the windows blazed with light and many doors along the curving terrace were open. From one of the houses came the strains of sweet music as a trio of young girls, caped against the chill, stood in the hallway and enticed their friends to join them by playing waltzes on their violins. There were many people in the street, more restrained than in Canada Road but no less intent on celebration. Kirsty glimpsed all this as she followed David,

Bobby snugly wrapped in his arms, across the pavement and up the shallow steps to the door of No. 19. The door was ajar but there was little jollity within, hardly light enough to see by and all the front windows, up and down, were dark. It seemed to her as if the house too was in process of dying, fading down to one last glimmer, one memory of the past, that would be soon extinguished.

Hugh Affleck met them at the bottom of the stairs. It was many months since Kirsty had last encountered the superintendent for his visits to his sister had become less and less frequent, for a variety of reasons; Nessie had company in David, and a decent servant in Peggie, and, perhaps, he could not abide to see her go before his eyes, to confront that inevitable decline that would be his to know soon enough. Kirsty thought too that there was some resentment in the man towards her or, through her, towards Craig, as if Hugh Affleck had not quite forgiven her husband for his brashness and the sensational manner in which he had gained attention in the Burgh police force. Tonight there was no evidence of the rough-and-tumble charm that was so much part of the detective's stock-in-trade. He had clearly been here for some time and wore a dark brown knitted cardigan over his striped vest, his rigid collar and thick black tie showing. He looked haggard, rumpled, not himself.

"What's that?" he said by way of greeting. "Is that your baby?"

"Yes, we couldn't – " David began.

"Put him in Peggie's bed. I'm sure she won't mind. It's the only room that's been warmed," Hugh said.

"How is Nessie now?" Kirsty said.

"There's no more the doctor can do. He's gone."

Behind them, to their left, Kirsty noticed that the gas had not been lighted behind the painted glass, that St Andrew's screen was darkened too. She did not know why but she felt moved to borrow a match from Hughie Affleck and go up and light the tiny jet. It was a sentimental, superstitious urge and she resisted it, with the pragmatical detective there, and David.

David said, "Is Aunt Nessie conscious?"

"In and out," said Hugh Affleck.

He ran his hands over his thinning hair and stuck them back into the deep pouchy pockets of the cardigan.

He said, "I didn't realise that she was so bad."

"I think," said David, "that none of us realised how rapidly she was slipping."

"Oh, I should have known. I should have spotted it."

"I'll take Bobby into the room," David said.

"If you please," said Kirsty.

She felt awkward in the house now, in that place where she had once been so comfortable and secure. Both she and Hugh Affleck watched David carry the child into the corridor to the kitchen, but did not follow.

Hugh Affleck said, "Little did I think, when you first came here, that one day you'd be present at Nessie's death-bed."

"Do you not want me here?"

"No, no, lass," he said, more gently. "I didn't mean it to sound inhospitable. You did much for my sister. You brought her friendship. It's me, perhaps, who should not be here. Precious little attention I've given her this past year or two."

"It wasn't easy, times," said Kirsty.

"Bea's with her," Hugh Affleck said. "If she ever regains consciousness, I think it would be your face she would like to see, though."

"I'm — I'm sorry."

"For what? It's a pretty enough sight," said Hugh Affleck with something of his former easiness. "Besides, we never really got on, any of us, even when we were children."

"Her sister Edith?"

"She has been informed, of course, but she is unwell too and in this treacherous weather cannot leave her house."

"And your daughters?"

He paused. "This is no place for them."

Kirsty became suddenly aware how isolated she had been, how lonely, without any kin to call her own. She wanted Craig to be with her, as well as David. She wanted Craig to assure her that when her time came she would not pass away without the favour of a family about her. There was Bobby, of course, but she could not yet imagine him as grown. She would protect him, even in her last moment of shallow and sad meditation, from the loss that lay at the back of everything.

"Will you sit with her?" Hugh Affleck said.

"Yes, of course, but are you — "

"Leaving? Lord, no. But I think Bea could do with a breather."

He opened the door of the back parlour, Nessie's sickroom,

and slipped in before her. Kirsty heard him whisper, "Kirsty Nicholson and David are here, dear. You can leave it to them for a while."

She heard the soft rustle of skirts and that cautious movement. Beatrice, Hugh's wife, came out of the sickroom. She was tall, pretty, dressed in a wine-red velvet gown, not at all suited to the duty that had descended upon her.

Bea said, "Ah, Mrs Nicholson. I'm glad you got here."

"David brought me."

"Yes, we weren't sure what to do for the best. Mr Graham's called on two occasions. You know Mr Graham, I take it?"

"Yes. May I go in now?"

David was behind her. He put a hand on her shoulder. The woman looked at them, head canted slightly. It was too ill-lit in the hallway for Kirsty to read her expression but there was speculation in it if not disapproval. Hugh Affleck drew the sickroom door open a little and beckoned. It was like a strange, upsetting parody of first-footing, of being invited across a threshold. She felt, heard, David draw in breath as he guided her forward.

The room was not at all gloomy, however. It seemed cheerful, a refuge, a quiet haven in the chill of midwinter. The fire was flame-bright in the polished grate and the big lamp had been carefully veiled with a three-sided screen of dyed gauze that made the light ruddy and cast soft whorls upon the polished table, the knobs of the bed, the ornaments upon the mantelshelf. A huge embroidered cushion lay on the rug where it had fallen when Bea Affleck had got up from the chair. It lay there as if waiting for a cat to curl and sleep upon it in the fall of light from the fire. In all of this Nessie Frew seemed almost as inconsequential as one of the crochet-work antimacassars that draped the chairbacks. She was hardly visible. She imposed not at all upon the comfortable, decent order of the room. Her lace-trimmed cap was perfect and neat over her hair, framing her small white face, with lips that looked as if they had been rouged and eyelashes that seemed lightly brushed with blue mascara. Only two springs of grey hair, falling upon her ears, appeared coarse in the delicate image. The pillow that supported her, for ease of breathing, was spotless and the edge of the sheet exact across her collarbones. There was hardly a wrinkle in the quilt, and no visible inspiration, no lift and fall of the chest.

"David?"

He went to her and said, "Auntie? Aunt Nessie?"

"David, is she – "

Lightly he touched two fingers to the side of her neck, not even disturbing the coarse curl that clung to her ear, just the balls of his fingers on her skin.

"No, there's a pulse. Thready but there."

"Can she hear us at all?"

"No."

Kirsty unbuttoned her coat and took off her hat. She put them into a corner, out of sight, reluctant to spoil the tidiness of the sickroom. There was no odour now, no corporeality at all. It was, she thought, a highly respectable way to die. She wished that it might be over, not out of selfishness or impatience but for Nessie Frew's sake, to relieve the old woman not of suffering but of indignity. She went to the bed and stood close, not touching it, though, and looked down.

"Mrs Frew?" She was surprised at the firmness of her voice. "Nessie?"

"It's no use," said David. "All we can do now is wait, and pray for her."

He still held a finger against the old woman's neck, as lightly and tenderly as if it was the petal of a rose that, late in season, might break and crumble at his touch. He put his left hand over his face, fingers bridged. Kirsty did not close her eyes. She listened to the murmur of his voice, a fluent expression of words and phrases that he found within himself, an intercession to a God in whom, at the last, Nessie had not quite managed to believe.

He stopped, paused, then said, "Bobby's in Peggie's bed, by the way. I expect he's asleep by now."

"Come, David. Come an' sit down."

"I'm fine here."

"You look so tired, dear."

"Somebody must be close to her," he said, "in case she wakens and needs help."

"She'll be glad it's you," Kirsty said.

"She'll be glad it's both of us," said David.

Kirsty brought a chair from behind the round table and placed it carefully near the bed. David settled on the edge of the bed, poised forward to take weight off the mattress. Kirsty sat close to him, the warmth of the fire on her cheek and the backs of her hands.

"Will you say another prayer?" she asked.

"No, I've prayed enough," David answered.

Knees touching, hands too, they sat close together for a time that seemed to have no duration and in the course of it, without waking, Nessie Frew passed on.

*   *   *

For Gordon it had been a hell of a good night. He could not remember ever having felt so at ease, so arrogant. He had been at the dining-table in the house on Great Western Terrace, his mother presiding, his sister by his side, all those wealthy folk about him when he had realised that they were not so different from him after all, that the Adairs were just Nicholsons with money and a bit of the surface polish that money brings with it.

The strength of his position had been slow to dawn on him but that Hogmanay the sun had surely come over the horizon at last. He had seen himself in a new light, seen that he was indeed the heir apparent, stepson to the top dog, though he would not inherit the kingdom without merit and effort. Even the autocratic Donnie had thawed somewhat, had deigned to laugh at one of the tales that Madge had told about her days as a servant at Bankhead.

There were twenty for dinner, pretty, well-groomed women and girls, all the men in evening dress, even the family's other bachelor uncle, Sinclair Smith. Madge was imposing in a great, trained dress with broad shoulders and tight sleeves that came down to her wrists, and Lorna had on an evening blouse that made her seem womanly, a girl no more. Madge had bought the blouse for Lorna and he, Gordon, had been given a credit line by Breezy in lieu of a New Year present and had gone with Eric to James Sobers' cutting-warehouse and had been fitted for the monkey suit and its accessories. He felt good in the rig with its satin collar and single button which, Johnnie Whiteside told him, must never be fastened. He had bought himself – at discount, of course – a silver cigarette case, fine, slim and scrolled, and felt himself no end of a toff when he flashed it in the smoking-room.

Breezy's household servants had been supplemented by a team of four hired from a catering firm. Madge did not feel herself ready just yet to plan and govern an entire dinner party and it would not have been seemly to leave it all to Cook, a skinny Yorkshire woman named Rowland who had been with Breezy for fifteen years and did not take too kindly to being supervised by a woman.

Dinner was served promptly at eight o'clock for there were some present who would not stay for the ringing of the bells but would want home to welcome the New Year at their own firesides. Breezy respected the sanctity of the occasion and kept the courses coming with an alacrity that would have been considered terribly impolite in the ranks of the Upper Thousand.

The talk was general and quite hilarious. Madge held forth from time to time, confident of herself since, Gordon suspected, his stepfather had found her to be a good wife behind the bedroom door. He certainly seemed contented with marriage. But when conversation broke into exchanges between partners the subject turned to money and the making of it, to chat about bloodstock, placed horses, trainers and jockeys, the secret abbreviated language of the racing set, little of which Gordon understood. He had a strange lack of enthusiasm for the Turf and no particular desire to learn the tricks of betting and bookmaking, though, God knows, there were five or six men at the table that night who could have given him expert tuition.

He had not lost his liking for gambling, far from it, but he preferred to play card games or to make his wagers on football results which he felt he understood. To him a horse was still a big clumsy creature that pulled a plough or a haycart and he could not quite separate that image from the proper one of sleek, pampered streaks of chestnut or black, with lineages like kings, who brought home the bacon on courses all across Europe, and whose prowess was fed to punters by means of the pink Press and a skein of specially installed wires. He listened to the exchanges indulgently, wished that he had been seated nearer to brother Donald for he had more interest in what went on in the Royal Exchange than at Newmarket or Lingfield or Ayr and needed instruction on how a man could make money from stocks and shares and the buying and selling of paper commodities.

He did not feel out of it, however. He sustained his arrogance, his assurance throughout dinner, stroked now and then by the attentions of Amanda Adair, a blossom now out of bud and, according to Eric and Johnnie, just dying to be plucked from the bough. It certainly seemed like it. She came on so strongly, across the breadth of the table, that Gordon fancied he could see the heat rising from her bare shoulders like sunshine on a boulder.

He would give her the eye now and then, lean across the silver and pretend to be fascinated by her chatter. He was conscious that Johnnie and Eric were envious of him for she would give neither of them a twirl, no matter how provocative she seemed.

It was all so civilised, without being stiff, without being inhibiting, and Gordon loved it. He did not think, not once, of his stubborn brother or, oddly, of his attractive sister-in-law down in Canada Road. Kirsty would never be for him. He would never entertain her to a grand dinner, just the two of them, or ever be with her in the bed in the kitchen of the tenement. He had reconciled himself to that sad fact and had managed to compartmentalise what he felt for her, to separate it from the life he lived in Breezy's house.

It was a half-hour before midnight when something occurred to which he should not have been privy, to which sheer chance exposed him; an incident that would eventually come to seem important.

Guests were departing, though not all of them. It was twenty-five minutes to twelve. In the dining-room servants were whisking away dishes, the clatter of their activity loud in the hall. Madge did not complain about their noisy haste. She was no tyrant. She knew that they were keen to be off to their homes too, all except Miss Rowland who had no relatives to visit, and the maid, Jean, who had come from an orphanage. Overcoats and capes were being dug out of the cloakroom on the ground floor and Gordon drifted down from the upper drawing-room along with everybody else for the leave-taking, a round of handshakes and kisses that would be a rehearsal for greetings to be given when the clock struck midnight. He was exhilarated but not tipsy. Madge was with Lorna at the open door. He could smell the night air, the faint luxurious dampness from the trees and grass of the Botanical Gardens across the broad highway. A carriage and a hack were out against the cobbled stoup, and just for an instant the snicker of the horses was like an echo from the past.

Amanda had put on a black cape with a red silk lining. Gordon thought that she looked like something from off the stage of the Gem, only she had a fuller figure than most of the chorines there, and was more dramatic. He had a sudden urge to kiss her and, acting on impulse, did.

The gesture was unexpected. It disconcerted her, though she had been asking for it all evening long. She gasped, blushed and then, recovering, kissed him on the mouth in return. Uncle Sinclair Smith guffawed and Eric Adair called out, "You. dog, Nicholson," and another girl cousin giggled, and then Amanda was tugged away by her mother and would have been gone if she had not called out, "My fan. My fan. I've left it upstairs."

"Ah!" said Gordon. "Allow me."

"Curled ostrich," Amanda called.

"I hope you're not bein' personal," said Gordon, half-way to the stairs.

The remark made Amanda laugh. She seemed quite different when she forgot how beautiful she was and Gordon, looking back as he took the stairs two at a time, was rewarded for his wit and gallantry. He experienced a queer wee sensation at the base of his throat, like a cherry stone that he could not swallow, and suspected that he might be on the brink of falling in love.

At the rail of the top balcony he paused and called down, "Is it a large ostrich?"

"No, a small one," Amanda informed him.

She was directly below him, looking up. He could see the soft fold of her breasts and, for an instant, he felt as if the cherry stone might choke him. The girl laughed again and waved to him; it was wonderful to be young and daft on Hogmanay. He turned towards the drawing-room, depressed the door handle and burst into the room without warning.

They were alone in the room, just the pair of them. He had not missed their presence in the hall, though he should have noticed that Breezy was not in the gathering since Breezy was the host. At first he hardly recognised his stepfather for Breezy had a fist about John Whiteside's collar, perhaps even his throat. Whiteside was pale and scared, almost cowering. He did nothing to protect himself from Breezy's fury and clearly had no thought for the line of his evening jacket or the damage that Breezy was doing to his shirt. Gordon had caught them at a high point of argument, though they had not been shouting. Breezy's cheeks were purple with rage, his mouth twisted unrecognisably. When he spun to face Gordon he did not have sufficient control to erase his furious expression.

"What the hell d'you want?" he shouted.

"I – I – I came for Mandy's fan."

John Whiteside's eyes rolled in relief when Breezy released him and, stroking the front of his dinner jacket, snapped at Gordon, "Get the damned thing then and get out."

It was like the voice of a stranger, harsh and coarse. Hinges of foam marked the corners of Breezy's mouth and his eyes were as hard and piercing as awls. Even though he had let go of Whiteside his hands still worked, balling into fists by his sides. "There, it's there," Breezy shouted, jerking. "On the stool."

Gordon snatched up the curled ostrich-feather fan from the piano stool and, flushed, crept out of the drawing-room. He closed the door softly behind him and paused, listening. But, it seemed, Breezy was too crafty now to raise his voice and Gordon could hear nothing save a furious drone of recriminations broken now and then by an apologetic monosyllable from Whiteside.

He had no idea what had suddenly thrown his stepfather into such a foul and violent mood, what Johnnie had done to incur such a dressing-down, but he was thoroughly stunned by it and did not forget the episode, though no reference was made to it, not by Johnnie and not by Breezy who, come midnight, seemed entirely himself again, equitable and smiling and innocent.

*　　*　　*

It was Kirsty's first experience of a funeral and it seemed to her a very strange rite indeed, over-solemn, formal and protracted, so that the minister's assurances of joy in heaven and of a life everlasting were at odds with the weight and oppression of the setting.

The New Year holiday had had to be accommodated and it was the fourth day of January before Agnes Frew's family and friends gathered in St Anne's at the unusual hour of noon for the first of the two religious services that would see Nessie finally to her rest.

The church was crowded with women and elderly men. Some of the latter were dignified and important-looking and, Kirsty guessed, had once been associates of Agnes' husband, the late Andrew Frew. It was also the first time that Kirsty had clapped eyes on Hugh Affleck's daughters, to whom Nessie had had such antipathy. Kirsty was surprised to discover that they were not pretty or stylish but rather dumpy young women who were patently bored by the proceedings.

It was a cold raw sort of day with occasional spots of rain coming unannounced out of the cloud. The church was chilly and grey. Mr Graham, however, would not short-change such a stalwart member of the kirk, even if she was but a woman, and went on at great length about Agnes' loyalty, devotion, sense of duty and the depth of her faith in God. David offered a reading from Hebrews and, later, another passage from First Corinthians and, later still, was invited to deliver a brief personal remembrance of his aunt which seemed to Kirsty too fond and too warm to fit properly into the old Scottish service.

Poor Nessie's body had been on its travels since the night on which she died. After due certification and formalities, seen to by Hugh Affleck, the body had been taken from No. 19 Walbrook Street to the funeral office in Byres Road, later to a laying-out room, and on the day of the service brought, unusually, to the door of the kirk where it reposed, closed, on draped trestles in accordance with some daft request that Nessie had once made to Harry Graham; a request, Kirsty suspected, that Nessie had not meant to be taken too seriously.

At the end of the service the coffin was put into the hearse again and all the men loaded themselves into hired conveyances, including a black-varnished omnibus which the undertakers furnished on request, and set out on the long drive to the old cemetery in Groves Road, a matter of six or seven miles away. Here, so David had told Kirsty, Aunt Nessie would be buried next to Andrew, among Frews and not Afflecks. At first Kirsty thought that it would be comforting for Nessie to lie at rest by her husband's side, until she discovered that the first Mrs Frew lay there too, on Andrew's right; that knowledge made her sad, somehow. She was relieved that only menfolk went to a committal. She feared the sight of the coffin being lowered into the crowded, unfeminine earth.

Craig accompanied her to the funeral. With his dour, pursed expression he was a perfect mourner. He climbed into the black omnibus along with elders and distant relatives without saying a word to anyone and the procession duly rolled off along Walbrook Street while the women, dark-clad and hatted, dispersed. Kirsty went along to No. 19 with Bea Affleck and her daughters.

As soon as the men returned from Groves Road a meal would be served: soup, shepherd's pie and thick Scotch trifle, the sort of dinner that Nessie used to make for her Presbyterian guests. Warmed by odours of cooking, it seemed odd to Kirsty that she would not find Nessie primly directing operations in the kitchen.

She helped Peggie and Bea prepare the table in the dining-room while the Affleck daughters lounged in the parlour, sipped sherry and kept three or four ladies from the kirk involved in casual conversation.

Once the table had been set and decanters filled – the men would be thirsty as well as hungry – Kirsty went into the bathroom on the ground floor, washed her face and combed and pinned her hair. Safe behind a locked door she shed tears for the woman who had first taken her in and who had taught her so much, one way and another. It was unlikely that she would be in Walbrook Street again. She wasn't conceited enough to suppose that she would inherit the place. If, however, she was offered a keepsake, a memento, she would ask for the book on China that David had given to his aunt one Christmas a long time ago.

The carriages returned about twenty past two o'clock, bringing Hugh Affleck, David, Harry Graham and four or five others. None of them gave any sign of suffering that a trip to the lavatory and a stiff whisky would not cure. Craig was not with them. Kirsty was neither surprised nor disappointed. Hugh Affleck told her that Craig had had to report for work; she knew that to be a lie as he was on night shift and not due to muster until ten thirty. She nodded, though, and went back into the kitchen to help Peggie serve lunch.

Hot food and good whisky relaxed the company. There was a certain restrained heartiness about the long table. Jokes were told, reminiscences about Nessie, enquiries about the other sister, Edith, who had pleaded ill-health as an excuse for not being present. Nessie would not have minded that. She would have taken pleasure in the sight of the dining-room so filled, even if Hughie was being too liberal with the whisky and her nieces too pernickety to eat the golden-brown pie but sat together, plain and supercilious, as if they were too refined to talk to anyone there. Only David was subdued. Kirsty noticed that he hardly touched his food. He sat with a faraway look in his eyes as if he was remembering his childhood, that time when he had first returned from China and had found a welcome in this house. She wanted to show him that she understood but he was withdrawn even from her and she had no opportunity to talk with him alone in the course of the afternoon. It was well after four before the mourners began to leave. Kirsty helped Peggie wash dishes and put them away again in the cabinets in kitchen and hall. She wondered what would become of the plates and tureens, who would eat from them next when they were sold.

It was growing late. She would have to leave soon to get back to Canada Road to prepare supper for Craig and to put Bobby to bed. She wanted to depart Walbrook Street before it became empty, before the loss of this haven made her cry again. The Nicholsons were gone, Nessie was gone; it would only be a matter of time, surely, before David left her too. She would be a prisoner in the tenement in Canada Road then, without company except neighbours, without contrast; a police wife, Bobby's mother, submerged in the humdrum routines of looking after her husband. She went into the cloakroom, found her coat and hat and put them on.

"Are you leaving us, then, Kirsty?" Hugh Affleck said.

"I am, Mr Affleck."

"I suppose you have your son to fetch home and put to bed?"

"Aye."

"We'll meet again soon."

"Will we?" she said.

"I believe you'll be required to attend a reading of Nessie's will."

"Me?"

"Yes. Did you not know? Nessie left you something. What I don't know but according to Mr Marlowe, her lawyer, you'll be invited to the reading next Thursday."

"Oh, I don't want to intrude."

Hugh Affleck put a hand on her shoulder. Even in the half-light of the long hall she could see that Hugh Affleck had been much affected by his sister's death, that weariness had blunted the edge of his affability.

She said, "I'll miss her too, Mr Affleck."

"Aye." He sighed. "Aye, so will I, lass. I'll miss her more than I ever thought I would. It's true, you know. Blood is thicker than water when you come down to it in the end."

The man's tears came thick and fast, made him ashamed all of a sudden so that he brushed past her, went into the bathroom and locked the door.

She went towards the kitchen to say goodbye to Bea and have a parting word with David. But he had forestalled her, had been waiting in the back parlour, in Nessie's room, with the door half open and the light out. It seemed furtive, too stealthy a thing for David to do. She recoiled a little when he came out.

"Are you leaving now?" he asked.

"Yes," she said. "I have to get home."

"I've hardly seen you all day."

"What will you do, David?" she said. "Will you stay here?"

"Until the house is sold, yes. Peggie will come in during the day and look after me. It'll only be for a month or so, I expect. Moves are already afoot to put the place on the market."

"Can't you buy it?"

He laughed. "I wish I could, Kirsty. But I'd have no use for it. What would I do? Run a boarding-house?"

"No, I can't see you doin' that," Kirsty admitted.

David had on his jacket and a scarf was wound about his neck, the old scarf bearing the arms of the University.

"I'll walk the length of Walbrook Street with you, if I may," he said.

She nodded. She wanted that bit of closeness to erase the strange, uncertain sadness of the afternoon. There was so much loss involved, so much change at this time. It was as if some divinity had planned it with a calendar. By the beginning of the next century she would be set on a steady course, and that would be her life, all of it, with its ups and downs, its hours of suffering and boredom and its moments of satisfaction and pleasure. She was reconciled to it.

He took her arm and led her to the door, opened it and went with her down the steps into the street. It was close to first whistles, to that hour when early-starters would be released from their benches and machines and would trail back home, when public houses would throw open their doors and when children, in this dark period of the year, would come in from play voluntarily, oppressed by the cold and gloom before the lamps were all lighted.

"You don't mind walking, do you?"

"No," she said.

David said, "Kirsty, I think I'll be leaving in a month or two. I wanted to tell you first."

"Do you have a parish?"

"No," he said. "No parish."

He held her very tightly by the arm, his body pressed against hers as if he was courting her ardently and clumsily like one of the bright sparks on the Kelvin Way, a hot young lover rubbing himself against her to persuade her to give way. He did not seem to care who saw them, the softness too had gone out of him.

Kirsty said, "You've changed your mind, David, haven't you?"

"Almost," he said.

"It's China, isn't it?"

"I wanted to explain – "

"You don't have to explain."

"I can't stay here now, dearest. It would be too obvious to everyone. I'm not running away." He slowed his pace, made her walk slowly. "I'm not running away from *you*."

Half the lamps were lighted along the curved street. She had once thought of Walbrook Street as elegant and genteel. Now she saw it for what it was, a respectable neighbourhood but not grand. Did her mother-in-law not live in a house in a terrace that would put these comfortable dwellings to shame? It wasn't right for her to be strung between so many poles, draped empty like a dress or petticoat, waiting to be shaped by other folk's ambitions.

"You're going back to China," Kirsty said, nodding.

"I have to," David said. "I have to go."

"Because they want you to?"

"I'm not *obeying* them. It isn't that," he said. "Father's not snapping his fingers and making me dance like a little dog."

"How long have you had it in mind?"

"Some months now. I had another letter from Jack last week. He's worried. There's trouble, the sort of trouble that isn't going to resolve itself without – well, without bloodshed."

"Bloodshed?"

"The Chinese Empress has deposed her nephew; I knew that from newspaper accounts. Jack tells me that she is full of a blind wilfulness, however, and will stop at nothing to be rid of the foreigners."

"Missionaries too?"

"All of them, even the Americans who do so much good with their schools and hospitals. Jack says the word is that the Boxers and their accomplices have a list of targets and objectives. Churches in outlying areas will be first on the list, I'm certain."

"What can *you* do, David? I mean, do you want to take up arms, to fight?"

"God knows, Kirsty. At least I can stop my father sacrificing himself and the rest of the family out of stupidity."

"He'll not leave his Mission, then?"

"He'll die there – if we let him."

"David – "

"How can I possibly live with *that* for the rest of my life?"

They were past the fence of the bowling-green and opposite the long wall above and beyond which lay the railway embankment, snaking in from the goods depot. The rattle of wagons sounded like armour and Kirsty felt herself grow cold. David stopped, took her in his arms, pressed her to him, not to comfort her this time but to take comfort from her. She knew that he wanted her, though she could not fathom the true reason for it, the nature of the love he shared with her, separated from touching and reticent desire. Loving David would not be like being loved by Craig. Craig had never held her so, had never made his need of her known.

She straightened. "You can't."

"Kirsty, do you mean – "

"I mean you can't. You must go to them. Will there be time? I mean, will you be able to get back to China in time?"

"Lord, yes. In fact," he relented, "there may be no war, no uprising, no attacks on churches at all. Circumstances may change for the better."

"Once you're there, you'll stay, won't you?"

"Perhaps."

"Have you told the Presbytery?" Kirsty said.

"I will, very soon. Gussie will help. He worships the distant missions. He's always thought me strange for giving up so easily."

"When will you leave?" she said.

"March. I'll sail from Tilbury in March."

"If there is a battle – the Boxers – will you be able to get out of China?"

"We'll be summoned to withdraw from Fanshi to the protection of the Legation in Peking, I expect."

"You want to go, don't you?" Kirsty said. "The prospect excites you, doesn't it?"

"No, it doesn't excite me," he said, "but I hope it'll give me peace."

"Oh, David, David!" She did not know whether she cried for

him, for Nessie or for herself as she clung to him in the shadows
between the street lamps and sobbed as if her heart would break.

"I can't ask you to wait for me," he said, "but you'll always
be here, won't you?"

"Yes," Kirsty assured him. "Always."

*   *   *

It was after six o'clock before she got home. After David left her
she wandered into Partick to the Ladies' Conveniences at the
Cross, where she washed her face and made herself right before
she went back to the Greenfield and the tenement in Canada
Road. Craig seemed almost startled to see her. He was in process
of buckling on his belt, dressed in his uniform already and with
his helmet on the table. There was no evidence that he had found
himself something to eat, and there was no sign of Bobby.

"I thought you'd gone to work," said Kirsty.

"Naw, I made a mistake. I'm on night shift, after all."

Kirsty said, "I'll make your supper."

"I'm not hungry," Craig said. "I'll get a bite before I go on
duty."

"Where?" Kirsty said.

He did not answer her question. "What's wrong with you?
Have you been cryin'?" he said.

"I've just been to a funeral, in case you hadn't noticed,"
Kirsty told him.

"Ach, she was an old woman, an' she went peaceful."

"I'll miss her."

Craig put on his helmet, carefully adjusting the strap. He
glanced at her. "Did a lawyer turn up, by any chance?"

"What lawyer?"

"Her lawyer," Craig said. "I thought somebody might've come
to read her will."

"No, nobody came to read her will."

"I thought she might have left you somethin'."

"Why should she?"

Craig shrugged. "Bein' her friend an' all."

"Whatever Nessie had will go to her family."

"We did more than her family to keep her happy."

"Are you sure you don't want supper?" Kirsty said.

"I'm goin' to the gymnasium for a while," Craig said.

"Who with?"

"Are you questionin' me?" Craig said. "With Archie, if you must know."

"Is Bobby still downstairs?"

"Aye."

Craig made no offer to collect his son from the Walkers' house and when Kirsty returned with the little boy some minutes later she found that her husband had gone. She was not angry at his early departure, at the lie he had told to duck the funeral lunch. She was relieved to be alone. She took off her hat, coat and black Sunday-best stockings. Bobby was on the carpet, chattering and playing with a broken toy that one of the Walkers had given him, a three-legged wooden horse on wheels. She would feed Bobby shortly and then herself, would sit by the fire with her mending, would try not to think about David and the void that his departure would leave in her life.

"Mammy?"

"Aye, son, what is it?"

Bobby held up the horse and thrust it towards her.

"Name?" he demanded.

She smiled and got down by him on the carpet. He leaned against her as casually as if she was a post, his elbow on her shoulder. She felt a rush of guilt at her neglect of him these past days, and a tenderness towards him that had been missing in her since that night in December when she had lost her second child.

"Cuddy's name?" Bobby asked again, scowling.

"Let me see," she said. "I think his name is Nero."

"Nnn . . ."

"Neee-ro. You can say it."

"Neee-ro."

"That's it," Kirsty said.

Bobby brought the toy close to his face and told the horse, "You're Neee-ro, see."

Kirsty laughed and hugged her son. In a matter of weeks, with David gone, she would only have her love of her son to sustain her. In a sense, Bobby would be all that she would have left. She remembered the days of hope, of optimism, that train ride from Bankhead to Glasgow when she believed that she was in love with Craig and he with her. Most of her illusions were gone now. She had so little to cling to, so very, very little.

"I had charge of a horse once," she said, "when I lived on a farm near Daddy."

"Neee-ro."

"Uh-huh, that was his name. He was a plough-horse, a great big fellow. He would – "

But Bobby had lost interest and, disengaging himself from her arms, went back to his play on the carpet.

*   *   *

Since his run-in with Billy King, Gordon tended to steer clear of the streets that lay west of the Kingdom Road. He could not quite put the small, sad, dark-haired woman out of his mind, however, and when he found himself in the vicinity he would make sure that he walked along Benedict Street. He felt embarrassed, almost demeaned by his curiosity about the street-woman. He would not have dreamed of calling at her house but he saw no harm in walking up the street now and then, particularly as King Billy's cohorts were not active in the winter and had no common stamping-ground. Since he had gone to live with his mother and Breezy on Great Western Terrace Gordon had lost his sentimental attachment to the mean back streets of the Greenfield. Now he could see just how dismal life was for the average working man. He did not blame the folk of the nether world for their condition but he did not wish to return to live among them, not now that he had tasted better.

Business, however, was business. He fixed on his charming smile as naturally as possible and kept all hint of patronage out of his voice when he dealt with customers, talked them into parting with their hard-earned cash in exchange for a carpet or an item of furniture. In the wake of the New Year spree, though, nobody was interested in the goods he had to offer and he had made only two modest sales that week.

It would have been easier to resist the lure of forbidden fruit, to avoid Benedict Street entirely, if Johnnie and Eric had tried to foster his interest in Greta. But as far as his peers were concerned the episode was gone and forgotten. It was a perverse urge, a sense of reluctant daring, that dragged him now and then to Benedict Street. His brief New Year encounter with Amanda Adair had not dimmed his recollection of the street-woman. On the contrary; sometimes, just before he fell asleep, wrapped in

fine Irish linen sheets and pure wool blankets, he would confuse
the two in his mind and imagine that it was Amanda Adair and
not Greta who dwelled in a house in Benedict Street and might
be his just for the asking.

It was almost seven o'clock. Shops were open, pubs lighted.
Older children stepped out in the direction of church halls where
there would be some organised activity to keep them amused.
Workers slouched homeward from shipyard and foundries. Carriers' wagons clattered empty and forlorn over the cobbles. The
district reeked of kippers and cabbage and the smoke of too
many fires, gas and drains and horse manure and the constant
brown undercurrent of the Clyde. On Great Western Terrace,
in contrast, would be the aroma of basting joints, the rustle of
servants' starched aprons, the glint of crystal and silver and,
at home, the faint gentlemanly fragrance of cigar smoke in the
marble hall where Breezy had passed through on his return from
a jaunt downtown. Even Madge would be soft and hospitable
now that she was freed from the burden of attending to pots and
pans. She would smile and make him welcome and preside over
the supper table like a fine lady, while servants danced to her
beck and call.

Gordon quickened his pace, heading for Benedict Street. It was
as if passing along it had become an obligation, like something a
Roman Catholic might have to do as a penance for evil deeds. It
was true that he hoped that he might catch a glimpse of Greta,
might even meet her face to face. Perhaps it was in his mind
that she would remember him, take pity on his innocence, invite
him back to her kitchen and show him the ropes, make a man of
him, even if he was unfortunate enough to be a copper's brother.
Toting his sample bag he rounded the corner into Benedict Street
just in time to see Craig duck into Greta's close.

Gordon had no doubt at all that it was Craig, though his
brother had covered up his tunic with a shabby overcoat and
wore no helmet. The fact that Craig had disguised himself
horrified Gordon for it indicated that Craig did not wish to be
recognised. In that split second all sorts of things fell into
place. *Out. Out. Out*, Greta had shouted, the moment she learned
that his name was Nicholson. But she had placed him beforehand,
had recognised his features. Clearly Craig was known to her,
familiar, and that could mean only one thing.

Gordon did not behave rationally. The subversive guilt that

had simmered in him boiled over into rage. He stalked across the street and into the close with no plan in mind at all. He was furious with disappointment for he had never doubted his brother's integrity, however much he disliked other traits in Craig's character. He felt that he had been deceived, that Craig had cheated them all. He dropped his heavy sample bag by the side of the door, raised his fist and battered on the woodwork, went on battering until the door was thrown open. It was gratifying to see the look of utter astonishment on the woman's face. He gave her a shove with his palm and went past her into the kitchen.

The sight that met his eyes stopped him dead in his tracks. Divested of his coat, the helmet looming on the table, Craig had a girl child in his arms, a four-year-old, Gordon guessed, with ringlets and shining eyes. She clung to his brother tightly and, fleetingly, it crossed Gordon's mind that Craig had fathered her. Impossible, of course; but the image of affectionate welcome was striking and, in its way, more obscene than anything that he might have anticipated.

"What the hell're you doin' here?" Craig demanded.

"I could ask the same damned thing of you."

"I'm here – on – on police business."

"Aye, it looks like it, I must say."

"What d'you think I'm doin' here, then?"

"She's your bunty, isn't she?" Gordon said.

The woman cried, "I wouldn't be his bunty if he was the last man on earth."

"There you are," said Craig.

The child did not cry. She slung her arms about Craig's neck as if he would protect her from this strange, shouting man. Craig made no attempt to put the child from him and Gordon thought how weird it was for Craig to adopt this paternal role for he had seldom, if ever, seen his brother cuddle his own small son.

Gordon said, "Does Kirsty know you come here?"

"I don't have to tell Kirsty what I do."

"I bet you bloody don't," said Gordon.

Craig placed the child in one of the wooden chairs at the table. He did it gently in spite of the abruptness of the motion and when he swung round again Gordon involuntarily raised an arm to protect himself. Craig had no intention of striking him, however, and planted his hands on his hips and swayed on the balls of his feet, very much the copper, justice on the hoof.

"You know not a thing about what's goin' on here," Craig said.

"I know more than you suppose."

"For your information, I was checkin' on this lady's bairn."

"That's right," said Greta. "She is awful prone to wander off an' Constable Nicholson keeps findin' her."

"Did she wander off tonight?" said Gordon.

"No, but I was in the neighbourhood – "

"What were you doin' in the neighbourhood?" Gordon said.

"Police business," said Craig.

"Sufferin' hell!" Gordon exclaimed. "Look, Craig, I know what she is, what she does. I've been brought here in the dead o' bloody night, for a good time. Explain that, eh."

Craig kept his composure. He gave no hint that the information caught him off guard. He rocked again, arms folded now. The wee girl tucked herself down in the chair and stared up at the constable admiringly.

"Is this accusation true, Mrs Taylor?" Craig said.

"He's been here, aye," Greta answered. "But it was a mistake."

"You told the Sheriff last time that you wouldn't get up to that sort of thing again," said Craig.

"I haven't," Greta said.

Gordon heard himself say, "Nothin' happened, Craig. It was – I mean, she's right. It was a mistake."

The exchange had drained off much of Gordon's priggish outrage. He felt deflated, unsure now.

Craig said, "Who brought you here?"

Gordon hesitated. Out of the corner of his eye he saw that Greta Taylor was frowning and shaking her head at him; tiny, urgent gestures hidden from Craig by her position.

"You don't know the chap," Gordon said.

"Was it Whiteside?" Craig said.

Greta's shoulders were hunched and she looked scared. She shook her head again.

"No," Gordon said. "All right, I'll tell you the truth. I asked Jimmy Moffatt for an address."

"Moffatt?"

"The cornet player in the Gem."

"Oh, him!"

"But it was the wrong address. I got it wrong."

It was obvious that the mare's-nest of lies had grown too

tangled to be comfortable for any of them and Craig did not interrogate his brother further. He had neatly turned the tables on Gordon, and Gordon realised it. The motives that had driven him into this house had been switched off by Craig's authority. If he had not been in uniform, if it had been later into the night, it might have been different. As it was, Gordon only wanted out now. All lingering desire for Greta Taylor had been dissipated by the incident.

"What do you need 'addresses' for, son?" said Craig. "You shouldn't have any trouble findin' girls, not in your position. Aren't they all tarts up on the Terrace?"

"No," said Gordon thinly, "not them all."

Craig laughed, a cold, insincere sound. He lifted his helmet and put it on, tucking the band under his chin.

"Come on," he said. "I'll escort you safe out o' the district."

"I can manage fine, thanks."

"Good night to you, Mrs Taylor," Craig said.

"Good night, Constable Nicholson."

"Ba-bye," said the girl child coyly, and blew the policeman a kiss from off the tips of her fingers.

"Bye-bye, love," said Craig.

*   *   *

It was winter now with a vengeance. Snell winds swept the streets of the Greenfield and cut at the ankles like scythes. The sky had changed from grey to chalk white. Amateur forecasters predicted snow before dusk and newspapers reported blizzards to the north. Kirsty wrapped up well, kitting herself for warmth as well as appearance for the afternoon walk to Walbrook Street.

Once more Jess Walker had proved herself to be a good neighbour and had agreed, quite willingly, to look after Bobby. Craig, on day shift, had gone out that morning without a word of farewell. He had not even wished her luck in the meeting with the lawyer, though he had speculated greedily on what they might gain from old Frew's will and testament and what preposterously large sum might fall on them as a result of the widow's eccentric affection for Kirsty. He did not truly expect it, however, though he had revelled in an hour of make-believe over supper and had become cheerful and garrulous as he had spent the fortune that would never be theirs. To Kirsty the reading of the will was an ordeal in prospect. She felt like a character in a serial story that had only one page to run, that her destiny was about to be tied up whether she wished it or not. That afternoon the final paragraphs would be written and she would end her connection with Walbrook Street, with the values and traditions that Nessie Frew had represented. She would also begin the process of separation from David. As she walked from Canada Road along the familiar route she was unaccountably upset. Shyness and uncertainty came crowding back. If it had not been so numbingly cold she would have presented herself at the door of No. 19 with flushed cheeks and eyes cast down.

David let her in. He did not kiss her, did not touch her, only murmured a greeting. He was dressed in a black three-piece. The colour of the cloth did not suit him and made the dog-collar appear stark and constricting. He was muted and solemn and the atmosphere in the house was even more funereal than it had been on the day of the burial. Hugh Affleck, his wife and daughters, Mr Marlowe, the legal executor, and Mr Hamilton, a lawyer there to represent Edith Affleck, were all clad in black too. Even Peggie wore her sombre Sunday-best overcoat indoors and a black straw hat that clung like a strawberry basket to her hair. The servant appeared unsure of her role and hung about in the corridor outside the dining-room where the meeting was to be held. Kirsty, though not late, was last to arrive and David ushered her at once into the dining-room where, after perfunctory greetings, Mr Marlowe got down to business.

Mr Marlowe was an elderly man, thin and pallid, with a high-pitched, craking voice. Mr Hamilton, on the other hand, was younger, square and stolid. It was obvious that the legal gentlemen had discussed the ins and outs of the will beforehand for Mr Hamilton put not a single question to his colleague and made no quibble at the interpretation of the wishes of the deceased.

Seated between David and Hugh Affleck, Kirsty listened to the preliminary rigmarole with detachment. The Affleck girls, however, had lost their aloofness and were alert and bright-eyed, hanging on every word that issued from the lawyer's mouth. David, hands flat upon the table, gaze fixed on his thumbnails, remained motionless during the quarter of an hour it took to disperse the goods and chattels of the late Agnes Frew.

It was soon done, without surprises. No. 19 Walbrook Street had been valued in the year of 1896 and was offered at that price to any member of the immediate family who wished to purchase it. None did. When the question was put to the table, for an instant Kirsty felt her heart pound. She could not help but glance at David, surging with the impossible hope that he would raise his hand, would make a bid. But he did not. He did not so much as lift his gaze from his thumbs. The house would now be sold. The sum raised would be divided in equal portion between Hugh and Edith Affleck. The household goods, with nominated exceptions, would be sold by auction and the sum thus made would be again divided equally between the surviving brother and sister.

Four parcels of stock in limited companies were left to each of the Affleck girls who did not seem in the least disappointed. Perhaps, Kirsty thought, they had been placated by the large sums inherited by their father and elderly aunt. Edith, she'd gathered, was ailing and might not last long and the money would accumulate again and dribble down to them. They would be the inheritors of other folk's thrift and endeavour and could not be denied their rights.

It was time now for the legacies. Peggie was sent for. She entered timidly and stood by the door, wringing her hands, more frightened than expectant. A little of her fear and sense of inferiority communicated itself to Kirsty who felt suddenly weak and cramped at the long table in the cold dining-room.

Peggie had been left the sum of twenty guineas.

The Affleck girls would have been insulted to receive such a paltry sum, even though they had done nothing to deserve it. To Peggie, however, the windfall was a fortune and she thanked Mr Marlowe profoundly as if he, and not Nessie Frew, was responsible for it.

To David Lockhart – five hundred pounds.

To Kirsty Nicholson – two hundred pounds.

All that remained of the cash holdings after deduction of legal fees was to go to the fabric fund of St Anne's. Mr Marlowe estimated that the church would inherit about three hundred pounds. Harry Graham had been left the two glass screens of St Andrew, and Jesus walking on the water. What the minister would do with them Kirsty could not imagine. There had been no flowery phrases, no last messages. The substance of the will had been concerned with money and not farewells. There were no objections, no grumbles even. The company repaired quickly to the large front room where a fire had been lighted and drink laid out. Peggie appeared with tea-things, and the men smoked.

"Are you pleased, Kirsty?" David asked her.

"Aye, of course. I didn't expect anythin'."

"Come on now, you know she liked you."

"I suppose so," Kirsty said. "But — two hundred pounds. Her family — "

"Well provided for," said David. "What will you do with it, the money?"

"I don't know. I haven't had time to think."

"Give it to Craig?"

"It'll go into the bank, I expect."

"In his name?"

"He is my husband."

"No, he isn't," said David.

They were standing by the window, teacups in hand, looking out at the bleached surface of the bowling-green behind its wooden fence, at a fretwork of masts and cranes that cloud almost obliterated.

Kirsty said, "If he knows it's — "

"Put it in your name, Kirsty," David said.

"I can't."

"What's to stop you?"

"Craig will want to know — "

"Let him have a share, if you wish, but don't let him get his hands on it all."

"I'm surprised at you, David."

"Nessie wanted you to have some volition of your own, Kirsty. You could almost survive on the interest on two hundred pounds if you invested it wisely."

"I know nothin' about investments, any of that."

"Nessie asked me to look out for you."

"I know she meant well," Kirsty said, "but she had no right to put that burden upon you."

"Ask Mr Marlowe when you'll receive the money and in what form."

"What will you do with your share?" Kirsty said.

"Leave it in Scotland, in the Royal Bank."

"You'll have no need for money in China, I expect."

"It'll be here when I get back, with some accrued interest."

"Will you come back?"

"Yes, when the trouble's blown over."

"I thought there had been trouble for years."

David sipped tea. His solemn mood had lightened. She could not be at all sure that he wasn't teasing her, though that had never been his style.

She said, "What if – "

He said, "Go on. What if what?"

"If I used the two hundred pounds to leave him?"

"You won't."

"I've nothin' much to untangle. I *can* leave him."

"But you won't. I know you won't."

"With you gone, David, I've nothin' to leave him for."

"Kirsty, I have to go back to see to it that my family comes to no harm. I can't trust my father to behave sensibly or responsibly; nor can I leave it all to poor Jack."

"Don't you – don't you want me?" she whispered.

"Of course I do."

"Have you told the Presbytery you're resigning?"

"I have."

"And?"

"Oh, Augustus is fair delighted. Mission work is considered to be a higher calling than plain preacher. The more you suffer and endure in the name of the Church the more you are favoured."

"I see."

"Kirsty, please do have a word with Mr Marlowe."

"And tell a lie to Craig?"

David paused. "Not the whole truth."

"Is this what you call 'looking out for me', David?"

"No, it's selfishness, that's all," he said. "I want you to be here so that I'll have something to bring me back to Scotland."

"However it is with me in the meantime?"

"Why won't you leave him?"

"I've a son, in case you've forgotten."

"I haven't forgotten."

"No, David. I won't lie an' I won't leave him."

"At least talk with Mr Marlowe."

"About what?"

"About money."

The conversation was interrupted by Hugh Affleck. He had got wind of David's intentions somehow and was keenly interested in the state of the rebellion in China. The detective, it seemed, was sufficiently well informed to discuss China and its Empress as if the place was a district of Glasgow and that powerful and terrible woman just another character on the books.

Kirsty stepped away from the window bay. David had said nothing to comfort her. Everything was inconclusive, not like a story where the ending was bound to be happy or, at least, complete. Life had no shape, no definition, especially for women like her who were caught in the territory between two worlds. Small wonder that she was discontented; that was her punishment for aspirations above her station. She could never be ruthless like Madge Nicholson. She could not demand love. Indeed, she did not understand that word now, confused as it was with longing and the need to be secure.

She dallied by the table, listening to the chatter of the Affleck girls who were deep in conversation with their mother, and to the mutter of the lawyers' voices. David had told her to talk to Mr Marlowe and now she began to see in his advice a grain of sense. She lifted the heavy teapot and carried it to the fireplace where the lawyers stood.

"Ah, Mrs Nicholson! Yes, a drop more, if you will."

Mr Marlowe did not seem daunting. She poured tea for both the gentlemen and then, casually, said, "I wonder if I might have a word, sir?"

"Of course, lass, of course."

Mr Hamilton discreetly turned and sidled off to talk with Hugh Affleck's daughters. Kirsty put the teapot down and let the lawyer lead her into a corner of the room where they would not be heard.

She said, "The sum of money that's due to me – "

"Yes?"

"Might I enquire when it'll be paid over?"

"In a couple of weeks. I'll send you a letter."

Kirsty nodded. "How will it be paid, Mr Marlowe?"

He shrugged. "By banker's order, by cheque. However you wish."

Kirsty put a hand to her throat. She felt a slight constriction there, a tightening of the muscles, as if she could not bring herself, quite, to say it. "Might I have it – might I have the money paid on two cheques?"

He gave no sign of surprise at the request.

"Certainly."

Kirsty said, "One cheque for fifty pounds, and the other for the balance?"

"Certainly, certainly."

"It's not illegal?"

Mr Marlowe laughed. "Heavens, no, lass. Might I ask what you'll do with this new-found wealth?"

"Put it away," said Kirsty.

At that moment, before the money had even come into her possession, she saw what David meant, what Nessie Frew had intended, and felt a strange little surge of confidence and something akin to power.

*   *   *

At first the snow came down as a sifting and uncertain dust that billowed along Dumbarton Road and obscured the landmarks one by one. Gordon had been expecting it and had gravitated towards the warehouse as the short winter day dwindled into dusk. But it was not just the threat of inclement weather that prompted him to curtail his commercial calls. He had been trying to catch John Whiteside for several days now and reckoned that his best chance would be at this unexpected hour of the afternoon. He had the distinct impression that Johnnie was avoiding him. He had found the office locked early these past nights, though the warehouse was a hive of activity with the arrival of great quantities of ironmongery that Eric had purchased at near knock-down prices from an outlet in Falkirk.

Shaking the snow from his coat Gordon entered the warehouse by the front door, letting it swing behind him on its big pneumatic hinges. New electrical lights gave a queer caustic tinge to everything, though the fittings minimised the risk of fire and were safer than gas or the old hanging oil-lamps. It was just as well, for the air was flecked with fragments of straw and the floor area, between racks and shelves, was strewn with lengths of pine and plyboard that the boys had levered from carriers' crates that the Railway Company had delivered that afternoon. Four chest-high, dry-air cabinet refrigerators stood among the packing debris and two cold-store rooms, taller than a man, were emerging, enamelled and mineralite surfaces gleaming as the boys brushed them carefully with horsehair brooms. Breezy had told him of the purchase and had asked him to prepare a list of the larger hotels and restaurants in the city to whom the wares could be offered for sale, undercutting Kent & Clarkson by thirty per cent. Anxious though he was to nab Whiteside, Gordon paused long enough to admire the cabinets. He would make a thorough examination of the models tomorrow morning, find out what the snags were, what might go wrong, so that he could skate round deficiencies in his prepared pitch.

"Mr Whiteside in?"

"Aye, Mr Nicholson. In the office."

"On his own?"

"I think so, Mr Nicholson."

"Right. Take care with those, Peter. No scratches."

"I'll see t'it, sir."

Gordon skirted the refrigerators and squeezed himself past racks of brass and copper coal vases and the assortment of pans and pots that had rolled into the store during the past days. He ducked under a column of carpet that was awaiting delivery to the Victoria Hotel. There was a light on in the office and he entered without knocking.

Johnnie wore a quilted green jacket and melton trousers, though the room was warmed by a bright coal fire and heat from the spirit lamp under the man's latest acquisition, a *Kaffee Kanne*. The machine percolated roasted beans in no time at all and gave out not only a stream of delicious black liquid from its brass tap but a rich fragrance which filled the office and seeped out to taunt the lads in the warehouse. A cigar in a stubby ivory holder was clenched in Johnnie's teeth. He had a cup of coffee in one hand and a pencil in the other. He was hard at work, calculating percentages from a sheaf of invoices. Papers and accordion files were piled high on the desk and six or seven squashed cigar butts lay dead in a metal ashtray shaped like a female hand.

"What the hell are you doing here so early?" Johnnie asked, glancing up with a scowl.

"It's snowin'," Gordon said.

"So what?"

"The town'll be white in an hour."

"You can help with the unpacking, in that case."

"I'll thank you for a coffee first."

"Help yourself."

Gordon found a cup on a tray on top of a cabinet and drew

coffee from the tap. He sugared it and stirred and drank, lit a cigarette. Johnnie pretended to go on with his work but his attention was not on the figures now.

Gordon said, "I also want a quiet word with you, Johnnie."

"Hey, I'm busy. Can't you see?"

Gordon leaned on the desk and, with his left hand, tapped Whiteside lightly on the crown of the head.

"Look at me, Johnnie."

"What?"

"Tell me about Greta Taylor."

"Who?"

"The girl – the woman – you took me to after Breezy's party."

Johnnie tried to contrive a grin but it did not seem at all convincing. "Want to see her again, is that it?"

"I have seen her again. With my brother, as it happens."

"When?"

"Last week."

Johnnie brought the cigar holder into the centre of his mouth and puffed out smoke. His eyes had that hooded, hawk-like glitter to them again but the grin had been wiped away.

"So Greta knows your brother. That's nothing to do with me, Gordon."

"Who is she?"

Johnnie Whiteside said, "Just a girl."

"A whore?"

"No. Indeed, no. I wouldn't call her that."

"How come you know her well enough to drop in after midnight and have a friend made welcome?"

"None of your damned business."

"Come on, John, tell me the truth for once."

"She isn't *my* bunty, you know. Never has been."

"Did you know she was acquainted with my brother?"

"I don't keep up with the affairs of policemen."

Gordon said, "If you've nothin' to hide why are you being so reticent about her?"

"There's nothing to tell," Whiteside snapped. "Nothing that remotely concerns you."

"Who is the father of her child?"

Johnnie Whiteside laughed. "Dear God! Is that it? You suspect some dark secret. Well, I can tell you, Gordon, you're barking up the wrong tree."

"Perhaps I should ask my stepfather."

"No," Johnnie said quickly. "No, I wouldn't do that if I were you."

"Is the child his?"

"Don't be damned ridiculous."

"Tell me, then." .

"The child was fathered by some sailorman who later drowned. No, she wasn't wed to him. Look, I only know Greta Taylor casually. It's true I've had a good time with her, but not for a while. I thought we were doing you a favour. I thought you'd enjoyed yourself. Look, old son, she's not the sort of person one gets attached to, if you know what I mean. Particularly a chap in your position."

"My position?"

"Gordon, you're a gentleman now."

"Did you know she was acquainted with my brother?" Gordon asked evenly.

"No, I did not."

"I thought, perhaps, that it was your intention to embarrass me – or him."

"Gordon, Gordon! I'm your friend, aren't I? What possible reason could I have for wanting to do the dirty on you?"

"That's what I'm askin', Johnnie."

"Well, I don't have an answer – because there isn't an answer," Johnnie Whiteside said. "I took you to Greta's because she's clean and personable. I didn't know that your brother had been there too."

"He hasn't, not like you mean it. He knows her because her daughter runs off from time to time, and she lives close to his beat."

"Ah, yes, of course."

"I believe Craig."

"Of course, of course."

"But I'm not so bloody sure I believe you, Johnnie."

"I would suggest that you ask Uncle Breezy," John Whiteside said, "only I doubt if he would take too kindly to the question."

"Did he go there too?"

"May have done, yes, but not since he met your mother. Uncle Breezy's an honourable type."

"Was Greta his bunty?"

"What damned difference does it make?" Johnnie Whiteside

said, showing impatience at Gordon's persistence. "It was all a long time ago. Years ago. Before you and your damned — before you came on the scene."

"You wouldn't be trying to get a screw into my brother, would you?"

"Dear God!" Whiteside shouted, outraged. "Neither you nor your precious brother have any importance at all as far as the Adairs are concerned. Oh, you may have your feet under Breezy's table, no help for that, but you've a lot to learn, old son. A *lot* to learn."

"A lot that you're not goin' to tell me."

"I've told you all there is to tell, about Greta Taylor at any rate."

Gordon put down the coffee cup, dabbed out his cigarette in the metal hand. He put on his most disarming smile, his professional, boyish, innocent smile.

"Thank you, Johnnie," he said. "Thank you for your honesty."

"All right, all right, say no more about it, what?"

"Not another word, old son," said Gordon.

*   *   *

She reached home just as the blizzard thickened and the streets of the Greenfield became dense with flying flakes. She was relieved to reach the safety of the close and thought of those unfortunates who were out there, far from shelter; shipwrights and shop-hands, children kept in school or sent out to buy something from one of the shops on Dumbarton Road. The weather made the district seem not just inhospitable but dangerous. She hoped that Jess Walker had not been caught out in it with Bobby. But Jess had been sensible and had shopped early and had been home with her children since mid-afternoon. Not only that; Craig had returned, had collected his son and taken him upstairs.

Kirsty climbed the stairs and let herself into her house without loitering for conversation with Jess. She was still tense, for some reason, and the breaking of the snowstorm had not helped her mood. Craig's cape hung in the hall, his helmet was on the coal-bunker lid. She went into the kitchen. He had lighted the fire afresh, stoked it up, and flames danced in the grate and on the throat of the flue. The kettle, set on the hob, purled steam and the table was set for supper.

Bobby was perched on the board by the sink, his little hands flattened against the window glass, his eyes round with wonder as he gazed out at the snow. The shadows of the whirling flakes danced over his face and she could see the swarm, lighted and shallow, all about the space above the backcourt. In ten or twenty minutes every aspect of the city would be changed, temporarily transformed, its patterns and contours altered to give relief from the stark familiar geometry of its verticals.

Craig stood behind his son, holding him by the waist lest he become too excited and topple backwards or fall to the left into the stone sink. Bobby was too entranced to give Kirsty much attention but Craig, smiling, glanced over his shoulder.

"Thank God I'm not out tonight," he said.

"It'll be bad enough in the mornin'," Kirsty said.

She took off her hat and coat and went with them into the bedroom, hung them up on the hook behind the door to lose their dampness before she put them away in the closet. Craig came behind her, treading softly in stockinged feet. He put his arms about her, nuzzled her cheek with his chin.

She said, "You didn't leave Bobby – "

"Nah, nah. He's down."

His arms were about her waist, one hand on her breast, his body pressed against hers.

He said, "Are we rich, dear?"

She said, "No."

He said, "How much? Tell me."

Kirsty said, "Fifty pounds."

He released her. "Fifty miserable pounds? Is that all? Jesus, it shows how much she really thought o' you, after all. That kind are all the same."

"Fifty pounds is nearly a year's wage," Kirsty said.

She did not regret her lie. Craig's reaction to her news strengthened the conviction that she had been right to hold back something for herself.

"Nothin' bloody like it," Craig said.

He had stepped away from her, slouched in the doorway of the bedroom with the light from the hall behind him. Seated on the bed Kirsty removed her boots and rolled down her stockings. She should change out of the Sunday-best skirt and shirt but she could not be bothered, could not bring herself to undress in front of him.

Outside, the street lamps shed light through waves of snow

and the wall of the bedroom was dappled with the motion of a million flakes just as the kitchen and the air above the close had been. She stared at the shadows without wonder or enjoyment. Three or four years ago this weather would have brought threat but also pleasure. How had she lost that, and where had it gone?

"Ach," Craig said, his disappointment palpable, "she cheated you, Kirsty. It should have been more, a lot more."

"Well – " she said, shrugging.

He seated himself by her on the bed, put an arm about her shoulders. She sensed in him some strange mockery of desire, mingled with other emotions which she could not separate or fathom. Tonight, when Bobby was in bed, she knew that he would make love to her again, would be her husband. She felt no more than mild curiosity and a shadowy apprehension at what he might do to her, what irreconcilable anger might not be vented upon her to give him relief. She also wondered if he would sleep with her, lie by her side and let her put her arms about him, snuggle close, now that there were only the two of them, and Bobby, and the snow outside.

She rested her head on Craig's shoulder.

"What'll we do with it?" he said.

"Put it away for a rainy day, I suppose."

"I expected it to be more."

"I know you did."

"I thought it might be enough to let us look her in the eye again."

"What?" Kirsty jerked upright. "Who?"

"Mam."

"Is that – "

"Anyway, it's a long way short o' that," Craig said. "When do you get this fifty quid?"

Kirsty brushed her skirt with the palms of her hands and gradually separated herself from him again.

She said, "In two or three weeks, when the legalities have been settled."

"You will get it, won't you?"

"Oh, yes." She pushed herself from the bed. "It's my entitlement an' it'll come in due course."

Craig sought her hand. She permitted him to grasp her fingers for a moment and then slipped from him. He gave a little grunt and said, "You're disappointed too, aren't you?"

"Yes, Craig. I'm disappointed too."

"Aye, they're all the same, that lot."

He got to his feet and, leaving her, went back into the kitchen.

Kirsty found dry stockings in the dresser drawer and, seated again, put them on. Her legs looked thin and pale in the snow-light from the window. She thought of David. Like as not he would be alone in No. 19 Walbrook Street by now, for Peggie would have gone home. She wondered what he was doing, David. How he would feel in the empty house. She visualised him there in the kitchen, a book propped against the cruet set, the fire warm on his back, as he ate sausages for supper.

"Kirsty?"

"What?"

"Are you comin'?"

"Yes, in a minute."

"Shake a leg, then. Bobby wants his tea."

*　　*　　*

Craig had never visited the Irish Market before. He had heard all about it, of course, for the market was famous in Glasgow's West End and, among the better-off, the source of many a joke and light-hearted insult.

"Here, Jimmy, I like your bunnet. Been down at the Irish Market, eh?"

"I say, Jeannie, that's a spiffin' blouse you're sportin' the day. Must've been a sale at the Irish Market."

"See you, ye wee nuisance, if ye don't shut your face I'll tak' ye down the Irish Market an' sell ye tae the tinks."

The cobbled ground on which the market existed was defined by three walls of the old Belfast cattle dock, now abandoned for more modern premises. It was approached by a broad, greasy ramp from the bottom end of Thomas Street where the horse-trams turned. Stables close by allowed stall-holders to stow their cuddies and unload their carts and from there to lug boards and baskets of clothes and bric-à-brac to the trestles under the brown sailcloth awnings that Mrs Fitzgerald rented out at the rate of one shilling per stance per day.

How Ma Fitzgerald had come into possession of the lease of that section of urban wasteland was a mystery but her legal entitlement had been checked by police and even challenged now and then in court and nobody doubted that she operated strictly within the law. Besides, it would be a bold man indeed who would dare argue law with Ma Fitzgerald, a tiny ferocious woman with a tongue like a whiplash and five enormous sons to back her up in argument. The sons did the work. Ma collected the cash. She also owned the prime arcade on the site, a rank of real-oak tables close to the mouth of the ramp upon and about which were displayed not junk but *Selected Items of Fine Domestic Furniture*. Abbotsford chairs, some pieces of Royal Crown Derby that the gypsies hadn't snatched up for themselves, or antiques that had some minor flaw or defect that a skilled craftsman could repair or disguise.

For the rest, though, it was a poor person's hunting-ground, with masses of second-hand clothing, gnarled boots, shoes with no heels, broken toys, broken screens, shoogly chairs and divans that looked as if they had been rescued from the bottom of a cliff. There were vases marled with horse-glue and knives with no handles, plates that would have made a mongrel sick, trays of dirty bottles and chipped jam-jars, pins by the thousand and buttons by the hundred score. There was a stall that sold unwashed chicken feathers for anyone who fancied stuffing pillows and knew how to treat the damnable things, stalls that sold tea the colour of the Kelvin and coffee the colour of the Clyde; toffee balls, gingerbread, sugar sticks and hot meat pies, all crust and gristle, and broth boiled from a bone that had been dug up with a dinosaur; trotters and tripe and basins of seafood as unappetising as carpet liner. On that Saturday afternoon, about three, before the lamps were lit to lend the market a goblin charm, even the mounds of snow that had been shovelled from the cobbles seemed second-hand, dusty, pitted, widdled on by dogs and worse, and the heavy over-ripe odour that pervaded the place had increased, not lessened, in the first trailing whisper of a thaw.

Craig wore an old reefer jacket and roll-necked jersey, moleskins and boots that he had brought from the farm when he first came north; yet his disguise was not perfect and he saw raised eyebrows, jerked thumbs, the knowing twitch of a moustache as he wandered among the trestles. Copper, it seemed, was written all over him no matter what he wore. He was not the only officer in the crowd. Two on-duty uniforms surveyed the scene from the dank arch of the public lavatories and he also spotted Jim Sloan and Sergeant Maddox from Percy Street scrounging, in mufti, for bargains.

Craig ignored the beckoning stall-holders. He did not want his palm read, or five volumes out of six on diseases of the alimentary tract, or a bowl of peas and vinegar, or a kilt worn at Tel-el-Kebir. He did not like it here. He wanted only to find Greta Taylor and get on home. Unwittingly he strode on at his beat pace while he searched for sheets on ropes or a cluster of women to show him where Greta had her stall. At last he found it at the rear of the site, hard against the streaming brick of the cattle lading; two long tables on which was displayed Greta's stock of clean, patched cast-offs. He did not charge up to her at once but watched her from the shelter of the stalls.

She had already lighted the wicks in the lanterns that over-hung her tables and stood behind these with her hands on her hips. Four or five women, not young, picked about among the garments that were lumped in a wicker basket, holding up old vests and drawers and stitched stockings to gauge size and state of wear. Greta, Craig noticed, watched them like a hawk, her dark eyes slanted. She was as vigilant and as suspicious as the average copper. She looked, he thought, rougher and more real than in the warm kitchen in Benedict Street. He felt an unexpected heat in his loins. He dug his hands into his pockets, and scowled across the space. But he also felt a certain tenderness towards her, regret that she had to earn her bread here in the groin of the Greenfield. He shifted position, searching for the child. Jen was on her knees under the counter. She had a rag-doll and an improvised cradle, a broken basket. She was mothering the doll with a series of mimed, theatrical gestures as if rehearsing for a part in the penny-geggie, the street entertainment that would strike up soon behind a canvas apron and add the jolly sounds of fiddle and cornet to the darkening afternoon.

Craig stooped, caught Jen's eye and waved to her almost at ground level. She stared at him, peering like a kitten in the gloaming, then grinned and curled her fingers at him. She was dirty, but it was 'clean dirt', just child's-play mud from the cobbles, not the ingrained grime that many of the girls and boys wore in their coarse pores. Craig rose and went to the front of the stall. The women melted away, without appearing even to notice him.

Greta wore a cape of brown tweed over a high-necked woollen dress, and mittens. A colourful scarf, not a shawl, protected her head. The child was dressed in padded pantaloons and a neat, tight, red coat.

Greta said, "You're a stranger."

Craig said, "I've been busy."

He did not feel resentful towards her because of the shameful episode with Gordon. In fact he felt a strong rapport with Greta now, admiration for her quick-wittedness in supporting the lies he had told his brother.

Craig said, "I came t'thank you."

Greta said, "Could you not do that at the house?"

Craig said, "All right, I admit it. I've been steerin' clear, a bit."

"I thought as much," Greta said. "I wondered if I'd ever see you again."

"Would that make you fret? Not to see me again?"

She shrugged. "Aye, it would."

Her candour surprised him, pleased him too.

Craig said, "I take it my brother didn't bother you again?"

"No."

"I think he swallowed it," Craig said.

"He didn't tell your wife?"

"Hell, no. He knows better. I'd punch him daft if he did that."

Greta said, "Will you not be comin' round to see us any more? Is that why you're here?"

Craig said, "I have to be careful, Greta."

He glanced down. Jen had crawled out from beneath the table, the rag-doll tucked under her arm. She peeped up at him from the cobbles by his ankles. He bent his knees, took her gently by the waist and lifted her into his arms. He had no idea of who might be in the crowd, of the identity of the two coppers by the lavatory. It was natural for him to lift the little girl, to let her clasp him with her arms and legs, to hold her for a while.

Greta said, "Come right out an' say it, Craig."

"I'm sorry."

He had the question ready, the question he had put to her just once before and which she had evaded. But he found that he could not ask her, could not say outright, "Tell me about Johnnie Whiteside," for she was crying. The tear, one tear, trickled down her cheek and clung to the fine dark hair at the corner of her mouth. It glistened in the spluttering light from the overhead lantern until she wiped it self-consciously away.

She said, "I've got a cold, that's all."

He said, "Greta, I am sorry – but you see how it is."

"Aye, I see how it is, how it'll always be."

"I didn't mean to – "

"Give her here."

He swung Jen and held her in between his hands and let Greta take her over the counter. He watched the little girl settle against her mother's breast and then, with a gesture that almost broke into his heart, saw her lick at the trail of the teardrop with her tiny, pink, kittenish tongue.

"A' better, Mammy," Jen said. "A' better now."

"It's – it's better this way," Craig said thickly.

"For you it is," said Greta.

He looked at her for a moment longer then turned and walked away, upright, it seemed, and unhurried.

He slipped between the laden trestles, heading for the ramp. He did not glance back. He did not wish to see her cry, did not want it stamped upon his conscience that he was capable of hurting her to this degree. He was afraid of that sort of power and of the knowledge that he had used it blindly.

He walked the streets until the pubs opened, then went into some cramped and smoky den away along the nether reaches of Argyle Street, miles from the Irish Market, miles from Greta Taylor and her child. He struggled through the pack of football supporters who had been at the taps for twenty minutes or so and stuck up his hand to attract the barman's attention.

"Aye, what'll you have?"

"Whisky," Craig said.

"A half?"

"Naw," Craig said, "a double."

* * *

The month of January was almost out before the letter from the lawyer arrived. Craig, on late shift, was asleep in bed in the front room when the letterbox rattled. Kirsty had been expecting the letter for days now. She dropped the black-lead brush, wiped her hands on her apron and hurried into the hall. The letter was in a long cream-coloured envelope, addressed in perfect copperplate handwriting. She took it immediately down to the water closet on the landing and there, by the faint light from the ventilator, scanned it.

In the matter of the estate of the late Mistress Agnes Affleck Frew, the letter stated, and her share thereof, Mr Alexander Marlowe would be obliged if Mrs Craig Nicholson would present herself at his chambers in St Vincent Street on Tuesday first at the hour of 2 o'clock p.m., at which time she would receive the sum of two hundred pounds, upon signature of a prepared letter of receipt for same.

Kirsty read the letter carefully, then, folding the sheet, tore off the top portion which gave Mr Marlowe's address. She crumpled the rest, dropped it into the lavatory bowl and flushed it away, making absolutely sure that it had gone. She tucked the slip into her bodice, returned to the kitchen and resumed her morning's chores as if nothing at all had happened. Later, when Craig asked her, as he usually did, if she had heard from the lawyer yet she just shook her head.

Fortunately Craig was on night shift on Tuesday. He was buried deep in bedclothes when the time came for her to leave. She dressed herself in a sober skirt and blouse and put on her black coat and hat. She dressed Bobby too. She put an ashet pie to heat in the side oven and left a pencilled note upon the table for Craig, informing him that she had gone to the lawyer's office. If he had been up and about he might have insisted on going with her and she would have had to invent more complicated lies to prevent it.

She left the house about half past twelve, Bobby toddling excitedly by her side, his hand in hers. She caught a tram at the end of Canada Road and, at Bobby's insistence, went up on to the open deck where her son sat on the wooden bench at the front and pretended to steer the horses. She hung on to the belt at the back of his coat tightly for he was as agile as a goat kid now, bobbing and bouncing up and down, crowing with delight at his lofty position. Warm winds had taken away the snow and brought parcels of cloud rolling and chasing over the city, but no rain so far. Roofs glistened with snow-melt and gutters ran with water and, though it was far too early, there was just the faintest promise of spring in the smell of the moist parkland as the car ground past the Groveries and on into the bustle of the city.

Craig had been quiet and indrawn these past days, not scowling and sulky, though. She had not known this mood on him before but she had no great curiosity about it or about him now. He seemed to have recognised that his plan for wreaking revenge on Breezy Adair had been misguided; to say the least of it, and she wondered if, in the course of the year, Craig would relent and re-establish relations with his mother. Neither of them had seen hilt nor hide of Madge since the day of the wedding and even Gordon and Lorna seemed to have forgotten of their existence these past weeks. Perhaps it was regret and remorse for his silly stubborn behaviour that had dampened her husband's temper.

She was not at all sure of the geography of the city but kept her eyes peeled and, noticing that the tram skirted right at the bottom of St Vincent Street to avoid the long steep hill, got off at the next stop. She walked up a side-street, steep enough to tax her lungs, and had to carry Bobby the last few yards. She found herself on the crest of St Vincent Street with the swoop down into the city's commercial centre before her and away to her right, visible over and between the buildings, a panorama of the city's docklands and ring of southern hills.

It was too early for her appointment but she made a point of locating Mr Marlowe's office, in an unimposing terrace, before she went in search of a tea-room. Bobby was most impressed by the 'luncheon'. He ate his soup and bread and steamed fish without a murmur of complaint and sat up on an extra cushion at the table with her like a perfect little gentleman. It was his first adventure in the city and he loved every minute of it. He was not intimidated by the din and clamour, the parade of businessmen, clerks and office girls along the pavements, not cowed by the height of the new buildings. After they finished eating Kirsty took him into the ladies' room and washed his face at the sink there and dried it with her handkerchief, then they went out again and climbed the hill to Mr Marlowe's chambers and, at exactly two o'clock, were shown into his room.

Dark wood and brass were the keynotes, though the window, even through a heavy net curtain, gave glimpses of the street. A small fire burned in an iron fireplace. The long desk behind which Mr Marlowe was seated was devoid of any documents except a letter and its copy and two cheques. The ink in the iron pot in the iron well was black and splashy, Kirsty noticed, as if it had been poured out fresh in her honour and the steel nib on the pen that Mr Marlowe gave her was brand new. Bobby stood beside her chair, quite contained and decently subdued. He seemed to be taking in every detail, to be assessing the elderly man with critical concentration and did not respond to the lawyer's lame attempt to amuse him.

Kirsty inspected the cheques. Both were drawn on the Bank of Scotland, she noted, rectangular, handsomely printed, signed with a flourish by Marlowe and Kearney. She read the letter of receipt and, with great care, penned her name to the original and to the copy, signed *Kirsty Barnes Nicholson (Mrs)*, as Mr Marlowe instructed. The lawyer blotted both letter and copy with a roller, put the original into a drawer and folded the copy and gave it over the desk, together with the cheques.

Kirsty moistened her dry lips. "I have it in mind to open a bank account with the big sum, Mr Marlowe. Is that a difficult thing for a person in my position to do?"

"Not at all," said the lawyer. "Do you have any particular bank in view, Mrs Nicholson?"

"No."

"In that case may I suggest that I accompany you to the St Vincent Street branch of the Bank of Scotland, where my account is held, and give you a personal introduction. You'll then be able to lodge the cheque immediately. In a day or two you'll receive a Pass-book which will show the state of your account and upon which you may draw to the limit of your credit at any time."

"How will I get the Pass-book?"

"By post, since you live some distance from the branch."

"Could I arrange with the bank to collect the book?"

"If you wish," said Mr Marlowe impassively. "May I enquire what you intend to do with the smaller cheque?"

"Take it home to my husband."

Mr Marlowe blinked, just once. "I see."

Kirsty said, "We'll put the fifty pounds into another bank, one nearer home. He's a policeman, my husband, so he'll not have any bother openin' an account, will he?"

"None at all."

"If that's all, Mr Marlowe, an' if it's convenient, perhaps we can go an' do it now," Kirsty said.

"By all means, Mrs Nicholson," the lawyer said. "I – ah – I take it you wish this transaction to remain confidential?"

"I do, Mr Marlowe. Completely confidential."

"Even from your husband?"

"Especially from my husband."

"I see," said the lawyer again and, trying to hide a wry little smile, got up to fetch his overcoat.

If she had not known him as well as she did she might have
supposed that he was grieving at last for the child she had lost
or that he was filled with regret for his behaviour towards his
mother. He was still too proud to call on her or write a placatory
letter and Kirsty, though it would have been easy for her, would
not do it for him. In fact Craig's mood was not one of surly
brooding but was almost dreamy and the tail-end of the winter
passed peacefully with the tenor of life in No. 154 more even than
it had ever been before.

Kirsty occupied herself with household duties and attended to
her son and her husband without complaint. Craig went out on
shift and returned, invariably, on time. He spent long hours in
bed, buried in the blankets, or sprawled drowsily by the kitchen
fire, smoking cigarettes and staring into the flames as if he could
discern there whatever it was that he desired, his castle in Spain.
He no longer went to the swimming-baths or to the gymnasium or
to play billiards with Archie Flynn, though now and then Kirsty
detected the odour of whisky on his breath or the faint sourness
of beer on his clothing.

He had lain with her four or five times but did not take her
with his old demanding insistence. He was hesitant, almost coy,
and would not accompany her to her bed unless she invited him
to do so. Even then his love-making was unsatisfactory. He did
not seem to be making love to her at all, really, and remained
distanced even at the most intimate moment.

The fifty-pound cheque had pleased him. He had displayed
not the slightest suspicion when she returned from the lawyer's
office with it and merely asked, "What'll you do with all that
money, Kirsty?"

"Give it to you to put into the bank."

"Is there nothin' you fancy? A new gas stove or a water-
heater?"

"No, I'd rather put it away safe," she had told him, "unless,
that is, there's something you need."

He had paused, a slight cynical smile upon his lips, before he had answered, "Nope, nothin'."

To Kirsty's surprise she did not suffer pangs of guilt at having deceived him. She felt that she had gained strength from the complicated deception. It had thrilled her to enter the huge Greek-style building in St Vincent Street, to be introduced to a teller, a young man in a starched collar and vested suit, who had treated her with considerable deference when he learned just how much she had to deposit. The young man had been even more polite when she had gone there again, with Bobby by the hand but without Mr Marlowe's protection, to collect the green-covered, new-smelling Pass-book with her name printed upon it in florid letters. She had bought a buckram wallet from a gift-shop in Renfield Street and had tucked the Pass-book into it and had hidden it beneath newspaper lining in the drawer of her dresser, where Craig would not find it. It was the Pass-book that gave her strength, an odd sort of courage. Sometimes when Craig was out she would break off her chores and fish out the book and read her name and the sum penned in the column, would hold it in her fingers for a while and draw security from it, and confidence and daring too.

Hugh Affleck was the only person who might reveal to Craig exactly how much she had inherited from Nessie Frew but Craig saw little or nothing of the Glasgow superintendent now and Kirsty reckoned it was worth the risk of discovery to have something that belonged to her and to her alone. It did not annoy her in the slightest when Craig opened an account in the local branch of the Royal Bank of Scotland with the fifty-pound cheque, an account registered in his name. In a strange way she felt that he was entitled to it, that she had paid him off for those early days. She did not regard any of the money as spendable, did not equate it with goods. Instead she transposed it arithmetically into a weekly wage, a period of time, calculated that it would purchase her one hundred and fifty weeks of independence at about a pound a week. Nessie Frew had gifted her Time not Money, and she would be eternally grateful to her old friend for that treasure.

One evening, after supper, Craig said, "It strikes me you haven't been to the kirk for ages. Have you given up religion?"

"It's not the same without Nessie."

"I'm surprised Lockhart hasn't been callin' on you to see what's happened, to redeem one o' his wandered flock."

"I'm not wandered," Kirsty said. "I expect I'll join a local church quite soon. In any case, David's too busy to think much about lost sheep. He's goin' back to China."

"Is he now," said Craig. "How soon?"

"March, I think."

She was sewing, and peered down at the thread, the fine needle, at the button stiff against the cloth. She kept her fingers still, waiting for more questions, for sarcasm or a wounding insult. But Craig said no more about David and when she glanced up at him a moment later she found that he was staring at the ceiling, at the pulley ropes overhead, his head resting against the chairback and that sad, dreamy look upon him again. She could not fathom Craig at all, could not imagine what strange schemes were evolving in his head now. She had expected him to be relieved that David was going out of her life and would not be there, like a shadow, much longer. But it occurred to her that Craig had never really known that she had fallen in love with David Lockhart, that he was too self-centred to believe that she could ever be attracted to another man or that another man could possibly want her as she was. All along, she realised, Craig had been indifferent to the threat that David Lockhart had posed to him, had not understood it.

"I think I might go to St Anne's this Sunday," she said.

Craig tilted his head and regarded her dispassionately.

"What?"

"I said I think I'll go to church on Sunday."

"What about Bobby?"

"You're not on duty, are you?"

"Nope."

"In that case you can look after Bobby for a couple of hours, can't you?"

"Aye." He sighed. "Aye, I suppose so."

With that concession he let his neck slacken, his head tip and fell to contemplating the ceiling in silence once more.

Kirsty, puzzled, watched him for a moment longer and then went on with her mending.

*   *   *

Uncertain weather continued over the weekend and the pews in St Anne's were anything but filled that Sunday morning. Even the bells that summoned the faithful to worship had a sodden, irresolute sound, smothered by hanging clouds and gusts of wind that cuffed and stirred them about. The church was chilly, smelled of damp wool and fur, of mothballs and peppermints. Kirsty felt empty and depressed without Nessie Frew's company; it came to her then that death was a very final thing, that she really would never see her friend again.

There was no consolation in the service. Indeed it made her even more depressed to hear Harry Graham's announcement that the assistant minister, Mr Lockhart, would shortly be leaving for foreign fields and would be greatly missed by the congregation. She had heard these same platitudes before in another context and it struck her as graceless of the minister to repeat them with no attempt at sincerity. Mr Lockhart had been invited to preach the sermon that morning, Harry Graham said, and Kirsty felt a prickle of excitement at the prospect, as if David would be moved by the finality of the occasion and would expound some great and original truth that would startle her, and everyone, out of their listless chill.

Sitting taller in the pew, Kirsty watched David climb the five steps to the pulpit. He put down his bible, opened it and shuffled the foolscap notes that he had prepared. For a second he vanished from view, seating himself on the narrow bench at the back of the pulpit to offer a private prayer and commend his preaching to God; then he stood up again, tall and dignified and full of authority. Without announcing a text he read lines from one of Martin Luther's letters, a source that did not please some of the congregation and that made Mr Graham frown as if he suspected that young Mr Lockhart was about to leave in a blaze of imprudent heresy. Kirsty shifted uneasily. David drew the sting from his words, however, put them forth in a neutral and undeclamatory tone, a take-it-or-leave-it manner that fooled most of the congregation, lulled them back into that jaded state to which, over the years, they had become accustomed.

"Cursed is the righteousness of the man who is unwilling to assist others on the grounds that they are worse than he is, and who thinks of fleeing from and forsaking those whom he ought now to be helping with prayer and patience and example," David said. "This would be burying the Lord's talent and not paying what is due." He let the foolscap sheet fall and, looking at Kirsty, almost smiled. "Luther tells us that Christ dwells only in sinners and that if we meditate on this love of His we will see His sweet consolation. Is this statement true? Is it worth examination? Is it something that will not bear too much study for you and for me?"

They wanted him, Kirsty sensed, to talk of sin, of deep, dark, unremitting sin, the kind of sin of which they had no personal knowledge. Perhaps they wanted him to talk of China too, to tell them how he would convert the heathen, how much he would have to sacrifice to perform the Lord's work in that benighted land. David, however, had no reason to wish to please them now. He went on with the sermon, almost casually, in a conversational tone.

The best that could be said about it was that it was brief. He was done in a quarter of an hour and the congregation was out on the street and headed home for hot dinners a full thirty minutes earlier than usual.

Kirsty went out with the last of the worshippers. David was in the vestibule with Harry Graham. He was shaking the hands of those members who had come to like him or for whom he had done some pastoral service. They were wishing him luck. Kirsty had an odd feeling that Nessie Frew was loitering just behind her and had to resist an urge to turn around and stretch out her hand. Ahead of her was David, framed against the arch of daylight at the door. She moved towards him. She felt both vulnerable and calculating when she smiled and touched his hand.

"Kirsty, I'm delighted that you came."

"You preached well today, David."

"Thank you," he said. "By the way, I have something for you."

"Oh?"

"Something that Nessie left with me, for you. Can you find time to call in and collect it before Thursday?"

"Today?"

"No, I'm taking lunch with Harry Graham today. Would Wednesday afternoon be suitable, perhaps?"

"Are you still there, at number nineteen?"

"Yes."

He looked into her face, into her eyes. All else was excluded, the people, the minister, the elders. It was as if they were completely alone. She did not know if there was truth in his statement that Nessie had left something to be given to her or if that was a gentle excuse, a lie made necessary by his uncertainty. He wanted to be with her, in Walbrook Street, alone for the last time.

271

"Will you come, Kirsty?"

"I'll come," she said.

*   *   *

Later, when he had time to think of it, Craig would thank God
that he had put on his uniform that February afternoon. If he
had been in mufti he would have been sunk, without doubt.
He had no reason to make himself ready for the back-shift for
he had already made his decision and was moving towards its
implementation as if in a trance. If Kirsty had been at home he
would have told her that he was going to the gymnasium but he
had no need to prevaricate for, that Wednesday, she had gone
out, and his need for self-deception had waned, shed like the
petals of a flower that had come at last to seed.

He had clothes in a locker in the Percy Street gymnasium, one
of everything that he would need to do it, and he could, if all
went well, leave the uniform there too and all the accoutrements.
He would not need to confront Kirsty, the duty officer or Chief
Constable Organ. He would not even have to write a letter, just
up and go. He would vanish into thin air, disappear from the
Greenfield and from the lives of all the people who had rejected
him and who did not need him. He could even take off that
uniform and desert the brotherhood of constables and sergeants
without too much regret. In fact, he suspected that when it was
done, when he had acted, he would suffer much less than he
had done when he ran away from Dalnavert with the girl, with
Kirsty, not because he loved her but because he wanted to have
her, and because his father had pushed him into it.

As he shaved he could see the sunshine from the window,
soft and hazy, though experience told him that the evening
would bring down frost out of the clear sky and that the night
would be bitterly cold. All smart and clean, looking out at
the sunshine, he felt as if he was coming out of hibernation,
and knew that he was about to do the right thing, no matter how much grief it caused, not to him but to others. He
had spent weeks testing his feelings, trying to imagine what
it would be like to be with her, cut off by choice from the
life he had built for himself, not to see Madge or Gordon or
Lorna again, not to see Bobby, not to be with Kirsty. It did
not seem to trouble him; the void that should have been filled

272

with anguish and loss was a void indeed, empty of all trouble-some emotion.

Kirsty and Bobby would not miss him, nor would they be plunged down into hardship. However selfish Madge might be she would not see her grandson starve; and if Madge did not take on the responsibility then Gordon would. Gordon would do it because Gordon was too decent for his own good. And none of them, not one of them, would ever speak to him again. They would not understand what it was that drew him to folly, why he could give up everything for a woman off the street, to be with a clothes-wife and her bastard bairn. It was not a sudden whim either; he had been manoeuvring himself towards it since that Saturday afternoon in the Irish Market, since he had seen the tear upon her cheek.

He poured himself a whisky from the bottle he kept hidden under a board under the bed, where Kirsty would not discover it. He drank the whisky and ate the meal that Kirsty had left in the oven for him. He did not even know where she had gone; the Forrester Park maybe, since the weather was fine. He did not know and, damn it all, he did not really care. He cleared the table of dishes and put them on the board by the sink. He poured and drank a second stiff whisky, put the bottle away in its hiding place, washed the glass, then finished dressing. He felt good, relaxed not tense. He took the Royal Bank of Scotland Pass-book from the envelope behind the clock and buttoned it into his notebook pocket. He put on his boots and then his helmet, smoked half a cigarette and then went out of the house and down the stairs into the street.

He did not so much as glance back at the windows of the house he had left, at the close, at the tenement that he might never clap eyes on again. His mind was full of optimism, his thoughts on Greta who, he was sure, would be loyal to him and, now that he had some cash, would run off with him and be his love until her dying day.

At the upper end of Canada Road he veered left and, with a jauntiness he had not felt in years, strode towards the bank to clear the whole account.

*   *   *

Stripped of furnishings and carpets, devoid of ornaments, the house at No. 19 Walbrook Street seemed totally unfamiliar, no more than a shell, and her excitement and determination waned as soon as David admitted her.

"It's all gone," Kirsty said.

"Yes, almost all," David said.

He wore his grey suit and collar and was more formal than she had supposed he would be.

"Where did it go?"

"To the saleroom, all except the screens; Harry Graham got those."

"Did the family take nothing?"

"Only some old photographs," said David. "The sister, Edith, asked if she might have some of the lace. Hugh agreed, of course."

"But the – the beds, everything?"

"Sold."

Kirsty shook her head in amazement at the speed with which Nessie Frew's comfortable home had been dismantled. New lives would soon begin here, she realised, and she would have no part in them. She walked down the hall, heels clicking on the bare wooden boards, and went into the kitchen. To her relief everything there was almost as it had been, table, chairs, pots and cutlery all in their places, only the clock missing. A drying-towel was neatly folded on the wire above the stove as if Nessie had just popped in to make things tidy.

"Is Peggie – "

"No, Peggie left last Friday," David said. "I'm fending for myself for a day or two, until tomorrow. I'll travel to Inverness to say goodbye to Uncle George and then go to London. I sail from there on the ninth of March."

"Are you excited?" Kirsty said.

"I'll be relieved to be on my way."

"Out of Glasgow, out of Scotland?"

"Kirsty, I have to do it."

"I know you do."

"Won't you take off your coat and stay for a while?"

She had put on her prettiest dress, the only one she owned. She had pinned up her hair, lifting it from her neck, and wore a silver pendant that Nessie had given her. She had taken great care with her appearance. She wanted him to remember her as she was that day, the last time that they would be together. He put her coat and hat into the closet and returned.

"Shortly, I'll make us some tea," he said.

"I'll do it, if you like."

"I thought you might have brought Bobby with you."

"I – I thought it best to come alone."

She realised, with trembling excitement, that even now he expected nothing from her. It was enough that they had met, talked, walked, had touched and kissed. The intimacy that they had shared, the birth, had no bearing on the relationship that had enveloped them and her feelings towards David were complicated and not reassuring.

"I asked you here to give you this," David said.

The parcel was wrapped in brown paper and tied with pink string. Kirsty recognised the soft knot and loose feminine bow; Nessie had made up the parcel herself. She glanced questioningly at David.

"She gave it to me last November and instructed me not to declare it as part of her estate, to make sure you got it if and when she passed away. I've no idea what's inside."

"Shall I open it now?" Kirsty said.

"That's why you're here, isn't it?"

She seated herself at the table and placed the parcel before her. She tugged at the string and let it fall away, took off the wrapping and exposed a book, the book of pictures of China that David had given Aunt Nessie and Uncle Andrew as a gift for Christmas, many years ago.

It was a genuine memento, something that Nessie had known she would treasure. Kirsty turned the pages of the quarto volume and vividly recalled the night when she had lain alone in the big warm bed in the servant's room and had studied these same pictures for the first time. She had been pregnant with Bobby but that had not stopped her dreaming wistfully of David. She turned again to the flyleaf and read the familiar inscription, *With All My Love, From David*, written in a large open hand. She glanced over her shoulder. David, standing close, saw it too. He was not in China yet, not yet parted from her, not yet far away.

"Why did Nessie give you that?" he murmured.

"She showed it to me once, to help me understand you."

"I'd forgotten about that book. Look at the date: eighteen eighty-three. Lord, I was only a child then, just off the boat from China. I purchased the book in Shanghai, I remember, with money my mother gave me; a gift for two people I had never seen before."

"Now they're both dead."

"Yes."

She lifted her hand and he took it. He put his fingers against the side of her neck and she felt the fine hair lift and prickle and tightened her grip of his hand as he stooped. She parted her lips a little to receive his kiss.

She experienced no sorrow, protected by the suspicion that she, not David, was the exploiter of their parting, that none of it would be happening if she sincerely believed that they would ever meet again. All the rest of it was a pretence; only the kiss mattered, and the moments that contained it.

There was nobody to disturb them. The house had been cleared of its disapproving ghosts and if any remained they were recent arrivals, and benign.

She did not release him, did not break contact between them as she rose. She clung to him, let him kiss her mouth, her brow and neck. Perhaps it had been to avoid this that he had surrendered his ministry in Glasgow and had booked a passage to China, to evade his desire to love her completely and fully. She separated herself from him and stood back a little. He looked abashed, unsmiling, tense beyond measure. She realised that he did not know how to proceed. It was not a weakness, not unmanly, but a kind of politeness added to the fear that he had misunderstood her.

"David, where do you sleep?"

"Where once you slept."

"In the servant's room?"

"Yes," he said. "Kirsty, this isn't what — "

"Hush, dearest," she said and went out of the kitchen and into the bedroom that snuggled beneath the stairs.

* * *

Sunshine hinted that spring was just around the corner but it was cool, almost cold, in the shadows and the sky over the tenement tops was glazed and icy. The haze that overhung the street's end was composed of smoke and granular dust and all the afternoon's sounds were sharply magnified: a coalman's cry, the clatter of the fish-seller's bell, the grumble of big carts on the riverside cobbles, young children shrieking in one of the backcourts.

Craig paused to listen, to make sure that it was high spirits and not distress that prompted those piercing screams. Satisfied that it was only a noisy game, he walked on. He had paused out of habit, out of the goodness of his heart, for he was not on duty and, if all went well with Greta, would never be at the beck and call of bloody Jock Public again. Never again would he have to brave the horrors of middens and vennels and midnight steps, to walk the railway on the scout for a mangled corpse, to wade into the icy river at the ferry steps to help lift out something so bloated that it was hardly recognisable as human. He wanted a cigarette but did not dare smoke while in uniform, just in case John Boyle or the duty officer spotted him and challenged him and somehow guessed what was on his mind. He must be patient for a wee bit longer.

Soon he would be in Greta's kitchen, in Greta's arms, a free man, free to do anything he wished. He touched his hand nervously to his back trouser pocket to make sure that the neatly folded wad of banknotes was still there, though how he could have lost them in a quarter of an hour was more than he could imagine. He was just being cautious, daft really. But the money was vital to his plan; he could not ask Greta to give up her house and her stall at the Irish Market, just to abandon everything for love alone. He would have to prove to her that he could offer her a better life, and the forty pounds that he had signed out of the current account in the Royal Bank would do it, would show that his promise was not false.

The fact that it was Kirsty's money did not stop him, though he took no pleasure in the irony of it, no added spice to the act of domestic larceny. He almost managed to convince himself that Kirsty would be glad to see the back of him and that forty pounds was a reasonable price to pay for a painless separation. He had not stolen the money; it was legally registered in his name and Kirsty had endorsed the original cheque to enable him to deposit it. He had even taken the precaution of leaving the Pass-book with a teller in an envelope with Kirsty's name on it and a signed form that transferred the balance of the account to her. When she realised that he had gone for good and rushed, as she would, to check on the money she would know that he had not been entirely heartless, had not left her without a penny to her name as many a man would have done under similar circumstances.

Unconsciously he had slackened his pace. He did not stride eagerly down Benedict Street. Instinct told him that this would be his final opportunity to change his mind, to find his conscience and recant his intention. Once Greta opened the door and let him in and heard what he had to say, and saw the money, then there could be no going back to Kirsty, not unless Greta turned him down flat, which he did not think she would. The tear, that unwilling tear, was his promise, his assurance, and this thing that he was about to do came from it. Greta loved him, and he was in love with her and had been deluded into believing that it was all and only what she did under the blankets that counted.

They would go away, go tonight, go anywhere that Greta fancied. He didn't give a damn where it was, though he would prefer the country to a city or even a town; some place like Dalnavert, a small-holding in the Borders or in the Mearns where he had heard that rents were not too high and the ground was fertile.

Considering that Kirsty was not his wife at all, he had done all right by her. Ten pounds, and his lying wages, would see her through for a month or six weeks. By that time there would have been a big family pow-wow and the truth would have come seeping out, that she had never been his bloody wife at all; and Gordon or Adair would have made decisions and would shoulder the burden and foot the bill. God, Kirsty would be better off without him, and Bobby too.

To hell with them, to hell with them all.

He turned into the close of No. 13, and rapped loudly on the door.

"Greta," he called. "Greta, it's Craig. Your Craig."

*   *   *

She let the dress slither about her feet and stepped out of it. She had bought pretty garters to hold up her stockings and, because she was unsure of David, had left her stockings on. Her petticoat had a deep square neckline and she had dabbed Lily-of-the-Valley across the tops of her breasts. She had done it to please him, with calculation, a quality that had lain dormant in her until love, one way or another, had brought it out. She did not think of Craig, only of herself, her private feelings about her body and how David would respond to it.

The servant's room was dominated by a solid double bed. She had slept here with Craig. Under mounded bedclothes Craig had taken her in furtive couplings that had filled her with shame and apprehension, the fear that Mrs Frew would hear what they were doing. Though unchanged, the room did not seem the same. The bed was neatly made; a book, not a bible, lay on the dressing-table, a pipe and a box of matches by it.

She lighted the oil-lamp to add warmth and give light. She wanted David to see her, to look on her body and admire it. She needed to be sure that if he chose to reject her it would not be because he found her physically displeasing. She was prepared for rejection; how could she understand what changes were made in a man who had a spiritual vocation and who had studied the nature of sin and its meanings? She had a faint recollection of David's hands upon her at the time of her labour but in that memory there could be no trace of shame. He had helped her, as few men will, to realise the unsubtle nature of femaleness. If he had not been given to the service of the Father, driven by unselfishness to do what he believed to be right, he would have made a wonderful doctor. But was this not right? Was her intention too a sin? Had she made herself part of some insinuating scheme to spoil David and to bring him down? Her doubts were numbed by vanity, and the vanity protected her. She did not fear that he would harm her, that there would be repercussions. They would kiss now and join, cleave and part; and would never be parted again, no matter where he was or she was, or how much time passed.

"Kirsty, may I come in?"

"Yes."

Hesitantly he pushed against the door and peeped into the room. He was trying so hard to be suave, to pretend that he could equal her confidence and the ease of her desire; but he could not. Shyly he remained by the door and let it close behind him of its own accord.

"You're quite beautiful, Kirsty," he said.

"Only quite?"

"Very beautiful."

He had already indicated that he wanted her, wanted to love her, and had put aside the notion that the act would be a stern and damning wickedness. He had taken off his collar and grey vest, had unbuttoned his shirt and removed his shoes. He stood before her now all dishevelled, like a practised lover, and yet he was still David, endearing in his eagerness and courtesy.

"Take me in your arms, David, please."

She moved to him, the bed at her back. She lifted her face and parted her lips. He did not, however, wrap his arms about her, not at first. He touched her chin with his fingertips and kissed her brow, her nose, while his right hand caressed her breast. She was instantly on fire, gasped and pressed herself against him. She had never known such strength of feeling, had never guessed that it was possible to release so many emotions in the course of this ordinary act, that it could mean so much more than pleasure.

Leaning, she drew him down upon her upon the bed. She gasped his name, again, again. He got his shirt off and tossed it away. He bared her breasts and touched his flesh against her softness, all the old round doubts cast aside now that he was with her. He was tender, though, not impatient, caring not selfish. She felt him ready and plucked up her petticoat. He held himself over her, poised, and looked into her eyes. She realised that he was waiting for her permission, that he would not take her surrender for granted even now.

"Wait," she said.

She slipped the ring from her finger, the wedding band that Craig had given her in lieu of marriage. She dropped it on to the dresser by the bed where it spun and glittered for an instant before it wobbled and fell still.

"Now, Kirsty?" David, smiling, asked.

"Now," she told him and, at the moment of union, closed her eyes tight.